HUSTLERS

← **A Ronald Quincy Novel** →

BLACK PEARL BOOKS PUBLISHING
www.BlackPearlBooks.com

HUSTLERS

A Ronald Quincy Novel

Published By:

BLACK PEARL BOOKS INC.

3653-F Flakes Mill Road – PMB 306
Atlanta, GA 30034
404-735-3553

Copyright 2005 © Ronald Quincy

All Black Pearl Books titles, imprints and distributed lines are available at special quantity discounts for bulk purchases for sales promotion, premiums, fund raising, educational or institutional use.

Special book excerpts or customized printings can also be created to fit specific needs. For details, write to Black Pearl Books: Attention Senior Publisher, 3653-F Flakes Mill Road, PMB-306, Atlanta, Georgia 30034 or visit website: www. BlackPearlBooks. com

For DISTRIBUTOR INFO & BULK ORDERING

Contact: **Black Pearl Books, Inc.**
3653-F Flakes Mill Road
PMB 306
Atlanta, Georgia 30034
404-735-3553

Discount Book-Club Orders via website:
www. BlackPearlBooks. com

ISBN: 0-9766007-3-0   LCCN: 2005928073

Publication Date: July 2005

ACKNOWLEDGEMENTS

Ron Jones:

I dedicate this book to J. Marie --- and to Family and Friendship

Quincy Penn:

First and foremost, I would like to thank the most devoted person I've encountered, Ron Jones. Thanks for your encouragements, support, undying devotion and motivational inspiration. One Love!

Last but not least, I want to thank my mother, Ms. Elizabeth Ann Penn. One, for holding me down and doing all that she could do, and demonstrating Real Love! I Love you Moms!

HUSTLERS

← **A Ronald Quincy Novel** →

 Black Pearl Books Publishing
www.BlackPearlBooks.com

CHAPTER 1

Popcorn

When I was six years old, I got caught stealing three bags of cheese popcorn from the corner store that some Arabs ran, down the street from where I was living at that time. The owner, an Osama-bin-Laden looking muthafucka, didn't call the cops. He did something much worst, he locked me in a bathroom that smelled like listerine and garlic until his wife went and got my Moms. Need I say, she whipped my ass, all the way home --- and then some, for making her miss the last part of "The Young and the Restless." After that, everybody, up and down the block started calling me 'Popcorn.' A name that has stuck like glue to this day --- along with my belief that that Arab was a damn terrorist, if ever there was one.

Nevertheless, I grew up in a battle torn section of Richmond, Virginia, called Jackson Ward. For the first seventeen years of my life, Donte 'Bay-Bay' Curry and I was boyz. In fact, our fathers had been partnas for life, long before we were born, which had given us even more of a reason to bond like brothers. Although our mothers didn't fuck with one another, for reasons I don't understand to this day, they never interfered with our friendship in any way. So we hung out practically everyday, especially when we became teenagers. That's when we use to drop rhymes mainly at the recreation center in 'Gilpen Court Projects', flaunt our skills on the basketball court, and chase the honies like we had been a couple of Rottweilers in-heat.

Unfortunately, '96 wasn't a good year for either of us, because we lost the backbones of our families. Our fathers! They were slaughtered exactly six weeks apart. It had taken a while for me to accept, but at some point, I realized that it came with the territory. You see, our fathers had been 'dope boyz'. They had sewn up Jackson Ward, and were spreading their wings in other areas of the city, as well.

Shit was lovely for a minute.

Up until some young-guns tried to set up shop on our Pops' turf. Them niggas wasn't having that! So the beef was serious and bloody. Mad niggas got slumped over a period of a few months, including our bread-winners. It was no concellation to Bay-Bay, our families, or myself, that they had put in 'major work', before they were gunned down. Just because of the fact that they went out in a blaze of glory, it still wasn't going to bring them back. Shit, it couldn't even stop Bay-Bay's Moms from suffering a vicious nervous breakdown. When she recovered, the spring of that year, she moved to Florida where her sister was already living, taking my man and his four siblings with her to the 'Sunshine State'.

Need I say, it was a crushing blow to Bay-Bay and I. Because we had made plans to lay down some tracks, and push the joints out the trunk of our hoopties, like every other muthafucka that believes in themselves when nobody else does. But unfortunately, we were being robbed of that opportunity. So on the day before my nigga bounced, we did the next best thing ---- we made 'a pact'. We promised each other, whoever made it 'spitting on wax', would find the other and get him in the door. After that, we didn't so much as shake hands, pound fist, or any of that other cute shit niggas do as farewell gestures. We simply backed away from each other, before we turned and went in opposite directions.

Now, eight years later, I opened the door to the apartment that belonged to my bun-bun, Peaches, and saw that nigga standing on the stoop. You can all but imagine the excitement I felt when I shouted, "When the fuck you get in, Yo!!!" After that, I attacked his ass with fervor ---- shaking his hand and hugging him like a straight bitch.

"What'sup, Playa??" He asked, when we finally let go of each other.

"Ain't shit." I replied, before inquiring, once more, "When you get in?"

He looked at his Jacob's Jeweler timepiece, before saying, "About twenty minutes ago. I went by your Moms, first. Your little grown-ass sister said you was cribbed up down here in 'Gilpen' with a 'stunna' --- is how she put it." He smiled. "When I asked her for the address, she gave it up with her lips twisted like a female with mad issues. Man, I laughed my ass off, because I can remember when she was knee-high to a duck's ass, eating mud pies and sucking her thumb."

I pictured in my mind, my twelve-year-old sister trying to impress Bay-Bay, whom she probably don't recall, and I cracked a smile too. "Yeah, Rainy a trip, yo." Over his right shoulder, I could see the full body of a pearl-gray '6' parked at the curb with it's Sprewell's still spinning, so I assumed that O'boy was pushing that 'big boy joint'. I didn't comment though, instead, I said, "Come on in, yo, and give a nigga some game, because, it looks like you doing 'big thangs'!"

I was trying to collect myself, because Bay-Bay had caught me off guard. It was obvious that he was there to help me get on in the recording industry, because the platinum, with blue and white ice lacing his neck and wrist, told me that much of the story. The problem, however, is that I hadn't thought of writing or dropping rhymes, for more than two years. All of my time and energy had been devoted to establishing my little landscape business. There had come a time when I felt like I needed to do something more realistic than waiting for a break that might not ever come. Now that it was sitting across from me, lurking in those smily eyes of ole-boys, I realized that I was just as excited about it, as if I was fully prepared. I knew he saw the excitement swimming-up-and-down my face, saw it clearly as he did the cheap furniture we were sitting on.

Especially when he said, "I know what you're thinking and part of it is true."

He was laid back, settled so comfortably in that raggedy-ass chair, I thought to myself, 'At least the nigga still hood.' Then I said, from being somewhat confused, "And what part is that?"

He looked thoughtful for a moment, before asking, "Are we alone?"

"Yeah. My girl, Peaches, she does hair on the weekends.

Every Saturday, her and her daughter be roaming all over the projects, getting money."

"Oh.... so the 'stunna' got a little hustle about herself, huh?" We both laughed. "Check this ---- Popcorn. I know you probably thinking that a nigga done signed wit 'Cash Money' or one of those other giant labels ---- and that I'm here to put you on. Right?"

My heart was racing and my throat was as dry as a bucket of sand. Still. I said, "True that."

4

"Well, the part you got right is that I'm here alright to put you on, but it don't got a muthafucking thing to do with spitting on wax. For me, Playa, those days are over.

I caught his drift, but I still asked, "So a brotha down --- what'sup?"

For what seemed an eternity, we stared at one another. In that stare, was his whole pitch. You and I, we were born and bred to the blood-and-guts of the game, in the same way that a blueblooded American is born into ten generations of wealth. Yes, our fathers were gunned down and literally slaughtered like dogs, in the end. But lets not you and I forget our heritage, or our own responsibility to our families.

They need us, muthafucka!!

That is what I had accepted, a long time ago. Hopefully, it is what you will accept, now ---- your calling. Your oppor-

tunity to step up to the plate and do some special things for your Moms, sisters   and your goddamn self!

Beyond his eyes giving me the 'beautiful truth', he said,

"I got that work, my nigga. As much as you want, as often as you need and for however long."

Damn! The thought of him being plugged like that scared the shit out of me. I was up and out my seat, before I knew it, peeping out the window. I knew he was probably tripping off me, yet he just sat as a portrait of calm and patience.

"I don't know, Bay-Bay, I'ma have to think this shit thru."

He slowly looked around the room, prior to staring me in the face and saying, "I feel ya. Take as long as you need. I just want you to know 'it's all gravy' if you trying to 'do that'."

I appreciate that, good looking out. But forreal, forreal, even if I wanted to right now, my bank fucked-up." I wasn't the least bit embarrassed when I went on to say, "Right now, Yo, I'm living from paycheck-to-paycheck."

He smiled, "You don't need no bread, to get down with me, Playa ---- even when you get caked-up." He made clear, before adding, "All I need is ya word and I'll have them joints delivered to you, anytime you want, for eighteen a brick. All I ask, is that you get me 'off top'."

"Goddamn, Bay-Bay, that's generous as a muthafucka!" I said because kilos of bomb cocaine, in V-A was hitting for twenty-five, twenty-six a pop, easy. "Still, I'ma have to give this shit some vicious thought."

He gave his eyes another grand tour of my surroundings, in an obvious way, before he said, "Take all the time you need. I'ma give you my hook-up, before I leave. That way, you can get at me ----- whenever!" He stood up, stretched and prompted, "Now come on, Nigga, let's go down on Chamberlain to Ms. Maggie's Restaurant, and eat come real food, before I get back to the highway."

"Ms. Maggie's!" I said, with astonishment, because she sold the best soul food in all of Richmond. I would've thought O'boy was hooked on those mid-level joint's, like Applebee's, Bennington, and Red Lobster. That's why, as we headed for the door, I cracked, "I guess having plenty of paper don't change a nigga's appetite, huh?"

He knew I was joking, yet he stopped dead in his tracks and looked me directly in the eyes, "In some ways it do, in some it don't. But with niggas .....ain't no tellin'".

◆◆◆◆◆◆◆◆◆◆◆◆◆◆◆◆◆◆◆◆◆

It's funny how when major decisions have to be made in a person's life, there will be signs appearing out of nowhere, giving that person reasons why they should do one thing or the other. Take my situation, by the time I got back to the crib, after riding in that plush-ass Benz, listening to all the 'big boy' moves Bay-Bay had made since being in the game ---- I was sold on the idea of 'slingin " like a muthafucka. Yet, before I got to the front door of the apartment, I spied this female name, Crystal, getting of a blinged-out Suburban that belonged to a wild-ass

6

'balla' whom everybody called 'Choo-Choo'. Seeing babygirl reminded me of Lil Dee, a good nigga she used to fuck with --- but who was now in the Feds doing a life sentence. Need I say, by the time I closed the door and sat down on the dingy sofa, in the dark, I had told myself, 'fuck that'! I'ma just stay at it with my business --- and wait for a better come-up.

A legal one, at that.

That night, however, I still couldn't get my mind off the sweet offer my man had made me, even when Peaches had sucked my dick, rock hard, and rode it like she was trying to fuck some money out of me, like she normally tries. When I got up the next morning, which was Sunday, I was back in that maybe I will, maybe I won't mode. That is, until I got a call from my sister Rainy, asking if she could get some money to buy her some new summer gear. She had said that our mother told her that she didn't have any money to spare. Next week was Memorial Day Weekend, so I knew babygirl wanted something 'fresh' for the holiday. My bank was fucked-up, still, I promised her that I would come through. I made that vow, because I knew there was a rack of niggas I could hit-up ---- especially my half-brother, Silk. He and I, we both had the same father, but different Moms. We grew up on opposite sides of the city, and didn't fuck with each other until about five years ago. Since that time, we've become cool as shit! What locked us in, I think, is that I used to visit him when he was doing a state bid. I did it out of love and respect for my blood. But still, he viewed it as a debt he can never repay. Anytime I ask, he breaks me off. He talks a whole rack of shit, of course, but that's his way of reminding me, he's big bro.

Anyway, I knew that I would have to see Silk in the next few days for a loan, after making that promise to Rainy. He lived in a infamous part of the city called Churchhill. And believe me, niggas over there are retarded as hell. When Richmond was rated 'The Murder Capital' of America, in the early nineties, Churchhill had been the primary killing fields.

Since that time, the city's ratings have dropped slightly, but my brother, Silk's stomping grounds remain a killing field. Especially, for niggas who was in the game, and faking.

Need I say, I hated going over there. And damn sure hated to drive up in 'Wilcom Court Projects', where that fool lived. Of course, everybody was hipped to the fact that I was Silk's brother, but that wasn't always a comforting thought, being that he was, at every turn, beefing with somebody without my knowledge. Trust me, when you petty hustle with crack or any other narcotic, drama becomes company, and a part of the territory.

Being in that position, at that moment, had me looking favorably, once more, at opening up shop. Pretty much, that was how my thoughts ran back-and-forth for the next couple of days.

◆◆◆◆◆◆◆◆◆◆◆◆◆◆◆◆◆◆◆◆◆◆

Tuesday evening, two situations completely tilted the scales in favor of me reaching out to my man, Bay-Bay. First, I swung through Momdukes after I secured my landscaping equipment in the garage I rented across the street from that little building the Arabs use to own. It's vacant now, however ---- those blood sucking muthafuckas milked the neighborhood for all it was worth, and showed their appreciation by leaving a condemned building standing on the corner.

Ain't that a bitch!

Anyway, my Mom and two sisters still live in the house on Clay Street my Pops copped back in the nineties. When I walked in the house, I could tell she had just gotten off work, because she still was wearing her uniform she wore as custodian at Virginia Commonwealth University. Plus, she was sitting on the sofa, with her shoes kicked off, while my youngest sister, Precious, rubbed her feet. It was about a quarter past five, so I knew she only had a couple of hours before she headed to her part time gig, cleaning offices at First Union Bank.

"What you doing here, boy ---- checking up on us?" She said, teasing me like she always do, about being too protective of her and my sisters.

"Yeah, you checking up on us?" Lil Precious echoed, with a big ole sweet smile on her face. She was nine years old, but almost as tall as Rainy.

I enjoyed Precious' innocent glow, for a moment, before, I looked back at Moms to say something devious. But the words got caught in my throat, because, that quickly, she had fallen asleep. That portrait of her sitting there with her features looking so tired and worn out, broke my heart into a thousand pieces. Especially when I heard that uncharacteristic snore escape her throat. All I could think, at that moment, was that Baby was dog-tired, and barely living above the poverty line.

That did it.

I left there knowing that my course was set. Shit was getting ready to change. It was as Bay--Bay had said, they needed me. They always have. Only, up to that point, I had elected to turn a blind eye to that reality. If I knew my father, he was probably turning flips in his grave, from the way I've shelved my responsibility for my mother and sisters. As I drove home, I felt ashamed.

That is, until I pulled up in my old battered truck and saw my girl Peaches leaning into the passenger window of that nigga, Choo-Choo's 'phat-ass Lexus'. That shit infuriated me in the worst way. Especially the sight of her wiggling her little cute ass, in them tight-ass Apple Bottom's Jeans ---- and smiling like that black-ass nigga was spitting gold.

Although she couldn't see me, he could. No doubt, he was creaming on himself from the belief that I was going to straight play myself. But clearly, he had me twisted I   was smarter than that. I parked my '88 Ford F-150, smooth and straight, before I got out and closed the drivers' door without drawing her attention. In my mind, that scenario of her and him, only boasted my determination to handle my business. As I walked toward the apartment, I even shook my head at her stupidity. Because, since she had chosen to blatantly disrespect me with a nigga that's probably fucking half of Richmond, she was definitely not a part of my equation from that day forward. That's not to say that she ever was, only then, she didn't have a snowball's chance in hell.

A fucking ho!

I shut the front door behind me, pulled out Bay-Bay's digits, and grabbed the cordless. I was posted at the picture window watching Peaches continue to have a fabulous time with O'boy, when Bay-Bay answered my call. I got right to the point, "Let's do that."

I could feel him smiling through the receiver, when he responded, "What took you so long, Nigga --- I was ready to cancel you out."

"It's like I said, Yo, I had to give it some serious thought. I almost added, 'Plus, I just caught my bitch wiggling her phat ass for a 'balla'', Instead, I asked, "So what'sup?"

"I got'cha as soon as I hang up." After a second of thought, he asked, "How many?"

"I 'ma leave that up to you." I said, mainly from not knowing how many I should have cracked for, since he was fronting them to me. "Just know that I'ma get you off the rip, and that's word!" I meant that.

Peaches swerved her head around in my direction with such lightning speed, I was sure that Choo-Choo had finally told her I was looking out the window at them. She stared at me as if I was the one out of pocket, right when Bay-Bay said, "Cool! Just keep ya head up, Playa --- it's gonna get greater, later."

That's fo-sho!, I thought.

I hung up the phone, at the instant that Peaches charged in the crib and demanded, "Why was you spying on me like that? I wasn't doing a damn thang wrong ---- just talking to my

10

gurrl, Crystal's, man. He didn't say nothing out-the-way to me, so I don't know why you was trippin' like that."

But she knew.

I could tell by the way she was standing, that if I was able to prove that she was lying, she was ready to take flight. I didn't realize until about a month after we started living together, that she was such a vicious liar. She had been in a few crazy relationships, prior to ours. And according to her, each of them cats used to beat her, for nothing. But it hadn't taken me long to figure out, each of those ass-kickings, she had endured, was more than justified. That is, for niggas that believe in beating women.

I didn't.

I think it's some coward-ass shit for a brotha to beat a sista, for any reason. If he's not equipped to deal with her mentally, then he should just call it quits. Of course, there are a lot of females, like that nut who stood before me lying her ass off, who like for niggers to smack that dome around. In their twisted little minds, it's supposed to confirm feelings. That's why I knew I fucked Peaches up when I merely went, Phpht!!", right in her face and walked the hell out of there.

I felt her eyes on me as I climbed back into my truck, and she was probably biting her bottom lip, from wondering if I was going to return. But that was her least worry, right then. I wasn't going to get ghost just because I caught her talking to a nigga --- not yet, I wasn't. I still felt Babygirl, I just wasn't going to stand there and allow my intelligence to be insulted. I had other shit to do, anyway. I had set my come-up in motion, therefore, I needed to line up all my ducks. Because … it was on!!

CHAPTER 2

Silk

"I told'cha punk-ass what I was gon duo if I caught you back ova here, didn't I muthafucka!!" I barked down at a nigga named Putty, who was layed on the ground, broke-up and bleeding. I had deep-checked his ass, two days ago, about pitching his shit on my block. I'd been in this game long enough to know, that if you let one fool set-up shop in your hood, and getaway with it, you was a bigger fool than he was. Because, inside of forty-eight hours, niggas from all four corners of the city will be hugging your block and clocking your dough.

I wasn't having it!

Muthafucka's was going to respect me and mines --- point blank.

Putty must've thought I was a joke, because he brought his bitch ass back over here, after he was warned not to. Therefore, me and my dawg, Tiny, tricked his dumb-ass back between two buildings, which, unbeknownst to him, was the best blind spot in all of Wilcom Court Projects. But his ass found out soon enough --- right when Tiny, who had been standing behind him, split his dome to the white meat. He fell to the pavement with one of those [OH SHIT!!] looks printed on his mug.

I almost felt sorry for O'boy. But my Pops, the fake-ass nigga that he was, taught me that you never feel sympathy for anyone who violates you. He had said that that was a sign of weakness---- and weakness was something that a blind man could see.

I had locks on the whole south side of 'The Court'. A fat jet black homie, named Frenchie, was holding down the north end. It wasn't like either of us were scoring heavy, or anything like that, because, I'm sure he was only copping 'big eights' just like me. Still, if a nigga came to Wilcom to score, they had to get 'flav' from either me or Frenchie --- case closed!

I was just going to leave Putty where he laid --- shit, he was broke all the fuck up and no threat at all. Plus, I was confident that he would rather walk on a crowded street in 'Baghdad' wearing an 'I Love George Bush' tee-shirt, than to ever bring his ass back to my hood. But the nigga sealed his own fate, when he muttered through swollen lips, "Yeah, but Choo-Choo said it was cool."

"Fuck that black muthafucka!!!" I screamed, because I hated Choo-Choo with a passion. In my mind, that nigga was some straight shit! The kind of nigga that tried to squeeze every ounce of blood from a nigga. Like then, the city was experiencing a drought, as it did every year around that time. And since he was the only muthafucka with 'yayo', he was pushing pure garbage, for top dollar. Yesterday, me and Tiny had to give-up forty-five hundred for a funky-ass big-eight. Basically, that's a whole grand, per ounce.

A straight stick-up.

But what could a nigga do, but kick it out. I damn sure wasn't going to turn my clientele away, if there was an alternative in keeping them on locks. Even if it meant I wasn't going to hardly make enough profit for my time and effort.

In light of that and some more shit, Choo-Choo had life twisted, if he thought he had done a nigga a favor. Even moreso, if he was under the misguided impression that he could send niggas on my block, without my permission.

Fuck that!

That was my only thought when I reached and pulled my bowie knife from its case at the small of my back.

Although I didn't need motivation, I heard Tiny when he said, "Fuck'em, Silk --- slump his bitch-ass!" He was standing off to the left where I had my knees pinning down O'boy, still holding the baseball bats we had put work in with a moment ago, while beating Putty beyond recognition.

Putty's eyes got so fucking huge when he saw me draw back that six inch blade and push the joint straight into his chest cavity. I did it twice more before he tried to scream. But that was a wasted effort, because thick gobs of blood clogged his throat and spilled from his mouth. However, it didn't stop me from twisting the blade, that final time, before I pulled the joint from his body. I glanced at Tiny as I done it and he looked as though he was busting off in his jeans. Probably because the only thing he enjoyed more than watching a good killing, was committing the act his damn self.

I got up and swiped my bloody knife across that slumped nigga's shorts. I leaned against the building and told Tiny, "Hurry up! Let's get the fuck out of here." Because he was busy digging in Putty's pockets and stripping O'boy of his jewels.

I didn't like doing that kind of shit, myself. But I didn't trip whenever he elected to rob a dead man --- that was on him! Plus, it fit right in with all the other weird shit he had done, all our lives. Like, when we was eight years old, he ate bird shit, merely because I asked him to. Even at a young age, I had enough sense to know he was, for sure, a muthafucka that would die for me. Something he has proven on several occasions, since that day, by pushing me out the way of a speeding car, and being hit himself. And taking a bullet intended for me, at two different points in time.

He's a funny-looking muthafucka, that don't like taking baths that often. Nor did he give a fuck about dressing in the latest shit. Still, he was my dawg ---- my partna for life! I knew a lot a people couldn't understand why I fucked with him. Especially my girl, Toi. She detested the way 'she said' he looked at her. But, it wasn't a secret, Toi was a 'freak-a-leek' --- the only kind of broad, I digged. She might say that stupid shit about anybody.

Including my brother, Popcorn.

Speaking of which, as soon as Tiny and I walked out from between the buildings, where Putty was left laid, clocked-out, I saw little bro parking in front of my building. So I turned to Tiny and said, "Go clean them joints up and stash'em. Then, just chill until I get back at'cha."

He didn't say nothing, he only walked toward his building with those bloody bats hoisted on his shoulder, whistling some crazy-ass tune he always blew when he was happy about something. As I highstepped toward my brother's truck, honestly, I didn't know if Tiny's joy had more to do with the killin', the goods he had jacked from O'boy, or the fact that he knew, Tracy, the two hundred pounder he lived with, was going to try and fuck his little frail hundred and forty pound ass, to death ..

◆◆◆◆◆◆◆◆◆◆◆◆◆◆◆◆◆◆◆◆◆◆

16

"What'sup, Nigga!" I said when I got close to where Popcorn was parked and still sitting in his truck.

I already figured he was there for one of two reasons, either to borrow some dough, or because he was having problems out of one of them niggas in Gilpen. So when he said, "Ain't shit. Get in, though, I need to holla' at you." I assumed it was about drama.

I warned his ass, before he moved in with that trick, that it was going to be a lot of problems. Because Peaches was one of those 'pretty bitches' that wasn't going to be nothing but trouble for a nigga ----- everyday of the week.

No matter, I got in as he requested, and watched him back out of the parking space. I couldn't help thinking how much he favored our father. They both were high-yellow, slim, with that silky fine hair. Where as me I was light brown, chubby, with a grade of hair a step above 'Kuta Kinte". I used to be jealous that Popcorn had gotten all of our father's features, and most of his attention, too. After all, he raised Popcorn, while I only saw him in spurts. Even though he's dead and gone, I still don't respect no shit like that --- he could've been a better father to me. But I can say, I'm glad I got over being pissed at O'boy. Because, being raised as an only child, I've discovered that it's cool having a younger brother.

Yeah ….. I knew I had younger sisters, too.

But I didn't fuck with those little bitches. They had a tendency of looking at me like I didn't exist or something. I knew they were young, and that they would've probably grown out of it. But the way I felt right at that moment, fuck them little red stuck-up ho's!

Popcorn didn't say anything, until we drove out of Wilcom, onto Wilcom Street. Then he promptly stated,

"I 'ma have 'some work' in a few days ---- you down or what?"

I almost laughed right in his face. Because I couldn't picture him selling nothing, much less, some damn narcotics. Yet, I kept a straight face when I asked, " How much 'work' you talkin' bout?"

As he made a jazzy right turn onto Mechanicsville Road, it looked as though he was giving my question a lot of thought. Then, he said with the most serious tone of voice I knew he possessed, "As much as you want, as often as you need, and for however long."

Need I say, I sat up much straighter on the truck seat. Because I knew in all four corners of my heart --- the nigga wasn't bullshitting! In fact, I was so sure about it, I began visualizing the lookof-shock that would be printed on Choo-Choo's ugly-ass face, when he found out I was holding 'like that'. The nigga might have a cardiac, because I was going to be 'nothing nice'.

Nevertheless, I came back down to earth, right at the instant Popcorn stopped at the red-light, the one just before you get to the Moseby Court Projects. My nigga, Fat Joe's new joint [Lean Back], was popping on the radio, when I smoothly said, "Damn, my Nigga, you are the 'answer to cancer'." I noticed he was suppressing a smile, because, like anyone else, he enjoyed a good stroking. Plus, I had, in essence, just told him, I was on his team. "When this shit suppose to jump off?"

The light turned green. He U-turned and headed back the way we came, before he said, "It's in motion, as we speak."

I looked up at the moon. It was clear and bright, and for some reason, it seemed to be smiling. Or it could've been all in my head, because, I felt like what Tiny must've felt from watching me break off that blade in Putty's chest. Being that, I felt like busting-off in my jeans, as well. However, my joy dimmed a little, prior to me asking, "What them joints gon be goin for?" I had some paper, but not enough to score a whole bird.

"Don't worry, Big Bro, I'm frontin'em to you for twenty-three, a pop." His eyes were smiling, as he made the left turn back onto Wilcom St., and said, "I'ma just need mine off the muscle."

'Goddamn!!' I thought to myself. I even raised my ass up off the seat, a few inches, that time. Because it felt like 'I had' in fact, skeeted forreal! Still, I used a calm voice to say, "I guess a nigga can work wit dat." Maybe it wasn't my buisness, but I asked anyway, "Who else you gon be fuckin' wit?"

He had already turned up in Wilcom, and was cruising past the buildings where Putty still laid, dead as shit, when he furrowed his brow and said, "Nobody! You the only person I trust."

I awarded the nigga a genuine smile, that time. Plus, I didn't trip or talk fly, when after we parked back in front of my building, he cracked for three hundred bucks. If truth be told, I tore my pockets off giving him those kibbles-n-bits. Why not? The nigga had just offered me the come-up of a lifetime…

CHAPTER 3

Peaches

"Peaches, you got something cold and sweet to drink?" This female named, Carla, asked. She was sitting on the floor in my livingroom, between my legs, while I painstakingly micro-braided her hair.

"Yeah, some ice water, Bitch." I said,.because that was the only language those hookers down there in the projects understood. They thought because they gave you a hundred fifty dollars to twist they shit,   it meant, also, a free meal, a massage, and a right to fuck your man, too, if you wasn't careful.

"Gurl, you cold." She said, before she gingerly went back to humming a few bars of Alicia Keys' [If I Ain't Got You

Baby], that was evenly flowing from my stereo. In other words, her feelings wasn't hurt, in the least.

I went back to concentrating on my task at hand, and enjoying the fact that Popcorn and I had worked thru our disagreement. Things were perfect between us again ---- and that was a good feeling! I had been highly surprised, that when he came back home last night, after walking out and not saying jack-shit when I tried to explain about me kicking it with Choo-Choo, he was in a very forgiving mood. He had pretended as though none of it had happened, which had been fine with me.

He had even climbed in bed 'butt bald naked'. That had been a clear enough message that he wanted to 'wax this ass'. Inside, I was smiling my ass off. That was, until I had looked down at his big hefty dick, that had hung from his slim body. There was nothing to grin about, at that point, because my pussy had swollen and throbbed and ran like a nose bleed. All, before he had even touched me.

I'm not bragging, or anything like that, but my kitty-cat must've been extra good to him. Being that he had kept right on fucking the shit out of me, twice, after he had cum. When he had finally pulled out, he went straight to sleep ---- bless his heart! I had not gotten angry, like a lot of females do, when their man falls out after having sex. Because, me, I prided myself on knocking my man the-fuck-out. In my mind, it said two things ---- one, he had put in major work. And, my pussy, to him, was still the bomb!

I had laid awake, however, for a long time, afterwards, trying to figure out why I liked flirting so damn much. It always got me in deep shit, one way or the other. After all, being a vicious dick-tease was what had got me pregnant by my High School Drama Teacher, which had gotten me black-balled by my uppity-ass parents, because I wouldn't get an abortion. And of course, all of that had landed me down here in the projects, hoping I would get a firmer grip back on life.

Don't get me wrong, I wasn't complaining about the direction my life took. I mean, I loved my daughter, Tondra, and I was glad that I had had the courage to give birth to her. To me, she was worth more than the love of my parents and three sisters --- and far more than the college education my mother and father refused me, because of her.

But fuck them!

I planned on providing Tondra with a good life, without their help. In fact, from doing those hookers' hair, in Gilpen Court, I had already saved up over four thousand dollars.

No one knew that, but me.

I wasn't sure if I was saving for college, or to start me a small business of some type. And hell naw!! I was most certainly not going to open a damn hair salon. I was tired of all the bitching and complaining that comes with doing women's hair. Whatever choice of business I chose, if that be the case, it would have to be something that I enjoyed, as well.

I looked at the small patch of hair I had left to do on Carla's head, and realized that my damn fingers were hurting like shit. I envied her and all females like her, who had them a nigga 'in the game'. Especially a brotha that had the sense to get in the game, stack his money, and get out before he got caught. I didn't think that Carla's man was that smart, though. Because he's been selling drugs for quite some time, yet they were still living in the projects. To me, that was stupid! Along with the fact that he kept buying all those new cars, and she was sitting on my raggedy-ass carpet, with all those diamond rings on her fingers. If the bitch got it like that, she should've brought me something cold and sweet to drink.

Anyway, my daughter, Tondra, was seven years old. I had her when I was seventeen, and still a damn child, myself. She was in the second grade, and looking forward to the upcoming Memorial Day Weekend. I had promised her that I was going to take her to that theme park, Kings Dominion, which was only a spit from Richmond. After that, she was even more elated by the fact that, once school was officially out, she was going to spend the summer with her father, who now lives in Atlanta. As a man, he wasn't shit, in my book, because he wouldn't stand up to my parents. Yes, he had been my teacher, but still, he was only six years older than me ---- but I'm not going to get started on that. My point was, he was a good father to our daughter, I couldn't take that from him.

A bastard!

As far as Popcorn was concerned, we hooked-up at a R.Kelly concert, last August. However, we had only been living together for five months. If I were to be totally honest about things, I would have to confess that I fell in love with his fine-ass, on sight. Since that time, my feelings for him have grown in ways I would never have imagined. He was sooo different from the other guys, I've' dealt with. He was kind, considerate toward me and my daughter, and no matter what I've done, he had never laid a hand on me.

Not once!

I wasn't perfect. I knew I had done some really stupid shit, sometime. Yet, I didn't want a man who believed smacking me was going to change my behavior. Popcorn had been the first man I've been in a relationship with, who knew how to fuck with my mental. That man could just look at me 'a certain way' and make me regret whatever it was I had done that had not sat well with him. He understood, the only way a person would change, was if they wanted to. Also, that that person could only change from within --- not from how many times they took a beating up-side the head.

Take yesterday, the way he looked at me, before he walked out, made me feel how disrespected he felt from watching me flirt with Choo-Choo ---- and that shit hurt me, that I had hurt him so deeply. What made matters worse was that I lied about it, although I knew he could see right thru my tall-tale. When he walked out, I hadn't blamed him. I had been sure I would've did the same, had someone stood and told such a blatant lie as I had. Truthfully, I thought I had lost him for good, that time. I had even curled up on my bed, and cried, before I had prayed for him to return. In my prayers, I had promised that, if he came back, I wasn't going to flirt with other men, or lie to him again, ever!

But who in the hell was I fooling?

I got to 'do me'.

In my mind, as long as I don't actually fuck any of the guys I flirt with, then, it's all good. He does his dirt, and I don't trip. Like this morning, he called up that bitch, Yolonda, and invited her to lunch ---- right in my damn face. He even had the nerve to smile the whole goddamn time they talked.

Of course, he had claimed that the two of them were 'just friends' --- and that may be the case in his mind. But I've been around that bitch enough that I've witnessed the lust glowing in her eyes.

And why wouldn't it be?

Yolonda was a gorgeous deep-chocolate bitch, just like me, with the same big ass and shapely legs. Quite honestly, I had yet to meet a super-black bitch, who wouldn't 'die twice' trying to get themselves a suave high-yellow nigga, like Popcorn. O'girl, no matter how she pretended otherwise, was no exception to that rule.

Sure, I knew they had known each other since grade school. So therefore, she had had a million opportunities to get at him, long before he and I. Yet, I also understood that 'females like her' would freak-the-fuck-out, the instant her so-called 'male friend' hooked-up with someone who was equally as fine as they were. In our case, it didn't matter that she had her chance, before me, or that she had a college degree, and I didn't. And not even that she owned a fabulous townhouse, and I lived in the fucking projects. In spite of those advantages, she felt inferior to me, because I had Popcorn, and she didn't…..

◆◆◆◆◆◆◆◆◆◆◆◆◆◆◆◆◆◆◆◆◆◆

25

Finally, I finished braiding Carla's hair. She pulled a damn knott of money out of her purse that looked like enough to feed the whole Gilpen Court for a week. After she handed me three fifty-dollar bills, she asked, "Did it hurt when you got your tongue pierced Peaches, 'cause I'm thinking about getting mine done?"

"Naw, not really," I said, before I flicked the tip of my tongue backwards and touched the small piece of metal that resembled a dumbbell. Then I smiled, because I knew I had lied. That shit had hurt like hell.

"Oh, auight. I'll probably do it, then. Because Tre been worrying me to death about doing it. He said 'he heard' a female gives better head, with a pierced tongue." Carla rolled her eyes, as she said, "But I don't know who he think he's fooling ---- somebody done sucked his dick with some metal in their mouth, now he pushing that shit on me, like he ain't never had it done. Picture that!"

When Carla left, I put that buck-fifty in my stash, under the floorboard in my closet. After that, I was getting ready to do a little house cleaning. But when I walked past my front window, and caught sight of Choo-Choo parking his Suburban at the curb, I ran to a mirror and pushed my hair around, some. I knew he was probably stopping through to get at Crystal, but I had seen her leave with another nigga, earlier. Therefore, I figured I may as well have me some fun also.

I waited just as patiently, until he knocked on her door, which was right across the court from mine. Then, I pulled up my skimpy shorts to a point where my ass cheeks were proudly on display, opened my door, and said, "She's not home, Choo!"

His face lit-up. The afternoon sunshine made it seem like he had thirty-two gold teeth in his mouth, instead of the four he actually sported. The closer he got to my stoop, the faster my heart raced because he was a big crazy looking motherfucker, forreal. The kind of nigga I wouldn't have minded fucking just once. You know, just to see how it felt.

"What'sup Shawty!" He said, before he licked my legs with his eyes.

"Just working, that's all." I said, out loud. But in the back of my mind, I was asking myself, *'What the fuck are you doing? Having me some damn fun ---- that's what! Suppose Popcorn drive up and see you like this? That's not gonna happen. He's having lunch with that bitch ----- remember!'*

"You don't do no work!" He said with a Don Juan glow to his face.

"Yes I do, Silly. I do hair, remember?"

"Oh shit! That's right." He said while he tapped his forehead with his open palm.

W both laughed, but I was dying for him to get a look at my ass ---- just to see how he would react. After all, he was off the hook just fiending off my legs and the fact that he could see my pussy print.

He solved all of that by running his hand thru his course afro, and asking, "When you gon hook a nigga up wit some of those micros, Shautie?"

"When you want me to?" I volleyed back at him, but hoped that he wouldn't say that he wanted them done, right then and there. That's why I turned, abruptly, leaving the door wide open, and said over my shoulder, "Let me get something, so that I can write down your appointment."

And let me tell you, when I heard that nigga gasp, as if he was choking with desire, my ass got soo damn hot, I thought I was sitting on a red-hot-poker. I knew I was working those hoochie shorts, but I hadn't known that it would garner such a crazed reaction from Choo-Choo. Until I felt him towering over me, with his huge hands cupping my ass.

Oh shit!!

CHAPTER 4

Popcorn

I awoke on Thursday, two days after kicking it with Bay-Bay, feeling as though I should've been in the game, a long time ago. I mean, that's how smoothly everything was coming together. I had a vicious connect, a dependable person I felt I could rely on to push the shit and keep my money straight. Plus, after talking it over with Yolonda, yesterday, at lunch, I had the perfect spot to stash 'my work'. I brushed my teeth, showered, and got dressed. Yet, the whole time, I kept thinking how it couldn't get any better than this.

I looked over at Peaches, who was still lying in bed, and wondered, 'What the fuck is wrong with her?' After all, she was normally up before, both, Tondra and I. I merely shrugged my shoulders, though, and figured that she was entitled to sleep in, like I have done more times than I care to count.

"Are you excited about going to Atlanta, Ms. Tondra?" I asked as she and I sat eating cereal, across from one another.

Her eyes lit up like Christmas lights, "Yep! My daddy brought me a rabbit."

"Really!!" I said with my voice full of her enthusiasm.

She nodded her head, up-and-down, because she was chewing her Cheerios. But then, she asked, "Can I bring my rabbit back home with me?"

"Yep!" I mimicked the way she had said it, a moment before. She smiled so truly, she had to wait before putting another spoonful in her mouth.

I walked her to her school-bus stop, and waved back when she flapped her hands at me from her bus seat by the window. I liked her as if she was my own kid. I didn't have any of my own, but I treated her as if she was my seed.

I didn't go back into the crib. Instead, I got in my truck right at the moment Carla, who had walked her children to the bus stop, as well, walked pass me and flashed one of those I-bet-I-know-something-you-don't-know looks. Still, I shrugged my shoulders for the second time that morning, and drove away.

The corner of Chamberlain and Clay Streets, where I stored my equipment, was only a few minutes ride from Gilpen Court. When I got there, my crew was already there, standing around. The only one who said something about me being a few minutes late, was Lil Rob. What happened, Popcorn, you catch a flat tire, or something?"

One of the two females that worked for me, Tisha laughed because she was trying to get at O'boy. Nobody else, including me, paid any attention to his lame-ass comment. Shit, I wrote his checks out every week --- he wasn't writing mine.

I got my 'get back' when I said, "Ok, we got a busy schedule, today. So we gonna break down into two teams." I turned and looked at Smokey, he was like my second in charge. "You take Lynda, Shun, and Mitch with you. Ya'll go to Northside and handle those three jobs off of Chamberlain. And if you got time, catch those two jobs on Woodrows Ave., too." I knew that they would, I just didn't want to sound like a slave-driver, or something. Because, cutting those lawns on that side of the city, was no joke. When I swerved my attention to Lil Rob and Tisha, they already figured, by then, that his wise crack and her enjoyment of it, had landed them on the shit detail of the day.

Literally!

"And ya'll two", I said, "Ya'll going with me over to Mrs. Jones' house." I didn't need to elaborate any further. They already knew that Mrs. Jones was the widow, who lived not far from Byrd Park, who had a contract with me, every year. One where I would have a truck load of manure delivered to her yard, and then, we would carefully rake the smelly substance over her complete two acre lawn.

They both hung their heads and climbed in the truck with me, after we loaded the rakes and wheelbarrow onto the back of the pick-up. Twenty minutes later, I dropped them off, got them started, and with a shit-eating grin on my face, I told them I would be back. Normally, I would've hung around and worked side-by-side with them ---- but not that day! Their asses were being reminded who was the boss.

I drove to the Post Office on Chamberlain, and checked my P.O. Box that I used for the business. There were several pieces of junk mail, but no check payment from any of the establishments who owed money for services rendered. Quite honestly, I didn't think that it would have been before the first of the month. I only hoped that some of those payments would've arrived before the holiday.

I walked out of the Post office with my eyes glued to a notice informing me that I was one of three people who were finalist of a ten million dollar drawing.

Imagine that!

I thought, right at the point of looking up and seeing, Julie, Silk's mom, walking down the sidewalk toward me. She was wearing a pussy-pink and white sundress with white sandals. I couldn't help but admire how smooth and soft looking her skin was. All I could think was, my pop was a beast when it came to women, because Julie was a fine-ass woman. She was a little too aggressive for my taste, but pure eye-candy, forreal!

"What'sup, Julie?" I asked.

She walked right up so that she and I stood face-to-face. "Damn boy, you look just like your father. You know that?"

"Yeah, I guess." I said, a little intimidated by the way she looked at me. Because she always looked at me like she would fuck me in a heartbeat. Some kind of way that just didn't seem right. But it didn't stop my joint from getting stiff as a board.

Especially when she said, what she always would say, "Come'mere and give Julie a kiss."

'Come where?' I thought to myself, because there wasn't one inch of space between us, already. I watched her lean in and place her lips on mine. She darted her tongue in and around inside my mouth, so quick and passionately, I wasn't sure whether she had actually done it, until afterwards, I tasted that peppermint flavor she always left lingering on my tongue.

"You want a ride somewhere, Julie?" I asked in as about an awkward manner as anyone who had just tongue kissed his half-brother's Mom', and his dead father's ex-girlfriend.

"Naw, Sweetie, I'm just out walking, getting me some air. Maybe next time, though," she said, after backing up and eyeballing me like I was desert.

"Cool," I said. Although, I knew she wasn't out, just for a leisurely stroll, as she stated.

She was, no doubt, heading to 'Blends', a tobacco store, a few blocks away. It was an establishment owned by Mr. Cool.

He was a old-head, whom my father use to get work from, back in the day. Yet, he had been smart enough, and lucky enough to retire from the game, without ever doing a bid. Plus the nigga was caked-the-fuckup! It was no secret that he owned businesses and properties all over the city.

Streetlore holds, that when that brotha was in the game, he never had any problems with a nigga giving him his ends.

But once.

A sheisty-ass nigga by the name of, Crispy, got a package from Mr. Cool ---- fucked it up, and tried to justify his move with some fifteen dollar game. Mr. Cool had merely taken a puff of his exquisite Cuban, blown out a cloud of smoke, before he had said, "We'll work it out."

And they did. Mr. Cool slaughtered his wife and three kids. Plus, he did the worst thing of all -- he left Crispy alive to live with his loss. He had even smiled when he stood over his pitiful body as he had wept, and told him in a true voice, "We straight, now. If you want another 'package' you can get that."

After that, Mr. Cool never had another problem with anyone about his dough. Crispy stuck the barrel of a thirty-eight special in his mouth, on the day of the funeral, and blew his own brains out. As for myself, however, I was glad that my Pop had the sense of mind to do good business with Mr. Cool. They even became cool over the years. Enough that, whenever I got a little nostalgic about my Pop, I would stop thru and holler at the 'O.G.'. The nigga spitted 'good game', the kind that always brought me out of my slump.

Standing on that sidewalk, in front of the Post Office, watching Julie's sexy walk --- I knew Mr. Cool was her Sugar Dad-Dad. He had been fucking her for years, even before my father got killed. He and Silk didn't fuck with each other, that tough. Silk just gave the nigga ten feet, because he knew that Mr. Cool took care of his mother's needs. Plus, Silk knew that fool was just as sick as he was.

I got back into my truck. I looked at my watch, and decided to swing by the crib. Maybe Peaches was up and I could hit that ass real quick, before heading back over to where Lil Rob and Tisha was.

◆◆◆◆◆◆◆◆◆◆◆◆◆◆◆◆◆◆◆◆◆

Peaches was wide awake. But to my dismay, she was still lying in bed looking like it might be that time of the month. She can be a real bitch on those occasions. So cautiously I asked, "What'sup, you aught?"

I could've been tripping, but it looked like she batted back the flow of tears, before she replied, "Yeah, I'm ok. I just wanna lay here and think for awhile ---- if that's ok?"

In other words, she was telling me to put my dick and my tongue away, and carry my ass. "Yeah, that's cool," I lied. "I just came back to check on you.--- that's all."

Her head came up off the pillow, and she looked at me for the first time. "That's so sweet!!"

I felt like a crud-ball, that my lie had garnered such a candy-sweet response from her. Particularly since, I was standing there with the peppermint flavor of Julie's mouth, still smeared on my tongue, knowing perfectly well, I wanted to fuck. Still, I said, I'll call you later, to see if you're feeling better, ok!"

"Thank you, Boo!" She said to my back. I didn't reply, because, I did as she requested ----- carried my ass.

When I got outside, it was my luck to run into Donnell and Donte, twin brothers who lived two doors down from where I lived with Peaches. They were doing what they did, most of the time ---- fight!! And those two muthafuckas could rumble, too. Both of them was about six-four, and weighed over two and a quarter. They wore bald heads, and gold rings in their noses, like fighting bulls. And those niggas were so goddamn black, it looked like they sweated motor oil.

It would take a complete fool to try and get between them while they mixed-it-up. This cock-diesel ass nigga named Big Frank, tried that shit about a month ago ---- and they tore that niggas ass up. Therefore, I gave them brothas their space. That's not to say that I enjoyed any parts of it, like Carla and some others seemed to be doing. The twins were good peeps, as far as I was concerned.

I hated to see them at each other, like that --- so I brought them a move, by saying, "Hey ya'll --- I think five-O might circle the block. So ya'll better chill out.

By that time, they had been locked like two sets of bullhorns, forreal, and tired as shit. I even noticed some relief when I gave them a reason to disengage. I didn't wait to see if they were going to resume; I got in my truck and drove away. It was only after I had gotten a half a block away that I realized, Carla hadn't enjoyed watching the fight, half as much as she had relished glancing at me. The few times I caught her doing so, she had been wearing that self-same look she wore that morning. One that was starting to fuck with my head......

CHAPTER 5

Peaches

When Popcorn left, I got up and ran me some bath water. I saw no need in me lying in bed. After all, everytime I closed my eyes, I saw that motherfucker, Choo-Choo, raping me. Cause, that's what he did --- he took the pussy. I didn't give him shit!

I eased my body down into the steaming hot bubbles, and tried not to think of the role I played in Choo-Choo literally ripping my favorite shorts from my lower body and gangsta' fucking me like I was one of those ho's that strolled up-and-down Chamberlain St. In fact, my shit was still sore from the way he had plowed in and out of me, yesterday. I was so glad that Popcorn hadn't wanted a repeat performance of what he had done the night before. This morning, I had known that he had returned for some mid-morning sex, but turning him away, I knew, would be easy. That's not to say that I enjoyed saying no to my man --- I didn't! I've never turned down his direct or indirect approaches, because again, I'm a firm believer that a woman should open her legs for her man, as often as he wants. That way, she has a right to get 'gangsterette' on the nigga if he creeps on her.

The steam from the bath was rising and cleansing the pores on my face, while the warmth from the water soothed all of my aches and pains, especially between my legs. That nigga had a big dick. He tried to put it in my ass, but I wouldn't let him. Thank God, he had not forced the issue, because he would've pulled my insides out. Shit, he damn near did that to my pussy.

I sat up in the shower-tub and slowly washed the top of my body. I didn't want to, but I had to also admit that there was a point in time, after I had gotten pass the initial shock, when

I was loving what that bastard was doing. He fucked like an untamed animal ---- with a camel's hump in his back, and the craziest look I've ever seen, printed on his face. If I didn't get four orgasms in the fifteen minutes he 'waxed that ass', I didn't get one.

I was out of the bath, patting myself with a towel, when I thought of how Carla had unluckily showed back up at my apartment, right when that nigga was leaving. She had claimed that she had forgotten to ask where I had gotten my tongue pierced. Yet, the way her eyes had scanned Choo-Choo's face and mine, it had been obvious to me, that her ass was just being nosy. It became all the more clear, when she pointed and told that fool his zipper was open. I had felt like dying, right then and there. Because that bitch had given me a look that had said, I was at her mercy. And worse, I was no better than she was.

Believe me, I hated that expression on Carla's face, equally as much as I despised what Choo-Choo had done. Perhaps, that had been the primary reason why I had resolved to tell Popcorn, no sooner than he walked in the door. I was going to tell him 'all of it'!

I swear.

But when that motherfucker walked in and first thing out of his mouth had been, "Did Yolonda call?" It had drained me of whatever need I had felt toward giving him the honesty I had previously felt he deserved. I mean, there I was, a rape victim, and all he could think about was if his other bitch had called. If truth be told, and it must, I got so goddamn angry, I took the cordless into the bathroom and called Choo-Choo on his cell. When he answered, I quickly stroked his ego, by cooing in his ear about how fabulous that dick was. That part, I wasn't lying about. But I regretted telling his crazy-ass that I wanted to see him again, especially upon Popcorn being so sweet and thoughtful that morning.

By twelve o'clock, I was dressed and headed out with the tote bag that contained all my hair styling essentials. I had a perm to do, two streets over from where I lived. This female named, Kiki, who fucked with this 'balla' named, Cash, always wanted something done to her head. With all the chemical I've put in her hair over the last six months, I'm surprised she still had a thread of hair growing from her scalp.

The twins, Donnell and Donte, were sitting on their porch smoking a blunt and sharing a forty ounce bottle of beer. I was surprised that they wasn't arguing or beefing like they normally do. When I saw that Donte had, what looked like, a fresh black eye ---- and Donnell had a cherry-sized knot on his forehead, I figured that they must've already mixed it up.

"What'sup ya'll!" I said. I liked them, they were sweet.

"Just gettin' twisted, Shautie. That's all!," said Donnell, with a king-size smile on his face.

"Yo, Peaches, tell Popcorn, that was good-looking-out." Donte pitched in, before taking another hefty swig from the beer bottle.

I didn't have a clue what he was talking about, but I said, "Ok!"

I was wearing white capris and a sky-blue belly shirt. That shit was fitting me, too. I wasn't surprised, when I got about four feet away, enough for both of them to get a wide-screen view of my 'phat ass', Donnell said, "Peaches, you all that ---- my man, Popcorn a lucky nigga!"

That made my day. Popcorn was lucky. He just didn't know how much. Even with some of the mistakes I've made, I was still a better woman than a whole shipload of Yolondas. His ass just hadn't figured it out yet.

But he had better!

Because, I wasn't going to keep putting up with him acting like Yolonda was 'something special'. When the truth was, she was nothing but a 'hoodrat' with a college degree and a little Assistant Manager's job at the Wachovia Branch Bank, on Chamberlain. She probably requested that particular location, so that she could be close to her 'sister' that be turning the same tricks her ass would've flipped, had she not gotten that scholarship to college.

I was glad as hell to finish Kiki's hair ---- that bitch's apartment stunk like shit. I told her ass, too. She only laughed and told me I was crazy. But in my book, she was the one that was nutty and trifling and had life fucked-up. Not me.

◆◆◆◆◆◆◆◆◆◆◆◆◆◆◆◆◆◆◆◆◆

When I got back to my crib, my sister, Toni was knocking on my door. The bitch had the nerve to be using a handkerchief, as if she might catch an incurable disease, or something. I couldn't imagine what she was doing down there, in the first place. Because none of my family had come within a five-mile radius of Gilpen Court, since I moved there.

I'm glad, when I came up behind her and snapped, "What you want!" She almost jumped out of her linen suit.

With her diamond studded hand placed above her breast, she said, "Girl, don't scare me, like that!"

"Scare you like that?" I asked. "It's broad daylight, and all of the thugs, robbers, and murderers are still sleep." That was my way of reminding her how ridiculous it was that she, along with the rest of my family, thought those were the only kinds of people that resided in projects. It never occurred to them that those types of individuals lived everywhere.

She didn't comment, she knew I was being sarcastic. "Can we go inside?" She asked when she saw the twins coming our way.

I took my time unlocking the door, just to prove to that fool, you can't judge people by their looks. They drove my point home when Donte asked, "Yo, Peaches, we going down to Micky D's, you and your friend want something?"

"Yeah, just don't order no apple pie ---- those joints are whacked," said Donnell, who was checking out Toni as though she was a better meal to eat.

She felt his heat, before she rushed pass me into the apartment. Because her chocolate cheeks had a rosy hue to them. "Naw, ya'll, we straight. But thanks anyway."

I closed the door and was insulted by the fact that Toni had elected to stand, rather than sit her uppity-ass on my furniture. Granted, my shit wasn't the best in the world, but I didn't appreciate her reminding me of it.

"The reason I'm down here, is to -----"

She tried to say, but I cut her ass short. "Whatever you came here for, if you too damn stuck-up to sit down, then you can get the fuck out." I wasn't going to sugar-coat my feelings. They sure as hell didn't when they cut me off. The person I felt I owed a lot to, was my Aunt Reba. She was cool. A class act of a lady, who didn't judge people or turn her back on family --for any reason.

Toni must've known that I wasn't joking, because she sat her sweet ass down, and crossed her legs. 'Now, what was so damn hard about that?' I thought, right when she said, " As I was saying, I'm here to offer you a chance to purchase this cute little three bedroom house, I have listed." She must've sensed I was prepared to say something smart, because she held up her hand, as if to say, 'Wait a minute, I'm not finished.' Then she imparted, "The owner has just lowered their asking price, for the third time. I think it's a excellent buy. When I heard it, I thought of you."

'This bitch is lying!', was the first thing that ran thru my mind. "What makes you think I can afford to buy a home? Don't you think I would've been done moved my daughter out of these projects, if I could?"

She reached in her purse and pulled out a sleek cigarette case. She lit a Virginia Slim, and said, "Because, I'm going to help you --- that's how I know you can afford it."

My lower-jaw almost landed in my lap. When did this greedy bitch buy herself a heart? She was two years older than me. Since I was the youngest in the family and had gotten most of the attention from our parents, and two older sisters, she was always envious of me. In fact, it had given her pleasure when I got blackballed.

She got her Real Estate and Finance Degree, four years ago, and became a Platinum Sales Agent, overnight. Her true aspiration, if I knew her, was to start her own Realty Company, before long. But for now, she was sitting in my living room, offering to help me buy a house.

That shit didn't fit.

That's why I asked her, "What's in it for you?"

She thought about it for a quick moment, before she said, "Let's just say, I owe you, and leave it at that." She spied an ashtray on the coffee table and plucked her ashes.

I looked at my watch. It was time for Tondra's school bus to arrive. "Well, let me think about it, and talk it over with my man." She looked as though she had an objection to make, when I said, 'my man', so I asked with a serious tone, "You got a problem with that?"

Apparently, she thought better of it, because she only shook her head, indicating that she didn't. I thought to myself, 'You bet not!' Then I said, "Well, I gotta go, my daughter's bus should be coming."

We both went out the door. When we got to her car, I could tell she wanted me to ask her to wait and see Tondra ---- but I didn't! In my mind, it was going to take a whole lot more, in order for me to invite her into my daughter's life. So, she gave me her business card, and left.

As I walked toward the bus stop, I had to admit, it felt good having something special to tell Popcorn, tonight. Thanks to Toni, I may be able to put that shit with Choo-Choo behind me.

But then, ain't no tellin'.

CHAPTER 6

Popcorn

At five-thirty that evening, the sun was riding low, but luminously toward the western horizon. I dropped Lil Rob and Tisha off on Broad Street, with a firm belief that they understood who the boss was, at that point. They had a shitty day, but they both smiled and said they would see me in the morning.

When I arrived at the garage where I stored my equipment at, Smokey was already there. I unloaded the wheelbarrow and rakes from my truck, first. Then, as I helped him down load what was stacked on his Chevy pickup, I asked, "Did ya'll finish up everything?"

"No doubt!" Smokey replied. He was the first person I hired and had proved to be the most reliable. Especially in the wintertime, when our sole source of income came from snow plowing. That brotha didn't mind hitching one of those snow blades to the front of his truck, like I did, and hustled all over the city, clearing off parking lots, private roads, and even small driveways.

Smokey was my kind of nigga.

We locked up, pounded fist, and drove off to enjoy the rest of our day.

I swung by my Moms, as I normally did. Rainy was sitting out on the porch as though she was waiting for me. I didn't like the look on her face, when she said, "I need to talk to you ---- it's important!"

"Aught." I said. "What is it?"

She got up off the step and started walking toward my truck, so I followed her. It was obvious that she didn't want anyone overhearing our conversation. She turned and faced me with her lips twisted the way Bay-B'ay had described. If she had perfected that look before, I had never noticed it. Or that she had breast and hips and a woman's behind, until she said, "There's this guy that wanna have sex with me, I like him, but he's much older than I am. So what you think?"

I didn't realize that I had sat down on the bumper of my truck as though someone had punched me in the gut. All I could think at that moment was, 'I'ma kill the muthafucka!! Whoever the over-grown, perverted son of a bitch ---- I'ma break his goddamn neck!'

Yet, when I looked at her and realized the degree of trust she was placing in me, I knew I had to maintain my composure. If I didn't, the next time, she wouldn't ask my advice. Which would only increase the chance of some nigga having her pregnant before she turned thirteen. Therefore, with as much calmness as I could give to my voice, I said, "Well, it sounds to me like it's not something that you really wanna do, right now. So it'll probably be best that you don't. Because, when a woman do something 'that important', she should be absolutely sure it's

46

what she wants to do." I noticed, when I said 'woman', she stood up a little straighter, as though she was glad that somebody had finally realized that she wasn't a little girl anymore. Someone besides that nigga who was trying to fuck her, that is.

But then, without realizing it, she sounded just like the child she still was, when she looked off to one side of me and said, "But suppose he don't want me, after that."

"Fuck'em!!" I thought I may have said it a tad-bit stronger than I should've. "That'll only mean he wanted you for the wrong reasons in the first place." I said, with a strong desire to ask who this mystery muthafucka was. I refrained from asking, however, because I didn't want to spook her. I did ask, "How old is he, anyway?"

"Twenty-something," She said, as if his age was supposed to prove she was a woman.

I hoped she couldn't see the blood in my eyes. Because, at that moment, I desperately wanted to kill!

"But you right, I think that's what Pop would've said." That was the best compliment for me, that she had ever awarded me. That and the fact that she agreed with my advice, placed me at ease. She also said, "Come on, I wanna show you my new gear." Right when my cell rang.

"Yo!" I answered.

I felt my pulse speed up, upon hearing, what sounded like a cracker, a old one at that, say, "What's happening, Popcorn! The wife and I are at the Comfort Inn., on a street called Chamberlain. When you get a chance, stop thru. We're in room 338. We got a message from Bay-Bay."

I merely said, "I'll be right there."

Rainy had been looking me right in the mouth, the whole time. She said, with her hands on her hips, "You don't have time to look at my stuff, first?" She twisted them lips, again.

I've been waiting all my life for this, I figured I could cool my heels long enough for babygirl to show me her gear. After all, the respect she had just given to me, by trusting in my judgment, was something else I've been anticipating. Now that I had her respect, it was up to me to hold on to it.....

I knocked cautiously on door 338, because I knew of those sting operations where the Feds would bait you in, give you drugs, and then arrest you as if it had been all your idea. I didn't believe that my man, Bay-Bay, would fuck me like that. But hearing that cracker on the phone had me a little 'noid'.

A white woman who stood as tall as my six-foot frame, door. "Popcorn!" She almost shouted, as if she knew me like that. "Come on in, Sugar." She had to be damn close to sixty, but that black cat-suit she was wearing, with three-inch heels, made me think, *'Daaamn!! Grandma is 'phat to death!'*

A much older guy, who seemed to be in good shape for his age, strolled out of the bathroom with a towel wrapped around his mid section. His hair was matted to his head, and when he walked over to get the two black canvas bags from the far side of the bed, I noticed a slew of freshly made whips on his back. I glanced at a bushytail whip, as long as a baseball bat, lying on the bed, and I understood why.

"They all should be there, Brotha. You can count'em if you like. He said as though Bay-Bay had them believing I knew the amount.

Rather than tilt my hand, I said, "It's cool! If we gonna be doing business, we gotta trust one another, right?"

The man stuck his hand out and said, "I'm J.R., and that's my wife, Big Titty Rose."

I gripped his hand, while wondering, *Where did she ever get a name like that?*, because she barely had a mouthful of breast. "Well, it's nice meeting y'a'll." I said. But I was ready to get my ass out of there. I liked them ---- they seemed cool. Yet, I felt uncomfortable as hell being around half naked white people, whips, and I'm sure it was some handcuffs lying around in that room, somewhere.

"We look forward to doing business with you." J.R. said as he walked over and put his arm around his wife.

She was smiling when she said, "Yeah, Popcorn, you call us anytime."

I reached and grabbed the two bags, before saying, "Well, I'll see ya'll next time, then. Be cool!" I rolled out.

When I got in my truck, I peeped inside one of the bags, and said, "Goddamn!!" Because my partna had hooked me up ---- forreal!

From Chamberlain, I cruised across Lumbard St. and made a left on Lee St., that took me straight to Yolonda's. By then, it was about a quarter to eight, and approaching darkness.

I was hyper as shit, once I parked and walked to her door with the two bags full of brick cocaine. She answered the doorbell wearing Baby-Phat jeans and a tank-top. "What'sup!" I said, as I breezed on in pass her.

"Nothing much." She replied, while closing the door. "Is that what you was telling me about?" She pointed at the bags.

"Yeah. Where you want me to put'em."

She thought about it for a second. "Come on ---- you can put those up in one of the spare bedrooms."

"Are you sure you cool wit this, Londa?" I asked, once we were standing in the bedroom of her two-story townhouse.

"Tsk!! Yeah I'm alright with it, boy. I said I was, didn't I?" She replied. Yet, deep down inside, I was wondering if she was regretting the fact that she had agreed to allow me to stash my drugs at her house. I was thinking she may have felt she had no alternative, being that we had been best buddies, forever.

"A nigga know what you said, yesterday. But still, I gotta be sure we on the same page, 'cause this shit ain't no joke."

I almost picked up the bags and walked out, because she didn't respond for a full moment. She even averted her eyes from my cat-green gaze, down to the canvas bags that sat beside the beat-up 'Timbs' I worked in. But then, she said in almost a whisper, "I know all of is serious business, Kevin." She always called me by my real name when she was dead serious about something. "So believe me, if I was uncomfortable with any parts of this --- I would tell you." She looked at her Gucci time-piece after that. I didn't know if she was trying to hide something in her eyes from me, or if she truly wanted to know what time it was.

In either case, I smiled and started stacking the bricks in the empty chest-of-drawers. When I finished, I knew Bay-Bay, a generous muthafucka, had sent me twenty-five joints to get my feet wet. That meant, I owed him four-hundred and fifty G's. That realization made my head swim, some, before I flung five of the bricks` back into one of the bags, so that I could get at Silk, as soon as I left.

Yolonda had left me to handle my business. When I walked back down stairs, she was lounging on her sofa, watching television. I looked around at how neat and orderly her den was --- and the plants she had in there grew their leaves straight and neat as though they understood her taste.

"What you looking at?" I asked before I could see the screen.

"CNN News," she replied, without taking her attention from the newscast. "I can't believe they're talking about giving the governing power back to the Iraqi's in thirty days." I didn't know what she was talking about, because I wasn't keeping up with that crazy-ass war. Still, she added, "Those people aren't stupid! They know that Governing Council will be made up of puppeteers for the American Government." She shook her head. "I just hope George Bush don't steal another election because our asses are in big trouble if he do."

I wasn't trying to talk politics. I was on a mission, that if it came off, George W. could kiss my ass! "I 'm out of here, Baby."

She got off the sofa and walked toward me with her hand extended. At first, I thought she wanted me to shake her hand like I done with J.R., but then, I saw she was handing me a door key. "I guess you're going to need this, right?"

That caught me off guard, because I hadn't thought of the fact that, every time I needed to get something, she may not be home. I accepted the key with a full belief that 'she had' thought 'it over, completely, and knew exactly how serious things were. No doubt, she was demonstrating her trust in me. In her eyes, I could see that she was relying on me to keep drama away from her and her home. With my own, I was promising her that I would. Then, I left.

CHAPTER 7

Silk

"I'm tellin' you, Shautie, you don't need to give that nigga no mo' dough for that slum he's dealing. I'ma be 'that nigga' real soon ---- and I got'cha!" I said to a gangsta broad named Fame. She owned the crack-house I was parked in front of on Brooklyn Park St., and another one on Norfolk Ave.

She smiled, "Silk, you always talkin' 'bout pluggin' big, and I ain't seen that happen, yet." She was leaning down with her arms on the open window frame of my hoopty. She was a thick chocolate honie, who didn't mind showing a brotha plenty of cleavage. She and I had never done any of that freaky shit, yet she knew I was trying to get at her. She was fucking with this bitch-ass nigga, named Winky, who called himself pimping at her 'cause she was getting' it' for a female on that level. From what I could see, he was coming off, but so was she. Because she was dragging his ass, every chance she got.

Me, I wasn't over there for no romance shit. I was hollering at her, like I had been doing all day with niggas in all sections of the city. Like her, everybody thought I was stuntin'. That's why, if Popcorn didn't come thru like he had said, me and that nigga was gonna' have some serious problems.

I kept my eyes on her breast as I said, "Yeah, but them niggas fakin', Shautie, not me. This time, though, it's 'bout to go down ---- and that's on all I love."

She ran her tongue across her top front teeth, not knowing how much I liked that cute shit. Before she said, "Well .... since I've never heard you say it like that, maybe I'll believe you this time." I was thinking to myself, 'This bitch likes me fo'sho!', right when she went on to say, "If you 'come up' before Choo-Choo score some better quality shit, then I'll be down wit'choo. Ok Boo!"

"I'm feelin' that." I said, as I started up my '76 Duce-and-a-Quarter. I idled for ten seconds, long enough to watch her work those hip-hugger jeans, back toward the little white house .... with a picket fence.

As soon as I pulled off, my cellphone rang, "What up!" I barked into the reciever, like I was already holdin' weight.

"Where you at?" Popcorn asked.

"Heading toward Norfolk Ave --- why??" I snapped back to let his ass know, I was getting tired of all the goddamn questions. Because I had one of my own ---- 'Where's that shit at??'

"Meet me at Byrd --- - lets feed some ducks."

I made a right turn onto Norfolk Ave, before it fully dawned on me that that nigga might be holding. But then, I had the common sense not to let my imagination run wild. I needed to see with my own eyes what he was working with prior to me getting excited about it. On the forrealla', when he came thru like he claimed, he may only have a couple bricks --- and that shit might be pure garbage. I thought to myself, if that was the case, he could count me out.

But who was I bullshitting.

Right at that point, that nigga could offer me some Pillsbury flour, and I'd accept it with a smile.

Just as I crossed the 'Dime Bridge', I thought of Putty, for the first time that day. My hands started sweating, as they always do when I ruminate about one of those bitch-ass niggas I had to slump. It's not like I was having regrets about what I did to him, because, in my mind, he brought the roof down on himself. It's just that I was thinking about how it had taken all that night and half the next day, before somebody had discovered his stankin' ass. After that, a few plain-clothes detectives had knocked on a few doors pretending that they gave a fuck. When no one seemed enthused about snitchin', they packed up and got the hell out of there.

I cruised up into Byrd Park, and followed the road around to the duck pond, with a murderous grit published on my face. Because, the fact that Putty had been beaten, and then stabbed, had left little doubt in anybody's mind, who lived in Wilcom Court, that that had been my work. Yet, like a few other times I had to slaughter a nigga on the home-front, they was holding me down.

Protecting they own.

I was sitting in my parked car, with the music blasting, thinking about how much I loved that kind of shit, right when Popcorn drove up and parked right beside me. He got out the truck with no expression on his face, but I didn't need to see anything there to know what was on his mind. That nigga was holding a black canvas bag --- that said it all!

He flung that joint onto the back seat, before he opened my passenger door and copped-a-squat. I turned down the CD player, before I said, "Is that it?"

"Yeah, but not all of it." He made clear. "That's only five of what I got. When you got that hundred-fifteen, get at me, and I'll bring you five more."

"Then you must be plannin' on drivin' back-and-forth to this duck pond, all night." I said with a baby-grit on my mug. Although, I wasn't mad at the nigga for trying to spoon feed me, a little at a time. Because, it only proved that he had paid close attention to our Pop, who had said on numerous occasions, *'Never front all your product coming out the gate. That's bad karma, and stupid'*.

"What you mean by that?"

I could tell by that look on his face, he didn't have a clue that the city was experiencing a vicious cocaine drought. So I served him like this, "Nigga, this whole set, is fucked-up! Right now, we the only muthafuckas that's holdin', besides Choo-Choo. And he got straight slum. So, if you holdin' like that, we gettin' ready to lock this shit down!"

"We straight, Yo." he said.

But I tested his ass, by saying, "Good! Cause I'm gonna run thru forty or fifty of these joints, in forty-eight hours."

The nigga didn't flinch or nothing. So I thought, 'Goddamn!! This shit is on!' Before I started up the Buick, and said, "I'm out of here, my nigga --- I got major shit to do." I waited until he was out of the car before I said, "When I holla', quit fakin' and bring me ten of them joints." I backed up and drove off, before he could respond.

◆◆◆◆◆◆◆◆◆◆◆◆◆◆◆◆◆◆◆◆◆◆

"Taste that shit, Nigga! I ain't fakin' ---- I just got a whole tractor trailer load of this fish-scale from Columbia, this morning." I said as me, Tiny and Frenchie stood in Frenchie's kitchen.

I had already used my knife to slit the vaccum-seald wrapper of the brick that was on his jelly-stained kitchen table. So he wetted the tip of his fat finger, and tapped the brick hard coke, before he dabbed it on his tongue. "Shit!!" He said as though that powder had been the best shit he'd tasted all day. "I love you, Nigga. This shit is the bomb!"

Tiny was smiling as if that was the proudest moment of his life. I knew, like fame, he hadn't believed that I was going to come off, that time. Because, in the past, I had told his ass that certain things was going to happen, that had never materialized. He never tripped about it, or threw any of that shit back in my face. He just rolled with it, like I did, pumping those big eights and keeping our noses above water. Now that that moment had arrived, I was just as happy for him, as I was for myself. On all I love, I was going to take that shit to the highest level. And my dawg was going to be with me, every step of the way.

I volleyed back to Frenchie, "Well, let's do this then, nigga. Give me twenty-eight, so you can handle your business."

"Twenty-eight! Damn, Silk, let a nigga eat, too." Frenchie said, although, he knew, under the circumstances, twenty-eight was a sweet ticket.

That's why, the best I could tell him was, "Don't worry, my nigga. When this drought is over, I'ma look-out."I didn't tell him how much, though, I just left it at that. Either way, he was coming off, and we both knew it.

Frenchie licked his lips, as he eyed the brick, one more time, ahead of him saying, "Give me a coupla' minutes, Silk --- let me see if I got that kinda' dough." He wobbled his fat-ass back to his bedroom, and fifteen seconds flat, he was back at the table where he carefully counted out twenty-eight stacks of cheddar. Once he finished, he said, "There's a grand in each stack, Silk."

"I'm hip to you, nigga." I said as I scooped the dough into the dote bag Tiny was holding. "Your money be so correct, you stack them bitches by the dates and serial numbers."

He laughed so hard, his big belly shook like jelly. But that didn't stop him from pulling out his purex containers and huge box of baking-soda. He was ready to perfect his 'cook up' skills, whether we stood there or not.

I hate the smell of that shit, so we tore-ass getting the fuck out of there.

◆◆◆◆◆◆◆◆◆◆◆◆◆◆◆◆◆◆◆◆◆◆

We left Frenchie's crib and drove straight over to Fairfield Court. It was after ten p.m., but out in front of the red brick structure, a ole-head named Bunky lived in, a gang of school age kids were hanging out ---- smoking cigarettes and talking shit. I parked and Tiny and I scooped past the ruckas those little toughlooking wannabes were making.

After knocking on Bunky's badly dented door, I scanned the area and noticed that the niggas in Fairfield were just as restless as the ones had been down in Wilcom before I laced up Frenchie. Now, those niggas on the home-front were back at being wide the fuck open. The same way that joint was going to be, as soon as I finished getting at Bunky.

He opened his door and I cracked out the side of my mouth, "What up, O.G.?"

"Ain't nothin' goin' on, Silk. Jus' the same ole same." He was wearing a wife-beater, beige slacks, and his signature, big block gators. I've never seen Bunky without a pair of gators on, since he moved to V-A from Baltimore, in the early nineties ---- and joined my Pop's crew. I was young, then, but I always liked the old timer. Maybe, because I had never seen him smile, and the fact that he was a 'good nigga' that knew precisely how the hustling game went. In my opinion, his only flaw was, he loved a young and freaky bitch. Perhaps that was why he had never bothered to move from the projects, he understood that the hood was a breeding ground for the kind of chicken-heads he liked.

But, maybe not.

I did know, however, that a twenty-anything broad with mad sex skills, could get that nigga's last dollar. All she would need was a half-ass story to spoon feed him, after sucking his dick and licking his ass.

He opened the door wider and said, "Come on in ---- ya'll want some Remy, or somethin'?"

"Yeah, let us get that." I squatted on the sofa, with my dawg, Tiny, standing off to my left. I knew Tiny wasn't hipped to that nineteen-sixty-nine grit that Bunky wore all the time, which was why he was posted up in a manner that would enable him to get to those two P.89 Rugers he had tucked in his waist band. I didn't bother to tell him to be cool and chill out. Because with him posted like he was, it made me feel more like 'that nigga' I was on my way to becoming.

Bunky handed me my drink, but sat Tiny's on the coffee table, which proved that Tiny's grit was just as fierce as his. He seated himself across from us, crossed his leg, and said,"I heard you da ' man, Silk."

I took a quick sip of the Remy, and smoothly replied, "You heard right, O-G. You tryin' to get down wit it, or what?" Then I thought to myself, 'Goddamn!!! Frenchie must be cookin' up that shit with one hand, and dialing up every muthafucka in Richmond, with his other.' But it was all good, though. In truth, that had been the main reason I had got at his ass, first. I had known he would put the word out quicker than a mean-spirited whore could spread AIDS. That way, niggas like Bunky and some others I planned on getting at in Churchhill, would already have their ends counted out and waiting.

Bunky pretended like it required some 'hellacious' thought, before he said, "Yeah, Silk, I'm tryin' to do somethin' wit'cha. But I hope you know, Choo-Choo ain't gon preciate you workin' on his turf."

Tiny downed his drink and almost slammed the glass back on the coffee table, and I smiled to myself before I said, "No disrespect to you Bunky, but do it look like I give a fuck about what that bitch-ass nigga appreciates?"

Bunky was one of those older coons that had a habit of doing exactly what you ask. I had been around him often enough that I knew he wasn't being sarcastic when he looked at me and then Tiny, as if he was taking inventory of who we were, forreal. After that, his hard face formed the closest thing he possessed of a smile, before he said, "Naw, I guess not. Ya'll two niggas look like ya'll don't give a flyin' fuck 'bout nobody."

Now, that's why I liked that muthafucka, he called it the way he saw it. I reached in the bag and pulled out a brick of that coke. I placed it on the glass table. "They twenty-eight a pop, O.G.. If you don't have the whole thing, you can get at me later. Cause word carries weight wit me."

He was back at gritting, again, when he reached under the chair cushion he was sitting on, and pulled out a brown paper bag. He placed it beside the solid brick of cocaine, before he looked at me, and said, "If you wanna do somethin' for me, young Prince, then let me get two of them joints, for that."

I thought to myself, 'Oh, you good, nigga.' Because he had stroked the shit out of me, just then, by calling me by my Pops name. He knew that, although I've talked mad shit about not liking my father, I've strived my whole life to be like that nigga, on some level. And Bunky was smart enough to use that, at that moment to get himself a little play on the price. "How much dough you workin' wit in that bag?"

"Fifty-four Gs."

"Aught, I can do that for you, O.G. Just make sho' you correct the next time. That's all I ask." I said. Not merely from the stroke game he had put down, but also, because I figured that that two grand was going to motivate Bunky to keep me plugged with whatever ChooChoo might say in his presence. That kind of shit was priceless, in my mind.

I stacked the other 'key' on the coffee table, got my dough, and we left. When we got outside, a few of those kids were sitting on the hood of somebody's 'STS', like they didn't care or believe that niggas got slumped for shit like that.

"Why you let'em get away wit that short money, Silk?" Tiny asked. Probably due to the fact that, when we was slinging dime bags of crack, we didn't believe in taking no shorts. And everybody knew they had to come correct.

I didn't bother to give a full explanation, but I did say,"We on a different level now, Dawg. The rules we used yesterday, don't apply today. You feel what I'm sayin'."

He chewed it over as we got into the car, then he said, "But some rules stay the same, no matter what. Right!"

I knew he was talking about the killing part, when a nigga violated. So I responded, "That's f o'sho!"

As we headed for Creighton Court Projects to get at this nigga named Pancake, I called Popcorn and said, "Quack, quack, nigga ---- lets roll!!"

CHAPTER 8

Popcorn

Around eleven a.m., Saturday morning of the Labor Day Weekend, Peaches and Tondra were gone to King's Dominion with Carla and her three sweet little daughters. Therefore, I told Silk it was cool for him to drop thru, instead of us meeting at the duck pond. I had taken him ten more kilos of coke, that same night I had given him the five joints, beforehand. For a minute, I had been worried about running out. That's why I had gotten right on the cell and called Bay-Bay. He proved decisively, that he wasn't faking about what he had vowed he could do. Because, at exactly seven o'clock that morning, I had met J.R. and Big Titty Rose at the Comfort Inn, again. They had helped me carry down five large suitcases and well-baked bricks of premium 'yayo', and loaded it into the back of my pickup. They both had been wearing lightweight jogging suits and well-baked tans that had given them the appearances of that of a brotha and a sista.

Especially Grandma!

In that outfit, she had still looked 'phat to death'. Believe it or not, even more so than she had looked in that catsuit she had worn two days ago.

Nevertheless, we chatted for three seconds flat, beyond loading up my work. Being that I had already given them the tote bag containing the four hundred and fifty Gs I owed Bay-Bay. All I could think at that time was, O'boy must really have a lot of confidence in those two. Because, shit, that was enough dough to retire them if they decided to 'get ghost' with his ends.

When I arrived at Yolonda's, she wasn't home. I felt a little strange being in her house, without her being there. But that feeling quickly dissolved after I reminded myself, she 'gave me' her house key, I didn't ask for it.

I had carefully stacked the bricks in all of the drawers of that spare bedroom. Except for the fifteen I was holding for Silk at that moment.

For some reason, I can't explain, the crib seemed extra quiet and that Anthony Hamilton Cd that was smoothly flowing from the stereo, felt like it was warming every fiber of my being. Perhaps it had a lot to do with the fact that I was squatting on a hundred twenty five grand, already, and I had only been in the game for a 'hot second.'

I did know that I had better keep my goals and objectives clear in my head. Because, I had no intentions of staying in that shit, forever. I was knee-deep in the game, for all kinds of reasons, at that point. Yet, none of my 'becauses' were related to the knuckle-headed shit that a lot of niggas hustle for. Like cars, jewelry, freakin' with a million honies ---- and worst of all, for the fame. In my mind, that shit was nothing! Because, what good would it do a muthafucka to have had all of those things, but ends up in a federal prison with forever. Or, dead. None.

That's why I've promised myself that I was going to at least try to make all the right moves. At the end of the day, I wanted to be caked and still free to enjoy what I've put everything on the line for. At the rate things were going, I felt assured that I could stack a 'mil', plus, before the end of the summer. I realized then in that day in time, a million dollars wasn't much to brag about. But for a nigga with vision, like I had, it could help to take me where I wanted to go in life.

Fo sho!

◆◆◆◆◆◆◆◆◆◆◆◆◆◆◆◆◆◆◆◆◆

Silk knocked on the door like he was being chased by the feds. Or, like he was simply being the goddamn fool that he was. In either case, I spied him thru the peep hole, before I opened it.

"Fuck you doing up in that tip ---- sleepin' or somethin'?" He asked, as he and Tiny walked pass me.

I was wearing baggy shorts, Air Force 1's, and a throw-back Jordan jersey. Plus, I knew that I looked fresh and wide awake. Therefore, I didn't feed into his sarcasm. I couldn't say the same for him and his man, because those fools looked like they hadn't been between a set of sheets in days. And if I wasn't mistaken, it looked like they were still rocking the same clothes from Thursday night.

"Cause don't nothin' come to a sleeper, but dreams. You got to be in it, to win it ---- like me and my dawg." He cliched his ass all the way into the kitchen, where he started digging around in the refrigerator for something to snack on.

I watched him pitch a big juicy apple to Tiny and began to munch on one himself, before I said, "How long you think the drought is gonna last?"

He sat at the table beside Tiny and said, "Ain't gon matter, 'cause we sewin' shit up. Therefore, for the rest of the niggas, the drought ain't gon ever end." He slapped a high-five with his man.

It surprised me that he couldn't see what was wrong with that picture. Especially since, our Pops always told me, and I know he told him as well, the worst time in a dealers life, was when he was lucky enough to be that supreme muthafucka in a city. Because that also made him 'that nigga' that niggas loved to hate, and the feds became focused upon until they locked him up ---- and boosted their careers.

Since he was my brotha, I felt obligated to say, "You think that's a good idea ----- not lettin' another nigga get his?" It looked like he had taken what I said, the wrong way, so I added, "I mean, goddamn, yo, it's enough cheddar out there for everybody,"

He was still exasperated by my logical stance, because he said, "Nigga, just get me that shit you got for me   and let me worry about the rest." He threw the apple core into the waste basket, and went back to the food box and snagged some grapes. When Peaches asked what the fuck happened to all the fruit, I was going to snitch his ass out since he had chosen to get flip-out-the-mouth.

I went and got the fifteen 'keys' and dropped the canvas bag at his feet. He looked inside and tried to appear as nonchalant as he had been about the other shit I had given him over the last few days.

But who was he fooling?

He was a nigga that had been accustomed to copping four and a half ounces at a time. And then, overnight, he slingin' bricks. So tell the nigga to give a break, and stop trying to look like he wasn't as impressed as I was about the amount that was in that bag.

I don't think I've ever heard Tiny say over three words, so I didn't trip in the least, by him just sitting there not humming a word. Only looking at Silk like he thought him God or something. It's all good though. I wish I had me a friend like that.

"You owe me three forty-five for that one, Yo." I said, just to make sure he and I was clear about the ticket. That was one thing I learned, you always made clear. Even when it seemed obvious. Because a misunderstanding about that dough could make the best muthafuckas fall out and be trying to split each other's wigs.

"Auight, we outta here!" Silk barked, as they stood from the table and Tiny hoisted the huge bag of drugs, as though it was a bag full of feathers.

◆◆◆◆◆◆◆◆◆◆◆◆◆◆◆◆◆◆◆◆◆◆

After that, I got in my truck and drove over to Momdukes. Although it was the weekend, and a holiday at that, I knew she would be at home, chilling. Being that those were the only times that she had gotten the chance to catch up on the things around the house that needed her attention. Sure, Rainy was a big help, in terms of cooking and cleaning and keeping the laundry with that special touch of a mother.

I parked at the curb of my family's house, and was pleased that Smokey had already been thru like he normally does on Saturdays, and cut the grass. It looked good and smelled great ---- nothing could beat the aroma of freshly cut grass. At least, in my mind it couldn't.

I found my Moms back in the kitchen listening to Kiss FM radio, an oldies but goodies station. Al Green's 'Let Stay Together' had her singing right along and swaying her hips ---- probably thinking about one of those occasions when her and my Pop had slow grinded on that classic tune. She had that look on her face, plus it seemed to me that she had forgotten that her hands were holding a cloth and a dirty dish in some dish-water.

"Oooh yeah!! You still got it like that?" I asked as I sat the glass top kitchen table.

She was smiling as though she was a tad-bit embarrassed that I had caught her in her groove. Still, she said, "Don't you let these few gray hairs fool you --- I can still dance circles around you."

She probably could have, too. Because, seeing her wearing something other than one of those damn uniforms she worked in, helped me to remember how in-shape, and shapely my Moms was. I'm not going to front, she couldn't get in Julies business, no way, no how. But in her own right, Momdukes was a strong eight and three-quarters on a scale from one to ten. Of course, that was in appearance alone. Every other kind of attribute you could think of, Moms was a straight dime piece!

"I hear you, Babygirl." I said, with a true smile.

She dried her hands and walked over to the 'fridge'. She didn't ask if I wanted something to eat, she just started hooking me up with one of those hokie joints that couldn't nobody fix for me, like she could. During that time, she and I, we kicked it about Precious and Rainy and everything else under the sun. Although, I didn't share with her what Rainy had confided in me. I figured that was meant to be my headache, and mine alone.

I polished off that sandwich and drunk the ice cold lemonade she served with it, before I gathered the strength to look her in the face and say, "You gonna have a right to be upset with me, but I got to tell you this, anyway." I watched her turn serious and motherly all at once. It broke my heart for me to have to give her the 411 about me slinging. But after what she went thru, having to deal with my father's death, I felt I owed her the heads up on me. Especially, since we've always kept it real with each other. And because, if shit went wrong in any way with me, she would be the one person, for sure, I knew would be there ---- no matter what. That's why, in spite of me preferring not to, I continued by saying, "I'm in the game, for a minute."

She got up from the table, walked over and got a cigarette from the cookie jar I knew she kept stashed there. She lit up and I could see that her hands shook. Her eyes weren't mean looking like I imagined that they would be, nor did she respond with the anger that I anticipated.

68

"You not mad at me?" I had to ask.

"Of course not ---- why should I be? That's what you were brought up around, all your life." She took a strong pull of the Newport. "I'm just grateful, I guess, that at least you waited until you were old enough to make this decision, knowing what the consequences bring. And you do know what they are, right?"

"Yes Mama, I've looked at everything, including what happened to Pop, in the end ---- and still believe it's worth it." I shook the ice cubes around in the large glass, as though I was studying the cubes. Before I added, "Plus, I think it's what Pop would've wanted."

What you mean by that?" She shot back like a pistol.

"For me to step-up, and look out for you and the girls." I got up from the table, after saying that, and put my arms around her. She was shaking, a little, and I knew why. She knew there were no words to change my frame of mind.

It was a done deal.

I was tired of her struggling and barely making it. I had tried to do shit the right way, and she knew it. Just as she knew, if I didn't step up to the plate, at some point, we could all drown.

She broke free of my embrace, and smashed her cigarette out, as if she was trying to rub out all of the obstacles that, even in the new millennium, still prevented a young black man from living a good life ---- unless he sold drugs. After that, she gripped my face with both her hands, and said, "You better be careful because, if any harm comes to you, it's going to kill me."

I felt her, but I didn't respond. There were too many uncertainties in the game, and I knew that she understood that better than I did. I only said, "I gotta use the bathroom, and then I gotta go. Auight?"

She smiled for the first time since I started that discussion, prior to her saying, "Well, at least some things never change. Your food still running right through you, no sooner than you eat it." She went hack to washing the dishes that were in the sudsy water.

I felt better. Like a vicious load had been lifted from my shoulders. My favorite girl had been apprised, and she wasn't mad as hell at me for trying to 'do da damn thang.' When I got to the bathroom door, I listened and heard clearly that she was still in the kitchen humming another tune from back in her day. Therefore, I dotted into her bedroom quickly, placed the pouch I had tucked in my waistband under her pillow. She always got down on her knees before she crawled into bed. That night after she finished whispering her prayers, I knew some of them would be answered. That twenty-five Gs I had just given her assured me of that.

CHAPTER 9

Peaches

I was tired as if I had run a marathon of some type, once Tondra and I returned from the amusement park. I even said to her, "Girl, you wore your Mama out!", while I was unlocking the door to the apartment.

She, with her ineffable smile, said, "Yeah, but didn't you have a good time, though?"

I flopped down on the sofa, kicked off my shoes, and agreed by saying, "I sure did! But that don't stop my damn feet from hurting."

She started laughing and hugging her stuffed animals we won for her, a little tighter, before she raced for her room. I was happy that we had a fun day, especially since she was flying off to be with her father in a few more days. I wanted her to have something warm and memorable, that we had done recently, tucked behind her heart. That had been the main reason I hadn't tripped when Popcorn told me he wasn't going, because he had something to do. I simply looked at it as an opportunity for Tondra and I to enjoy some quality time.

But I had thought, however, I had better not discover that his 'something to do' was with that bitch, Yolonda. I knew I would have no understanding about that shit.

I got up off the sofa and drug my tired ass upstairs to my bedroom. As soon as I flopped on the bed and reached for the remote, I heard Popcorn come in and close the front door. I glanced at the clock, it was half pass nine. I don't know why, but I had thought it much later than that.

I heard him coming up the stairs, so I kept the television off. I wanted to ask him, once more, if he was about.

"Ya'll have a good time?" He asked, as soon as he walked into the room serious about us buying that house my sister, Toni, had told me

"It would've been better, if you came along," I lied. But it was ok!"

He didn't comment. He seemed just as remote as he had appeared over the last few days. Almost as if he had a ton of shit on his mind ---- all of a sudden.

So I casually said, while he was removing his clothes, "I'ma try to get in touch with Toni, tomorrow, to see if that house is still available. But are you sure that I should tell her we don't need her financial help?"

He didn't look upset from the fact that I was questioning his stance from the other night. He merely laid his clothes in the chair, as he always did, before he said, "Yeah, I'm sure. I think we can handle that shit on our own. The down payment can't be no more than ten percent. Whatever that is, I should be able to come up with that."

My heart felt like it was brimming with love for that nigga, at that moment. Because I loved a man that wasn't afraid of a challenge. In my mind, that's what purchasing that house was going to be, a pure test of our strengths. After all, his earning power with his landscaping business, hadn't been all that impressive.

"What about furniture?" I asked, as I stood up to undress, myself.

"What about it?" He volleyed back at me.

"You know we gonna need some new stuff. I mean, this furniture I got now was some hand-me-down shit my Aunt Reba was nice enough to give me. It was cool for this, but we gonna need some different things for a house."

"I agree, so maybe you oughta think about throwing in all that dough you got bama'd in the floor, in the closet." After that, he smiled at me, before he walked out to the upstairs bathroom, wearing his robe. Tondra had caught him once, coming out of the bathroom one morning with nothing on, but his underwear. It made him feel fucked-up. So he's probably the only nigga in the projects with a silk-bordered robe.

I had liked that in him.

That it was important that he showed my daughter respect. I know it had a lot to do with the fact that he had sisters, whom he would want niggas to respect. But still, I believed it went further than that.

"How long have you known about my stash?" I asked, while being a little pissed that he had snooped around in my shit like that.

"Well let me see," he said, as he flung his robe onto the same chair as his clothes. "I think it was over a month ago that you left the floorboard off to the side, for the whole world to see that you're caked." He looked like he was enjoying the fact that I had tilted my own hand, without knowing that I had.

"Well why haven't you said anything?" I was trying not to sound upset.

"Why should I? It's your business if you want to hide money from me, and cry broke." By that time, he was lying on his side of the bed, under the blanket and sheet.

What he said, and the way he articulated it, made me feel petty as hell. Still, I tried to defend myself, by saying, "I wasn't just hiding that money from you, I was hiding it from myself, as well."

"Whatever, Peaches." He said as he laid his folded arms behind his head. "Don't trip, Yo. Your reasons are 'your reasons' ---- I don't have to know what they are. It's cool!"

I didn't like any parts of that. One minute, he and I were talking about buying a home together. And the next, he busted me out about that money I had concealed from him. Yet, he was telling me it was cool.

Something was going on.

I couldn't put my finger on it. But some kind of way, I had a feeling that I was going to regret hiding that four grand from him. And worst, being stupid enough to slip and let him find it.

"You crazy." I said, before I went to the bathroom, myself.

While I sat on the toilet, it occurred to me that he and I hadn't made love, not one time, since Choo-Choo raped me. Well ... since he half-raped me, I guess that would be a more honest assessment of that situation. Anyway, Popcorn hadn't tried to touch me since that morning after O'boy.

I wondered why.

I knew he hadn't heard about Choo-Choo being up in the crib, gangsta' fucking me like I belonged to him. If he had, I'm sure he wouldn't have made plans for a future with me. Because, buying a house together, was some serious business. If truth be told, I was expecting him to, at some point, soon, bring up the topic of marriage.

I wiped myself, brushed my teeth, and cold rinsed my face, At that point, I needed to be wide awake and rejuvenated. He was going to fuck me real good tonight, or my name wasn't Peaches.

◆◆◆◆◆◆◆◆◆◆◆◆◆◆◆◆◆◆◆◆◆◆

Peaches was a trip-and-a-half. How could she think that it was cool for her to hold out on me, all these months, and then had looked at me a moment ago as if I was the one that had life fucked-up. Of course, I knew she would think, off the whistle, that I had snooped around her crib, looking for shit. That was why I had taken such pleasure in pointing out it was her own carelessness that had placed me on point, as to how conniving she was. Because, at every turn since I've been with her, she had tried to keep her polished fingers in my pocket.

For one thing or the other.

My Pop had always repeated to me that there wasn't a creature created by God, more cunning than a woman, when she chose to be. My affiliation with Peaches had given new meaning to that bit of wisdom handed down from father-to-son. Babygirl, as sweet and sexy and loving as she had been during our months together, was also, a stupid bitch with a greedy little heart.

As I laid in bed waiting for her to return from the bathroom, I had to laugh inside, from her asking why I hadn't pulled her coat about my knowledge of her secret bank.

Picture that!

Even a fool knew that I was suppose to leave her asleep, right where she had believed I was. It had given me a higher ground than where she had thought she was standing. I was sorry that I appeared that gullible to her. And yes, I was stunned when I had reached my hand down into that hole in the floor, and pulled out all those five, tens, and twenty dollar bills.

But I had recovered, at the blink-of-an-eye, when I thought of Mr. Cool. He was the one whom, once, had taken a delicious toke from his Cuban cigar, and said, "Motherfuckers will always bring the weakest game, to the strongest nigga. A wise brotha will not bust it out, immediately. He will hold it close to his chest and wait for the right time to drop it like a royal flush."

Like I'd done that night.

Because, make no mistake, I knew that Peaches was in the bathroom trying to regroup. She knew her ass had been 'found out'. Knowing her as well as I had came to know her over those nine months of being with her, I was confident that her plan, once she returned to the bedroom, would be to engage me in some of that 'freaky shit'.

I was 'all game'.

Plus, I was so sure about her intentions that, after she walked back into the room, and said, "It's still early, ain't it?", like I couldn't see right through that bullshit.

I said, "Cut the jokes."

She understood me clearly, because she slid out of her lemon yellow bra and panties, in a flash. Once she cuddled up close to me, I moved in for a kiss, but stopped an inch from her lips. I just stared at her, without saying a word. To me, she was a beautiful woman, with so much potential, as far as being all that a nigga needed in his life. But she was so full of shit, it was preventing me from getting all the way into her. Sure, I had agreed to buy that house with her ---- but that wasn't shit, in my mind. Just some small shit to the giant I was planning on becoming.

She reached and gripped my dick, but her eyes never left mine. In them, I saw the raw heat and passion she was feeling at that moment. Even the love I knew she felt for me. In turn, I stroked her creamy soft thighs, and slowly ran my middle finger up-and-down the wet slit of her sweet pussy. I was feeling her so truly, I thought of screaming, *'BLACK BITCH BE REAL WITH ME!!!'*

But I didn't.

I knew that was something she had to want to do, on her own. So instead, I simply kissed her and finger-fucked her, while she smoothly stroked my full-grown dick.

I loved that she didn't play around in bed. She knew how to give a muthafucka a piece of heaven. Like, when she finally put that slab of dick in her mouth, she moaned almost immediately, knowing that kind of shit got a nigga off. Especially while she sucked and slurped with that piece of metal in her tongue, sliding in-and-out of my pee-hole. It was enough to make me want to moan like a bitch, myself.

Yet, I held J. my composure, played in her hair, and fought myself from blowing the back of her throat out with the explosion of my juices. I was determined her ass wasn't going to get away that easily. The lamplight was turned low. After I straddled her from the back and looked down at her pretty black ass, I gave in to that tremendous urge to smack it, while I was long-dicking her real slow. At first, I thought I may have connected with her cheeks, perhaps a little too hard. But when I saw her turn her face so that I could see what was a 'pleasurable smile' published on her features, I let it rip. In fact, I began slapping that ass ---- and pushing that dick as if I had gone lustfully insane. Just: like she had.

When I skeeted, I knew she had creamed, as well. Because she uttered it as she normally did, as her slim fingers opened and closed, and searched for something to claw at. Yet, what amazed me more than anything, Babygirl fell the fuck out as if she had been clubbed upside her dome. All I could think at that time was, 'Nigga, you a beast!!'

◆◆◆◆◆◆◆◆◆◆◆◆◆◆◆◆◆◆◆◆◆

The next day, we slept late. Tondra did her regular for breakfast, some cereal and 'O.J'. And then, she and her new stuffed animals camped out in front of the television watching an old Loonie Tunes video tape. Shautie was real cool like that. She didn't mind her Moms and I sleeping in.

But Silk, now that was a whole different matter. Because by ten o'clock, that nigga was screaming in my ear, 'Right now, Nigga!'

So I got up and headed for Yolonda's. When I got there, I took note that her car and some other car were parked in front of her house. It had never occurred to me that she was seeing someone. Because she never talked about having a man, nor had I seen her with anyone, since she stopped allowing herself to be played by a wannabe gangsta named Chase. I doubted very seriously if that's who it was at her crib. Because that nigga wouldn't be caught dead in a whip, if it wasn't foreign. Especially in a Lincoln like the one that was parked behind her sandy-beige Camry. And parked a way that a keen eye could quickly tell it had been staged there overnight.

My suspicions were confirmed when, just before I got to her stoop, her front door opened and a brotha, who was just as light skinned as I was, but not quite as tall, came strolling out toward me. The nigga was dressed like an insurance man, in my opinion --and sported a paper-thin mustache above his lip, like a damn fool.

I didn't know why, but I felt more jealousy from knowing that buster had slept with Yolonda, than I had from watching Peaches kick it with Choo-Choo. The bitch-ass nigga had a nerve to say, "Good morning!", as we passed each other. He even said it like he was preparing to give me his pitch about some fucking term life insurance. So I merely gritted on him, while thinking to myself, 'Fuck you mean, good morning!' But he seemed as though he hadn't given my diss of him any consideration. He only stuck his hand in his pocket, and kept right on stepping toward his car.

She was standing in the doorway with some cutershorts on, and a tee-shirt. She held the door open for me and asked, "Why you didn't speak to him?"

I didn't have an appropriate enough answer to give, so I merely said, "It's too early for that speaking shit, Yo."

She followed me up the stairs, "Yeah, but don't you think you may have offended him?'

I almost said, 'Fuck him!!' But I didn't want to keep talking about something that, even I hadn't understood. After all, she was entitled to 'get busy' with whom ever she pleased. Therefore, I said, "My bad, Yo. Next time you see O'boy, tell him I said it wasn't even like that."

She was posted just inside the bedroom, with her arms folded, when she responded, "Uh huh."

The way she said it, got my attention. She was hip to me. She knew I had been jealous. I didn't feed into it, though. I continued loading the bricks into a garbage bag I had gotten from a box in one of the drawers, where I had put it. When I was straight, I turned and said, "Look, I know you aren't charging me for laying my work here, but I would like to give you something, from time-to-time, anyway."

"Whatever, Popcorn, that's on you."

All I could think was what in the fuck did she see in that funny looking nigga that I had just seen, when I said, "Cool, so take this."' I handed her two grand. Enough, I figured would've easily covered her monthly expenses. Something else my Pops taught me, always lookout for people on your team, even when they give you the impression that you don't have to. Because loyalty, he said, was priceless.

She seemed surprised by the neat stack of twenties, almost as if she hadn't had a clue that I still had over one point five mil worth of drugs stacked in the drawers of that room.

But she knew it was a lot. So in my mind, a funky two grand shouldn't have garnered that type of reaction from her.

She held it in her hand, and walked back down the steps with me to the door. When I started out, she grabbed hold of my arm, with her free hand. I paused long enough for her to say, in a whispery voice, "We didn't do anything, Kevin."

I held a straight face, and hoped that she hadn't saw in my eyes the jubilation those words caused me to feel. Because, I walked out that door knowing that I felt Shautie like that. Knowing it for the first time. Yet, because of our friendship, I wasn't sure if I would ever do a muthafucking thing about it.

CHAPTER 10

Silk

"Toi, quit bitchin' and complainin'. Bitch, I told your ass, I'ma make it up to you." I said, to my bun-bun. She'd been trippin' all morning, now that the Memorial Day Weekend was over, because I didn't take her out to no clubs, or make it over to her Moms for that fake-ass cookout that they have every year. I just couldn't seem to get it thru her hard head, that chasing that scratch was far more important than eating hamburgers and hotdogs. The city was as dry as a soup bone. Therefore, it was like my Pops use to say, you gots to strike while the anvil is hot. And that's exactly what me and my dawg, Tiny, had done ----- sewed that bitch up. Shit, we had every nigga and they uncle copping from us. That's why, as of that morning, we ran thru about sixty joints since we started slingin' weight last Thursday.

Not bad for a couple of niggas that had been serving dime bags a week ago.

Toi, Tiny, and I were cruising down Jefferson Davis Highway, when she looked over at me with pouty lips, and said, "Yeah, but everybody was looking at me funny, at the cookout. Especially my damn sister, Cherry, that bitch make me sick!" She pulled out her glossy lipstick and hit those fabulous set of lips after she said that.

I had tuned her ass out, like I'm sure Tiny, who was sitting on the backseat, had done. We had more pertinent things to be thinking about, than to be concerned about her sis giving her a 'funny look'. That's why I looked up into the rearview mirror, before I asked Tiny, "You check on those joints like I asked? " He knew I was referring to those bulletproof vests, and those additional weapons I requested. The way we was laying down work, and violating niggas territories, shit could get ridiculous at any time.

When it does, I wanted to be ready to bring the drama because the first impression was a lasting one, forreal. Niggas was going to find out, real quick, we weren't faking.

Tiny didn't say anything. He didn't like talking at all around my girl. He just shook his head in the affirmative, as I made a bumpy turn into the huge parking area of a Cadillac dealership. Toi's neck was turning her wide eyes in every direction. I thought to myself, "I know this bitch ain't thinking 'this' is how I'ma make it up to her. If she does, she got life twisted!'

I parked and the three of us was out the car, barely, before a bowtie looking cracker strolled up and said, "Can I help you folks today?"

"Yeah", I said, "You can tell my man Frank, he got some customers out here."

He threw his nose up in the air, before he went and did what he was told. In a hot second, Frank fast paced it over to where we were standing in a sea of Escalades. He stuck his hand out and said, "I'm Frank, but I don't believe we've met."

Frank had a rep for helping niggas get one of those phat-ass trucks or any of those Caddys on the lot, without a lot of hassle. "We haven't," I replied. "But I'm just a good brotha that's tryin' to cop a couple of these joints, without a lotta dumb shit. You feel what I'm sayin'?"

He did.

The way he licked his lips, said it all, before he said, "I think I can get you taken care of, my friend. Which ones are you interested in?"

From my peripheral view, Toi looked like she had to piss or something, the way she was moving her lower body. In fact, I've never seen her so excited, and for what, I didn't know. She might, at some point, land her one of those cute little Hondas, but she damn sure wasn't about to get her a 'Lac' of any kind.

Tiny must've thought I was considering her, as well. Because when I turned to him and said, "Which one you want, Dawg?", a smile cracked across his face, like I had never seen before. We had been 'at it' so consistently and hard, I hadn't taken the time to break him off, yet. I figured, that was a good way to start.

He pointed at a blood-red one off to our left. I thought to myself, *'That figures.'*, before I looked at Frank and said, "Auight, that one, and that silver bitch, right there." I indicated a four door 'big-boy joint'.

"No problem." Frank said. He wrote down some information off the invoice. We went to his office, and true to his word, we got the paperwork done without a hitch. Toi pouted the whole time, but I had to give her credit, she knew better than to say anything out of order. Because it was no secret to her, I would break my foot off in her ass, anytime, and anywhere.

Frank hooked us up with a lender that catered to 'dope boyz'. In so many words, it was made clear that it would be cool to make up to nine thousand dollar payments, every week, if I chose, until the loan was paid off. It made sense to me that the interest rates would be sky-high. After all, institutions like that were no more than loan-sharks with a license.

We got back in the hoopty, and I drove off. Because we had picked out some smoking rims for both of them, and made plans to scoop up our trucks, tomorrow.

I made a right turn off of Jefferson Davis Highway, as soon as I passed the Destiny Club. That section of the city was called, Blackwell. The niggas over there were just as simple as the ones from Churchill or Jackson Ward. Perhaps that's why I smiled to myself, when I heard Tiny chamber a round in both of his nines. Plus, I almost laughed out loud when Toi, who heard it too, swung around in her seat as if she had thought he was intending to split her wig.

She even found something, she thought, was pleasant to say, "My gurl, Tonya said ya'll the shit, Baby."

"Oh yeah!" I fed into it to calm her scared ass down. Because, no way was I going to let my man slaughter all that good pussy. I didn't give a fuck how much she got on my nerves, sometimes ---- that shit wasn't happening.

I parked in front of a money-green crib on Pilot Street, right as she went on to say, "Fo sho, Boo. That bitch said ya'll got the whole state on locks." She unwrapped and put a folded stick of gum into her mouth. She done it as though she knew her stroke game was on fifty thousand.

"Well, this time, that skeezer got it right." I replied, before I turned to Tiny and said, "Come on Dawg, and bring that shit." Toi acted like that meant her too, so I said, "Sit your ass in the car, we'll be right back."

She didn't fake an attitude, that time. We merely turned on the ignition so that she could listen to the radio. It made me think perhaps I should make Tiny chamber a round in her presence more often.

Tiny and I walked up on some concrete steps first, and then about five wooden ones, onto a swing, glider, and plant infested porch. Before we could knock on the door, a tall nigga with designer braids on his head, opened it wide and walked back farther into the house without saying a word. Of course, we followed him, and ended up down in a basement that looked like some shit off that show, 'How I'm Living'. The walls were swirled in such a rich and harmonious design, it seemed like the finisher must have taken a lifetime to perfect.

Also, the carpet was so thick and plush, when I looked at Tiny, he was checking, as I had, to see if we were walking on air.

My best guess was, that since Peewee had only been home from Levenworth Penitentiary, only three or four months, he was probably cribbing with his Moms, for a minute. But goddamn, with all the glass and rich leather that was down in that basement, that nigga was still carrying it like he had before that ten-year bid he'd just squashed.

We squatted in his sitting area. A flat screen dominated the wall in front of me, as I said, "What up, my Nigga?"

He had his hands locked together and his legs crossed as if he was boating a fresh pair of those 'big blocks' he was sporting back when he was taking down his. "Nigga, I'm fucked up wit you --that's what's up!"

I thought he was dead serious for a moment, but his low volume smile told me otherwise. So I smiled, too, and said, "Why is dat?"

"Cause you doin' it 'like dat' and just now hollerin' at a nigga ---- that's why!"

Me and that nigga use to chase hos together, back in the day when he was living in Churchhill. I fucked with him, real tough. And quite honestly, the only reason I hadn't got at him, until then, was because I was under the misguided impression that the feds had broken him. After all, doing a dime piece in one of the most notorious penitentiary in the country, was no joke.

Therefore, I said, "I thought the feds had broke your back. That shit happens, you know, especially when a nigga do it, like you done it. "

Tiny knew Peewee, too. He knew the nigga was good 'peeps'. Yet, he was still standing up and on guard like he had been at Bunky's.

"Yeah, ok, I feel you on dat." Peewee said. "So what's happenin', 'cause a nigga tryin' to get in where he fit in?"

I looked at Tiny and he understood. He walked over and handed O'boy the two bricks out of the tote bag.

Peewee was one of those niggas that wasn't faking if he was on the come-up, I was sure of that about him. I wanted him on the team, permanently. That's why I said, "I know your bank is a little fucked-up right now. So I'ma give you these joints for fifty, instead of the fixty-six I'm taxin' everybody else. But the next time, Playa, we do this shit, straight up."

He looked at me for a full minute, before he said, "I been home a hundred and fifteen days. And it's a sad thing to say, but in all that time, not one muthafucka has offered to help a brotha get on board, the way a nigga like me deserves." He paused, prior to him saying, "Except you."

That basement was as quiet as a prayer service, while he and I just stared one another. In my mind, that was a real moment among real niggas.

When Tiny and I left that house, there was no doubt in my mind that Peewee was on my team. And that, before the sun rose again, he was going to have Blackwell on locks. After that, it ain't no tellin' ……..

CHAPTER 11

Peaches

I didn't get in contact with my sister, Toni, until, yesterday, the day after the holiday. She said that she went to Myrtle Beach for three days. According to that unusual glow she was wearing, I had assumed that she had gotten herself plenty of dick, as well.

Nonetheless, I caught her that morning on her cell. She was headed to her office at Parker Properties Northside Branch. She was happy and obviously surprised that I called. And yes, that house she had told me about, was still available. So we made plans for her to pick up Popcorn, Tondra, and I at six that evening, so that we could do a walk thru.

I informed Popcorn of our plans when he stopped by the crib around noon. Still, I was not expecting him to be around, being that he had been so damn busy, lately.

But he was.

In retrospect, it may have been better, all the way around, if he hadn't been, because he and Toni had not mixed well. That bitch had always had a sneaky little way of trying to talk down to people. Therefore, it shouldn't have stunned me as clearly as it had when she glanced over her shoulder at Popcorn, who had been sitting in the back seat with Tondra, and said, "Corn Chips, how is your little business coming along?"

I had braced myself from feeling the intense heat of his stare. But I had relaxed some, and even smiled when he replied, "Not bad, Tiquitta. Thanks for asking."

Need I say, Toni's chocolate cheeks had acquired that selfsame rosy tint that it had the day that Donnell had eye-fucked her fabulous-body. In fact, as she had gripped the steering wheel tighter and drove the remainder of the way in virtual silence. I couldn't help thinking about how much her cheeks reminded me of ripe black cherries. I guess she hadn't enjoyed being called what she had assumed was a project name.

The house was located in the Northside area, on North Ave. It was okay, but not at all like I had envisioned in my head. The best part was that the neighborhood was quiet and clean, the kind of environment that would have been much better for Tondra.

At that time, I hadn't been able to gauge Popcorn's true reaction. But I had had a strong suspicion that his high hopes were just as deflated as mine had been. Being that we both had seen, for the sixty-seven-thousand dollar asking price, we would barely be getting our money's worth.

It hadn't helped that just before Toni had dropped us back at Gilpen Court, she made a stop at a dream-come-true for me. At least not at that point in life. It was a fantastic cedar and smoke glass Townhouse, down the street from where that bitch,

Yolonda lived. But I hadn't cared if it had been right beside her's ---I loved it! I tried not to show how much, because I didn't want to appear ungrateful toward what had been offered. Because, believe me, moving out of that projects into a house of any kind, would've been an answer to one of my oldest prayers.

Popcorn and I talked it over last night, as we had told Toni we would. In the end, we both had agreed that it was time to move. So he had said he was going to get on top of things today. What that meant, I had not been sure.

What was it he was going to get on top of?

I've checked his bank savings and checking accounts, as recent as a week ago, and was sorry that I had. Because it had almost made me fork over that four grand I had saved. Meaning, Boo was broke as shit!

Still and all, I had the faith that he was going to pull it off. In the past, he had never told me he was going to do something, and didn't handle his business. Therefore, I placed the vacuum cleaner back in the closet that particular morning with the belief, in the upcoming weeks, we was going to be hauling our shit over to the Northside of town.

◆◆◆◆◆◆◆◆◆◆◆◆◆◆◆◆◆◆◆◆◆◆

Around two p.m., someone knocked on my door. I opened it and wasn't surprised by the sight of Carla standing on my stoop, smiling. She and I had been hanging out a little since that day she stumbled up on Choo-Choo leaving my apartment with his zipper open. I'm sure her reason was quite different from mine, because I was trying to keep the bitch close so that she wouldn't breathe my business to any of those other hoochies in Gilpen Court. Especially, Crystal.

She used to be my girl. But I hadn't seen her, nor had I been looking for her, for that matter, since before Choo-Choo threw himself on me, literally. I knew she hadn't heard nothing about it, because she was the kind of female that would approach Popcorn about it, if she had.

"What'sup, Diva!" Carla said, as she breezed by me into the crib. She was wearing a white short---set and flat sandals, and carrying a Prada white straw bag.

"Nothin' much," I responded. "Just cleaning up my crib, like you should be doing."

"Gurl, Pleez! I do that shit twice a month. If Tre don't like it, he can tell one of those tricks to come ova and do it. Shit! Since I'm sharing him, I might as well share that shit, too."

'Damn!', I thought, *'I just made a simple statement -----*

wasn't asking for no damn sermon.' I flopped down on the chair across from where she sat, but I didn't feed into that nonsense she had just puked up.

Therefore, she dove into something else I wasn't interested in, by saying, "What you think?" Then she stuck out her tongue for me to see that it was pierced and still bruised around the area she had a ring inserted thru.

"Not bad." Was all I thought to say, while awaiting her to bitch about how much I had lied about the potential pain. Yet, she did no such thing.

Instead, she said, "Gurl, Tre told me Popcorn's brother, Silk, is doing it!"

"What you mean?" I said, while wondering if my feet would look that good in those flats she was wearing.

"What -------- you'on know?? Tre said that nigga got the whole city on locks. I think he said don't nobody else got no coke, but Choo-Choo. And his shit supposed to be pure garbage. That's why he thinks ain't nobody seen that crazy-ass nigga since before the weekend." She said, before she had the nerve to cross her leg and ask, "Have you?"

I was mindful of the fact that she was studying my features, for a hint of discomfiture. In her mind, that would've confirmed what she believed she already knew. So I concentrated on maintaining a arrow straight--face, as I said, "Naw, Girl, I haven't seen that fool since he was over here trying to get me to do his hair." Although that was the truth, the guilt I felt from what he and had done, was what made it seem like I was articulating a lie.

"Mmmm..........!," she said with shady eyes.

"What you hummin..'bout?"

"Nothing ----- nothing at all." She had the corners of her mouth upturned. But I didn't give a fuck at that point, whether she believed me, or not. She knew it, too. I think that's why she shifted directions, by saying, "Maybe you ought to get Popcorn to holla' at his brother. 'Cause I know ya'll tired of strugglin'. Silk'll probably look out for him, real good, on the strength that they brothers, too."

I was thinking to myself, 'Why don't this bitch mind her own fuckin' business, and get the hell out of mine.' But deep down inside, I knew she was right   I was tired of struggling! Plus, I wanted that townhouse, bad as shit. But no matter, there was no way I could fix my mouth to ask my man to sling drugs. That was something that a stackhead would do. I knew better. To me, a man had to make that choice, all on his own.

Still, to get her out of my business, I said, "I'll think about it. "

"Well, you ought to, "she said, ahead of looking at her stainless steel Movado, and saying, "Shit! I gotta go. I got some bizness I gotta take care of."

'Thank goodness! Carry your ass.' I thought. She was quickly becoming my main reason for wanting to get the hell out of Gilpen Court. I certainly had no plans of telling her I was moving, and I damn sure wasn't ever going to tell her where I lived, once I did my disappearing act.

When she got to the door, she turned and asked, "Say Girlfriend, you wanna go to the mall later. And you don't have to worry, if you see something you like ---------I got' cha! 'Cause I know how it is when your man only workin' a nine-to-five. Plus, who knows, Popcorn might end up being Tre's hook-up ----- then you can do us a favor. Right! "

I was almost starting to like that bitch, but I could see right thru her bullshit. I wouldn't have been surprised to discover that Tre had sent her around there with that weak game, in the first place. In either case, I said, "Not today, maybe some other time, Carla. But thanks, here. "

"Ain't nothin'-------- we down like that." She slung back over her shoulder as she went out the door.

I sat down on the sofa, hard, and thought, 'Bitch pleez!', before I laid back and began to ruminate about all the nice shit I could do if Popcorn took it upon himself to hook-up with Silk. But high up on a tree limb in my thoughts, a little birdie was telling me .... that shit ain't gonna' happen.

CHAPTER 12

Popcorn

"Goddamn!! I said out loud to no one, but myself. "A million dollars." I never imagined that I would be in the same room with that kind of cheddar. But there I stood, looking at that beautiful, beautiful pile of paper.

I was up in the spare bedroom of Yolonda's home. She wasn't there. She was down at her gig probably doing what I had just finished doing, counting big faces. Since I received those hundred 'keys' from Bay-Bay, the dough had been coming at me with such lightning speed, I had been cramming mad stacks in a canvas bag, without actually counting any of it, myself. I hadn't tripped because, if the count was off, there was only one person I needed to 'get at' to get it straight.

I zipped the bag and placed it on the floor of the closet. I had to smile, because, if truth be told, I was placing just as much confidence in Yolonda, as Bay-Bay awarded in J.R. and Big Titty Rose. On that level, I presumed, more than on any other plane in life, you had to trust people. If they violated that trust, in any way, than forreal, forreal, you only had one choice ------ to kill! To slaughter they grimy-ass like a muthafucking dog.

I grabbed the twenty-Gs off the dresser that I had set aside, and stuffed the bills into a brown manila envelope. I walked out to my truck and wondered if Smokey and the crew had gotten that huge planting job done around the Administration Building on the campus of VCU. My moms knew all the Professors and other personnel from working there for all those years. Therefore, she always made a pitch for my business with anyone who would listen. Believe me, I've gotten some decent contracts from her hustle, and up in-your-face approach.

I climbed in the truck believing that they had, if I knew Smokey. He hadn't appeared bothered by the fact that I'd been missing in action a lot, over the last few days. Neither had Lil Rob and Keisha, for that matter. I appreciated my workers, enough that I had thought of smashing them with a little bonus, around the fourth of July.

But I hadn't decided, yet.

I drove over to Chamberlain and parked in front of 'Blends'. The blue sky had a few white clouds floating like balloons across a placid blue sea. Yet, it was hot and humid as a muthafucka, because there wasn't a tender breeze to be felt, for miles. That's why it felt so good once I walked into the tobacco shop where the central air had the building as cool and comfortable as a Eskimo's hut.

"Yo, Chubby, is Mr. Cool around?" I asked the albino looking brotha that was sitting behind the counter. But I already knew that he was, because Mr. Cool never went anywhere

94

without Chubby. Chubby was his 'juss'. Meaning, he did just what the fuck Mr. Cool told him to do.

"He's in the back, Lil Prince." He gave the once over with his eyes, as if he could tell whether I was strapped, prior to him saying, "You can go 'head on back. He'll be glad to see you."

I walked thru some beaded curtains into a open room that smelled more like the natural blend of tobacco than it had out front. Mr. Cool was in a much smaller room that looked more like a miniature bar, than an office. Because it had soft lighting, low volume jazz playing, and two shelves of every kind of alcohol you could think of, across the long wall behind the desk where Mr. Cool sat.

I saw in his eyes that he was happy to see me. But he wouldn't be 'Mr Cool' if he showed it any other way. How could he not have been elated about seeing me ----- my presence always gave him a chance to relive his past, by telling me about the highs and lows of his life. In either case, I was always a eager listener. I learned early on that all O.G.'s loved that quality in a young nigga. That ability to just set and keep your mouth shut, listen and learn.

"What's up Mr. Cool!" I said as I stood in the doorway of his office. I wasn't going to take for granted that I could just walk into his office, uninvited. Fuck that shit Chubby said.

"Just trying to make a dollar, Young Prince how are things going with you? I haven't seen you in a while."

"I been -----" I was about to say, before he cut me off.

"Come on in, and have a seat: Don't be acting like you're a stranger around here."

"Thank you, Mr. Cool." I said while I copped-a-squat. "As I was saying, I been at the grind so hard, I haven't really had time to do much of nothing. Except stay at it. "

"So you 'grindin' now, huh?" He asked with a relaxed look to his face. He opened a sterling silver cigar box and took out one of the tasteful Cubans he loved to puff on, before he went on to ask, "What kind of 'grindin' you doing, 'Young Prince'?"

I knew from experience with Mr. Cool that was a test of some sort. Also, I somehow knew that the only answer he would be satisfied with, was no response at all. Therefore, I merely sat and stared at him while he carefully lit his cigar.

After he enjoyed about three incredible tokes, he looked at me and said, "That's a good answer."

At that moment I remembered why I knew it would be. It was he who had told me on numerous occasions that no one, outside your mother and God, needed to know your business, unless they were playing a active role in it.

Apparently, he saw right thru to the core of my intentions, because he rodded back in his plush leather chair and asked, "So tell me young Playa, what brings you by today? Do you need something?"

Mr. Cool must've seen that look of 'need' printed on so many faces in his lifetime that he could've spotted it a mile off. Because he had no reason to suspect that I required something from him, being that I'd never asked him for anything before.

I leaned forward and rubbed my hands together, ahead of me saying, "I need a favor, Mr. Cool." It tripped me out that my palms had been sweaty.

"What is it?" His tune was unchanged.

"I need a legitimate check for twenty thousand dollars, so that I can deposit it into my bank account."

Without the slightest hesitation, he laid aside his Cuba, took out a photo album size book of blank checks. In an even hand, he wrote out the twenty grand I requested. With one finger, he slid it across the desk toward me and said, "I'm giving you this money without interest. And I mean it when I say take your time paying it back. Your Pops was a good man ----- and you're cut from that same cloth. I can tell!"

'Goddamn! He has missed the whole point. He thinks I want to borrow the money.' I thought to myself, while my hand was under my tee--shirt preparing to pull the brown envelope from my waistband. He had such a self-satisfying look on his face, that I felt that there was no way I could take that away from him. So I pulled my hand away free and empty. I saw nothing wrong with owing someone, such as the notorious Mr. Cool, as long as I had his dough to fork up whenever I chose.

"I'm speechless, Yo. I don't know what to say."

He puffed his cigar and said, "Don't say nothing, then. Just go handle your business, Young Prince. I already know you're grateful."

I folded the check and stuffed it in my pocket. I showed Mr. Cool a genuine smile. And then, I left knowing that I didn't have to worry about him ever slaughtering my family, because I couldn't pay him his money, and telling me afterwards, 'We even now, Young Prince, so if you wanna borrow some more money, you can get it.' Naw, that shit wasn't going to happen ------- not to the O' boy, it wasn't.

◆◆◆◆◆◆◆◆◆◆◆◆◆◆◆◆◆◆◆◆◆

I went straight to my bank and deposited the check into my checking account. I was almost surprised by the fact that the company name on the check was that of a Pharmaceutical Supply Company, one that I had never heard of. But I had reached a point in my thinking, that when it came to Mr. Cool, nothing surprised or shocked me anymore.

That nigga was deep!

After that, I drove over to Northside and easily found the Realty Company Toni worked at. They were in a meeting of some type, so I waited. Nothing was going to prevent me from seeing that look on her face when I told her we wanted that townhouse instead of that crib she first showed us. I hadn't been able to get that joint off my mind, and I knew Peaches was captivated by it, as well. She hadn't fooled me by pretending otherwise.

Finally, after about fifteen minutes, Toni walked out into the reception area and invited me back to her office. Her's was the complete opposite of Mr. Cool's ---- bright, quiet, and without a hint of alcohol anywhere on the premise.

"We'll need to make this quick." She said, like she had a ton of things to do. But I knew she was faking. She was only trying to flex and get some 'get back' from me purposely calling her Tiquitta.

Therefore, I replied, "Yeah, I feel the same way. I got shit to do myself. " I reached in my back pocket and pulled out my check book. "We decided to move on that crib. So I wanna give you the ten percent, now, to lock it down."

"Oooh ....that's so sweet. I'm so glad that ya'll are taking advantage of that opportunity. I know it's not the best house in the world, but you must agree, it's a nice place to start. Right!"

I didn't respond because I had blotted that shit out. In my mind, she was still making a sells pitch, for no reason. I merely wrote out the ten percent amount to Parker Properties, and handed the check to her with a shit-eating-grin.

She accepted the check enthusiastically. But became more excited, it seemed, when she said, "I'm afraid your math is a little off, Kevin."

At least she got my name right that time. "No Toni", I said with emphasis, "My math is always on point."

She laid the check aside and wiggled around in her seat like she was enjoying things a little too much. Then she said, as though she were explaining to a child, "Sweetie, ten percent of sixty-seven thousand, is only sixty-seven hundred dollars ---- not the thousand five hundred you got written out."

"True that!" I said with an even brighter smile than hers. "But correct me if I'm wrong, Sweetie, twelve-five is ten percent of that town house you showed us, am I right?"

She looked just the way I had imagined she would, which was stupid as shit, as she said, "Yes. But I thought ….. I thought ya'll was busing the house I showed you first. "

"We was, Yo. But I decided your sister and niece deserved more than that." I spread it on thick. I was sure, next time, she wouldn't try to pre-judge a brotha because of what his circumstances seemed.

It looked like she was looking at me with a new set of eyes, as she said, "This is going to make Peaches and Tondra, very happy."

"I hope so," I said. While I looked at her and saw she was genuine, it occurred to me that maybe she wasn't a half-bad person, after all. Perhaps it was that brand of thinking that prompted me to say, "You don't seem like the type of female that has plans to work for someone else, your whole life." She was obviously flattered by that remark, which was cool, because I meant it. "If you got any ideas, let's do lunch, sometimes, and kick it." I almost smiled from the fact that I used one of Yolonda's 'white lines'. "After all, Toni, we family, right?"

She didn't try to argue with that. She only smiled and said, "You're something else, Kevin. But I'll give your invitation some thought, ok?"

I got up and said, "That's cool ----- just make sure it's some 'serious thought', aught!"

She nodded while she was still smiling. She handed me a receipt and I left. But as I walked out toward my truck, there was no doubt in my mind; Toni and I were going to be business partners and the best of friends…..

CHAPTER 13

Silk

"Put that dick back in yo mouf', Bitch! A nigga ain't skeeted yet," I said to Remy, a trick-bitch that use to be 'all that' until she started hittin' that pipe. Her appearance was still 'like that', that's why every nigga in the hood was at her.

She looked up at me with those hazel eyes that I used to dream about, and said, "But I been sucking it for over thirty minutes, Silk, and you only gave me a crumb."

"Yeah, but I'ma give you one of these when you finish, like I promised, Ho." I said, while I held up one of the fat grams Tiny and I had kept to the side for tricking. "So quit stunnin' and put that slab of dick back in yo throat where it belong."

She hesitated for a split-second, before she regripped my firmness and began to slob and bob on my joint. In fact, she was slurping and slobbing it like she was mad at me, or something. But I didn't give a fuck.

Fuck her!!

That stanking bitch hadn't given a nigga like me the time of day when she had her little office job at Phillip Morris. She had kept her nose pointed upward, like her shit hadn't stunk. That pipe pulled her head out of the clouds, though. Because it costed her her job and her marriage to a sucka' from Henrico Bounty, which was a breeding ground for nothing but money and busters. Nonetheless, since that time, Remy had sucked and fucked so many cats for a blast of crack, that personally, I wouldn't fuck her trifling ass with Tiny's dick.

That said a lot.

That nigga would fuck anything. He proved that when we were twelve years old and he gorilla fucked a frisky-ass German Sheppard, who had been in heat and kept looking at him.

"Oooh.....shit, Bitch ------goddamn!!" I said, while I was

skeetin' in her mouth. "You should've got mad sooner, if it makes you eat up a dick like that." Her head was fire!

I watched her swallow every driblet of my semen. I thought of not giving her the gram I had promised, especially when she said, "Mmmmm.... your shit taste like milkshake, Silk." Because, if that was the case, she 'needed' to be paying me. But since her dome was like that, and I was sure to wanna sample that joint again, somewhere down the road, I kicked her down, right when my cell buzzed. So I told her, "Get yo stankin'-ass up out'cheer, I got shit to do."

She broke out the crib as if Toi was back from the mall, and was threatening to kick her ass. The thought of my bun-bun deep checking Remy almost made me laugh, as I answered the phone. "What up?" I said, while I reach and fired up the dutch.

"Silk, this Mario, Man. Some fucked up shit just went down."

I sat up straight, and blew out the smoke from the dutch without inhaling it. Mario was Toi's cousin. She practically pleaded with me to put the nigga on, because I had been hesitant about it. I knew that he had Idlewood on locks, but I also had figured that since he was my girl's 'peeps', everytime he had a beef with them crazy-ass niggas in Westend, I would be slab-dab caught in the middle. Since his call came right after that fabulous dick sucking I had just gotten from Remy, I almost said, 'Nigga, handle that shit yo'self.' But.I didn't, because since I knew that Mario was a 'go hard' young nigga, his problems had to be with a major crew for him to feel like he needed my backing. Therefore, I said, "Just chill, my nigga, I'm coming at'cha.

◆◆◆◆◆◆◆◆◆◆◆◆◆◆◆◆◆◆◆◆

In no time flat, I had parked up beside Tiny's blood-red Escalade. Toi drove my joint to the mall. But no matter, I would've pushed my hoopty for that occasion. It's just that O'girl had found a lot of reasons to be flexing in my shit, over the last few days. But I had a vicious move for that, I was going to cop her one of those Honda's, a lot sooner than I had planned.

Tiny flung a duffle bag onto the back seat. It was full of the necessities I asked him to bring, and probably some extra shit he felt we might need. Once he settled on the passenger side, he passed me a forty-cal joint with infra red beams, before he displayed a calico fifty-shot automatic on his lap. He looked just as serene and at peace with himself as one would appear who was on their way to a revival of some sort. Perhaps, to him, we were. I was certain about one thing, however -- he had been waiting for an occasion like that in which we were headed for, since the day we blew up.

Maybe I was too, because we both were quiet and into our own personal thoughts, as I drove us to the Westend of town.

I had my CD thumping, though, with some of that 'G-Unit' flava. I was feeling them niggas from day one. But even more so, now that we were on a mission.

I turned off of Hill Street, onto Third Ave., with my head slightly bobbing to the beat of 'Popin' em Thangs, ' because I was ready to do whatever. If that shit with Mario required that Tiny and I put-in-some-work, then, at that point, I felt that that night was just as good as any to set an example. Niggas needed to know we would not stand for any disrespect, on any level.

We cruised pass Idlewood real slow. I wanted to take a reading of that particular block that Mario was raising so much hell from. I even turned down the music and had the windows open so as to hear anything that sounded unusually loud. Tiny's ears were so sensitive to sound, that nigga could hear a mosquito break wind ten spaces away. Yet, like me, he hadn't seen or heard anything that forewarned of drama. Therefore, we continued on a few blocks, to Maplewood where we normally met Mario to hit him off.

Mario was about five-foot eight and ripped like a muthafucka! His head was long as a football, but laced with those curly type waves. He was what the honies called a 'pretty boy'. He kept a rack of young Shanties on his dick, but for some reason, that nigga was big on 'vets'. He told me once, that older broads were the only kind of females that knew how to appreciate him. But I'm still trying to figure that one out. Because there was nothing a oldhead could do for me, but cook me a good meal and turn me on to her daughter.

Nevertheless, Mario was standing out by the curb with the older female he lived with. Her name was Terri and she was fine as shit. She obviously was trying to calm him down, because he looked more hyped than both Tiny and I.

"What'sup, Nigga?" I asked as soon as I got out the car.

He started to bounce around as he said, "That bitch-ass nigga, Troy, pulled up on my block with about five otha' niggas, and got gangsta' with the crew of young niggas I got workin' for me."

"So, why ya'll ain't just handle that shit right then and there, instead of lettin' them niggas live to drive outta there?" I asked. But I already knew the answer. Brothas like Mario were quick to put a youngin on his team, without giving any thought to the fact that, when the drama came ---- nine times out of ten, they were going to bitch up.

In any case, once Terri got a good view of how serious Tiny and I were looking, she scurried her ass back into the house and cut off all her lights. And Mario, he didn't even try to answer my question. Yet, unbeknownst to him, he said the right thing when he spit, "That nigga Troy thinks because he's one of Choo-Choo's flunkies, he can flex his muscles anywhere, and get away wit it."

Tiny shifted his weight as if he knew it was on and poppin', as I barked, "Where that bitch-ass nigga at?" 'Cause Choo-Choo don't run a muthafuckin' thang in this town no mo. We gon get 'dat shit' straight, tonight!"

"I know exactly where they ass at." Mario said, before he turned and started running toward the house. Over his shoulder he said, "Just let me get my shit!"

He was gone longer than I had expected. When he returned, I understood why ---- he had dressed in all dark clothes, like Tiny and I. That gesture assured me even more, he knew the score.

He jumped on the back seat and said, "Make a U-turn and go back the other way. I bet they down on First Street at that fake-ass crap house they be hangin' at."

I slammed on brakes, almost completely, and pulled my Buick over by the curb. "What, you taking us to a damn crap-house where a hundred niggas, at?" I shouted before I said, "Fucks wrong wit'choo!"

"Naw......naw Shauty, it ain't like that. Niggas only be hustlin' dice down at that joint Saturday and Sunday nights. Troy just be chillin' down there because his mans, Roc, jive holds the joint down, and he be pettlin' a little weed thru the week."

I said, "Yeah auight!", before I drove away from the curb.

We parked down the alley from the spot they were held-up in. We had already peeped the whip Troy and his homies were pushing earlier, so in our minds, it was on and poppin'!

Tiny reached in the duffle bag and handed me and Mario both a steel plated vest, before putting one on himself. Mario started gritting like a muthafucka ---- and I liked that! Even the fact that he was still mugging when Tiny handed him those goggles and he said, "What the fuck are these?"

"Night vision jaunts. Just put them joints on, and push that button, right there," I pointed.

"Goddamn!! Ya'll niggas ain't bullshittin'. Ya'll on some high-tec shit, on the realla'!"

Any other time, I would've smiled and relished that compliment he made ---- but right then, shit was too serious for that.

We crept along the graveled alley way in single file.

Mario led the way until we got to the yard. That's where Tiny stepped ahead of us and raced for the crib as if he intended on being the first one to 'set it off'. But that wasn't his purpose at all. He was scoping for the power box that was normally located on the back porch, or down in the basement of most older-style homes in the city.

He disappeared for a minute behind some high boards that blocked our view. But then, his greenish like figure, made by the night vision, stood above the two steps, waving us forward.

HUSTLERS

As soon as Mario and I stepped onto the wooden porch, we saw him standing over in a corner with his hands on a switch. He actually smiled for the first time that evening, before he pulled it downward, and killed all the juice that crib had.

We heard niggas hollering and jaunting on each other just before I put my size twelve foot through the door, and kicked the joint straight off the hinges. That was when them niggas stopped laughing, and began to ask each other, "What the fuck was that?"

When we charged in, we landed in the kitchen, first. But the house was so damn small and wide open, we were able to race through the next room and into the living room, where everybody was at, before they actually realized shit was about to be 'off the chain'.

I was in the middle with Tiny on my right, and Mario locked in tight on my left. I heard the snug breath of fear escape each of them cowards' mouths. I was amazed by the fact that we saw them so clearly, and yet, they couldn't see jack-shit. That is, until we pointed them infra-reds at several of their domes. Even Mario's jaunt was equipped with red beams, as well.

"Don't no muthafucking body move up in this bitch!!" I ordered like I was mad at the world. The two niggas that were sitting on the sofa started to reach for what was in their waist, but froze as if they had turned to statues. "Which one of ya'll Troy?"

"That's his faggot-ass right there in that chair." Mario made clear. But so did the other six cats that were in that room. Because, like a perfectly tuned drill team, all them niggas eyes pointed straight at slim, all at once.

"Fuck you want wit me, Shauty?" Troy asked, like he was a gangsta to the end.

The room was still pitch black to them. So without him seeing me, I walked right up on him with my knife gripped in my right hand. I drew the joint back, before I shouted, "This

107

Muthafucka!!" And stabbed him in the top of his mellon. Blood shot everywhere and he screamed like it was an outcry he had waited his whole life to let loose. But then, death gripped his throat and silenced that nigga. Making the room quieter than a seat on the moon. Until the other six stunt dummy's in that room must've thought, 'Fuck that!, before they tried their hands and reach for their heat.

Too late.

I clipped the other joker that stood nearby where I had slumped Troy's bitch-ass. I hit that nigga dead center in the forehead with that forty-cal. I had been strapped with, in my left hand. Mario defiantly won his props from me the instant he cut loose with his nine. Because he hit a fat bear-looking nigga that stood closest to the front door, so many times, he looked like he was doing the 'chicken-head', prior to his fat-ass crashing into the wall and sliding down it.

I didn't concern myself with the other four wannabe's that were in that joint, because I heard that Calico of Tiny's spit mad slugs, like crazy. I couldn't swear to it, but for one split second, I thought I heard that fool whistling that tune of his, as he aired them niggas out like mince meat.

When the banging stopped, it looked like a slaughtering house up in that tip. Blood and bodies laid everywhere. It was enough to make me smile inside, because that was the kind of message I wanted to send. One that made it clear to every muthafucka in that town, fuck with me on any level --- and you'll be fucking with your life!

Nonetheless, we got the hell up out of there. It wasn't until we were racing down the alley toward the car, however, that it occurred to me that Tiny hadn't bothered to rob the stiffs' before we bounced. I thought of asking him why, once we got back in the whip. But I already knew, he finally understood too, that the rules that had applied then, didn't apply anymore. In the case of him not robbing dead niggas no more, I was glad. Now, if I could've just gotten that nigga to clean his ass up and stop whistling that crazy-ass tune, I would've been a happy muthafucka.

CHAPTER 14

Peaches

It was Friday night and Popcorn, Tondra, and I were getting our eat on, up in Ms. Maggie's Soulfood Restaurant, down on Chamberlain St. Although I loved soul food myself, it was actually Tondra's idea for us to eat there that evening. Since she was leaving tomorrow to go stay with her father, we let her choose where we would have her farewell dinner at. When she promptly stated Ms. Maggie's, I knew her decision was based on those delicious pastries that the real 'queen of soul' had to top off one of her soulful meals.

Tondra and I were enjoying fried pork chops, while across from me Popcorn was munching on some barbeque ribs. They had to be good, because he was licking his fingers and kept saying, "Ummmm ------ huh!!"

When he had walked in yesterday evening and handed me that receipt for the down payment on that townhouse, that's what I had felt like saying. Plus, I had even felt like turning flips like I had done as a cheerleader, when our team had scored. At least, part of me, anyway. Because the other part wanted to know where in the hell did he get that damn money. He sure as hell hadn't volunteered that information.

I sat taking sneak peeps at him while I nibbled on my pork chop. I was even wondering, was he actually selling drugs for Silk. But I felt I knew the answer to that one already ----- hell naw! Therefore, he must've borrowed the money, as he normally did. Which means now he's going to be broker than he already was. But I shouldn't have complained, right?? Being that I was getting what I wanted.

That was how I had eventually looked at it last night. That's why I had showed him my appreciation by giving him the royal treatment. I believed when a man did something like that, he should be rewarded, bigtime. So I had ran a nice warm tub of water, lit some candles, and bathed him like he was a king. I had patted him down, afterwards, and gave him the most sensuous massage, I'm sure he had ever had.

He loved it!!

Especially when I had done something for him no man had been able to make me want to do. I had licked his ass. I had licked it real slow, and sucked it, too. I could tell he had fought it, but before the show was over, I had him moaning like a bitch. But it was all good. Because that had only inspired him to demonstrate a little later, just how much of a man he was.

"Mama, Popcorn sai`d it was ok for me to bring my rabbit back, when I come," Tondra said, with chocolate icing at each corner of her mouth.

"Well, I guess that means you can, then," I responded, with a smile. The fact that he had just put us in a house, to me, meant she could haul an elephant back, if he said so.

"Damn! That was good," Popcorn said, while he wiped his mouth. "Even better than the last time I was here."

I couldn't help it. "And when was that?" I said, because I assumed he was referring to his lunch date with Yolonda.

He frowned before he said, "A couple of weeks ago when a partna of mine was in town visiting. Why?"

That surprised me, because he hadn't said anything about a friend of his being in town. "No reason. Which one of your friends, because I don't believe I met him, did I?"

"You wouldn't know'em." He looked at his watch. Ya'll ready to bounce?"

'Oh! So he just gonna blow me off, huh. That can only mean that his ass was here with that bitch. Townhouse or no townhouse, I'm tired of that shit that's going on between them. If he wants to keep playing around with her, then maybe I should give Choo-Choo another call. Only this time, I won't be faking.'

He paid the check, and we left.

◆◆◆◆◆◆◆◆◆◆◆◆◆◆◆◆◆◆◆◆◆◆◆

The next day after we got back from boarding Tondra on the plane to 'ATL' with her stewardess that was responsible for her, he dropped me at home. He said he had to attend to some more damn business. All I wanted to know, was when did he start having so much to do on Saturdays and Sundays, when, at one time, those had been our days to do shit together.

'Well, I'ma fix his ass.', I thought the instant he left out that door. I didn't know who he thought I was, but I damn sure wasn't the fool he imagined.

I quickly punched in Choo-Choo's cell number with my lips twisted the way Popcorn said his sister, Rainy, had been doing. At that moment, I had a attitude more stronger than all of hers combined, I'm sure. 1 wasn't going to stand for 'my man' dissing me for another bitch.

Oh hell naw!

Choo-Choo's cell merely rang and rang. So I hung up my phone and flung the pillow across the room. But before it smacked the wall, I was busy dialing another number. That person answered on the second ring. So I said, "What you doin', Gurl?"

Carla replied, "Nothin' much, what up wit you?"

I didn't waste no time. "You wanna go see this townhouse, I might be moving into?" That should prove how pressed I was to see for myself if Popcorn was actually at Yolonda's crib, as I suspected.

"I'll be right around there." That nosey bitch rushed that out of her mouth, and hung up.

Ten minutes later, we cruised up Lee Street. I let her pass the townhouse I was moving in, by pretending I couldn't remember which one it was. Yet, before we actually got to Yolonda's house, I virtually shouted, "Turn into that driveway, right there", I pointed at one of about three houses from O'girls. "Because, I'm sure it was that one back there." I said. She eagerly did as I instructed. Plus, she seemed so preoccupied with getting her a look-see at my new crib, she hadn't noticed my man's truck parked behind Yolonda's Camry.

But I did.

I saw it just as plain as day. I was furious as hell by the time she parked at the townhouse. Still, I said, "Come on, Gurl, let's take a quick peep in the windows."

I didn't have to ask her twice, because she was out of her Nissan Maxima and peering thru the front picture window before my feet touched the ground. She made it clear, all the way around the dwelling that she was dying to see the upstairs. She said it as if she believed I actually had the fucking key, but was holding out on her.

By the time we got back in the car, I settled in my head --- for sure, that I was going to persist in calling Choo-Choo until I got hold of his ass that evening. Because, I wasn't going to let Popcorn, or no other nigga for that matter, get away with blowing me off for another female. That's why I asked Carla to just drive around for a while, I wanted to kill some time with the hopes that my next call would get thru.

It worked, too.

Carla was in Rite Aid on Jefferson Davis Highway buying up a few things. Therefore, I took that opportunity to call O'boy on my cell.

After about five rings, he clicked in. "Who diss?" He asked as though he was expecting it to be one of those telemarketers, so he could blast they ass out.

"Peaches, Choo, did I call at a bad time?" I had sugar and cinnamon coated each word.

"Naw Shautie, it's cool. What up!"

"Nuthin'." I responded in my best voice. "I was just thinking about you .... wondering what you was doing. That's all!"

"Why ----- you tryin' to see a nigga, or what?"

My heart was racing as I said, "Yeah, but not at my crib, no more. That shit ain't right."

"I feel dat. But what about at this Comfort Inn I'm at down on Chamberlain?"

I could feel that nigga smiling thru the phone. It was like he was too sure of the fact I was going to say, "Ok! That'll be fine. But you got to give me a little time, ok?"

"I ain't doin' nothin' but chillin', Shautie. So just do dat when you can. Auight?"

I felt myself getting moist below, as I asked, "What's your room number?"

"Sixty-nine, Shautie ---- and that's on the backside, up in the cut, where I like to be."

I was trying to figure out if he was trying to tell me something, right at the instant that Carla appeared from the drug store. So I hurriedly said, "I'll be there, bye!" I sneakingly pressed the off button, but kept right on talking as C.arla's signifying-ass started up the car with her ears wide open. Finally I said, "Look Popcorn, we can talk about that when I get home, ok?"

When I pretended to click off, Carla said, "That's right, Gurl, handle your business face-to-face. 'Cause a nigga will say anythang' ova the phone."

I just shook my head, because she had just fed into a fake conversation about something she didn't have a clue about, but had added her two cents, anyway.

It didn't help that by the time she stopped at my apartment, and Popcorn's truck was nowhere in sight, she said, "Look like you shook'em good Gurlfriend, cause his ass done got ghost."

"He'll be back." I said only to pacify her. Then, once I was completely out of her car, I added, "I'll see you later,

Diva."

She tapped her horn twice and drove off.

I rushed up stairs and freshened up, real quick. I was already wearing some white stretch Baby Phat jeans with a peach colored top. To me, that was appropriate enough for the occasion. And got the hell out of there.

By the time I got to the motel, I was experiencing the worst case of guilt possible. I felt as though I was overreacting, and that if I went through with that booty-call, I was going to regret it. But all of that was before I spied Popcorn driving his truck out of the parking area, with a pleasing look plastered on his face.

It had been over an hour since I had seen his truck at Yolonda's. Therefore, I figured the bastard must've been there to pick her up and brought her ass to that spot. I was fuming when I paid the cab driver, because my best guess was, she was probably still laid up in one of those rooms waiting for him to return. Which meant, he was probably leaving long enough to tell me, he had business to take care of.

Yeah right!!

A motherfucker!!

I was standing at room sixty-nine without realizing how I had gotten there. Still, I banged on that damn door like I was saying to Choo-Choo, "You better give me some of that damn dick ---- right now!!"

He opened the door in a manner that made it clear, he was ready to go slam off. Until he saw it was me, of course. That's when his face lit up like a neon sign, as he said, "Damn Shautie, you serious as shit, ain't you?"

I walked in without saying anything, one way or the other. I sat my hoochie bag on a chair by the window, before I faced him and recognized for the first time, he was butt--bald naked. As well as, his dick was rock-hard and seemed as though it was extending about two feet from his body. I almost shuddered from the thought of all that meat being inside of me.

"Take that shit off." He commanded like the animal he was noted for being.

I didn't know if I liked him talking rough-and-tough that day. After all, he had gotten gangsta' the last time he and I had done something. Therefore, that time, I was expecting him to be a little more loving and gentle.

What a fool I was to think that.

"Bitch, you hear what I said??" He almost shouted that time. "Ok, Choo, I'm doing it," I said, while I was unbuttoning my top. In the back of my mind, however, I was thinking, 'What in the hell have I gotten myself into?' Especially when I heard the toilet flush in the bathroom, before the door opened and this tall female named Moon came strutting into the room just as naked as Choo-Choo was. She was smiling at me as though I was dinner, as her eyes roamed my body.

I looked at Choo-Choo and his expression said it all. I was going to freak with them, or else. I didn't know what 'or else' would mean, nor did I care to find out. That's why I continued at removing my clothes, but cursing Popcorn every step of the way for pushing me in that direction.

"Both of ya'll get on the bed, 'cause I wanna watch for a while, first." He said, prior to him squatting on a chair and sparking up a damn funky-ass cigar.

"Ok Choo, but I can't stay long, because my man is expecting me to be home when he get there." I was trying to pave the way for a clean break, before long.

But he negated that reasoning, by replying, "That nigga ain't gon be thinking 'bout you, tonight." He puffed and blew smoke, before he added, "'Cause his mind gon be ofva places."

That puzzled me, that he would say something like that. It was like he knew Popcorn was in one of those rooms with Yolonda.

Nevertheless, none of that mattered the split second Moon licked evenly around my pussy lips, before she started darting her long tongue in-and-out of my excited vagina. Because that red-headed freckled face bitch had skills. In fact, she was so adapt at sucking pussy, she made me forget that Choo-Choo was in the room, and probably my damn name, too. Especially when she liplocked my clit, and began licking and sucking it like candy.

However, I didn't take kindly to her actually sitting her pussy on my face. Shit, for one thing, it looked like someone had split her shit with a battle axe. I mean, that's how big and raggedy looking her pussy appeared. And worse than that, however, was that she smelled like Choo-Choo had been screwing her all day long. But at some point of her slow fucking my face that shit started turning me on. I don't know if it was before or after Choo-Choo had begun fucking the shit out of me and calling me every kind of insulting name he could think of.

All I knew was that I was loving it! Enjoying it so much, I started believing what Choo said about Popcorn being preoccupied for the evening. Because, that's what I wanted ---- for him to stay with that bitch all night. Being that, as I flicked my tongue over the fat contours of Moons clit, and felt that crazy nigga's dick beating my pussy into a pleasurable state of submission; I knew I wasn't going to leave that damn room, until I was good and ready.......

CHAPTER 15

Popcorn

Around seven o'clock, that same evening, I sat out on the stoop in front of the apartment. The sun was close to it's setting position, and thereby, casting shadows all over the hood. To my left, the twins were kicking the bobo with some chicken-heads that lived across from the row of units we lived in. I cracked a smile, because I was glad that they were doing something, other than trying to bang each other up.

I glanced up-and-down the block, wondering where in the hell Peaches was at. Silk had asked me earlier that day to shoot thru Wilcom Court, because he and Tiny were putting down a vicious cookout that evening. I reluctantly agreed to swing by, but I didn't want to do so without asking Peaches to come along. I was sure it would be something she might enjoy, our first night alone for the summer. As for me, however, I would've been just as content with us chilling, watching a movie, or something.

Particularly from all the running around I had done that day.

Yesterday, I had had all of Bay-Bay's ends, and most of the five hundred Gs I was making myself off the hundred bricks I had gotten from him. In light of that, I had called and placed another order, because I hadn't wanted to hear Silk's mouth if, by chance, we ran out. I didn't believe that we would've, not after he had informed me last night, that Choo-Choo and a few other 'ballas' were back in pocket with 'flay' that, supposedly had just as much fire as ours. Still, in my mind, it was best to be safe and on top of the game, no matter the status of other niggas.

I looked up at the purple and orange and navy-blue streaks augmenting the sheer beauty of the sky, and I had to admit, life was lovely, once more. It felt good ---- incredibly good placing those hundred Gs underneath Momduke's pillows that morning. One might wonder why I just didn't hand her the scratch, straight up. Because I had wondered about that my damn self, at first. But then, I realized that that had been the manner in which my Pops had always given her 'dope money'. He had even told me one day when I was real young, yet, it was obvious I never forgot, "A man should always make it easy for his Mama and his woman to accept this kind of money", He had held up a few knots of cheddar, "Because, they are the only ones that might die from the guilt of accepting ends from you, if anything ever happened."

I got up off the concrete and went into the crib. I glanced at the telephone, and thought about calling Peaches on her cell. But decided all of a sudden, perhaps it might be better if I didn't take her with me. That way, I could just pop up, eat a few hotdogs, and get the hell out of there before them fools got too much alcohol in them ---- and got 'off the hook'.

I locked the front door and noticed that the honies were gone who the twins had been spitting at, so I asked, "Ya'll wanna ride over to Churchhill to a cookout? Some shit my brother puttin' down."

"Hell yeah!" Donnell prompted.

Donte, who joined him as he walked toward me and my truck, cosigned it when he said, "I'ma ride on the back where it's cool."

But before he could climb up into the bed of my F- 150, Donnell grabbed his arm, and said, "Oh hell naw, Nigga, you just wanna ride on the back because you knew that's what I was gon do."

Donte pushed his brother's hand away, and stood like he was ready to mix it up with his equally crazy-ass brother, prior to him saying, "You a mufucking lie!!"

'Yo!!!" I said as if I was the ref or something, "Why don't both of ya'll just get on the back and chill out. It don't matter who thought about it first ---- ya'll niggas are identical twins. Has it ever occurred to either of ya'll that it's natural for ya'll to think alike?" I was tired of their shit. I didn't give a fuck if they decided to beat me up, instead.

But they only looked at each other, and then at me as if I had been a rocket scientist, before Donnell said, "Dammmn.... Popcorn, that's some deep shit!"

"Fo sho!" Donte added.

'These niggas a trip.' I thought, ahead of saying, "So what up?" Ya'll gon keep standing there letting them steaks get cold, or what?"

They both climbed on up into the bed and settled back like a couple of trained Rotties would've done. I only shook my head and drove away.

◆◆◆◆◆◆◆◆◆◆◆◆◆◆◆◆◆◆◆◆◆◆◆

As I drove along Hospital Street, I ruminated about how surprised I had been when J.R. had called that afternoon and told me he and Big Titty Rose were at the Comfort Inn. But since we were taking Tondra to the airport, I told them to hold up a few hours. He didn't trip, he had said it would give them time to rest. And I had thought to myself, 'Yeah, and use that damn whip!'

Nevertheless, once I had dropped Peaches back at the apartment, I had went to Yolonda's to get Bay-Bay's grip packed-up and ready for delivery, first. Then I had zipped over to the motel and handled my business. When I got back to Yolonda's with the fresh shipment, she had been in one of her talkative moods, so I had hung-out there a little longer than I should have. After all, I knew Peaches was sporting a full-blown attitude when I had bounced, and I hadn't blamed her.

Especially since she was the only one, it seemed, that hadn't had a clue about what was going down. At that point, that was the way I desired it to be. To me, she still had life twisted. Asking me all those damn questions at the soulfood restaurant last evening, proved that. But that was how people were who couldn't be trusted themselves ----- they didn't trust anyone!

I turned up in Wilcom Court, and I swear to God, I thought I had taken a wrong turn. It looked like a'damn concert, festival, and circus, all rolled into one. Because niggas were everywhere!! So much so, I knew it would be hopeless to even try driving my truck up to Silk's building. Therefore, I backed out and parked along Wilcom St., so that I wouldn't have toworry about being blocked in.

"Goddamn!!" Both of the twins echoed from where they stood up on the bed of the truck.

"Is this that joint?" Donnell asked.

"I, guess so." I said. "It looks like my brother likes doing shit on a grand scale. Come on ya'll!"

It took us hardly no time to weave through the crowd up to the front of Silk's building where he and Tiny were laid back in recliners, like kings, drinking out of chilled bottles of Hypnotiq, There were some other individuals seated in their 'circle of gold' --- niggas whom I really wasn't hipped to, but had seen around.

Except for Bunky.

I remembered that O.G. from when he was hustling 'p-dope' with my Pop's and Bay-Bay's father.

Silk had a long-headed-nigga with waves in his hair, whispering something in his ear, so I turned to the twins, and said, "Ya'll can go ahead and get in the mix ---- I'll find ya'll when I'm ready to bounce."

"We'll holla', then." Donnell said, as he followed Donte over to get something to grub and drink.

I stood there for a moment, scanning the scene and shaking my head. Because in my mind, Silk was a damn fool to be setting it out, like that. I counted at least eight grills popping off steaks, hamburgers, hotdogs, and even some jumbo shrimps. Also, he had a whole collage of coolers spilling over with forty-ounce bottles of beer, Alize, and Hypnotiq. I saw why everybody was laughing and dancing and partying their asses off.

Silk was sweet!

I was sure that he hadn't taken the time to realize none of those muthafuckas were going to be anywhere around if the roof cabed on his ass. Meaning, if he caught a bid, or found his ass right back at the bottom, scrambling again.. I thought about telling him those exact sentiments, once I noticed him walking my way. But who was I to be telling him how to 'do him'.

◆◆◆◆◆◆◆◆◆◆◆◆◆◆◆◆◆◆◆◆◆

"What'sup, Nigga!!" I shouted out to my brother, over music that was thumping up-and-down the 'block party, slash, cookout'. Tiny and I were setting out for our crew ---- and all the other broke-ass niggas up in The Court.

"Nigga you doin' it, ain't'cha?" He replied, But I saw the disapproval in his eyes. But fuck it ---- it was my dough to splurge any damn way I pleased.

"Yeah, you can say that, Dawg, if you want to. But forreal, it's just a little sumthen' to get Toi off my back. She been trippin' 'bout a nigga not doin' shit with her ova' the holidays. So this is my way of killin' all that noise. You feel what I'm sayin'?"

"Yeah, aught nigga", he said, before he started smiling, and added, "But you can tell that shit to somebody else. Because you and I know you flexin' because that's what you do. This 'big boy' shit you doing ain't got nothun' to do with Toi or anyone else."

I took an easy sip of my 'notic' like I didn't hear any of that shit, being that he had me dead-to-the-right. Then I asked, "Why you ain't eatin' and sippin' on sumthen' cold." Toi was standing nearby smiling from something her sister Cherry was saying. But I killed that shit by saying, "Com'-ere Toi! Get Popcorn one of those steaks and a bottle of that Alize, Bitch. And pull that goddamn skirt down some. Fuck you think you at ------ one of those shake-yo-ass spots??"

She smiled and twisted her ass across the grass, to do what I said. That's why I was feeling her ----she appreciated a nigga that kept it gangsta with her ass. A freak bitch like her would be a nightmare for a busta or simple weak nigga, because she'd run circles around him. And fuck every nigga in his crew, behind his back. I turned back and faced Popcorn, because that was my least worry. Toi knew better. She knew I'd kill, and then kill again, if she brought me a move like that.

"I could've gotten that shit, myself, Yo "

"What!! Nigga, that's what a bitch fo', to cater to a man's needs. Which reminds me, "I said while looking around, "where Peaches at?"

He shrugged, then said, "Fuck if I know."

I hated that, that shrugging ass shit, and the fact that a muthafucka didn't have a clue where his bun-bun was at all times. "What, she don't have a cell or something?" I took a long swallow of my drink that time and waited for his answer.

126

"Yeah, she got one." He accepted his food from Toi and said, "Thanks!", before he looked back at me and said, "But I ain't tripping about where she at or what the fuck she doing, that I'ma check up on her. Fuck that!"

"Check up ---- Nigga that ain't checkin', that's stayin' on top of your game. For all you know, she could be somewhere, right now, jooking'another nigga."

He paid me no mind. He adjusted the Alize under his arm a little better, so that he could hold his paper plate and cut into that juicy steak. Therefore, I said 'fuck it' too. She wasn't my bitch, or my problem. Instead, I said, "You straight on your end?"

"Yeah. Why, what's up?" He countered, knowing I was talking about that 'yay'.

"Nothin', forreal. My man, Mario was just tellin' me, Choo-Choo trippin' bout some homies of his gettin' smoked the other night." I downed the rest of my drink, prior to stating, "Plus that crazy-ass nigga hinting that he thinks that's my work. 'Cause he made the statement that he gon shut me down. But picture that! That'll be like a Volkswagon trying to out run one of those Modenas ---- that shit ain't happenin'!"

He looked like he wasn't feeling that nigga Choo-Choo, either. Especially when he said, "so what you trying to do, keep him on locks, instead?"

I watched him put the last bite of the steak in his mouth, before I replied, "Yeah, that and some mo shit. Ain't no nigga on this planet gonna threaten me, and that be that."

"Everybody that was down with you, they still on your team?"

"Fo sho! That's most of'em, right there", I gestured, with my head over toward the group chilling around where I was parlaying beforehand.

"The broad, too?" He asked with a tinge of surprise in his voice.

I smiled and said, "Nigga, that ain't just any oh female --
-that's Fame. And Babygirl is gettin' it like any of those niggas
sitting over there. She done ran thru fifteen of those joints since

day one. So don't let all that ass fool you, she down like
a mu-fucka!"

He took a good look at her and commented, "I can see
that in her, now that you've set it out like that."

"Here, Boo, I thought you might want another one of
these," Toi said, while handing me another chilled bottle of
Hypnotiq. Plus she gave me a freakish look that conveyed what
she had in store for me that night.

"Yeah, good lookin', Baby." I swerved back to Popcorn,
and said, "I think it's time for us to renegotiate, 'cause, I'ma
have to show 'my peeps' betta love, now that ofva' niggas are
back-in-pocket." I took that fresh bottle of 'notic' straight to the
dome, after I gave my pitch.

"I feel that," he said, before he looked over at my crew.
Then, right after he sipped the chilled bottle of Alize, he asked,
"What kind of play you talking about? Because I'ma have to
holla at my mans."

"With the way we pushin' that shit, I think twenty-one to
me, is fair as a muthafucka. That way, I can drop it on them for
twenty-three. 'Cause I ain't no greedy ass nigga ---- I'm just
tryin' to look out for my peeps." Of course, I was wondering if
he saw how that big that lie was standing in my eyes. Being that
I was going to still tax them niggas, no matter what he did.

He said, "I'll get back at'cha", right when Peewee rolled
up thru the crowd flossing on a 1300 Hayabusa bike, real slow.

That bitch was hot!

Yet, I didn't know who the niggas was hawking the
most, that fly-ass bike, or that freshly minted dimepiece that
was riding on the back of that joint. I did know, however, she
was hugging that nigga, Peewee, like he was the best thing since
Prada.

"Look," I said, "I'ma go kick it wit a few muthafuckas. But don't leave without hollerin' at a nigga, aught!"

"Do you Fam'. I'ma just get my grub on and chill!" He replied, before he asked, "is that your Mom over there?"

I looked where he pointed and said, "Yeah. You know Momduke likes this kind of shit."

I didn't know why he asked about her, because after we pounded fist, he went in the other direction from where Julie had been standing, swaying to that joint "On Fire! by Lloyd Banks. But I didn't give it a whole hellava' lot of thought, because Popcorn could be a strange muthafucka, sometimes....

CHAPTER 16

Popcorn

At eleven o'clock, an hour before midnight, I was still at that cookout, funning like a muthafucka!! At first, I. had pretended to myself that I was holdin' fast because the twins were macking hard as shit, and I didn't want to rain on their parade, But who was I fooling? Once I had downed that whole joint of Alize ---man it was on! 1 started spitting mad shit to a group of honies that had pulled up on me, 'giving it up'.

What was the harm?

I had no plans of puttin' in work ---- I was just doing what a nigga do.

But then, somewhere along the line, I had ended up down between two buildings that this freak named Dovia had said, was the best blind spot in all of Wilcom Court. She made that pitch to me, before she got down on her knees and started spit shinin' my joint. Baby had some fire head, so I let her 'do her'. But I didn't have any plans of breaking off my platinum dome for her. However, when she had dug a jimmy out of her purse, I had been so goddamn excited, I had slipped into that joint with lightning speed. I plodded my way into those hot guts with a satisfying glow on my face. Being that Dovia, who was 'phat' as Mylissa Ford, had placed both her hands high up on the building wall, indicating that she wanted me to beat-that-pussy from the back.

Her shit had been so good that, just before I skeeted, I had thought about locking Babygirl down as my side piece. But right after the explosion, I cancelled that shit. I was even a little fucked up that I had put myself out there like that. Particularly since, for the most part, I had prided myself on giving a shautie a hundred percent. That way, I always felt justified in maintaining that expectation from her.

Don't get me wrong, I wasn't going to loose any sleep behind what I had done. It's just that, it had been the first time since I started living with Peaches that I violated her trust in us. Shit happens, though.

I had been fortunate enough to avoid Julie all evening. But at that moment, she had trapped me up in Silk's apartment. I had been using the bathroom. When I walked out, however, she was sitting on a sofa that was as new as all the other furniture in O'boys pad. In fact, it was as though Silk and Toi had emptied their apartment, and replaced everything ---- including the ashtray that Julie plucked her ashes in and said, "Hi, there. Aren't you going to say hello to Julie before the night's over?"

"Yeah, I was just waiting until I could catch you when you wasn't kicking it with somebody. That's all." I lied.

She didn't care if I was or I wasn't. She laid her nondescript cigarette in the ashtray, and stood up.

And man, did she stand tall.

The sight of her seasoned beauty and that belly-ring in full view by that belly-shirt she wore better than any female, half her age, had me drooling like a damn fool. Plus, thanking God for Dovia. Because, had I not enjoyed that splendid moment with her, I didn't know if I could've held back as I had toward Julie's advances.

Especially when she ordered, as she always does, "Come here and give Julie a kiss." She even opened her arms, exposing those luscious C-cups as an added incentive for me to come close.

I done as she asked. I walked up to her face-to-face, inhaled her sweet perfume, and allowed her to put her tongue in my mouth. Only this time, I knew full well what she was up to. Because, as she kissed me I kissed her back. I tasted her peppermint flavored tongue and lips, and grinded my hips into hers when she clawed at my back, gently. I figured, since she was always fuckin' with my head, I was going to use that occasion to fuck wit hers a little, myself. But don't misunderstand me, I had no plans of guttin' Silk's Mom---- I wasn't that gone off the Alize.

She pulled back from me and said, "Damn, Boye, I bet you a good lover like your father was. You need to come by and see ole Julie sometime." She winked real sexy like, before adding, "And let me be the judge of that."

"You off the hook, Yo." I said, because I didn't want to say what was really on my mind, which was, *'That shit'll never happen Julie!'*

She liked that response. Being that she touched my nose with her forefinger and a glowing smile, before she strutted past me toward the bathroom.

I went out the front door, and stood at the entry area of the building. Shit had died all the way down to only a few light groups of niggas, but Silk's crew had bounced. That nigga and Tiny were still laid back on their recliners, only now they were twisted from all the alcohol and drugs they consumed all evening. But if truth be told, I knew they were also drunk as shit off the success of their block-party-slash-cookout, as Silk had put it earlier. Because they had set-it-out in such a ghetto fabulous manner, they would be talked about for years beyond that day. I guess you could've said that was their fifteen minutes of fame. I couldn't argue with that, so many people lived a whole lifetime and never got that chance to touch the face of fame or greatness, on any level. Perhaps, that was why, as I stood on that concrete landing, I smiled and gave them niggas their's.

"Popcorn ----- Nigga, this joint was all that!" Donte said, as he and Donnell walked up from my right.

I watched Tiny get up off his seat and walk toward the corner of the building to do what looked like, take a piss. Being that as he staggered, he was unzipping his pants, as well. Then I turned toward the twins and said, "Tru dat. They damn sure set-it-out, that's fo'sho." I had wondered if they had saw me duck between those buildings with Dovia, before I went on to ask, "Ya'll brothasready to burn out?"

"Yeah, we straighter than a mu-fucka." Donnell said, before he and Donte high fived one another.

I was curious about what they were celebrating until Donte boasted, "We just freaked this little bowlegged shautie, down between those buildings, and she was like that!"

"Oh yeah." I said, while feeling somewhat crushed that Dovia had not felt satisfied enough by me, that she had to get with two other niggas, afterwards. Plus, it occurred to me that perhaps she had already gotten hammered by some other joker before me.

A fuckin' Skeezer!

Donnell cosigned his brothers remark by saying, "Yeah man, she put her hands up the wall, and told us to bring it on!"

I didn't want to hear anymore about that slut, whom I had contemplated being my woman on the side. So I said, to kill that shit, "Ya'll go on a head to the truck. I'ma holla at my brother real quick and then we outta here."

"That's word." Donte said right when I noted a P.T Cruiser, with chrome blickies and tinted windows, coast up pass where we were still standing on the wide stoop.

I watched the joint U-turn and was thinking how slick those joints probably were back in their day, right when it came to an abrupt halt crossways from where Silk laid chilling with his eyes closed and a pleasing glow to his grill. I even heard Julie come up behind me, and the twins once they said Damn!!", when they saw how good she was looking. Yet, for some reason I never took my eyes off that whip.

When all four doors of that joint flew open, 1 understood why.

Four niggas that were wrapped like ninjas, leaped out with some heavy shit, and pointed every barrel toward Silk. The hairs on my neck stood out like blades of grass an my heart raced like an olympian sprinter, with fear. But before I gave myself time to reason shit out, I was off that stoop ----- screaming at the top of my lungs, as I ran toward my brother....

◆◆◆◆◆◆◆◆◆◆◆◆◆◆◆◆◆◆◆◆◆◆◆

I was lying there almost smiling to myself at how smoothly Tiny and I pulled shit off that evening. It hadn't mattered that Toi and Big Tracy had been the ones to actually put everything together, niggas was going to still recount that night as the most fierce cookout-slash--block party a muthafucka had ever set-out in that city. When they do, my name, along with my homie, Tiny, would always be the ones remembered as the 'ballas"that did that'.

Tomorrow, we were planning to get back on our grind. We had fucked off a lot of dough, but that shit didn't mean nothin'. My Pops use to always say, you got to show niggas love, if you expecting some love in return. Popcorn may not have felt any of what I had done by jacking off all that paper I spent that night, but that's something he'll probably never be able to comprehend. But O.G.'s like Bunky did. That's why he never moved from the projects, even when he could've. He knew like I did, nobody showed love for a muthafucka, better than the niggas that squatted in them jungles. For instance, had I slaughtered niggas like Putty in that neighborhood Popcorn grew up in, my black ass would've been on death row five seconds after it happened because one of his neighbors from his old hood, would've felt it was their job to drop a dime, even if it was some shit that they wasn't even sure of. Yet, my 'fam' there in Wilcom, they didn't go out like that ----- them niggas kept it gangsta! Therefore, in my mind, they were worth every steak they ate and every ounce of alcohol they drank.

I gotta piss!'.

That's what I was thinking the exact moment I heard Popcorn screaming about somethin'. In fact, that nigga was hollering so loud, he was disturbing my flow. I hated that to, but I opened my eyes and raised my head to look in the direction of all of that damn racket. When I did, I saw that fool racing toward me, and he was looking as though the devil himself was chasing him.

Then, all at once, it sounded like the night had been lit up by the roar of thunder. I even thought for a split--second that it had started to rain some shit that was hot and painful and capable of knocking me off my damn recliner. Because by the time the thunder ceased, I was lying face down on the blood stained grass, thinking, 'Fuck was that!!'

♦♦♦♦♦♦♦♦♦♦♦♦♦♦♦♦♦♦♦♦♦♦♦

"Send a ambulance, right now, goddamit!!" Donnell yelled into the receiver of my cell.

I was blinded by tears and the utter pain of watching those grimy--ass niggas gun my brother down like he was a animal of some type. The sickening part for me was that, I had almost reached before the shooting started. I hadn't known what I could've done to prevent him from being banged up -----

I had merely felt that I needed to try.

136

And so I had.

Yet, before I had reached him, a bullet had hit me in my thigh. And then, another one had caught me in the shoulder, just prior to me crashing to the ground. For as long as I live, I wouldn't ever forget that look of pure wonderment on Silk's face when he was about to go down, at that moment, before all hell broke loose. Apparently, the twins had held Julie back from harms way because just before I had taken the first slug, I had heard her screaming, "Let go of me!!" Then, however, as I laid with my head craddled in Dovia's lap, of all people, I saw thru my tears, Julie hugging Silk's blood-stained body close to hers with no expression's on her face.

None.

As Toi kneeled beside them, seemingly in total shock.

I didn't know where Big Tracy was. But before I closed my eyes and buried my face into Dovia's embrace, I saw what looked like a glob of blood crawlin' toward Silk's slumped body. It took a minute for it to register that it was a shot-the-fuck-up Tiny who was making that low crawl to his mans side. Yet, I couldn't figure why the fuck he was smiling.....

CHAPTER 17

Peaches

At two fifteen a.m., I rushed thru my crib and raced for the bathroom. I turned on the faucets to the bathtub, full blast. I was thankful as hell that I had beat Popcorn home. But then, I had been certain that that bastard wasn't going to be there, that's why I surceased in freakin' out' at the motel with Choo--Choo and Moon. And got mines! In fact, when I left those two, not long ago, they both had been glad to see me bounce. Being that I had gotten so comfortable with what we had been doing, I had set out to demonstrate to them why it was me who had put the 'F' in freak.

I peeled out of my clothes and stuffed them down in the bottom of the hamper, because I knew I had leaked all the way home in that cab. I also made a mental note to do myself down into the bubbles of warmth. It felt so wonderful lying there, especially after such a lickerish evening. Still, I couldn't help thinking if, whether or not, I was on pussy, forreal, forreal ----- at that point. Because I had no regrets about what Moon had done to me, and vise-a-versa.

But fuck that.

I knew I loved men and dick and getting my black ass spanked by an ole rough hand, than for me to be completely off the hook over pussy.

"Damn!" I said once I heard my cell ring in my purse on the dresser, in the bedroom.

I reluctantly got out of the bathtub, wrapped a towel around my wetness, and tip-toed to answer it. The whole time, however, I was regretting the fact that I had turned it back on, just before I had gotten out of that cab. Even more so upon me hearing someone say, "Where the hell you been?? I been calling that damn house every fifteen minutes, because your damn cell phone was turned off."

"Who the hell you talkin' to like that, Rainy?" I shouted back into the receiver, and not acknowledging the warning signals that were starting to blink in my mind. After all, why was she calling there in the wee hours of the night, like that.

"I'm talking to you ----- that's who!" Her little smart ass persisted in saying.

I was going to curse her ass out, and hang up the damn phone on her little grown ass, until she promptly added, "My damn brother is in the hospital, and your ass -----"

"What you say??" I was hoping that I hadn't heard her correctly. "You heard what the hell I said -----he's right here in the emergency room, goddamit!"

"What hospital??" I shouted, before I asked, "For what!!" "He's been shot, that's what! And you better get your ass down here."

She had gotten on my last nerve, at that point. Still, I asked again, "Where at??'"

"MCV."

I hung up, after that, because I didn't care to hear anymore of her bullshit. Especially since, she had every right to be angry at me. Hell, I was livid with my damn self. Of all nights for something to happen to him, it had to be on that one night that I was somewhere doing something I shouldn't have been doin'.

But what about him?

'What had his ass been doing for someone to shoot him? I bet not find out that it had something to do with that damn Yolonda. I mean that.' I thought before I tried to decide who to call,' Carla or my sister, Toni. Of course, Carla was closer, but at that moment, I felt I needed Toni. Therefore, I punched in her digits, while I was toweling myself off.

She answered on the second ring, with a sleep tainted voice. All I could think to say was, "I need you!"

I felt no surprise when she replied in a more alive tone, "I'll be right there."

I didn't know how she done it, but fifteen minutes later, she was knockin' on my door. I rushed out dressed in a tank top, jeans, and sneakers, to find that she was wearing the same damn thang.

I gave her the brief information I had, after we loaded up in her car. Beyond that, however, we didn't talk the remainder of the ride over to MCV Hospital on Marshall St. What did amaze me, though, was how troubled she looked during the short ride, and as we rode the elevator to the sixth floor where we were told the family and friends could wait until Popcorn was brought out of surgery. It was almost like she was hurting as much as I was, from the thought of something this tragic happening to him. It made me feel closer to her -- it made us feel like sisters, again.

Once we got off the elevator, there were mad niggas everywhere! In truth, I didn't have a clue that everyone was there because of the shooting that related to my man that was injured. That is until Toi walked up to me and said in a tearful voice, "He's dead."

I almost fainted from what she said, but I held onto Toni and shrieked, "What!!!"

That crazy looking bitch just shook her head, up-and-down, and said, "Yep."

Yet Rainy came to my rescue, and she should've after all that shit she kicked over the phone, by saying, "She talking 'bout my otha brother, Silk ----- not Popcorn!"

I felt a mixture of happiness and sadness at that moment that I could never articulate in a thousand years. My man was alive, but his brother was dead and stinkin'. That's what I was thinking as Toni and I walked along the crowded corridor, looking for some place to sit. Because I didn't want to talk to anyone, not then, I didn't. Not even Popcorn's Moms.

But no one told Rainy that. She squatted on the opposite side of where Toni sat, and said, "His friend might die, too." I knew who she was referring to, but still, I didn't respond. That didn't stop her, though. She merely glanced around at some of the people there, and said, "Popcorn only got hit, twice." I didn't understand why she said 'only', as though that hadn't been made clear, "But that guy, Tiny, I think he got shot eight times. And Silk, well ..... ain't no tellin'."

I was thinking. 'Ooh my God!!', right at the instant that a doctor came out thru the swing-doors that lead back into the emergency room, and asked, "Is someone here that is immediate family members of Kevin Washington?"

I was shaking like a leaf, especially my legs, but I walked over to where he stood in front of Popcorn's Mom. She looked so sad, it made me feel ashamed about what I had done that evenin'. I couldn't look at her. That was why I had chosen to sit so far away from where she sat. I even wondered if she saw my shame. Because she reached out and grabbed my hand and squeezed it as though she was conveying her forgiveness of me freakin' with Choo--Choo and Moon, while her son had been somewhere being shot-the-hell-up.

Her gesture forced me to lower my head right when the doctor said, "He's doing great, Ms. Washington. Neither of his wounds were life threatening." He was smiling at Popcorn's Mom, warmly,

"Thank you Doctor!" She responded while giving my hand another squeeze.

"How long will he have to stay here?" I inquired, because I wanted to know. Plus, I felt I needed to speak up, also.

"Probably about two days, long enough for us to be sure that no infection has set in." After that, he rubbed his hands together, before he added, "Now, with that said, I suggest that all of you go home and get a good night's rest ---that's what he'll be doing for the remainder of the night. By tomorrow morning, he should be more alert, and in less pain. Ok!"

"Ok, Doctor." Ms. Washington said. "Thank you very much!"

He merely smiled and started to walk away, before a strong voice stopped him in his tracks, "What about my man!!" When the doctor looked confused about whom she was asking about, Big Tracy, who was hugging Tiny's Mom, said, "You know---- the short cute one!"

The doctor didn't miss a beat, "Oh yes, of course." His expression became grave as he stated, "All I know at this point,

is he's still in surgery ----- and he's fighting." He turned and walked back thru the swing doors.

Ms. Washington stood up and held my face with both her hands, ahead of saying, "you go on home and get some rest ----- here until you get back, ok!"

I couldn't argue with her, even if I wanted to. I was tired and guilt filled and in tremendous need of some time to think. Because, there was somethin' that had been nudging me from the moment I had gotten that call from Rainy, about Popcorn being shot. The problem, however, was that I had been unable to piece it together.

"Ok, Ms. Washington, but I'll be back real early." I made clear, because I planned on being there when my man opened his eyes.

"I'm going with her, Mama." Rainy stated -matter-of-factly.

Ms. Washington only looked at me, without saying anything. She was judging my expression to see if I felt as she had, that Rainy was maybe a little too aggressive in the way she pursued things. But I simply smiled and said, "It's ok."

Once Rainy, Toni, and I got out in the parking lot of the hospital, Rainy, who had already been talking Toni and I in a coma, said somethin' that stopped me dead center in my tracks. She said, "If I know my brother, he was probably too busy worrying about Silk, than his self or anything else. I mean, that's how he is, Gurl."

Toni was fascinated by Rainy and didn't mind her sitting up front, while I leaped on the back seat. They were chattering away, but their voices sounded far off, almost like in a dream. Because I was recounting what Choo-Choo had said when I first got to the motel, about Popcorn was going to be 'too busy' worrying about other shit, than to be concerned about where I was at, or what I was doin'.

My hands started trembling again, as Toni's BMW sailed down Clay St., toward Gilpen Court. Because there was no doubt in my mind Choo-Choo had been responsible for what had happened to Popcorn, Silk, and Tiny. Yet, I felt as though that was something I could never breathe a word about, to anyone…….

CHAPTER 18

Popcorn

Early that morning, after I had been moved to a regular room on the eighth floor, my eyes opened, slowly. I was still in a lot of pain, but no where near what I had felt while lying on that ground with those fresh hot balls in my ass. Those joints made me respect the power they held over life and death. Because, even though I knew I had only been hit-up in the shoulder and thigh, I still had wondered if I was going to live to see another day. A nigga just don't know how terrible that ordeal is, until he witness that shit. That was all I could say about it, at that time.

I was a little uncomfortable the way I was lying in bed, but I dared not move. I merely scanned the small room where I laid. The first persons I saw were my Moms and Julie sitting on opposite sides at the foot of my bed. Moms gave me one of her soft reassuring smiles, while Julie wore that selfsame blank expression she had been wearing when I saw her holding her dead son in her arms. To either of them, I didn't know what to say. Being that I could only imagine what my Moms had been thru worrying about how badly I had been injured. And as far as Julie went, what do you say to a woman whom has lost her one and only son. Nothin'.

Not a damn thing.

Perhaps that's why I looked off to the left, by the door and noticed that one of the twins, I think it was Donte, but I wasn't sho', was posted there with his big-ass arms folded. To me, he looked like he was praying for some ass to show thru that door that he could 'get at', for what had happened last night.

I felt that nigga -----I felt him like a mu--fucka! But the party was over, at that point. I didn't have a clue who it was that shot us, only that none of those niggas were big enough to have been Choo-Choo. Therefore, with all the niggas Silk was beefin' with, it could've been anyone of them.

I thought about telling Donte to unfold his arms and go the hell on home, right when my Moms said, "How you feel, Honey?"

My mouth was dry, but I still managed to say, "A little sore, but I'm okay"

"The doctor said you'll be up and about in no time." She said.

It amazed me that she sounded so cheerful, even though I knew it to be all for my benefit. The only thing that was more of a surprise than her it's-goin'-to-be-aught tone of voice, was that she and Julie were in the same room, without trying to kill each other. My Pops had given me that much about those two, a long time ago. In fact, he said that back in the days Julie and my Moms use to scratch and claw each other up so badly during their little cat--fights, that it would look like they had used switch-blade knives on each other, instead of those long pretty fingernails they both had been noted for. In either case, I believed that morning had been the first occasion that I had been in Julie's presence as a grown man, that she hadn't said, "Come'er, and give Julie a kiss."

My eyes got heavy again, so I closed them. But apparently, I must've gone straight out, because once I opened my lids again, Julie and my Moms were ghost. In place of those two were Peaches, Yolonda, Rainy, Toni, and you're not goin' to believe this ----- but that damn Dovia was sitting over by the window, as well. I thought to myself, 'Damn!!', from knowing if the wrong thing was said by any of the females in that room, shit could get real heated.

I spotted one of the twins standing over by the door, like before. But this one had to be Donnell, because he was dressed differently from the last one I saw.

'Fuck they tryin' to prove??'

I thought to myself before a whole barrage of questions were directed at me, all at once.

"You feelin' betta, Boo?" Peaches asked.

"You want me to raise your bed, Popcorn?" Rainy inquired with the remote control in her hand.

"You want another pillow, Kevin?" Yolonda posed in her sweetest voice.

"You want some 'hydro' to help wit that pain?" Dovia asked flat-out, and didn't seem bothered by the other females turning and staring her.

But my Moms hadn't raised a fool, I was on top of what situations like that brought about. Nothin' but pure drama! Therefore, I didn't answer any of those questions. I kept my damn mouth shut and slowly closed my eyes, as if the pain medication had taken hold of me, once more. It worked, too. The room became a chatterbox, all over again. Only that time, no one was tryin' to kick it wit me.

If truth be told, there was only one person I needed to holla' at in that room. That was Yolonda. Because I didn't want her to panic in any way, and start flushing my work down the toilet, from the belief that somethin' might happen to her, next. Yet, as I listened to her and Toni converse, it didn't sound she was trippin' like that. I hoped not, because I damn sho' didn't have it like that, to make shit right with Bay-Bay, if that pack got fucked--up.

Speaking of Bay-Bay, I knew the first chance I got, I was goin' to get at O'boy about sending J.R. and Big Titty Rose to scoop those hundred jaunts. Because I wasn't going to fool myself, without Silk, that shit was history!

But then, I thought of someone and my eyes flew open. I looked in the direction of Peaches and asked, "What'sup wit Tiny??"

"He's in intensive care. But what you expect ----- he was hit eight times." Rainy rattled out before Peaches could answer.I didn't say anything else. I merely closed my eyes, again. Only that time, I wasn't fakin' ----- I went slam out like a light. That is, after I muttered a little prayer for that lil' nigga with a giant's heart.

◆◆◆◆◆◆◆◆◆◆◆◆◆◆◆◆◆◆◆◆◆◆

Late that night after visiting hours were over, I was lying in that hard-ass-bed trying not to think about the fact that Silk, my only brother, had died just like my Pops had gotten slumped. That shit was 'erckin' the fuck outta me. He was gone and I knew I had to live with that much. But a loud voice in the back of my mind was telling me there was no way I could have any piece of mind, until I 'mercked' everyone of those muthafuckas that was mobbed--up in that P.T. Cruiser that had rolled down on us. If I knew Tiny, I knew if he survived, he's gonna be feelin' the same shit. I'm not going to front, at that point in time, I hadn't busted a grape when it came to puttin' in major work. Yet, as I laid there staring at the semi-dark

148

shadows of that room, I knew as well as I had known anything in my life, that shit was getting ready to change.

All of it!!

I had lost two soldiers whom I cherished, to that ruthless muthafucka ----- called the game. So how could I walk away without trying to at least avenge my brother's death? How could I do something like that, and still call myself a man? I couldn't, and I knew that there was no two ways about it ----- I would have to step up to the plate, and 'rep'. Earlier, I must've still been high or somethin' off that Percocet, for me to have even considered the idea of giving Bay-Bay back those hundred joints.

That was some ridiculous shit, on the realla!

Because, no matter what, it still had to be strictly about stackin' those big-faces and stepping up a niggas game.

For the first time since 1 awakened, I caught sight of a movement over by the door. I trained my focus until I realized that one of the twins were squatting in a chair with his big--ass arms still folded. I almost laughed out loud, because that nigga looked like one of those genies out of a bottle. Only he was bigger, blacker, and meaner looking. I was getting ready to ask him, why was he still there in my room? But the door opened and two other individuals walked in as though they were permitted to visit whenever they damn well pleased.

The twin was up and out of his seat, in one swift movement. He stood like he would pounce on both their asses, with ease, if either one of them looked like they were preparing to do something that would bring me additional harm. That was, until he apparently recognized who they were. At that point, he got the hell out of one of their way, but still posted up beside the other.

I was virtually shocked by the sight of Mr. Cool strolling toward my bed. I had no idea that I meant that much to him that he would take the time to visit me in a hospital. Especially at a half past midnight.

He walked up to my bedside, wearing pure silk and smelling like new money and a splash of Paul Sebastian cologne. He rolled a fresh, unlit cigar around between his lips, while he stared me. His eyes seemed to be alive with a million questions, but he only asked, "You want one of these, for later?"

"Yeah, auight." I replied, although we both knew I wasn't goin' to smoke it.

He merely produced one from his front pocket, and extended it to me. I smiled inside, because Mr. Cool was handing the Cuba to my hand that I had taken the slug in that particular shoulder. Of course, I could've just reach my other hand over and accepted it. But since I knew that was his manner in testing me, forreal, I painfully lifted my right hand and took the cigar.

He twirled that exquisite hand-rolled joint between his lips again, before he turned and left the room with his 'juss', Chubby right in step.

All I could think at that moment was, 'Cool Mu-tha-fucka!! '

CHAPTER 19

Choo-Choo

I got out of bed, Monday morning, feelin' like the weight of the world had been lifted from my mufuckin' shoulders. In a way, it had, being that that larceny-ass nigga, Silk, was no longer a threat to me or my 'bizness'. I felt like laughing until I passed-out my damn self, from imagining the look on that nigga's face when my peeps, whom had driven in from Tidewater, had rolled up on his fake-ass and wetted-his-ass-up. But I didn't laugh, smile, or any of that other dumb shit, because those niggas didn't handle that lil' nigga, Tiny, like I had specifically ordered them to do. I merely stretched and cut loose one of those loud and funky farts, before I started walking toward the bathroom.

"You act like you ain't got no damn home trainin' or somethin', Choo."

"Fuck that shit!" I said, because I don't be trippin' when her triflin'-ass be letting out those vicious joints while I be beating that pussy. It's just that, all of a sudden, since I brought us that quarter million dollar crib in Colonial Heights, she been jaw-ackin' about me doing shit I had been doing the whole time I had been fuckin' with her stuntin' ass. But I'on give a fuck ----- I ain't changing who I am, and how I do me, cause we living in some better shit than before.

That shit ain't happenin'.

On the forrealla, she best check herself with all that bullshit, anyhow. Because I'm starting to get burnt out on a lot of shit she been pulling lately. Especially that shit about her trying to dictate when I can get in them draws. Like when I came in this morning, I didn't want that ass, forreal. But because I knew she had just gotten her hair done, I intentionally ripped them panties off that phat-black-ass, for the hell of it. In my mind, I was daring her stankin' ass to say something. I was extra glad that I had freaked with them other two bitches before I had gotten home, because that had given me the staying power I had needed to fuck the shit out of her. If truth be told, that's what that bitch was mad about, more than the fact that I had broke wind, like I always did.

◆◆◆◆◆◆◆◆◆◆◆◆◆◆◆◆◆◆◆◆◆

By one o'clock, I was dressed and sitting in my Lexus, waiting for the garage door to open. I had already settled in my mind, who I needed to get at first. So I hopped on Interstate 95, and cruised down to Broad Street. From there, I turned off on Meadows, and hung a left onto Maplewood. I had DMX blasting from my speakers, the whole drive from my crib. That nigga, like Jada Kiss, spit nothin' but that fire ----- I loved both of them mufuckas.

I pulled my Beretta 9mm from under the seat and stuffed the joint down in my waist. I wasn't like a whole rack of niggas,

I didn't need a clan of mufuckas with me when I handled my bizness. Because, forreal, forreal, I was a small army my goddamn self. Especially when I was feelin' salty toward a mufuacka like I felt at that moment toward that coward-ass nigga, Mario. I knew his ass was down wit that shit that got my man, Troy, slumped last week. But even if he wasn't, I was still fucked up with him, Fame, and them other back stabbing ass niggas that was copping off of Silk, instead of me.

I knew my 'flay' may have been a little weak, for a minute, but that ain't the point. To me, it was all about keepin' it real with the nigga that breathed life in you, in the first place. Shit! He was suppose to be a family. I kept the wolves off them weak-ass mufuckas, when that nigga, Silk, was still slangin' 'rocs', and begging to get his black ass on my squad. I ain't gon' hate, I knew he was an outstanding hustler, the kind of nigga that would've blown me up quicker than a scud missile. But I also knew, he was an ambitious mufucka, too. I would've had to grow eyes in the back of my head, because he wouldn't have rested until he had become 'that nigga' that he knew I was.

I banged on that old head broad, Terri's, door and waited five seconds before I pounded on it again. I wanted Mario back on my team, but I also wanted to scare his ass to 'deaf ' first. That's why I had my face balled up like I was mad at the whole goddamn city, when I banged that bitch for the third time. In fact, I thought the glass was going to shatter out of it, that time.

To my right, I saw the curtain move in what was probably the living room, as though someone was peeping out to see who it was. Just in case they may have thought I didn't see them, I barked, "You betta open this bitch up, nigga, fo' I kick it off the hinges!"

After that, I heard Terri's scared-ass plead, "Wait a minute, he's comin'. She was a straight dime-piece as far as old heads went, but that bitch sounded like she was 'a hunnet' years old.

I looked down at my untied Timbs, and was thinkin' about whether or not I should kick him in his ass, when I heard the door open. I looked up with my mug still twisted, and was beyond surprise to see Mario standing sideways with one foot in front of the other, gripping his P89 Ruger like he was ready for some drama. "What'sup Shauty ----- why you knockin' on my shit like dat?"

'Oh so this lil mufucka done 'bought' some heart since the last time I saw his punk--ass, huh.' I thought to myself. Yet, my heart had already started beatin' like an african drum, before I said, "Nigga put that 'gat' away fo I get gangsta on your punk-ass."

He seemed a tad-bit hesitant, at first, but finally, he tucked that big joint down in his waist. I didn't trip from the fact that he kept his hand near the butt of it, 'cause, that's what a scared nigga would do. I merely sat out to get him back on my team by sayin', "I heard about O'boy gettin' slaughtered. So since I'm puttin' my shit back togetha', I wanna know, right now, if you wit it or not?"

That nigga had the nerve to act like he was giving it some thought before he said, "Yeah, I probably be gettin' at 'cha, Shauty, in a few days."

I felt like bitch slappin' that little long head mufucka, for trying to act tough, like I'on know who his bitch-ass is, forreal. But I held fast. In my mind, as long as he was going to be clockin' that dough_for a nigga, I'd get my chance, real soon to go upside his mufuckin' dome. Therefore, I said, "Yeah, well don't wait too mufuckin' long, Shauty, 'cause that shit movin'."

I turned and walked back to my whip fully convinced that he would most likely be blowing my two-way off the hook before the day was over. How could he not, with Silk deader than hell. I was the best thing that nigga had goin'. And, his worst nightmare, if he chose to fuck with somebody else.

'That's word!'

HUSTLERS

I thought to myself, as I bounced my head to 'X', and cruised toward Church Hill to pay my man, Bunky, a little visit as well.

CHAPTER 20

Yolonda

"Gurl, it's a damn shame what happened to them, especially Silk", my sister, Tinia, said. She popped and smacked on that chewing gum she had in her mouth, as always, as she went on to say, "Cause, that was one nigga that knew how to treat a ho. I mean, he had a way of makin' a bitch enjoy what she was doin'." She smiled before adding, "Plus, he was a generous nigga, too, even before he blew up. That's sayin' a lot, 'cause most niggas in the drug game, are some petty-ass muthafuckas when it came to payin' a bitch her's. In they mind, they hate to believe that when they get wit a ho, they just as much of a trick as your average busta'   ----- but they are! "

I wasn't interested in all that street shit she was babbling about, because I had just gotten home from work. Mondays was one of the busiest days at that Wachovia Bank I worked at. All I wanted to do at that point was find out if she had done what I requested of her, so that I could get me a quick nap in, before I went to Silk's wake that night. So I side-stepped Tinia's bullshit by asking, "So what up, Girl, did you take care of that for me?"

"Did I?? Gurl, I done got us a sweet hook-up." Her eyes had that greedy shine to it that they always reflect whenever there is a discussion of money.

"How much he gonna charge us?" I inquired, but knowing that it was going to be something completely ridiculous.

He ain't qon charge us shit, 'cause he gon be our customer." I must've looked like I didn't believe what the fuck she was saying, because she went on to say, "I ain't lyin'. His name is Tre, and he said, he'll cop everything I bring, as long as it's as good as what you gave me to give him."

I studied her features for a moment, to make sure I didn't see any larceny highlighting her face. She was my oldest sister, but she was one of the most larceny-hearted females I knew. 'Fo sho', that sister shit didn't mean a damn thing to her ----- that bitch was all about the Benjamins. I felt she wasn't a threat to me, because I knew her for what she was. That's why I had 'got at her' the moment I decided that I was going to 'get mine' off the top, from Popcorn's stash.

I may as well.

Especially since he was trying to play me like I was a chicken-head or somethin'. That's what I felt like when he gave me that measly ass two grand.

What, he thought I was going to put myself in harms way for that kind of dope-fiend shit. Well, he should've thought again. Because it wasn't that type of party ----- not with me, it wasn't. He should've seen that much in my damn face when he had the nerve to hand me that shit.

I could tell that Tinia was playing fair, but she had to be extra stupid not to. After all, if she tried to bring me a move, she would've just been cutting herself out of something that may have resulted in her getting out of ho'ing for a living.

Who knew?

Nevertheless, I said, "Did you tell him what the price was? Because we aren't taking any shorts."

She popped her gum and shook her crossed leg, up-and-down, like she was trying to entice a trick, before she answered, 'Of course ----- he know the deal. I been dealin' wit his ass for a couple years now, he know I don't play. Plus, he 'love it' when I suck his dick, 'cause I got this." She stuck her tongue out to show me her tongue-ring, as though I hadn't seen it before. Then she asked, "Why you sellin' that shit so cheap, though? We could get twenty-five Gs out that nigga's ass, easy."

"I know, but you did tell him that you was messin' with a guy from New York ----- right?"

"Yeah."

"Alright then. I just want him to believe that that's where it's coming from. As far as the money goes, ain't no need in being greedy. Not when we getting the shit free."

She smacked that gum like it was the juiciest shit she tasted, before she said, "I guess you right, I can live with the twenty grand. Especially since half that shit gon be mine." Then she smiled.

He was getting ready to get us some real money. And it was about time. She had gone straight into prostituting, right out of high school. Whereas, me, I had followed the straight and narrow path. Yet, as we sat in my living room, that day, I honestly didn't feel, even with my degree and position at a branch bank, that I was any betta' off than she was. As far as Popcorn and our friendship goes ----- fuck him!! And fuck that two thousand dollars he thought was suppose to make up for me putting my damn life and freedom on the line, so that he could give that hoodrat, Peaches a betta' life. Everytime I had thought about that shit today at work, I had almost wished that his ass would've been the one that got killed, instead of his brotha'.

Or both of'em, for all I care.

Because then, all of that damn 'coke' would've been mine.

"Come on, Tinia, I want you to check out the ones I've been in, and see if you can tell," I said, and walked toward the stairs.

When we got to the bedroom, I handed her two from the top drawer, and she said, "Daamn! You good, bitch. Both of'em don't look like they been touched."

That was what I wanted to hear. I smiled. Because, from that day forward, that nigga's shit was hit!

CHAPTER 21

Popcorn

I hadn't realized how much Silk's death had affected me, until I sat in J.W. Manning's Funeral Home that day of his burial service and felt a warm flow of tears coursing down my face, as the good Rev. Watson bellowed the closing remarks. I looked around at my Mom's, Peaches, and the other niggas who were there to pay their last respects, and wasn't surprised to see them cryin', as well. Julie was sitting ahead of me, however, shedding no tears, and showin' no outward emotions. I admired her, at that moment, because, basically, she was saying to everyone, your tears won't bring'em back.

As I had expected, Toi set-out to make a spectacle of herself, by screaming, crying and trying to climb in the damn casket with that nigga. I loved my brother, but I damn sho' wasn't feelin' nobody to that extent. Big Tracy pulled Toi away with her kicking and pleading for somebody to kill her, too, so she could be wit her man.

'Bitch, cut it out.'

I was thinking, right when I spotted Bay-Bay standing in the back of the large funeral parlor, by the exit where Tracy lead Toi out of. I called him yesterday as soon as I had gotten discharged from the hospital, and told him everything that went down. He never said he was coming up for the funeral, but I was glad as hell that he did.

My shoulder and leg was still sore as shit. But in spite of the soreness, I could still grip the one crutch I used to help me walk, instead of riding in a damn wheelchair, like everybody wanted me to do.

It was around two forty-five when we got to the grave site, and hot as shit. Especially in that black suit Peaches had brought for me out of her little stash she had 'bama'd'. Now, that was some shit that had left me at a loss of words ----- her tight-ass dippin' in her stash for the O'boy. But her generosity hadn't stopped there. Babygirl had actually pulled out every dollar bill she had hidden in her bank-under-the-planks, and handed it over to me, before she said, "I know it ain't much, but you probably gonna need this to help you with your business and other things, until you get back on your feet." Then, she had even lowered her head, and added, "We don't really need to move right now, either. So you can give that money back to whomever you borrowed it from, until we can afford it."

That shit made me look at her differently, after she sat-it-out like that. I had even thought, maybe she's not the little greedy-ass bitch I had imagined her to be. After all, only a loving and unselfish individual could come thru like she had last night, knowing that givin' up that scratch was gonna' kill whatever she had been saving for. It had been like she had chosen 'me' ova her dreams for the future. A honie don't make that kind of move, unless she was feelin' a nigga completely and 'fo sho'. Looking at shit from her perspective sent me on a vicious mission within myself. Because, I needed to know 'fo sho' how I was feelin' her. Especially since I always felt that she and I would make a hell-acious team. I just needed for her to find her way home to me. And maybe all that had happened was what she needed. In either case, I came out of myself admitting that, indeed, I was feelin' her 'fo sho' as well. Therefore, I was planning, at some point, real soon, to pull her up about what was happenin', forreal.

They lowered Silk's body into the ground, while the Rev. Watson recited that 'ashes to ashes' bullshit, and Toi took center stage again, by screaming her head off. I had to give that bitch one thing though -- she was dressed-to-kill in that black silk body-fitting dress. If I wasn't mistaken, she was sportin' a pair of those Manolo three inch heels that cost about eight hundred or more. That told me Silk must've had some ends lying around the pad, before he got hit-up. Probably no more than fifteen or twenty grand, though. Because, if I knew him, Julie was holdin' the stash. He fucked with his Moms like that, because she had never tripped about nothing he did -- and vice-a-versa.

After the Reverend said the final prayer, he announced that Julie would be receiving family and friends at her home. Still, everyone milled around at the grave site for a minute. Talking some of that fake-ass shit like how good Silk was and how much of a wonderful muthafucka he had been his whole life. One fool even had the nerve to suggest that my brother was 'in heaven' - knowing perfectly well, if there was a such place as heaven and hell, that nigga most of all wasn't below tryin' to push crack on Satan, himself.

I looked over at the hole where the casket was down in, and saw my two sisters, Rainy and Precious, standing over it, hugging each other. That was a sight that touched me. I hobbled with my crutch up to their side, and asked, "Ya'll ready to go?"

"Yeah, but do you think he knew we loved him." Rainy asked, before she turned her sad eyes in my direction, and added, "Me and Precious, I mean, 'cause, we didn't really get a chance to tell him."

I held her gaze and said, "No doubt! And guess what?" "What?" Precious prompted.

"He loved ya'll, too. He use to tell me that all the time. Said he was just waiting for ya'll to get a little older before he told you." They both looked at me as though they were feelin' what I said, but just to make sure that they did, I leaned in closer and whispered, "Don't tell nobody, but I think he was scared of little girls."

"Really!!" Rainy said, with a smile on her face that was so big it seemed to spread off of it. I guess that was one lie that explained for her why her older brother had started acting like she didn't exist. The same way she and Precious had treated him.

After that, it was easy getting them away from the grave site. They caught up with my Moms while I got trapped off by Toi and that lil' long head nigga that I had saw whispering in Silk's ear when I first got to the cookout the other night.

Toi didn't waste any time, she merely looked around to be sure that no one could hear us, before she said, "Popcorn, this is my cousin, Mario, and he wants to 'get in where he fit in'."

Her sayin' that, had solved the question I had had in my mind about whether or not Silk had hipped her about me being 'that nigga'. I wasn't trippin' or anything like that, it was just that I wasn't expecting to be kickin' drug business, ten feet from where my brother had just been laid to rest. Knowing Silk, though, he was probably feelin' honored. Perhaps that was why I had scanned our surroundings, as well, before I said, "What's your name, Fam?"

"Mario." He said with a baby-grit on his face.

I was diggin' Shauty, already. It seemed like he might have the kind of heart I liked in a nigga. Especially for what I had in mind.

"Auight, Mario, check this out. Give Toi your hook--up, and I'll get at'cha, real soon, so we can have a sit down."

He stuck one hand in the pocket of his fly-ass baggy suit, I think it was a 'Versace' joint, before he said, "She got all my info, already. So I'll be lookin' out fo' that."

I watched him turn and leave, but Toi, she stoodfast. Therefore, I said, "What'sup, Yo?"

"What you want me to tell the rest of'em?" She shifted her weight from one leg to the other, after asking me that question, like she was tired of the attention she was gettin'.

Imagine that!

"Who?"

"Them." She pointed in a sweeping sort of way, across the terrain of bodies that were standing all around.

Yet, as I looked more carefully, I could see clearly who she was talking about. Because they were watching us, I guess, and was waiting for her to tell them somethin', one way or the otha. So I shook my head up-and-down real slow, as a way of communicating to them as well, prior to me saying, "Tell'em the same thang, give you their hook--up, and I'll get at'em."

"What's in it for me? You gon pay that damn truck off that Silk brought me, and look out for a bitch, now that your brother gon?" She gave me 'that look' before she added, "I'm sure Silk would've done it for your bitch."

I knew she was probably lying about Silk coppin' her that joint, but I didn't bust her bubble, though. I smiled, because she was funny as shit, to me. Plus, she didn't have nuthin' that I wanted. Especially, after being with my brother, but I liked her, anyway. So I said, "I got you, Shautie. You handle your business, for me, and I'll look out. But stop the dumb shit, 'cause that shit ain't happenin' -----auight!!"

165

She laughed and switched that phat-ass, as she went in one direction, and I in another.

◆◆◆◆◆◆◆◆◆◆◆◆◆◆◆◆◆◆◆◆◆◆

I liked it that Peaches was hanging close to my Moms. I walked over to where they were waiting for me and said, "Ya'll go 'head, I'ma ride over wit my mans."

I was expecting Peaches to trip, but she didn't. She merely asked, "Is your leg okay?"

"Yeah, it's cool," I lied. That joint and my arm was killin' me.

"We'll see you at Julie's crib, then." She kissed me real quick, and got in my Mom's brand new Chevy Blazer, with my sisters.

I walked toward the rental that my mans, Bay-Bay, was leanin' against, with his arms folded. He had a kingsize smile on his grill as he said, "I guess that was the 'stunna', huh. Not bad."

"Yeah, that was her alright." I flung the crutch in the back and squatted on the passenger side.

He closed the door for me. As he started to drive off, he asked, "Who are those two big mean-muggin' muthafuckas with those rings in their nose?"

"They cool! They twin brothers that live in Gilpen, too. They was with me when all that crazy shit popped off.

He was looking thru the rearview mirror as he said, "So what'sup, now? They think they your bodyguards or somethin'? Because they was 'goosin' you all over that damn graveyard. Plus, they trailin' us, right now, in a raggedy-ass pickup truck."

"Yeah, I know. I let'em drive 'my truck' to the funeral."

He knew I wasn't trippin' off his remark, forreal. Still, he said, "My bad, Dawg." We both laughed. Then he got serious before saying, "It might not be a bad idea to put them two niggas on your payroll. Shit, they showin' that kind of love for free, it ain't no tellin' how far they're willing to go if you was looking out. "

I had already thought about dropping a grand a week on both of them anyway, for taking it upon themselves to hold a nigga down. Yet, Bay-Bay's encouragement had just sealed that payoff for them. I knew they was going to 'love it' because neither one of them had a gig, other than a part-time joint they worked on occasions. That's why I said to Bay-Bay, "I'm feelin' that. They some die-hard niggas, just what the fuck I'ma need in my life, right now."

That seemed to have pleased him, especially since I had turned down his offer to send up some of his peeps to wet-up whomever I ordered them to. To me, that would've been some coward-ass shit on my part, if I allowed some ova muthafuckas to do what I'm suppose to do my damn self. No way. Because as soon as I get a wiff of who slumped my brother, I was goin' to do what I gotta do.

Point blank.

We were cruisin' on Nine Mile Road. The temperature was still at its peak for that day, which was why the air-conditioner in that Lincoln LS felt good as shit. That soft leather seat was huggin' and caressing my sore-ass body so tenderly, I felt I could close my eyes and sleep forever.

"Where we headin', Slick?" He asked.

"Keep going, you heading the right way." I countered. "Julie lives in Henrico, a spot called Laurel Ridge."

He peeped out of his side view mirror, while saying, "I see she's still fine as ever."

"Yeah she's cool." I replied, from thinkin' he was kickin' it 'bout Peaches. Although, I didn't know why he would make a statement like that about her, because that was the first time he saw her.

"What!! Nigga, I don't know why ya'll haven't hooked-up, yet, that's on ya'll. But don't sit ova there tryin' to play-down how good Babygirl looks. Especially today, did you see her turn every head up in that jaunt? Nigga's tongues was droppin' to the floor." I was smiling at that point, because I knew he was referring to Yolonda. Then he asked, "Wasn't that her sister with her?"

"Yeah, that was Tinia." I almost told him that she was 'gettin' hers' flat on her back. But that shit wasn't his or my business. Baby got a right to 'do her' any way she pleases.

I ain't mad at her.

I showed him where to make his first turn, while he kicked it about me comin' down to the Pineapple State, real soon. I even told him that if I had felt up to it, I'd hop my yellow-ass on that plane with him, that afternoon. For one thing, layin' up in that damn hospital had a nigga lookin' pale as a 'Casper looking muthafucka'. For another, I felt I just needed to look at some different scenery for a minute -- something that would have helped me to regain some peace of mind and a little piece of heart.

We arrived at Julie's Townhouse in no time. When Bay-Bay put the rental in park, he looked at me and said, "I'ma send you up one of those money counters by J.R. the next time they come thru. "

"Good lookin', Yo. 'Cause that's some tiresome-ass shit, counting that dough."

He was still staring me when he said, "Yeah, that's part of the reason I'm doin' it. But the main point in me sending you that jaunt is so you won't keep coming up short. Because that shit startin' to add up."

I was looking dumb-founded, I'm sho', when I said, "Forreal, Yo!"

"Yeah, no joke. The first time it was some light shit. Probably about three or four grand, I'm not sure." He furrowed his eyebrow, before he went on to say, "But the last time, it was twenty—five Gs off it's mark. I ain't trippin' about it, though. I just don't want that kind of shit to keep happenin', because that 'little shit' cut's into a niggas pockets over a period of time. You feel what I'm sayin'?"

"No doubt!" I agreed. I felt him totally, and at that moment, I was mad-as--hell at Silk ----- a no countin' muthafucka! ! I felt fucked-up. I didn't want my mans, and connect, Bay--Bay, thinkin' that I was intentionally doin' no petty-ass shit like that. That wasn't my 'M.O.'.

I almost laughed though. As it turns out, it was my damn scratch that paid for the cookout-slash-blockparty, after all. Being that, I made it crystal-clear to homie, "I'ma get at'cha."

"Nah .... you don't -----"He tried to cut in.

But I killed that shit. "It ain't no debatin' the issue, Yo ---

I got that!! Case closed."

He smiled. But I knew it had nothin' to do with him being reimbursed for those funky-ass twenty-eight Gs. It was about me showing the nigga principles. That's what it was, makin' sho a nigga 'get his'.

Why not?

I damn sho wanted mine……

I knew I had shocked the shit out of Popcorn when I gave him all the money I had to my name. Shit, it had surprised the hell out of me, too, that I was handing that nigga all of my hopes and dreams. But deep down inside, however, I had known it was the right thing to do. He was a good man. A female of my caliber, don't get chances everyday to prove to a man that they down wit'em, by law. Especially when shit get shaky. Him gettin' shot and probably being disabled for a few weeks was my golden opportunity to say, "Look at what you got, Nigga ---- I'm the real thang! Not some fake-broad trying to come-up off a nigga." Sure, I hid my money and didn't say a damn thang to'em or no one else about me stacking for a better future. But it wasn't like I was stashing my hard earned money for some stupid shit, like clothes and jewelry. Uhuh ….Hell naw!!

Whatever I would've actually done with that money, would've benefited my daughter and Popcorn, as well, if he and I would've remained partners.

In either case, he had it now, and I'm glad that I gave it to him. I love that muthafucka! I'm sure he realizes that shit, now. There was nothin' I could've done to change it, even if I wanted to. The only thing that was important to me, at that moment, as I laid with my man that night after the funeral of his brother, was that he was alive and there with me. The only thing that I could say about the situation I had with Choo-Choo and Moon, was it was never goin' to happen again.

I meant that.

The apartment was soothingly quiet. I had Alicia Keys' 'Secrets' playing low on the stereo that was in the bedroom. I had just finished changing Popcorn's bandages and was sitting on the side of the bed sipping some ice cold water with pure lemon juice squirted in it -----I liked it like that! Anyway, he said, "We need to talk."

I don't know why, but my heart started beatin' like crazy. Maybe because I automatically thought he was going to interrogate me about my whereabouts the night he got shot. I wasn't feelin' that shit at all. Still, I swallowed the lemony water, and said, "Ok, lets talk then."

He smiled in a way that informed me he knew I wasn't as brave about holdin' that kind of conversation as I was pretending. Being that anyone whose ever been in a relationship before knew, that that 'we need to talk' shit could mean some super-crazy shit could fall out of that person's mouth after that. Like in our case, he could say, 'Check this out, Yo, I ain't feelin' this shit no mo'.' Instead, his voice was tender sweet when he said, "I wanna talk about us, and where we're plannin' on takin' thangs, from here."

I set my glass of ice water on the nightstand, because I felt my hands began to tremble. I faced himafter that, and said, "You know I'm down wit'cha, Boo, for whatever."

It looked like the lights went out in his eyes, before he said in a much harsher tone of voice, "This ain't no time for none of that cute shit. I need somethin' from the heart. I need commitment ----- some of that forever shit! 'Cause, if we gonna be together, we have to start being together, like yesterday!" I watched him scramble up to his feet without reaching for his crutch. I knew betta than to try and help him. He was on fire inside, burning with a need to be understood. So I merely sat like I was supposed to do at that moment. Butt kept my eyes glued to his, as Alicia was blowin' that 'I don't want nothing, if it ain't you Baby' joint in the background. I was feelin' homegirl betta than any bitch had ever felt her. Because, I swear, I didn't want nothin' and no one, if I couldn't have Popcorn.

He hobbled around the bed and stood ova me, before he ordered, "Stand up!" I did as he requested, in one smooth motion. He then said, "Listen to me. My brother is dead----he was the one muthafucka that I trusted most, in my life! The one muthafucka that I never had to second guess about whether or not he would be there if I needed him." He waited five clicks of the clock, before he said, "That's what I'm lookin' for in a female ----- that degree of dedication and loyalty. In other words, that's what I got'sta have from you 'if' we gonna step this shit up to the highest level. You gotta decide right here and now, if you can give me that. Because that's what I gotta have!"

He was studying my eyes as if he was sure he could tag a lie lurking there, if it showed itself. At that point, my whole body was shaking because that was a moment I had been waiting for. I didn't wanna fuck it up. That was, maybe, why I stuttered a little when I opened my mouth to speak, "Ba... baby I -----"

He scared the shit out of me, because he screamed, "Black Bitch, BE REAL WITH ME!!!!" Plus, he was tremblin' his damn self.

I believe that was what forced me to 'give it up'. Because, it was at that split-second, that if I could've, I would've given that nigga my soul. In place of that, however, I said, with Alicia rooting me forward, "Muthafucka, I love you!! Enough, that I gave you my passport to a betta life. Because, I would rather live here in these damn projects with you, forever, than to be anywhere without you. ." My Gurl was backin' up my outpouring, with 'Secrets' so I knew he was feelin' my love for him. "If that don't tell you that I wanna give you what you need, nothin' eva will."

He didn't say nothin' for a full fifteen seconds. But then, his cat-green eyes started smiling before he hugged me with his good arm, and stuck a mile of tongue down my throat…..

♦♦♦♦♦♦♦♦♦♦♦♦♦♦♦♦♦♦♦♦♦♦♦

I pulled my tongue out of Babygirls mouth, and said, "So we down now, right?"

She was brimming with heartfelt feelings. I could tell, as she responded, "Yes, Baby, we down."

"Auight." I said, sit down then, and let me give you game." For a second, she looked like she was about to order me to sit, instead. After all, I may have appeared to be in a lot of pain, being that I was standin' too long without my crutch. I wasn't going to allow that shit to stop me from serving her 'our situation' the right way. I didn't want any of what I had to say to loosen its impact. Therefore, after I watched her take a sit on the side of the bed, I said, "You might've already figured shit out, but in case you haven't -----I'm at it."

She knew what I meant, out the gate, but still she asked, "What, sellin' drugs?" Her voice was even, but by that time I knew she really didn't have a clue. Had not had a muthafuckin' idea. Especially when she crossed her leg, one-over-the-other, and started rockin' the top one, a little.

"Yeah, I been gettin' money for a few weeks now.

"Oh, so Silk had put you on, huh?" She asked, while I could see her wheels churning back over the last month, looking for the signs she missed.

"Nah.... not exactly. It would be better to say, I put him on." I wasn't bragging, I was just keepin' it real.

"You're kidding!" Her surprise was unveiled at that point. "But Carla told me that he had the city on locks -----that he was 'doin' the damn thang'." Her leg was rocking like crazy, by that time. "And you're sayin', all of that was coming from you??"

"Yeah, it's happenin' like that, Yo."

"Daaamn ……" She drug out real slow to express how impressed she was. But then, her leg stopped it's movement, before she asked, "So what happens now that your brother is gone, Baby?"

I'm sure I looked as though I drifted into deep thought, prior to me saying, "We still gotta eat and live, regardless, Yo. So shit still gon' be happenin'. Only now, I'ma have to step out there, and put it down myself. I just wanna know that you got my back, I mean as far as holdin' us down." I lifted her chin and looked deep into her eyes before adding, "I believe in my heart, that you got that."

Her leg cranked back up with its rocking movement, as she said, "I will Baby, I swear!!"

I didn't need for her to be swearin' and all that, because, she had already proven herself, as far as I was concerned. So to give her a much clearer portrait of the situation, I hobbled like a broken down old man toward the closet. "Come'er, I wanna show you somethin'." She followed and watched me push all of her clothes that were hanging on the left side of it, completely out of my way. Then, I painfully slid down the wall, before I reach with my good hand and arm, and pushed aside the empty shoe boxes that were stacked in that corner. When I did, I was sure she was able to see the two boards I had loosened, before I pulled them up to give her a picture perfect view of all that loot I had stashed there on Saturday when I returned from Yolonda's. At that time, I had decided that I wanted my bread close by, especially since I wasn't hot or anything like that.

Therefore, I had felt the best way to out-fox-a-fox, was to put that shit right under her nose. So that's what I had done, being that Peaches' stash was right over in the other corner of the closet.

Ooooh my god!!!" She said with her hand over her mouth. "Babee how did you get all that, so quick?"

I enjoyed her reaction, and answered her question by saying, "Stayin' at it, Yo. I know you was trippin' about me constantly on the go and shit, but as you see, it was all good."

She looked like she went somewhere, other than where we both sat in that closet, for a moment. Then, however, she said with a teasing smile, "You damn right I was pissed." She even hit my good shoulder, and added, "You should've told me Boye!"

I repaid her pretty smile with one of my own. "I'm tellin' you now ----- ain't no difference. Except, I know fo'sho where your head at."

"I hear'ya."

"Come'er, then." I said, while reaching for her dome. "I've never had no head in the closet."

She pealed off her panties and said, "Neither have I!", before she started gettin' her man, with her neatly shaved pussy laid in such a way, it was inviting. So I buried my scull 'uptwinxed' her legs and showed the O'girl some love.................

CHAPTER 22

Choo-Choo

"Fuck you mean, you auight, Mufucka??" I said to that soft-ass nigga, Frenchie.

His fat black ass was tremblin' like a bitch. But still, he stood in my damn grill and repeated what he said the first time. "I'm auight, Choo. But good lookin' out, anyway."

Fuck he thought I was. I was standin' there like a damn fool, holdin' those two bricks he gave me the indication he wanted when I had kicked it with his bitch-ass on Monday. Now, he gon' change-up like he believes he got that option.

'Fuck that!'

That's what I was thinkin', right when I hauled off and bitch-slapped that big-belly mufucka so hard, a line of spit flew from that nigga's jaws and smeared the opposite side of his face. Then I screamed, "You think I'ma joke, Nigga!!"

He sat his fat-ass down on that soft-lookin' sofa he had in his front room, and was holdin' his mug like my bitch, Wyndie does when I have to go upside her dome. Plus, he sounded just like a broad when he said, "Wait-a-minute Choo, please don't hit me no mo'. I can explain."

I hate a 'gel-ass' mufucka, that's why I yelled, "Ain't no fuckin' explainin' Nigga!! Jus' get your fat ass in there and get my ends, 'cause this shit your's now. "

His punk--ass looked and saw my big-ass hand still spreaded like I was ready to backhand his ass, so he said, "Auight, Choo, you got that. Jus'.... jus' let me get myself togetha, that's all I ask."

I was thinkin', *'What the fuck he mean by that?'*, right when that nigga's hand, that he had slipped down between the seat cushion, was pullin' out what looked like one of those old 44 mag. jaunts. I did know it had at least a ten inch barrel, 'cause he was still tryin' to clear that part of it while I dropped those two bricks of yayo, gripped his throat with one hand, and pinned down that hand holdin' the burner with my other.

When the nigga realized that I had his ass on locks, he started screamin', "DON"T KILL ME, CHOO!!! PLEASE.... PLEASE.... PLEASE, DON"T DO IT!!!"

But. I wasn't fazed at that shit. That nigga had life twisted if he thought I was gon' walk out that crib wit'em still breathin'.

Picture that!

I literally snapped the bones of his wrist, like I would a thick branch of a tree. The burner fell free, and his outcry became one agonizin' sound of utter pain. That shit was drivin' me crazy, so I head-butted his bitch-ass about three good times --- enough that he almost lost consciousness. In either case, his squeal turned into a throaty moan, as I reach and grabbed that antique lookin' pistol, and commenced to beatin' his fat face and meaty scull wit it.

His body was frailin' and kickin', buckin' like a wild stallion for the first few blows. But after that, his ass was out cold. That didn't stop the O'boy, though, because I was seeing blood. I must've hit that nigga about thirty times wit the handle of that joint. When I stopped and backed up from him, I was sweatin' like a mufucka. Also, I had so much of that nigga's blood on me, it looked like I had just slaughtered a hog wit my bare hands. But I didn't give a fuck. I just reach and pulled that three 'hunnet' and fifty pound nigga to the flo' and begun stumpin' his damn grill until I had broke every bone in it. His shit looked like a bloody-ass pancake pasted to the flo' when I got done wit.

Fo' some reason, I felt like slaughterin' that fat black bastard to make up fo' that shit Mario had pulled the otha' day, and fo' the fact that I hadn't been able to catch up wit Fame or that nigga Bunky. It had been like they asses were duckin' me or somethin'. But I bet when they hear about this massacre up in this bitch tonight, they gon' be on my 'jock' hard as a mufucka.

I went in Frenchie's kitchen and washed his blood off me with some dish detergent he had on the sink. After I toweled myself off, I looked in his fridge, and felt my mouth water from seein' a big ole country ham starin' back at me from a platter. I wasted no time hookin' up a double--decka' joint, wit lettuce, tomato, and mayo. I bit into that delicious mufucka, as I walked back toward that nigga's bedroom. I knew he had some paper hidden back there, somewhere, and I had no plans of bouncin' without it.

Soon as I marched into that triflin'--ass niggas room, I hurried up and chewed that mouth full of swine, before I barked, "Fuck you doin' back here?"

The little timid lookin' broad that was over in the far corner of the bedroom, shakin' like a wet puppy, replied,

"Non--thin."

"Get your stankin' ass ova here!" I shouted at her. When she scurried ova to where I stood, however, I felt a litte sorry that I had screamed on her. I mean, she was a pitiful lookin' bitch if I ever saw one, wit her little skinny-ass standin' there wit a tank-kini on and some damn runnin' shoes.

What the fuck was wrong wit that over-grown nigga?

"How old are you, Bitch?"

She trained her big scared-as-hell-eyes up at me and said, "Nineteen."

I took a wide-mouthbite of my sandwich, after she said that. Because she wasn't as young as I had thought she was, therefore, I felt no mo' pity. In fact, I was chewin' that delicious veggie joint tryin' to decide if I was gon slump her ass, too. But that lil' bitch saved herself when she said, "I know where his money and stuff is at."

"Get it, then! Fuck you standin' there waitin' on?"

She zipped over to the bed and flipped off the top mattress, befo' she stood the box spring up on its side. She got down on her knees wit her tongue hangin' out the side of her mouth like she was 'skeed-up' or somethin'. I guess, in a way she was. I had to give it to her, though, she was about her bizness. I liked that a bitch didn't talk back or ask questions ---- just jumped to it whenever a real nigga told'em to.

I was thinkin', 'I might keep this lil' stankin' bitch.' Right when she slid back the fake panels on that slumped niggas bed , an'showed me the money'! Where I stood, it looked like a few 'hunnet grand', easy.

That shit got my dick hard! Especially when she laid it out in clear view. That's why I walked up to where she was kneelin' and flung that dick out, right when I said, "Let me see what'cha workin' wit."

She got straight at that jaunt as though she knew that was her final exam, one in which she had to score high as a mufucka if she hoped to live.

And she did.

That lil hood bitch had the O'boy skeetin' in thirty-five seconds flat. We didn't leave out that crib until the wee hours of the night. We fucked, counted money, ate that nigga's grub, and then freaked some mo'. I ain't gon' front, when we walked out that jaunt, I was feelin' Shautie like a mufucka. I was even huggin' her lil' bony ass wit one arm, while I carried that nigga's shit wit the other. And I wasn't sho' which one was the betta' prize I had gotten from that bitch-ass nigga ----- her, or that bag full of dough.....

♦♦♦♦♦♦♦♦♦♦♦♦♦♦♦♦♦♦♦♦♦♦

Yolanda

I didn't like the idea that Popcorn brought that bitch, Peaches, to my damn house when I wasn't there. Nor the fact that she knew he was stashin' his shit there. I didn't like it, not one bit! Because, I was no fool, I knew her ass didn't like me. She was jealous of his and my friendship. Plus, her being a female, like I was, she knew there was a chance, at anytime he could end up in my bed, where, in all truthfulness, he belonged.

I mean, come on.

Just look at her. Sure, she was nice looking, ok. But what else did she have going on----nothin'!! That's what. He was selling himself short by not taking advantage of those opportunities I had given to him, the last few weeks, to be with the real thang. But I wasn't tripping because I was gettin' mine, all the way around the board.

Like at that moment, I was lying in bed, in the nude, waiting for Patrick to come out of the bathroom. He was the guy Popcorn bumped into the other day and got jealous as hell about ----- I saw it on his face, that's why I had pacified him by saying 'He didn't do nothing. '

But, imagine that!

If he believed that shit, he had life fucked up.

Patrick had been tappin' this ass for a few months. He may dress like a square-ass-nigga, but his sex game was on one-thousand! I ain't lying. That's why I was lying there, at that moment, with my coochie throbbing, hoping that he hurried the hell up. I wanted to 'get me', and still get some rest for work, tomorrow.

Nevertheless, there wasn't a lot I could say at that point in time about Popcorn having that trick in my damn house. Because, no way did I want him getting pissed off at me and stashing his shit somewhere else. So, although I didn't like it, I decided I could swallow that one. Particularly since I was 'coming off' decent as shit. Being that I had taken twenty-five grand out of that duffle bag of money he had kept up in my closet, before he moved that shit. Plus, Tinia had sold the kilo of coke I had skimmed off some of the bricks that were still stored in my spare bedroom. I wasn't the least bit worried about being 'found out' because I was on top of-my-game, by only shaving a ounce from each 'key'. I did it that way, because I remembered one of my cousins, saying, most kilos weighed out close to an ounce over the normal two-point-two pounds of a typical brick. Therefore, I was figuring that niggas Popcorn was 'hitting-off', wasn't going to be tripping about the weight. Anyway, if you count that petty-ass two grand Popcorn had the nerve to give me, I was thirty-seven Gs ahead of the game. Not bad for a few weeks of using my damn head, instead of letting a nigga use me.

Patrick walked out of the bathroom carrying his clothes, which he had folded real neat. He sat them straight and even on the armchair I had in my bedroom ----- and carefully lined up his shoes, under it.

I just watched his ass and thought what I always thought while watching him do that 'burnt-out' shit, 'Homeboy, you are country as shit.' Yet, when that nigga faced me with his five inch dick, that was brickhard and crooked as hell, my pussy made me forget all about how much of a neat-freak that nigga was. All I wanted was for him to be inside of me. Because, I wasn't like a lot of females, a big-dick--nigga wasn't necessarily what turned me on. Especially, if the nigga didn't know what to do inside-out.

I reach out for Patrick, as he climbed on the bed. He kissed and I felt his 'lil man' punch at my thigh, before it found the softest place on earth. He closed his eyes, put a camels hump in his back, and began fucking me like he was going to show my ass, 'he meant bizness'.

I wrapped my arms around him, tight, right when he asked, "Is that dick good, Baby?"

I smiled before I said with my sweetest voice, "Fo sho, Baby."

CHAPTER 23

Popcorn

Friday, around noon I was sittin' on the sofa in the front room, when Donte tapped on the door, before sticking his head in and sayin', "A O.G. named Bunky wanna holla' at'cha, Boss."

"It's cool, Yo, let'em in."

I didn't bother tryin' to tell him not to call me boss, because I had already told him and Donnell to kill that shit. But those knuckle-heads wasn't trying to hear that. Especially after I showed them niggas love with that G money that morning and told'em they were 'locked in' if they were trying to get down. Need I say, they tried to kiss my hand, after they pledged their lives to me. It sounded like some shit they were repeating from one of those hardcore gangsta jaunts they saw on television, but both of those muthafuckas 'gave it up' like it came from their hearts.

Bunky walked in wearing linen and full-skin gators. He copped-a-squat in the chair Bay--Bay had sat in almost a month ago ----- before he crossed his legs and said, "What's happenin' young Prince, you feelin' betta?"

"I'm straight O.G. --------------------what'sup wit you?"

"Just tryin' to get mine." His mug was set like he had just sniffed a blow of some P--dope, but I knew better. That nigga only got high off money and them young bitches.

"I'm feelin' that, Yo." I said before I reached off to the side of the sofa and grabbed the canvas bag I had waiting there for him. I placed it beside my feet, and said, "I don't know what you was doin' wit my brother Silk, but if you wanna 'get money' wit me, O.G., you got to be willing to pump at least ten joints a week."

His expression didn't change, when he said, "I ain't got that kinda dough, young Prince."

"That ain't what I'm sayin', Yo. I just need your word, and for you to be a slave to it ----- that's all!"

He studied me for a moment. Then, his eyes lit up, a little before he said, "You just like your father, more than Silk was --- that's not a stroke, either. I'm givin' you good money. I like your style and I love the way you gettin' ready to put it down. But .... I'ma have to pass, young Playa. Because I'm just a 'lil nigga' whose happy to stay in his place."

"You sho?" I inquired.

"Yeah, that's word, young Prince. Wit what happened to Frenchie, and now wit'chew steppin' this shit up, I think I'ma just sit this one out. 'Cause," he started to say, but dropped his long face to the canvas bag, first. "Shit gettin' ready to get ugly."

I didn't say anything in response, because maybe he was right. Fo sho, he had been around long enough to recognize a storm when he saw one comin'. As far as him not gettin' on my team, I was cool with that. I gained more respect for him on that day. Due to the fact, he had been straight up with me ---- and himself, about not wanting to blow up beyond the level he was on. To him, the price was too high. How in the fuck could anyone argue with that?

Nonetheless, I had already locked down everyone else who had stopped thru that morning. They were game lick a muthafucka! Especially that nigga, Peewee. When I had given that brotha the run down about the ten or more joints he had to do, to be locked ---- he had looked at me and said, "And!", as if, to him, that wasn't going to be no kind of problem. In fact, homie cracked for twenty of those 'blickies', right out the gate. I hadn't blinked when I told him I'd get at him later that day wit that other dime he wanted.

The best part, everybody was happy-as-shit about the twenty-three thousand dollar ticket I gave them for each jaunt. That shit was 'SWEET!!' and they all knew it. Fame had even said, "Boo 'fo dat' you get to tap this ass, anytime you wanna." I only smiled, because she was a little too thick for the O'boy. I'm sayin', she looked like the kind of broad, to me, that could break a nigga's back tryin' to please her.

Anyway, Bunky, stood up from the chair with his mug still twisted ----- 'jacked' his trousers, and said, "Keep your game tight, young Prince, because only the strongest and ruthless muthafuckas survives. Anytime you ova in Fairfield Court, stop by and holla', for any reason."

"I'll do that, O.G." I volleyed back out of respect.

I watched him bounce, before it occurred to me, Choo-Choo must've put his spook game down, real thick ......

◆◆◆◆◆◆◆◆◆◆◆◆◆◆◆◆◆◆◆◆◆◆

After O.G. left, Carla's man, Tre, swung thru, and I smashed him off with ten of those thangs, too. But not until I had heard that nigga spit some weak-ass shit to me about a nigga from NYC giving him the same 'flay' as what I was servin', but for a much lighter ticket. I had merely listened to that bullshit with no expression on my face, before I had asked, "Then why you ain't fuckin' wit him, then?" Of course, he had somethin' slick to say. All while he had gripped the canvas bag with those ten bricks I was putting on his face.

At that moment, however, I was out walking up-and-down the block, without my crutch. I was determined to get my stroll on, without looking like a damn handicap. I had been taking those walks three times a day since I returned home from the hospital, thanks to my Boo, Peaches. Because she was the one on top of me persuading me to get-my-ass-in--gear.

The twins were walking behind me 'grittin' like they were still madder than I was about me being fucked-up. But I doubted that.

Nobody was more pissed about what those cowards, whoever they were, had done to me and my peeps. If ever I find out who they were, they were going to wish they had never been born. That was word.

The afternoon sunshine was on blast, which was cool with me. Because my skin tone was returning to that golden glow the honies loved. I was wearing Guess shorts and a throwback jersey,

Yesterday, I told Smokey that I was thinking of turning over the landscaping business to him, and that nigga was grateful as hell, just from the idea of it. To me, he was a good muthafucka, who had already earned that joint. So forreal, forreal, I would only be awarding him somethin' that was already his. In either case, I told him I was going to let him know what'sup, real soon.

As I was walking back pass the apartment for the fourth time, and was thinking about how much of the pain in my leg was starting to let up, Big Tracy cruised up in Tiny's blood-colored Escalade. Her big ass was trying to look like she was all that, too. Because, even with her not getting out of the jaunt, I could see that her wig was freshly done, her nails painted, and

she even wore some purple blush to match her plum colored lip-
-gloss.

"What'sup Tracy!" I asked after I'd easy-walked over to
the whip.

"Not alot, Popcorn. You feelin' betta?", she said.

"Yeah, I'm gettin' back, Yo." I replied. But as I watched
her large bosom rise-and-fall, I wondered how in the hell could
that lil' nigga handle all that woman. In my mind, it was like
trying to imagine a monkey freakin' a damn elephant or
somethin'------ and lockin' that bitch down. Anyway, I went on
to ask, "when Tiny suppose be comin' up outta Intensive Care?"

She almost looked surprised, when she said, "what, Toi
didn't holla at'cha like I told'er to ----- he was moved to a
regular room, yesterday."

"Oh yeah!!" I prompted, as I made a mental note to get
in Toi's shit. Her ass had been tellin' me everything else, but
she couldn't remember something as important as that? Fuck
was wrong wit her!

"Uh huh. He the one told me to come thru here today
and drop you this stuff, he said you might need it."

"Like what?" I was curious and so was the twins who
were posted nearby.

"Some guns and thangs ----- they in the back! Ya gotta
get'em out, though, 'cause I hurt my damn back loadin'em up."
She was rumblin' around in her purse as she talked, like she was
looking for something important as hell. So I stood there
waiting, and so did the twins, to see what else she had for me.

That is, until she pulled out a damn Snickers candy bar,
and was smiling like she had found some money or somethin'.
But then, I guess that was some 'good money' to her. Especially
the way she ripped that paper wrapper away with her teeth, and
bit into that muthafucka like it had 'betta be good'.

I looked at the twins, and they returned my gaze with them both looking like they were fighting back the temptation to bust out laughing.

Donte opened the back door of the luxury SUV and snatched up two duffle bags, while Donnell grabbed the last one. They hustled them jaunts to the crib, but I went back to where Tracy was still sittin' chewing on the last bite of that candy bar.

"I appreciate it, Tracy." And I did. I didn't know why I hadn't copped me some hardware before then. I guess it was because, as I said earlier, I hadn't put in no major work, up to that point. Therefore, that kind of shit had been the farthest thing from my mind. I believe you could say, before all that shit with my brother being slaughtered and me getting banged up, I was one of those niggas that believed in finessing. Or, in extreme cases, tearin' a niggas head off.

But the tables had turned.

I had to comform with the world I was living in. Either that, or blow my come up and loose my muthafucking life. Trust me, that shit wasn't going to happen.

"I'll tell Tiny, that." She responded, before she patted her eyes with a tissue, and said, "I miss Silk, already. He was like

a brother to me wit his crazy ass. I ain't gon say he was the nicest nigga in the world, but he sure was nice to me

'Now, that's keepin' it real.' I thought, prior to me saying, "I feel you on that, Yo."

"Well I gotta go." She said as she started the truck.

"Tell. Tiny I'ma get at'em, and keep his head up, Yo."

"I will."

I was standing there watching her drive off, right when that nigga Choo-Choo came cruising by, real slow like. He had some DMX bangin' from the loud--ass speakers of his Suburban, and he was grittin' and rockin' his head to the beat of the song. I stared back at him with nothing printed on my grill.

For what reason?

No doubt, I didn't like his black-ass 'AT ALL!' but I wasn't going to put it on front street for him or no other nigga. To me, that was some sucka shit! The kind that I didn't have time for.

Just like, right when he almost got compl.etel.y pass me, I saw his midnight features crack into a ugly-ass smile. Sort've like the one he had shown me that day that Peaches was leaning on his Lex, wiggling her ass. Only this particular time, it was more to that grin. I didn't know what, nor did I actually give a fuck. Except, he had better hope that it didn't have a muthafuckin' thing to do with what happened at Wilcom Court. Because, if I ever found out that it did ….. ain't no tellin'.

"Gurrrl …..you the shit, now ----- ain't cha!" Carla said for the twentieth time since we hooked-up that morning. She wanted a bitch to believe that she was givin' props, but I knew better. Because, on the realla', she was 'hatin'.

I didn't even feed into it that time. I was enjoying my thoughts of how wonderfuleverything had been going, since after Silk's funeral. Like Popcorn and I having that heart-to-heart talk. Him believing in us enough to lay his hand on the table, and practically pledge his life to me. As I done to him. The only thing that had made me feel bad about that night, was the fact that I hadn't told him about what I had done with Choo--Choo and Moon. Plus the fact that that nigga had told me, plain as day, that he was responsible for what had taken place at that cookout. I mean, what more could he have said, after boasting to me that Popcorn was going to be busy.

The way I'd been justifying the fact that I hadn't breathed a word of it to my man was from me convincing myself that it would be better alll the way around, if I kept that from him. Because, just as sure as Carla and I were riding in her car, Popcorn would kill that black motherfucker, deader than hell. Sure, I knew that Choo-Choo deserved to die for what he had done to them. I even believed that there was a strong possibility that my man would get away with doing it, if he did kill him. But, I just didn't want to take that chance. He and I were on our way toward a splendid life together. Nothing and no one was worth sacrificing that. I knew that sounded selfish and cold, but so was life.

"That's it over there!" I pointed out to Carla. We had been riding along Jefferson Davis Highway looking for 'The Mattress Depot'.

My sister Toni dropped by the apartment the day after Popcorn showed me all that money he had stashed under the floorboard. She, to my surprise, produced the keys to the townhouse and said it was a done deal. She had said the closing would only be a formality. In other words, she had told me that fly-ass crib was ours! She even said we could move in anytime we liked.

I couldn't believe it!!

After all that time, I was finally moving the hell up out the damn projects. My head had swimmed a little as well. But that had been, when after Toni had left, Popcorn had handed me fifty Gs and said, "We probably won't live in that jaunt for more than a year or so, but take that and 'freak it', anyway you want to."

I'm not going to tell you what I did to him, after that. Because sucking the rim out of a nigga's ass, might be against the law.

Anyway, Gurlfriend had driven me all over the city, since the crack of dawn, and had even helped me pick out some super fly shit for my crib. She was one of those bipolar bitches, because one minute she was cool as shit, the next, she was hatin' on a championship level. I've never understood hos like her, the kind that had had every opportunity in the world to have a better life. But, choose to stay where in-the-fuck they were at, as long as they could get their hair done, or nails polished, and walk around with a pocket full of dough.

Fuck that shit!

Life was bigger than that, to me. That's why, even more, I was feeling Popcorn. He had left no thought that he and I thought alike about all the really important things. I had known that right after we had finished sexing each other in that closet, that night, and he explained to me that anybody can make money and spend that shit. But it takes a wise, patient, and strategic motherfucker, to stack those benjamines, and spend'em correctly. In other words, although we could afford some 'bigger shit' than what we were preparing to move into, nothing that we were doing to earn money 'on the legit tip' could justify us copping a three, four, or five hundred thousand dollar crib. Therefore, it would be wise for us to stay on our level, until we create other avenues for some cash flow.

I had listened to him, and felt myself bursting with joy, that he was nothing like the Tres and Choo-Choos, and even Silks of the world. In my eyes, he was a brotha who was aiming to get shit right and I was loving him for it!

He told me he was planning on giving his landscaping business to that guy Smokey, but only after he and I kicked it with my sister, Toni, about opening a small Real Estate Company. After all, Toni already had her Brokers Licences, and would probably be enthusiastic as hell about stepping out on her own. If that jumps off, though, he wants me to get my credentials, as well.

I picked out Posture Sealy mattresses and box springs for the new beds I had already brought earlier. I couldn't help but think how happy Tondra was going to be when she came back home. I had talked to her everyday since she left. But I hadn't mentioned anything about the move, or the fact that I had been planning on buying her that Princess bedroom suit she saw in a magazine, and loved. Now, that I had, however, I was going to decorate her new room with all of her favorite colors. Like pink and white and powder blue.

As soon as Carla and I loaded back into her car, she made clear, "I'm hungry ---- and you gon' feed me, Gurrl. I mean, forreal though, 'cause all that damn runnin' around I done done wit your ass, I'm 'bout to starve!"

I couldn't argue with that. Shit, I was hungry my damn self. So I replied, "That's cool, Hooker. Where you wanna eat at?" "I got a taste for some bangin' fried fish." She said. "I know what that means." I returned with a smile.

"You damn skippy!"

"Ms. Maggie's!!" We both said, and high-fived each other.

She zipped back across town, with 106.5 FM serving us up with the right kind of flavor we needed at that time. Because, at that point, we had that good soul food on our minds.

I knew I did!

So we just hummed along with Anthony Hamilton, and seemed to have drifted into our own thoughts. Mine were about my man, and how wonderful my life had become, overnight. With Carla, I didn't have a clue. But I knew one thing fo sho, it had something to do with making Tre move her the hell up out them projects…..

♦♦♦♦♦♦♦♦♦♦♦♦♦♦♦♦♦♦♦♦♦

"Uhuh ----- hell naw! Carla said as she whipped her cream colored Maxima over onto the wrong side of the street, and double parked in front of Tre's Nexus LX470 truck that was parked on Chamberlain --- a few blocks from Ms. Maggie's. She did that shit as if she hadn't noticed or cared about those damn cars that were blowing their horns and slamming on brakes to keep from tearing our asses up.

I was shook the fuck up, and speechless. Because it all had happened so quickly, I didn't have a clue as to what was going on. That is, until I watched her reach into her purse and grab a switchblade knife before she jumped out of the car, saying," Ain't no bitch gon' play me like that."

Some people might think that I was wrong, but I sat my ass right in that car, and just watched the whole thing. Because, who was I to have tried to stop her from doing what she felt she needed to. To me, that shit was between her and Tre and that female he was posted up talking to. So there was no logic in me putting myself in the mix. Especially since that crazy-looking bitch might try to 'get at me', for trying to stop her from handlin' her business.

Anyway, I couldn't believe what I saw. Carla ran upon'em so damn fast, that Tre's eyes got so fucking big, I thought they were going to pop-out-his-head. The female had her back to Carla's approach, therefore she didn't even see it comin' until she turned around enough to see that damn sharp-ass blade slice her across her shoulder and back.

That shit made me flinch. Even moreso, once I saw that it was Yolonda's sister, Tinia. In either case, she let out a damn scream that Yolonda probably could've heard at that branch bank she was working a few blocks from where we were. Then, she broke out running so fast, the bitch actually ran out of those stilettos she had been wearing with her micro-mini. Before I caught myself, I was laughing my ass off. Because, that was the funniest shit I had ever saw.

I knew my girl, Carla was a certified fool, but I hadn't had a clue that she was 'doin' it like that'. It looked like Tre hadn't known, either. Because she had his ass pinned with his back to his truck, sweating bullets trying to explain like his life depended on it.

'You go gurl!'

That was what I was thinking right when I heard a siren, and saw her come hauling ass back toward the car. She jumped in and started it up without saying a word. Yet, once we got a block away, she began laughing her behind off, before she said, "I knew it! I knew it goddamn it!"

"You knew what?" I had to ask.

"That his ass was fuckin' wit a bitch wit a tongue ring ---- that's what! Didn't you see it?" She asked like I was supposed to give a fuck.

"Nah, I couldn't see it from where I was at."

"Well, she got it, alright. When she started screamin' like a bitch, I got a good look at it. And I told his ass about it, too. I didn't respond, so she went on to say, "Guess what his ass tried to say to clean his shit up?"

"What?" I asked, while not believing that she was parking in front of Ms. Maggie's like ain't shit happen, a moment ago. I mean, I wasn't complaining, because I was still hungry as shit. But I felt that if it had been me that had just cut-a-bitch and had threatened to carve up my man as well, my appetite would've been long gone.

But not her's. She looked normal as hell, while unbuckling her seat belt, and saying, "He gon tell me, she his otha connect ---can you believe that shit??"

I was thinking how stupid his explanation sounded my damn self, until I quickly remembered that Tinia was Yolonda's sister. And that it didn't seem ridiculous at all. I wasn't going to hip Carla to all that, but I did say, "Make'em prove it to you, Gurl."

She looked at me like I was just as dense as Tre had thought she was, prior to her shouting, "For what!! I already know that triflin' ass nigga lyin'."

I shrugged my shoulders in a way that implied she might be making a mistake. "If you say so. It's just that, with me, I like to know fo' sho' that I got mine's dead wrong. That way, I'll make his ass pay, with no remorse."

"Com'on, Gurl, lets go get our eat on, 'cause you crazy." She said. But I saw it in her eyes -- she was going to do exactly what I said. I was sure of that, and the fact that she was going to hip me about it to.

As we strolled into Ms. Maggie's, I only hoped and prayed that that bitch wasn't sellin' Tre, no drugs. Because if she was, I would've had to bet my soul that, some kind of way, that shit belonged to my man..........

CHAPTER 24

I parked my whip in the crowded parkin' area of the 534 Club, on the corner of Harrison and Broad Street. I was flossin' in a fresh Gucci hook up -------------- and the little shautie I had copped at Frenchie's crib the otha' night, was ridin' shotgun, next to me, laced and dipped in Prada.

Why not?

Shautie was alll that, as far as I was concerned. In fact, everytime, ova' the last couple' days, that I had thought about how that fat-ass nigga had had that 'good bitch' and hadn't known what the fuck he had ----- I've wanted to find that nigga, brang his ass back to life, and slaughter that mufucka, again.

"Com'on, Slim Shautie, let's check dis jaunt out." I said, although I knew from all the 'big boy' shit on the lot, that it was balsa's up in that spot.

She got out the Lex, and started strollin' on those six inch heels, like she was the finest bitch alive. Which was a damn lie! I never said that she was a dime-piece. I said she was all that, and I meant it. Because, I was the kinda nigga that didn't get hung up ova' the way a broad looked. Wit me, she had to brang some otha' shit to the table if she wanted her props from me. For instance, Shalia, which was her name, she had the most vicious sex game than all the tricks I had been wit in that city.

No bullshit!!

Plus, Babygirl paid attention to 'errythang'! Meanin', she knew every nigga that Frenchie was hittin', which she happily passed my way. Plus, she gave me 'good money' about two young hungry niggas up in Wilcom Court, who she had said would be game to fill Frenchie's shoes, if I wanted to hit'em off. When I got at' em, them niggas was standin' and. pantin' like a couple happy-to-see-me mufuckas. Since yesterday, they'd been paper-chasin', already, like I like a nigga to 'go get it'.

Nevertheless, as we neared the front entrance of the jaunt, niggas was huddled aroun', mean muggin', and tryin' to cop 'em a freak for the night. So I reach out and hugged Shautie real. close, to make a statement to them niggas ----- and to make her feel special also. Because, in my mind, that's what you do for a 'good bitch' you give her 'her's'.

"What's up Choo--Choo, my nigga!" This stuntin'-ass nigga named Tree-Top shouted out like he was happy to see a mufucka. But he was frontin', 'cause ain't no nigga that owe another nigga eight Gs, glad to see'em. Especially when he been duckin' and hidin' from'em.

That's why I walked straight up on him, wit Babygirl still locked in my grip, and said, "You got my scratch, mufucka??"

"Nah, Big Money, bu….but I'm ------"

I cut that nigga 'shaut' by sayin', "Gimmie your car keys, Bitch, 'cause I'm tired of playin' wit your ass!" He looked like he was gon buck, for a second. But then he must've realized, real quick, that I didn't give a fuck 'bout gettin' his blood all ova my Gucci.

He dug in his pocket and handed me the keys to that phat—ass G35 Infiniti he was mashin'. It looked like he shrunk right befo' my eyes, from gettin' carried in front of the otha niggas that were ear hustlin' our altercation. But again, I didn't give a fuck That's why I showed him the six gold fronts I was sportin', before I said, "I'ma still- give you a chance to get your whip back --- but nigga, now it's gon cost you the eight Gs, and some."

I thought I saw my lil' bun-bun smile for a split-second and that was a first. Being that, that lil' bitch had been doin' everything wit a straight face. Which had been anotha' thang I liked about her. Still, that lightning quick glow I saw was cool, too. That told the O'boy, Slim Shautie knew how to enjoy drama, instead of 'kirkin--out' like Wyndie, my baby-mama, normally did.

I pocketed that niggas keys, and stepped off on his piteful lookin' ass. A few otha fools flung some fake-ass greetins' at a baila', before me and Shautie--girl walked on into the spot.

The first person I saw was this 'pink-toe' named Sandy, who works for the Richmond City Police Force. As always, she was wearin' her tight-ass uniform, as she stood buggin' niggas for ID, which was cool. Because I'm feelin' a mufucka that wants to make sho everybody legit in they shit. But the thang that irked the fuck out me, everytime I went to the jaunt, was the fact that that cracka' broad took shit to a fucked-up level. In otha words, she targeted certain mufuckas that she thought might be on the outlaw tip, by keyin' in their social security number into a computer that'll snitch out a nigga if he's outta pocket.

Ain't that a bitch.

Me, I must've had 'that look' because she tagged my black-ass every time I came thru. It never occurred to her, apparently, that I would've had to have been one dumb mufucka to show up at that club, if I was duckin' them folks.

Anyway, Slim Shautie and I watched as Sandy did her little harrassment thang, before she published a fake--ass smile, and waved us on in. I was grillin' hard as a bitch, as we strolled into the lower leve lof the buildin' where they had video games, pool jaunts, and a bar that was always busy as hell.

Word ----- niggas were deep as shit up in that tip and that nigga Lil Flip was gettin' his thang off.

Plus, the jaunt began to buzz Like a beehive, the farther we walked into the clusta' of niggas. That shit only made me smile inside. Because I knew they were kickin' it about me bein' the one that had gotten at Silk ----- and had iced Frenchie's faggot-ass wit my own bare hands. That had been the kind of reaction I had dreamt about last night. Because that meant those niggas were hipped to the fact that I was back. And that I wasn't goin' for a mufuckin' thang……….

◆◆◆◆◆◆◆◆◆◆◆◆◆◆◆◆◆◆◆◆◆◆

"But what happened??" I asked with utter concern printed on my face. "I don't understand."

"Tre's bitch tried to kill my ass, for no reason ----- that's what the fuck happened!" Tinia said from the passenger seat of my Camry.

I had just picked her up at the emergency room of MCV. She was sittin' sideways in the seat, to prevent her back from touching it. According to the doctors, she had thirty-two stitches that ran from the top of her shoulder, downward to the center of her back. I couldn't believe it!

Because, in my mind, nothing like that was suppose to have happened. I felt I had thought everything out, clear enough that neither of us was being placed in any sort of danger.

Needless to say, I was upset as hell. Perhaps that was why I said, "Maybe we just need to quit while we ahead."

"What!! Bitch, are you crazy??" Tinia shouted out in my car, like she was screaming at one of her tricks. "I ain't trippin' 'bout this shit to the point that we should pass upon this blessin'. "

I just thought ----" I tried to say.

"Well, thought wrong." She seemed to have calmed down before she went on to say, "I'ma be auight. If your ass wanna think about somethin', think about how you gon help a bitch pay for a little plastic surgery, once we get caked up. 'Cause you know how I love exposin' my back and shoulders, when I pit-in-on."

"Umm huh, that ain't all your ass like 'exposing'." I said with a smile. Because her attitude was infestious. She had lifted my spirits, just that quickly. Had it been me, though, that had gotten those damn stitches, our drug slangin' days would've ended right then and there.

"You got that right." She replied while changing positions in the car seat.

"What about him, though. Do you think he'll still wanna' do something?" I inquired while I was parking in front of a fairly decent crib that Tinia was sharing with another female, on the corner of Jackson and First Street.

"Hell yeah! That nigga ain't stupid. He gon' swear to that Chickenhead bitch of his that he ain't gon eva talk to me again. But, the first chance he gets, his ass gon be tryin' to find me for several reasons." She showcased one of those mischievious grins before she wewnt on to say, "Of course, one of those reasons will be for him to still get those bricks at a steal. Anotha' one would be about him wantin' some of this platinum dome. But the most important reason of all will be for him to beg me not to have that bitch, Carla, locked the fuck up!"

I watched her reach for the door handle, after she said that, before I asked, "Is that what you gonna do, take a warrant out on her?"

"Maybe I will, maybe I won't. At this point, it ain't no tellin'." She eased on out the car, and I waited until she was inside her house, before I cruised on off happy as hell that we were still 'at it'.

CHAPTER 25

I' ma leave ya'll to talk." Big Tracy said, as soon as she looked up and saw me walk into the hospital room, where Tiny was still laid up.

I still had a slight limp to my stroll, but the pain in both

My leg and shoulder, was just about gone. That's why it was fucked up, on a lot of levels, when I saw O'boy still lying on his back with that crazy-ass look on his mug.

"What'sup, Yo?" I finally asked when I stood by his bed.

Yet, it was obvious that he wasn't interested in no small talk. Because he got right to the point, out the gate, by asking, "You find out who them niggas was, yet?"

"Nah, not yet, Yo. And forreal, forreal, I ain' t been looking all that hard." Which was the truth.

He tried to reposition his body, a little, as he asked, "Why is that? You plannin' on lettin' that shit ride?"

I was staring him right in his shaggy-beard face, when I volleyed back, "Are you?"

His eyes looked like they became as red and heated and inflamed as a raging fire, before he snapped, "Fuck naw!! I'm gon slaughta' every one of them cowards ------and they families too, just as soon as I can stand on my feet." He shifted something under his pajama shirt, and went on to say, "They fucked tip when they left me wit breath in my body."

"I'm feelin' that, Yo."

"Then why you ain't lookin' real hard, like Silk would've been doin' if somethin' hadda happened to you, instead of him?" I felt his eyes burning a whole in my grill, waiting for me to respond. I was determined not to get angry by what he was insinuating, because I knew how shit must've appeared to him. In light of that, I tried to give him some understanding of where my head was, by saying, "My Pops taught me a long time ago, not to ever react to anything I wasn't positive of. Because if I did, I would be dancing to another muthafuckas tune." He looked like he wasn't feelin' that shit. So I gave it to him like this, "In other words, Yo, I got two choices I can make. I can start runnin' around broadcasting my intentions, like a damn fool or sit tight and wait for the shit to fall in my lap."

He looked at me like I sounded more of a bigger fool than I had a moment ago. Then he said, "Who you tryin' to bullshit, Popcorn ----- ain't shit gon fall in your lap, but some bird shit if you keep sittin' around waitin'. But that's cool! 'Cause I don't want nobdy fuckin' wit them niggas, unless I'm wit it, any how."

He and I wasn't seeing eye-to-eye as far as trying to handle that shit correctly. Therefore, I changed the subject, when I asked, "Any Detectives been by here to try and fuck wit your head?"

He raised his shirt up and was peering down at the 'shit bag' he was wearing, as he said, "Yeah, them fools don ben thru, twice, wit that fake-ass shit they be tal.kin'. I ain't even open my damn mouth, though. I know they don't give a fuck 'bout Silk being slumped. If anythin', they probably mad that they didn't get the chance to do it they damn self."

I was buggin' from the sight of that colostomy-bag that was attached to his mid-section that was why I only heard bits and pieces of his reply. Seeing that shit helped me to understand why he was so damn angry and dead-set on 'gettin' at' them fools that had 'hit us up'. Still, I looked over at the few 'get well' cards that were on his stand, while saying, "True dat! Because that was how I looked at it too, when they questioned me that one time, before I got released from the hospital. They were even asking me some off the wall shit about a nigga named Putty, and some other jokers that they thought Silk might've slumped."

Tiny had covered the bag with his shirt, prior to him crackin', "You back at it?"

"Fo Sho!" I promptly answered. I peeped at the door, which was still closed, and said, "I'ma still hit you off wit ten Gs a week, while you laid up ----- auight ! "

"I'on give a fuck 'bout no money, you can keep -----"

I cut his ass short. "Lil Nigga ----shut the fuck up!! I'm tired of hearin' all that negative shit. You ain't the only muthafucka that's hurtin' inside ----- I am too!" I was damn near screamin' at his ass. But he only folded his arms back behind his head, and laid there with his eyes shining like he had become a happy muthafucka, again. That's when it occurred to me, that that lil' crazy-ass fool was just in need of a nigga to step-up and tell'em what to do, like Silk had done their whole lives.' Therefore, I went on to say, "Fam, you gonna take that muthafuckin' scratch, plus you gonna clean your ass up, when you touch down. Because you on my team, now. It's simple as that!"

He was smiling like he had the night he had crawled toward Silk's dead body, bloody as hell. That made me ask'em, "Why was you smilin' when you was tryin' to make it over to where Julie was holdin' Silk?"

He shrugged his shoulders a little, and said, "I thought me and my dawg had got slumped, togetha. To me, that was some gangsta shit!"

I couldn't understand or argue with that so I merely said,

"I gotta bounce, Yo, but make sho you holla at a nigga if you need anything."

He didn't respond. He pressed the button to the nurse's station instead. A big breasted female, with a flat ass, appeared out of thin air. "What can I do for you, Mr. Dean?"

He folded his arms back, behind his head, as he said, "I'm ready for that bath, now, Shautie."

"Oh, so I don't have to drug you no more, for that?" She said it with surprise in her voice.

"Nah.... I"m on some otha shit, now."

I shook my head and went on out the door. As the twins fellin step with me, I felt beautiful my muthafuckin' self, from knowin' that I had some hard--knock niggas on my squad.

◆◆◆◆◆◆◆◆◆◆◆◆◆◆◆◆◆◆◆◆◆

When I got to the crib, Peaches was up in the bedroom counting that bag-of-cheddar I had gotten from Fame, before I went to visit Tiny. I almost couldn't beleive how quickly my peeps was runnin' thru them 'hunnet' jaunts I started frontin' to they ass five days ago. At the rate they were gettin'it, I figured I might have to start cracking for two hundred jaunts, from here on out. The thought of that, made me smile inside. Because, although Silk was puttin' his thang down, smashing a 'hunnet' plus in a one week period, I'm not sho he could've kept that pace going, now that the so-called drought was over. But me, there I was still layin' my lick down like a muthafucka, even though the city was flooded.

"Havin' fun?" I asked Peaches, because I knew she was tired and frustrated as hell, from trying to get an accurate count of all that dough Fame had stuffed loosely in a garbage bag.

She kept on counting until she got to a even amount, before she said, "Hell naw!!"

I squatted behind her and whispered in her ear, "Good! Now you know what I've been thru."

She pouted her lips as though she had a full blown attitude, and said, "You gonna have to get somebody else to do this shit, 'cause I ain't volunteerin' for it, no more."

I started laughing, "Don't worry, Yo. I got that shit already covered the next time 'roun. I just need for it to be 'on point' this time   auight??" She looked like she wanted to ask why, so I said, "My peeps told me that day after Silk's funeral, that my count been off everytime I've sent his ends to'em. He wasn't trippin about it, though. It's just that, the last time, that joint was twenty--five grand light."

"Oh really!" She promptly said as if something else was standin with her remark.

Still, I went on to say, "Yeah, no bullshit. At first, I blamed that shit on Silk. But then, when I had the time to about it, I had counted out all of Bay--Bay's dough my damn self. As a matter of fact, I had counted half of that shit out, one night ---- then I came back the next day and finished. It was no way the money could've gotten mixed up, because the ends that was uncounted was in one of the black canvas bags I keep on hand. But the other was in a duffle bag joint."

Peaches had gone back to playing with the money on the bed, as she said, "Hmmm .... that's strange."

"What' cha mean?"

She was making the stacks she already had counted and banded up, look neat, while she said, "It just seem funny o me that your count was off that much ---- and it was an even amount that was missin'."

It sounded to me like she may have been trying to point--a-finger at Yolonda, I think. But since I couldn't relate to no shit like that, I changed the subject. "How much you got, so far?"

She felt me blow that shit off, but she didn't flip the script. She only fell in step, by saying, "Whoever gave you this money like this is crazy as hell." She blew at a strand of hair that was lying down the center of her face. Then she pointed at two stacks, and said, "Those two right there, are an even fifty thousand ---- and they're right on the money, too. But that little pile is only twenty grand, so far."

Since there was sixty more thousand to be counted, I asked, "You want some help?"

"Say what!" She asked like I had lost my mind, or somethin'. "Your ass betta give me a hand with this crazy-persons money ------or we gonna be fightin' up in here."

"Yeah, auight." I said, as I got up from behind her and walked around to the other side of the bed, to get busy. "But I ain't doin' it 'cause I'm scared of your ass. So don't get it twisted." I added with a smile.

"Oh, I don't got it twisted. But I do know what you scared the death of, and it ain't got shit to do with me beating you up."

I watched her lick her fabulous lips, after that. Then, I started countin' that damn money like one of those tellers at that bank Yolonda works at. Because, fuck that shit ----- I wanted her to show a nigga what I'm supposed to be scared of........

CHAPTER 26

Saturday afternoon, Popcorn drove up and unloaded, what looked like, twice the amount of drugs he had stashed at my crib, the last two times. I was almost slobbing at the mouth, as I watched him stack that shit in all of the drawers and up on the top shelf of the spare bedroom closet. I had already decided that I was going to 'get mines' as soon as he left.

I was wearing a lemon-yellow wife-beater and some white Baby Phat sweat shorts, with matching sneakers. I was extra glad that I had dabbed some Chanel behind my ears, between my breast, and on the insides of each wrist. Because, I was lingering close enough to him that I knew he could smell that sexy-ass scent.

And it was driving him mad!

Especially when I was sitting up on the dresser with my legs opened wide enough that he had a picture perfect view of how fat and luscious looking it was between my legs. He thought I wasn't hipped to him sneaking peeps, down there. But I was. I saw his eyes sweeping across my thighs, an embracing the print of my pussy like they wanted to look at it and touch it and taste it ….. forever.

Right after he finished with his task, he stood in front of me, in such a sure-footed way, I thought to myself, 'Get ready, Girl, because here it comes!' I was so sure he was going to snatch me up off that damn furniture, rip that wife-beater from my body, and lick and suck on me, like I was rock-candy.

Boy, was I wrong.

That nigga merely dug into the back pocket of his Guess jeans and handed me a envelope with some money in it, and he said, "This is how it's gonna' be comin' from here on out, auight?"

I'm sure I was looking stupid and fucked up, all at the same time, because that was how I felt. "Yeah, but how much is it?" I asked as though I was still trying to entice him into roughing-off the pussy. Perhaps then, I would've felt like I had earned that money I had already taken from him.

"It's twenty-five Gs, Yo. But don't be actin' like you ain't gonna take it, 'cause I insist ----- case closed!" He said that with his cat-eyes reflecting the love he held for our friendship.

It was a look that made me want to die from the shame I felt, by me having clipped him. I realized at that moment that I should've trusted in him to do the right thing, when it came to looking out for me. But I didn't. I could only hope that he couldn't see my treachery illuminating from my features, as I held the hefty envelope and said, "Thank you."

He stepped in closer to me, and I enjoyed that wonderful feeling of my heart racing with pleasure and anticipation. Because, I was thinking that finally I had him. I could make

But guess what.

That motherfucker just kissed me on the forehead, like I imagined he would a child, before he said, "Ain't no 'thank yous' between me and you, Yo -----we like that!'"

He grabbed the big canvas bag that he had loaded some of that stuff in, and started out of the room, right when my telephone rang. Therefore, I leapt from the dresser, and said, "Be careful!"

"Fo sho." He said and kept right on stepping.

I ran into my bedroom and answered on the fifth ring, "Hello."

"I thought you was gon', Diva. I was gettin" ready to hang up and call your cell."

I was peeping thru the vertical blinds as Popcorn climbed up' into his old beat--up truck, and drove away. Then, I said to my sister, Tinia, "Nah, I'm here, Girl. I was kickin' it with O'boy."

"What, he still there?"

"Uhuh, he's gone. Why, what'sup?"

"Our boy said he 'want that' as soon as possible." She rattled that info while she was smacking on some chewing gum. Sometimes, that bitch could make me so damn mad with that kind of shit. Because, I didn't care what nobody said, a female could sell her body without acting like a two-dollar ho.

For one hot second, I thought of telling her, that slingin'

shit was dead. But thank goodness, that moment past, just as quickly as it had popped up in my head. That wasn't the time to be getting soft and developing a conscious. It was the occasion to be gettin' paid! That's why I said in a firm and even voice, "Come by in a hour and it'll be ready."

She quipped, "You preachin' to the choir, Bitch ---- I'll be there!"

I hung up the phone, broke out my cheater-tools, and got busy................

◆◆◆◆◆◆◆◆◆◆◆◆◆◆◆◆◆◆◆

I left Yolonda's crib ----- quick, fast, and in a muthafuckin' hurry, because I knew what she was trying to do. She was tryin' to give a nigga some of that 'goodd life' between her legs. She almost 'came off' too! I was feelin' that shit, especially when I had walked up close on her and kissed her on the dome. Being that the perfume she was wearing had made my knees buck and caused a vicious tingling sensation in the head of my dick.

No bullshit, Yo.

I didn't know why she had came so strong, that time, because, we both knew what the deal was between us. As far as that attraction shit went. Yet, we had kept our shit in check, even when it had felt like it was some impossible shit to do. When she had squatted up on that dresser with her legs open for the O'boy to feast on those lip prints, I knew, then, she was outta control. She best be glad I was locked in with Peaches at that point, forreal. Because I would've snatched her fine-ass up off that damn dresser, and chewed them sweats off that phat ass.

Anyway, I cruised straight down Lee Street and stopped in front of Maggie Walker High School to scoop the twins. That's where I always leave'em when I go to O'girls. I trusted them, but I didn't put that much faith in nobody. I had promised her that I wasn't going to hip nobody to what she was doing for me, I planned on standing on that.

What about Peaches?

That was some different shit. She had graduated to wify status. Therefore, she needed to know the whole hook-up, because I felt that was the only way she could have a nigga's back, all the way.

Donnell and Donte jumped on the back of the pickup and I took Chamberlain Street down to Hill ---- before taking a left turn onto Second Street. I parked in front of a big white house, right when a lanky looking woman stood up from the parked car in front of where we sat. "Ya'll looking for my son?"

210

She asked like she had a broom in her hand ready to chase our monkey-asses away from in front her door.

"Yes Maam." I answered, because that was how I was raised.

She smiled and showed us her three top teeth, and her bottom one, too, ahead of her saying, "Go head on in, then. He's waiting on you.

We did as we were told. Donte was carrying the bag with the ten jaunts of 'yay' in it, while Donnell walked in front of us, sniffin' for trouble. We walked inside and a young brotha who was tall and lanky like the woman out front, was standing by the window, waiting.

"What'sup Fam ----- you the brotha I kicked it wit over the cell?" He looked a little too jumpy for a nigga that was tryin' to go 'all out' for his.

I could tell Donnell felt the same way, that's probably why he had both hands under his 'Do tha damn thang' tee--shirt.

"Yeah, that was me, Big Money ----- my name Tree-Top." He bounced from one leg, to the other, and back again.

Toi had stopped thru yesterday, and gave me this nigga's digits. Plus, she had stamped his hustlin' rep ----- after she had given me the pitch about what had happened the other night at the 534 Club, between him and Choo-Choo. That's why I asked him straight up, "Why you owe Choo some dough ----- you fuck a 'pack' up?"

Tree--Top looked at me like I said somethin' fucked up about his Moms, before he began shifting his weight again, and said, "Hell naw, not fo--real."

"What'cha mean by that, Fam ----- either you did or you didn't?" I was wishing he stopped that fucking moving around. That shit was driving me crazy.

"Naw.... see, what happened was, he gave me some work that was pure garbage. I pushed that shit to some of my best customers. When they cooked it up and didn't hardly get nothin' back ----- I had to give they ends back to'em." He was still changing weight from foot-to-foot, as he added, "But Choo, he ain't tryin' to hear dat. He still sayin' I got to pay'em, anyway."

From what I had heard about Choo-Choo, that shit was makin' sense what Slim was saying. Still I said, "If you tryin' to get wit this, that's all good. But I'm not tryin' to put you on, only so you can pay your ticket off wit O'boy." He looked like he was feelin' me, but I asked him anyway, "You feelin' what I'm sayin'?"

"Yeah, Money, I feel ya. I ratha' be down wit'choo, anyway, than to be hustlin' wit a nigga that ain't got no understandin'." He slid his hands in his pockets and slowed his weight changing movement.

"Auight, as long as we got 'our understanin' -----that's all I'm concerned 'bout. Because I ain' t no rescue mission -----

I'm a nigga that's bout it' ----- forreal ." - I   watched Donte walk over and place the work at his feet, before I went on to say, "You got ten jaunts in that bag, at twenty-three a pop. Which means, your ticket two hundred thirty--ight Gs."

He looked like he did some quick math in his dome, before he said, "I don't think that's right, Money ----

"Nah, in the side slot of that bag is the eight grand I heard you owe that nigga Choo, also. Get at that nigga, get your whip back, and keep'em out your bizness.

That brotha showed me a smile I didn't think he possessed, ahead of him saying, "Word, good lookin' Money ----- you won't regret puttin' me down. But you'll see. "

We walked back out the front door and saw his Moms still chillin' in the front seat of her Grand AM, like it was far more comfortable for her to be parlayin' in her whip, than anywhere else. In either case, she showed me those four teeth again, and said, "You a spit image of your father, when he was your age."

"Thank you," I respond.

Donnell and Donte jumped up on the truck, right when she added, " I use to go wit' em , you know -----best man I eva had."

That shit gave me the chills. Being that I couldn't imagine Pops with them 'bag of bones'. She had to be tight, back in the day, if she was tellin' the truth. But still --- goddamn, Pops! He had just lost some major playa points, wit me, if he was slabbin'-that-ass.

I didn't even try responding to that shit, I just got up in my shit, and headed for home. It felt good as a muthafucka, though, knowing I had just locked in another major dope-boy in that town.

Fuck Choo-Choo !

◆◆◆◆◆◆◆◆◆◆◆◆◆◆◆◆◆◆◆◆◆◆

Peaches (from Florida)

How could he be so blind?

Because to me, it had seemed so obvious that Yolonda had been the one who had stolen that shit. Still, I knew that I couldn't say nothing, straight up, without it sounding like I was trying to hate on that bitch, and their friendship. Therefore, I had merely dropped a subtle hint, which I had been sure he had heard, loud and clear. He had just chosen not to feed into it, however, so I backed off. Because, in my mind, I felt I should've had some concrete evidence, my damn self, before Iactually pointed the finger at that bitch ---- - I wanted to be able to poke her straight between the motherfucking eyes.

Still and all, I didn't want Carla to be hipped to whatever was happening. That bitch would have had that shit all over Gilpen, before sundown. Therefore, I only said in a half interested tone, "Oh yeah. What did he say?"

"Some shit 'bout he ain't got to prove nuthin' to me." I felt my hopes for trappin' Yolonda's larceny-ass, began to evaporate, right when Carla furrowed her brow and added, "But I told his ass he was right, he don't have to prove shit to me. I'll just bitch and ask her my damn self."

We had placed all of the blue plastic loops thru the curtain holes. So I backed up to make certain that the heavy plastic hung straight and even, as I said, "Gurl, you crazy."

"No I'm not! I ain't gon stand for him makin' me get a damn hole in my tongue, for his ass - and he not keepin' it real wit a bitch. Fuck that shit!!"

She was upset, all over again. Because she dug through her purse that was on the vanity, and fired up a cigarette, even though I had warned her ass not to smoke in my crib. But I didn't trip, since she was helping me, and didn't have a clue. I merely said, "I feel you Gurl. Niggas be thinkin' they can say and do anythan' ---- especially when they ass gettin' money. But any female that care 'bout herself, will make her man, give her her's."

She must've felt that shit, completely, because she snapped, "You damn right ---- and Tre gon' give me mines! He gon' prove he's coppin' from that ho, or I'ma find her ass, and get in her shit my damn self."

"Peaches!! Where ya'll at?" That was Popcorn calling me from where he stood on the steps.

"In the bathroom, why ----- what's wrong?" I asked because it sounded like he needed me for somethin'.

"Ain't nothing wrong, Yo. Just come down here, for a second."

"Alright, I'll be right there." I said before I looked at Carla and said, "Gurl they helpless without us, ain't they?"

"You got that right!" She quipped and gave me a high-five. When we got down stairs, Popcorn grabbed my hand and said, "Come on, I wanna show you somethin'."

His eyes were smiling enough that I had to ask, "What's goin on?"

But he didn't reply, he merely led me out the front door, with Carla at our heels. Once we walked thru the doorway, though, I stopped dead in my tracks, because that brand spankin' new CLK 430 Mercedes, I was staring at, took my motherfuckin' breath away. I knew, immediately that it was mines, because it had a big red bow wrapped wrapped about its silver-gray body. I screamed thru both my hands that were covering my mouth. Popcorn, the twins, and my sister, Toni who had obviously driven it over, were all smiling their asses off. But Carla, that hatin' bitch, couldn't even fake a genuine smile, even if she had wanted to. That was what I meant about her being bipolar ---- one minute she was my sidekick, but the next, she was a bonifide hater.

But I wasn't seeing that.

I wrapped my arms around my man's neck, and gave him the sweetest kiss he ever had. I made sure he knew what was coming later that evening, by the seductive manner in which I sucked his big fat tongue.

Toni, who may have felt a little embarrassed by the way we were carrying on, said, " Alright ya'll, that's enough of that."

"I knew she probably played a role in me getting that fly-ass whip, so I cut her some slack. Yet, when I pulled my lips away from his, I poured my soul into it when I said, "I love you, Boye!"

◆◆◆◆◆◆◆◆◆◆◆◆◆◆◆◆◆◆◆◆◆◆

Popcorn

Toni had brought enough KFC fried chicken, slaw, and baked beans to feed a football team, when she dropped off Peaches' CLK 430 like I had asked her to. I was diggin' Shautie, Yo. She was cool and down by law, as far as I was concerned. I even told her that, yesterday, after she had agreed to cop that whip, for a nigga. In fact, I had told her, no matter what happens between Peaches and I, she was always going to be my big sis.

That had made her smile like she had done that day at her office, after I had given her that deposit for the crib.

Nonetheless, we all huddled around the kitchen table gettin' our eat on. Especially Donnell and Donte. Those niggas were puttin' in major work. I believe Tony may have felt a little uncomfortable by the penetrating manner in which Donnell stared at her, each time he licked and sucked chicken grease from his fingers. I started to check'em, but that shit was way too comical. Moreso that Toni's ebony cheeks were burning like mahogany. Plus, everybody else was 'lunchin' off that shit, too. Including Peaches. I guess she was figuring, like I was, that if Toni planned on being apart of our click, she was gonna have to learn how to straighten that shit herself.

About two days ago, I copped two-way jaunts for Peaches, the twins, and myself. Mine started buzzing, blowing up like crazy, right when the O'boy was thinking about smashin' another one of those crispy-ass breast and a buttered roll. Therefore, I was a little salty about having to just up and bounce.

But I did.

One thing my Pops made clear, no matter if you were grubbin', sleepin', or getting ready to lay-up in some pussy when that paper called your name, you had to go and get it. And he said, " Off the whistle!"

I backed away from the table and said, "I'll be right back, ya'll." The twins were getting up, too, but I made them niggas happy when I said, "Ya'll just chill. I'll scoop ya'll in about ten minutes."

They sat their happy asses back down and didn't miss a beat.

In a way, it was all good at that point being Yolonda was only a few blocks away. But on the other hand, niggas were in a much better position to get in mine's. Therefore, I drove toward o'girls spot, decided upon the fact that, real soon, I was gonna have to bama my work somewhere else.

It was just that simple.

She wasn't home when I got there. Which was no biggie, I just snatched up the twenty jaunts that Peewee had just hit me fo'. Being that he had printed out, 'Meet me at apartment 20b.' Also, I knew that the 'b' meant he was at his Moms over in Blackwell. He had a ride-or-die shautie that lived in Highland Springs, as well. So I knew that if he put apartment 20h in whatever statement he printed out, he would be posted at his bun-bun's pad, waiting for me to hit'em off.

I picked up the twins and Peaches walked out to the truck and said, "I'ma take Toni back to get her car, you want me to pick up any thing while I'm out?"

"Yeah, stop by Block-Busta and pick up that new DVD 'White Girls'.

"Didn't we see that, already?" She asked, like she was trippin' about watching that shit again.

"I know, Yo, but that joint funny-as-shit."

"Whatever!" She rolled her eyes slightly, before she said, "Anything else?"

She was aiming to show off her new wheels, so she wanted a whole list of errands to run. I merely smiled and said, "Nah, I'm straight. Unless you wanna drive down New Orleans and get some of those good Cajun ribs." I fought back a smile after that, because she knew I was hip to her wanting to floss in her new whip.

That's why she prompted ,"Forget'choo!", before she turned and headed back in the crib.

I sat there and watched her shake that phat ass for me, like she knew I would. After all, I had told her several times that day, that those skin-tight jeans she was sportin', was jive fuckin' wit a nigga's dome.

◆◆◆◆◆◆◆◆◆◆◆◆◆◆◆◆◆◆◆◆◆

Peewee was a smooth nigga. I liked fuckin' wit shanty, because he had that hustlin' shit down ---- ice cold! He even brought some class to the game. Like, when we got to his Moms, he took us down in a basement that was fly-as-shit. He popped a bottle of ' bubb' and poured four crystal flutes full, and said, "I propose this toast, My Nigga, to Silk, to you, and to the good life!"

We clanked glasses ---- him, the twins, and myself. After that, that smooth muthafucka, pulled out a Fendi briefcase, that probably cost twelve 'hunnet' or betta, and flipped it's lid, before he said, "That's four 'hunnet' sixty Gs, and not a dollar short."

I looked at how neat and pretty that cheddar looked piled high in that designer case, and it made me feel like a cheap uncouth muthafucka with no manners. After all, my mans Donnell was standing there grippin' a fifteen dollar canvas bag, with his work in it. Yet, a quick calculation of how many Fendi joints I would have to purchase to hold all those bricks, made me think, 'Fuck that shit!!' Before I said, "You ain't bullshittin' are you, Fam?"

"All the jokes been told. Now it's like what that nigga 'Young Bucks' be spittin', 'It's time for me to shine and get Mine!!"

"I heard'cha, Yo. " I served while we pounded fist. And then the twins and I got the fuck up outta` there.

I was creepin' down the tree lined street that I was cribbin' on, with Slim Shautie ridin' shotgun. It was after midnight, but as I turned up into the driveway leading into my double-car jaunt, I saw that my mufuckin' bedroom light was still on. I thought to my self, 'Good!', 'cause I planned on settin' some shit out, tonight. Especially since my little bad-ass kids were gone wit Wyndie's Moms and Pops on one of those fake-ass vacation's they go on every year.

I parked my Lex next to the Suburban and glanced ova at Lil' Boo. She was sittin' there wit no expression on her face ---none! I had been around her long enough, at that point, however, that in spite of that bland look she sported, I could still tell when she was trippin' 'bout somethin'. While I looked at her that moment, I was cocksure that Baby wasn't the least-bit upset 'bout me bringin' her to the crib. It was almost like she had already expected and accepted the fact that, at some point, she was goin' to end up here. In truth, the Lil' Bitch may have known it all along.

Anyway, I took my seat belt off, and barked, "Com'on!"

She did exactly as I had commanded her ass to do. She got out and walked aroun' to where I was. She was wearin' a silk top wit no bra on, which made her mouth-full of titties look appetizin' as shit. Plus, her hair was freshly braided, and I had paid for a manicure and pedicure, earlier that day for her. Maybe, somewhere in the back of my mind, I had known then that I was gon brang her ass out to my crib that night. Fo sho, I had been playin' wit that idea, for quite some time, 'bout brangin' a freak to the crib. Being that being with two or more broads all the mufuckin' time had made that shit with Wyndie and I seem like some weak-ass--shit. So eitha' Wyndie was gon get wit the program that night, or she was gon get her stankin' ass up outta there.

For serious.

"What the fuck you think you're doin'??" Wyndie shouted out when she looked away from the flick she was watching on t.v. and saw me and Lil' Shautie walk into the bedroom. That bitch had sure sounded tough as nails, but I saw in her eyes and the way her jaw muscles quivered ---- she was shook!

Therefore, I said, "Bitch, you know what time it is. I'm tired of your stankin' ass layin' up in he'a actin' like you like that, forreal. You don' moved out'chere aroun' these crackas, and fo'got some shit." I reach out after that and placed my mufuckin' arm aroun' Lil' Shautie's shoulders. But I made sho Wyndie could see my big black hand cuppin' and grippin' Shautie's peach-size jaunt, befo' I said, "When I first started fuckin' wit'choo, you was a (a ho!!) and a viscious freak -----

just what the fuck I liked. You don' tried to flip-the-script on a nigga. But tonight, Bitch, you gon' be all you can be, or you gon' get'chor stuntin' ass up out'chere."

I looked down at Lil Shautie and saw that quick smile race across her face again, like I had the otha night when I took that nigga Tree-Top's whip. I even felt it when she slid her hand down into my right back pocket. There was no doubt, she was bettin' on Wyndie nuttin' up, and so was I, so I could go upside that dome.

And that crazy--ass bitch didn't let us down, eitha. She jumped up off that mufuckin' bed, like that bitch was on fire, and ran toward a nigga, screamin' "I'ma kill your ass, motherfucka! ! You and that bitch!" She said, right before I caught her ass wit a vicious two piece, just like I had planned on. She was a big bitch, so that shit only dazed her stankin' ass, and made her fold and drop to her knee's. I knew I had to work fast, because she was gon keep at it until I knocked her ufuckin' ass out, anyway.

So I did just that.

I connected wit anotha jaunt, but this time, I landed that one right on her chin. She toppled over and laid on that thick-ass carpet wit her body twisted like a pretzel. Plus, that sexy-ass nightie she was wearin' was jacked up to her waist ---- exposin' nothin' but ass, thighs, and a picture-perfect portrait of that lemon-green thong that was buried 'uptwixt' her velvety soft cheeks.

Lookin' at that shit, as I stood ova her---- huffin' and puffin', got my dick hard as a mufucka. So I started takin' off my gear. I looked over at Lil Shautie, and she was doin' the same damn thang. In fact, that lil' bitch was so turned on, she seemed to be breathin' more aggressively than I was, as she pulled off her shit.

Wyndie stirred some, when I ripped that little cute shit off her bottom, but she didn't come fully awake. That is, until my Lil Boo buried her grill down between her legs and started

220

eatin' Wyndie's pussy, like she had gon' insane. I'm sayin', Shalia had gotten all outta character. Because she was tremblin' and moanin' and groanin', while she grinded her hips into one of Wyndie's legs ---- all with her lips locked to Baby's clit. I was sittin' back wit my dick facin' O'girl, but I was lookin' back at Shautie do her thang. Next thang I know, W'yndie was goin' bizirk, her damn self. That big bitch started movin' her hips like she was fuckin' my big dick, or some'um.

That shit turned me the fuck on!

Especially when my baby-mama started strokin' and suckin' my jaunt the Nasty way she use to slob-and-bob on that blickie, back in the day. That shit made a nigga rise up off her, grip her hair, and began movin' my mufuckin'waist. I even closed my eyes and listened to the beautiful sounds of both my bitches moanin' their pleasures. I felt like a nigga ought to feel that had caught 'blaze of two ghetto bitches'.

Special as a mufucka!

♦♦♦♦♦♦♦♦♦♦♦♦♦♦♦♦♦♦♦♦♦♦♦

Yolanda

"When did they do that?" My sister, Tinia, asked while sitting on my sofa with her barefoot tucked beneath her.

"All I know is, they moved in yesterday, and he told me about it last night." I tried to sound indifferent about it, but Tinia knew I was pissed.

And I was.

How could Popcorn have gone all that long and not breathe a word about him and that chickenhead moving a few blocks from where I lived. I mean, that's some disrespectful shit, forreal. You don't do a friend like that ---- I should've been one of the first persons he told. Next thing you know, he'll be moving his stash somewhere else without saying jack-shit about that, until it's done. Then I would be standing around looking stupid.

221

Besides all of that, I just didn't like the whole idea of him being that close to me, period. That shit infringed on my damn privacy. Because, at that point, he would be more prone to cruise by my house at any hour of the night and peep Patrick's car parked out front.

Then it would be no doubt that O'boy was getting at this pussy.

Shit!

That was something I just didn't want him to find out about---- not yet, anyway. Being that, in my mind, I felt there was still a tremendous possibility of me taking him from Peaches. For sure, that dumb bitch didn't know what she had -- especially with him being caked, now. He needed someone like me to show him what to do with that damn money.

"So what're we gon' do now, Babygirl? Do we keep gettin' ours, or what?" Tinia said while clawing at her stitches. I couldn't blame her, though, because they were probably itching like hell.

I was glad that she hadn't taken charges out on that bitch for slicing her up. That shit could've went somewhere we couldn't afford for it to have went. Like, if it came out about that guy Tre scoring drugs from Tinia. It may have sounded like some silly shit to imagine, but you never knew how some of those niggas pitched their business to their women.

I had been off work about an hour, before Tinia showed up. Still, I was wearing what I had worn to work, even some pointed toe sling-backs. Therefore, I slid my foot out of those damn things, ahead of me saying, "Baby pleez! That shit don't mean nothing. We just gonna have to be more about our bizness,-that's all."

"Heeey!" Tinia said, while snapping her fingers around in front of her body.

That was some more of that damn ho-stroll-shit, that I didn't like, but I didn't comment on it. Instead, I said, "What you

222

think about us staging a robbery or break-in--- do you think we could pull it off?"

That bitch brought her feet from beneath her and planted them on the floor, so damn quick and fast, I thought she was getting ready to get the hell up outta there. But boy was I wrong. She only sat on the edge of the sofa and appeared that she was giving my question the kind of serious thought required. Either that, or she was merely trying to 'snuff' me like her grimey-ass hadn't already been entertaining the idea of us doing that shit, way before then. Eitha' way, it didn't matter to me, because I had laid it all on the table, at that point, for us both to look at and hopefully come up with a master plan.

After a moment, she said, "Yeah, I believe it's possible. But I hope you know, that nigga is gon' 'slaughta' both our asses, if he eva catches wind." Her eyes were shining with greed, beyond her giving me that and licking her lips.

I looked off to the left of her, into the face of the beautiful truth she had just given up. Then I looked at her, and awarded her one of my most devious glows, as I said, "But it's still worth it, ain't it?"

She shook her head up-and-down like she had springs in it and replied, "You damn straight it is."

"Ok, but look." I prompted, while I stretched my legs out in front of me and wiggled my toes, "Let's not be in a hurry. We can sleep on it for a few days, and then we'll make a decision ---- alright!"

Those springs in her neck started working, again, as she said, "That's cool wit me. But forreal though, it ain't shit else to think about. Not for me it ain't. I don't mind deep-throatin' a dick sometime. Nut I'm burnt-out on trickin' for a livin'---- that shit don' got old as hell." She looked at her fingernails after that.

"Whateva, Gurl ! " I said and fought to keep from rolling my damn eyes at that bitch, because she was lying her ass off. She knew good and well, no amount of money was gonna stop her from fuckin' niggas for money. I realized that shit after she got cut-the-fuck--up the other night ---- and was right back at it, trickin', like shit hadn't happened to her ass.

But that was on her.

At that point, my focus was on tearing off Popcorn for his stash, and getting the hell away with my life…….

CHAPTER 27

Popcorn

"Goddamn Popcorn, I don't know what to say!" Smokey said when I informed him that the little landscaping joint that I, along with his help, had been trying to build, was all his.

"You done already earned it, Yo. So stop trippin.'" I showed him a genuinely warm smile, before I added, "Besides, you still gotta handle my Moms yard, plus swing through my new joint, and hit me off, too, so what's to be happy about!"

"You got dat!" He said, before he looked over at the rest of the crew and said, "Man, they gonna be happy-as-shit about this five hundred dollar bonus you givin' up. Especially since the Fourth of July weekend is jumpin' off." He scratched his head, prior to him saying, "But you sho you don't wanna give it to them, yourself? I mean, I don't have a problem about handlin' it for you, but it just seemed like something you might wanna do yourself."

I glanced over at Lil Rob and em hangin' out by Smokey's truck looking like they was restless about getting on with that days work, so they could enjoy the long holiday weekend that they were getting off. Then I said, "Yeah, Fam, I'm sho. In fact, I want you to hit'em off like it's coming from you. That way, you'll win their loyalty even more, now that I'll be outta the way." He looked like he was preparing to argue that point, as well, but I gated that shit by saying, "It ain't nothin' else to kick it 'bout, Yo ---- I'm outta here." I turned and walked back over to where my pickup with the twins on the back of it, was parked, and bailed out.

It was a good feelin', Yo, to give something to a muthafucka that you knew would appreciate the hell out of it. At least for me, it was. In truth, I had been discovering that a lot, lately, about how truly cool it was to be spreadin' love helping every muthafucka that 'I felt' had been down with me during my struggle. I wasn't sayin' that any of the shit I had done was some hellacious shit, only that, for those I had put on ----- that shit was right on time.

Anyway, I left the little storage building and went straight over to my Moms. She had quit her part-time gig cleaning offices at that bank at night. Plus, to my pleasure and utter surprise, she was on a two-week vacation from VCU. That was something that was foreign as hell to O'girl, every since my Pops died because the O'girl been going hard non-stop, trying to maintain a decent life for me and my sisters.

I parked and told the twins, "Com'on ya'll, let's see what Mom-dukes got burnin' in the kitchen."

Need I say, those two niggas fell in step wit me, before I had finished the statement. Especially since, they had been by the crib with me, enough at that point that they knew anytimewe dropped by the home front, we was gon' get our grub on.

We strolled in the house and went straight to where that delicious aroma of fried bacon and onion fried potatoes was luring our asses. My Moms was the only one in the kitchen and didn't seem all that surprised by us walking in and pullin' up a chair at the glass top table. In fact, she may have been expecting us, being that the table was already set and waiting. She tried to hold back that little sneaky smile of her's as she said, "Ya'll wash up, 'cause this stuff'll be ready in a minute."

Donte and Donnell said, "Yes Ma'am!", in unison as they rushed for the bathroom.

But me, I lingered for a moment, and said, "Mama, why don't you and the girls go down to Charlotte, and visit Aunt Sheryl for a week or sum'um?"

She turned around a little too quick for 'worry' not to be printed on her lovely middle-aged features, before she asked, "Why?? What's wrong?"

That shit fucked me up that she was still buggin', on the D--L about me gettin' hit up. She hadn't said anything, to that day about the shootin' ----- or about her true feeling's about her wanting me to get out the game. But as I stood there checking out the raw fear in her eyes about something like that happening to me again; or worse, I wanted to throw in my hand and give her back her peace of mind.

But I couldn't.

Not at that point, anyway. I had to ride-or-die, no matter what.

Therefore, I walked up on her and said, "Everythang cool, Mama." I even tilted her chin upward, a little so that she and I were looking eye-to-eye before I added, "Forreal Mama it's cool!"

The twins walked back into the room and sat at the table. They knew 'a moment' when they saw one. Therefore, they just enjoyed the bacon and potato smell.

She looked over at them, back at me, and apparently, she decided that I was keepin' it real. Because she then asked, What are you up to, then, that you want me to go to North Carolina?"

I almost said, 'Nothin!', but that would've kilt everything. So I came clean by sayin', "Me and Peaches flying out to Miami, tomorrow. I just was thinking how nice it would be if ya'll took a trip, too.

CHAPTER 28

Peaches

That following Tuesday, all of the furniture and appliances had been delivered to the townhouse. I made those damn delivery men a little mad, at one point, because I made they ass move that heavy-ass sofa and loveseat around, until I was feelin' it.

In any case, once every thing was in place, I was happy as hell. Because, even if I must say so myself ---- that joint was all that! I mean, flat-screens on the walls of the livingroom, family room, and in the master suite. The carpet was thick as Kentucky bluegrass, and the leather was soft as a baby's ass.

My girl Carla was there watching with an eagle's eye, how taste-fully everything blended together -- matching and complimenting each other. I smiled to myself, because I knew once she copped her a crib away from the projects, she was going to copy-cat my flava. Yet, I wasn't buggin'. Being that, according to my man, we were only going to be camping out in that joint, temporarily, anyway.

Popcorn and the twins were unloading the boxes of personal shit that I had packed up to be moved over to the spot. As far as the furniture and otha' mess, we were leaving that worn-out shit in Gilpen Court. We were still holding down that spot, for a minute.

I guess to keep his guns and thangs there ---- I didn't know!

Nevertheless, Carla was helping me hang shower curtains in the upstairs bathroom, as she said, "Yeah Gurl. I did like you said, I told that nigga he gon' have to prove that shit to me."

My ears perked, because I'd been waiting on her to bring that subject back up. Especially after what Popcorn had told me the other night about that damn money coming up short when he paid his friend, That's all.

Momedukes was no fool. That's why after she turned back stirring her onion flavored potatoes, she said, "In otha words, you don't want us in town, eitha, since you won't be around to protect us, right??"

"Right!" I said thru a smile, and went to wash my hands. While I was back there, though, I tucked those two hefty envelopes that was in my waistband, under her pillow. Each one of them was holdin' fifty thousand, enough, I figured, to insure that she and my sisters could have one hell-of-a-good-life whether they touched the Carolinas, or not.......

Donte, Donnell, and I left my Moms, full as a muthafucka! Since it was still early and I wasn't expecting nothin' to be poppin', we went by the apartment I still held down in Gilpen Court. As soon as I parked my truck, however, Kiki's man, Cash, pulled up on me sportin' a 'do rag' under his fitted ball-cap, with no shirt covering his frail ass, baggy Nautica shorts, and a pair of flav's. He had his slugged-up grill twisted as he said, "Yo, Red, I ------"

But I grilled his ass out, by saying, "How many I gotta tell your ass, my name ain't Red, Nigga!!"

He put his hand slightly over his mouth, and gripped his dick with the other, and said, "My bad!! Popcorn, you know a nigga don't mean no disrespect, Shauty. I'm just tryin' to holla at'cha, 'bout some of that 'flav' nigga's puttin' out you holdin'."

I didn't particularly care for O'boy, that's why it irked the shit outta me when that nigga pushed up on me, calling me Red. That's why I always put a straightenin' on that shit, when his ass jumped out there.

But, bullshit won't nothin.

It was no secret that Slim would hold face wit a muthafucka, betta' than any hustler hustlin', so I put my soaring dislike for him on the back burner, and said, "I thought you was gettin' it wit Choo-Choo and that otha' nigga, 'Flick'?"

"I was, you dig, but I'd rather get in the car wit'choo. 'Cause word is, you settin' shit out on the real." He slid both his hands down into the front of his Nautica's, after that, and stood like he was posing for a camera shot.

"Yeah, well they gave you good money', Yo. But did they also hip you to the fact that you can't 'play fifty' with me ----- you got to be all the way down wit a nigga, from here on out if I put you on."

He flashed that grill of his that I wasn't feelin', also, before he said, "I feel ya, Shauty." He said with his pose still intact. "That's the kinda shit I like ---- make a nigga feel like he straight mobbin' or som'um."

"I'on know all 'bout that, Yo. I'm just tellin' you how my flow is. And if you violate, shit gon' get hectic."

I looked at the twins who were mean muggin' and grittin' and damn near spittin' fire. That shit told me that they wasn't feelin' that nigga, eitha'.

It must've informed him of the same exact thang, because he said, "I ain't heard 'bout that drama shit, Popcorn. It's all about mackin' and stackin' grip wit me, ya heard."

I studied him for a split-second, and said, "You got that, Yo. I'll get at'cha in about an hour, at your crib and we'll take it from there."

"Word!!" He said while he pulled his right hand out from down inside his shorts, and gave an indication that he wanted to pound a nigga. But I only looked at that lame like he was crazy-as-shit. I wasn't suggestin' that he was playing wit his shit or nothin' while we kicked it, because most young cats that have that habit, normally hold their hands between their boxers and outer garment. Still, I really didn't play that shit, and he quickly realized it too. Because he put that same hand up to his mouth, like he had done earlier and quipped, "My bad", before he turned and swaggered back thru the hood to his spot, to await that work I was gon' hit'em off wit.

CHAPTER 29

Peaches

At approximately eight forty-five a.m., Saturday morning, Popcorn and I were chilling in First Class of U.S. Air Flight 113, as it raced down the runway, and took to the clear and ocean-blue-sky. We were on our way to Miami, Florida for the Fourth of July weekend. I was sooo excited about our trip, I could hardly retain the joy I felt. After all, that was the first time I had been to the Sunshine State, and the very first occasion that Popcorn and I had traveled anywhere togetha'.

My life was turning 'storybook' all of a sudden. I felt like Brandy must've felt in that movie Cinderalla. Because, one minute I had been cooped up in the projects, hustlin' my ass off doing hair, and wondering if I ever was gon' come-up.

Then, right under my nose, my Boo was gettin' his grind on without me knowing it, but doing all the right shit that a nigga suppose to be doing. So much so, that in almost no time flat, that nigga was the caked-the-fuck-up and trying to decide if I was worthy of being the female he wanted to place on wify status.

Something that I almost tricked off.

That shit made me shiver, some, as I looked out the window of the jetliner, down at the patches of earth that laid below. But fortunately for me, everything worked out for the best. There I was sitting on that plane with 'my man' holding hands and loving that motherfucker, with all of me.

We had a brief layova' in Charlotte, before we continued on down the coast. There was an older white couple sitting across the aisle from us who was arguing quietly about something. It made me wonder if Popcorn and I would be togetha', years from that point in time, and be in love enough to argue quietly like those oldheads were doing.

Our stewardess was slim as a pencil, but nice as shit' She was right there every time we needed something. Almost like she could read our minds or sum'um ---- let me find out! Anyway, she served us hot eggs and pancakes and bacon, with real juicy strawberries on the side. I ate all of mines, and most of Popcorn's, because they were delicious as I don't know what.

We touched down at Miami International at a quarter pass twelve. Popcorn grabbed our carry-on bags from the overhead compartment, and we headed for the main terminal where his friend, Bay--Bay was suppose to meet us. I was wearing some cream-colored Parasuco jeans, cream body-strap, and some Gucci sandals that matched the shoulder-strap purse I had flung across my body.

Popcorn, on the other hand, was looking fly-as-shit' in the bone-white Polo joint I had brought him, yesterday. I had known it would look good on him, because it was trimmed in the same cat-green hue of his eyes.

When we entered the main terminal, he was probably thinking the same damn thang I was ----- that   we   had landed in Cuba, Costa Rica, or one of those other Spanish speaking nations. Because, that joint was flooded with our South American brothas and sistas.

And those Hector's and Julio looking niggas was some fine-ass motherfuckers, too.

That wasn't to say that I had plans on violating my man, I was only givin'em theirs. The way Popcorn was sizing up those Mamies, I knew he was feelin that shit, too.

He had walked all the way thru the huge-ass Concourse, damn near, before a voice behind us said ..... "Welcome to Miami."

We turned around and saw Bay-Bay standing there with one of the most attractive females I had ever saw in my life. He was smiling his ass off. But shit, I couldn't blame him, not one bit. He and his woman, looked like money. I felt like their presence made me feel Popcorn and I were scrambling, country, and waay out classed.

But when I looked over at Popcorn, he looked like he wasn't seeing none-of-that-shit. Neither was his man Bay-Bay, because those two niggas stared at one another. The fact that she didn't try to break the ice, was enough to warn me about who and what I was gonna be dealing with.

A real bitch.

◆◆◆◆◆◆◆◆◆◆◆◆◆◆◆◆◆◆◆◆◆

Popcorn

I had always heard that there was nothing like that warm feeling of the Florida sunshine touching you for the first time. When Peaches, Bay-Bay and his broad, Zesty, and I walked out of the crowded Airport, and those beautiful

sunrays caressed my skin, I had to stamp that shit-----
forreal! That golden warmth felt lovely. Especially as I
walked toward my mans Maybach, with Peaches holdin' on
to a nigga like she was happy as hell to be down wit a
muthafucka.

We squatted in the back of that big body, and had
more leg room than if we were cruising in one of those
plush-ass stretched limos. Bay-Bay knew we were 'lovin'it'
because he peeped at me with smily eyes, thru his rearview
jaunt, as he drove away from the curb.

Peaches was probably trippin', as I was, from the
land being so damn flat and even and without a hill or
mountain to be seen in any direction we looked Only a
whole rack of palm trees and a lot of otha' crazy-looking plants that I
had never seen before. You can just about imagine my reaction to
seeing a fuckin' orange and lemon tree, as well ----- that shit was
off the hook, Yo . Because I was so use to coppin' those jaunts at
the grocery, it hadn't occurred to me that they grew on trees.

Bay-Bay had Jada Kiss breathing in our ears, spittin' that
knowledge in that 'Why' tune, when he turned it down, and asked,
"Ya'll wannna stop and get som'um to eat, or ya'll straight until
we get to the crib?"

I looked at Peaches and she just smiled and snuggled
closer me. Which I took to mean, she was hungry all right --- but
only wanted herself some Popcorn. As for me, I was auight. That
late breakfast we ate on the plane was still holdin' me down.
Therefore, I said, "We auight, Fam."

He merely nodded slightly, before he raised his cell to his
mouth and started talking. That joint must've vibrated in his hand,
the way my two–way had began to do at that same moment. My
heart started pounding outta control, because I felt it was too
soon for anyone to be hittin' me from the crib, unless somethin'
was wrong. After all, I had just gotten off the plane.

I tried to glance at that joint without Peaches pinnin' my move, but she caught on and leaned in to read my message when I did.

It was Donnell.

That nigga wanted to know if I was aught. I was thinking, suppose I'm not, right when I looked at Peaches ---- and we both fell out laughing. Because she must've been thinking the same exact thing. After I regained my composure, however, I signed off …..No doubt, Good lookin', Yo.

I should've assumed that it was one of the twins, because my click was nothin' but the truth. I made sho of that last night. Especially Peewee, I smashed that nigger wit a extra ten jaunts to add wit what he already had copped.

Bay-Bay was still politicin' on his cell, as we sailed the Bascayne Bay Bridge. His bun-bun, Zesty, was posed beside that nigga undisturbed by the fact that he was paying her no attention, at all. I guess she was use to him handlin' his business on the regular. In a way, she and Peaches were a lot alike. Perhaps, that explains why they hadn't clicked, off the muscle. Apparently they both were the kind of broads that were cautious as shit when it came to engaging another female for the first time. That was one of the other things I liked about Peaches ----- the way she handled herself when a broad tried to front on her. Because, that's what was happenin' at that moment---- Zesty was trying to gain the higher ground, because she was on her turf. Yet, my Boo was making it plain and clear that she wasn't stutin' who's turf it was ---- she wasn't having it. She wasn't gonna be kissin' no bitch's ass, regardless of how fine she was, how much ice she flossed, or the fact that she thought ----- 'her man' was'-that nigga'.

I knew Bay-Bay had peeped the little 'catty shit' they was doin', as well. But just like me, I was certain that he didn't give a fuck, either. I was down there to see my dawg, clear my dome, and to enjoy my muthafucking self. I figured by sometime tomorrow, the broads will have found their common ground ---- enough for' em to get wit the program.

But when it came to a couple of strong minded females, it ain't no tellin'........

♦♦♦♦♦♦♦♦♦♦♦♦♦♦♦♦♦♦♦♦

Bay-Bay dipped off of Ocean Bay Drive, up into a circular driveway of a multi-million dollar crib. Of course, I knew he was 'ballin "---- but goddamn!! Homie was doin' it forreal! That bitch looked like a mansion ----- straight outta Spain somewhere. I ain't even gon-' front, that jaunt had me open. Because, I was hoping that he was legit enough to be cribbing up in a jaunt that elaborate, without him tilting his head to the "Feds about what was 'really goin' on'.

Peaches and I got out the back of that 'big boy joint' and followed Bay-Bay and Zesty into the most glamorous foyer I had ever set foot in. I'm sayin', the shit was like that, I heard it take Peaches breath away. Yet, she showed nothing on her face for Zesty to see and relish in. Me, on the otha hand, I said to my mans, "Goddamn, Nigga you dloin' it, Yo!"

He looked around at all the marble, obsidian glass, and polished wood, before he said, "This ain't nothin' but some small shit, Champ. I want me one of those big joints like the ones further up the street." As an additional way of dismissing my compliment, he then turned to Zesty and said, "Show Peaches where their room is so she can freshen-up, if she want to ---- then show her around the place."

I watched them both climb the winding staircase, and when they disappeared down the hallway, I looked at homeboy and said, "They on some bullshit, ain't they Yo?"

"Yeah, but they'll be auight. He said with a knowing smile. "Com' on Dawg, lets goin myoffice, and kick it."

He led me into a room that was almost as big as my whole crib. I stood looking at the floor-to-ceiling windows that gave a true to life view of the ocean that was beyond the hundred foot of beach that separated. his crib from the Atlantic. All I could think at that instant was, if all of what I've seen so far, was some small shit --- then I figured I, must've been a 'small muthafucka". Because, that hook-up Bay-Bay was flossin' in, would've been all I could've ever wanted.

Word !

"Have a seat, Playa. He said as he poured us a splash of Louis XIII into one of those fat bubble lookin' glasses.

I pulled up a chair that looked like it's arms were seashells with pads on it. And in all honesty, it felt that way too, being that that joint was uncomfortable as shit. Still, I remained seated there and accepted my drink from him without complainin' 'bout it.

Especially since he slid down into an identical one, across from me, and asked, "You like that money counter?"

"Yeah, that jaunt takes a lotta weight off ' a nigga ---- and keeps it real." I took a sip of the drink and fought the temptation of askin' if my last count was on point. After all, I was sho that it was, because Peaches had been just as determined as I had been to 'straighten my face'.

He sipped his too, prior to giving me one of those penetrating stares, and sayin', "You know, I knew you was gonna be knee-deep in it. But you done stepped up your game, all the way. Quicker than I had thought you would. So I gotta ask you this, Champ ---- what's the most frustratin' thing 'bout bein' full-up?" He must've thought I hadn't understood what he was hittin' at, because he added, "I mean, you got'sta be sittin' on a mil, right?"

I thought about it for a second, and nodded my head. Because no doubt, with the work I had in the streets, and what I still had bama'd over O'girls, I was holdin' a mil plus, easy.

"So what's the most frustrating part about it, Dawg?" He persisted.

I held that niggas gaze, as I said, "Not bein' able to floss. And I ain't talkin' about on no dumb-shit, eitha."

He drained his glass and stood up for a refill, before he said, "So your Old-man taught you well, too huh."

"No doubt, Yo. That nigga gave me the game when I was young, I thought it was som'um every young nigga was gettin' from they Pops."

"Damn, me too, Dawg!" Bay-Bay said as he walked over to his desk and asked, "You probably thought I was wildin' out, when you first saw me pushin' that Benz ---- and even more when you peeped that Maybach today. Right!"

He was watching me closely, so I kept it real. "True dat! But what else could a nigga think?"

"I ain't mad at'cha. I would've thought the same thing about you, had I not had any dealin's wit'cha for all these years." He sat his drink on his desk and said, "Peep this."

I got up and walked over to where he stood. Plus, I had no plans of sittin' back in that joint, anyway, because my ass was sore as hell. Anyway, I said, "What'sup?"

He pointed at some photographs on his desk top, and said, "You see those beautiful faces right there?"

I looked at the portraits, but to me, there was nothing beautiful about any of'em. I mean, every person in those pictures had to be at least seventy or older. I wasn't saying that they were ugly or anything like that. It's just that I didn't see a muthafuckin' thing about none of'em that I would've called beautiful. Therefore, I simply said, "What about'em, Yo?"

"They're the reason a nigga legit." He knew I didn't have a clue what the fuck he was implying, so he said, "Take her for instance," He indicated a Winnie Mandella look-a-like. "She was the aunt of this broad I had on locks. Her name was Leona Smith."

He paused as though he was remembering her, before he went on to say, "She had moved down here from the Motor City, after her husband retired from Ford Motors. But unfortunately, one year after they settled in, her husband had a vicious stroke that left O'boy completely fucked-up. I mean, he had required a private nurse and the whole nine yards." Bay-Bay took a quick sip of his drink, and continued with, "I don't need to tell you, that shit ate their savings up in two years and slim hadn't clocked out. That nigga was lucky that he had a good bitch like Leona, because she held that nigga down, sacrificing everythang to make sho that brotha had the best care. Even his and her her life insurance policy."

I had been standing there with my drink in hand, wondering where he was goin' wit his story, until he said that. That was when everythang fell in place for me ---- and made all the sense in the world. I even looked back at the collage of framed pictures on his desk, and had to admit, at that point, everyone of them wrinkly-ass faces looked beautiful, after all.

Before I could comment either way, Bay-Bay said, "I know it may sound like some cold-blooded shit that I snatched-up them people's life insurance policies, but I don't look at it like that. For one thing, Leona was gonna sell her's and her husband's joints to an investment firm that was only gonna kick'em half the face value. But Me, I stepped in and gave her the full five hundred grand value of each jaunt. Her husband died three months later, and she, a year. In between that time, she told all her friends, and the rest is history, my brotha."

"Damn, Yo, that's some deep shit. Ain't shit cold-blooded 'bout that ---- you helped 'em and they returned the favor. In my mind, you deserve a medal f o that shit."

He smiled after hearing that. "I'm glad you feelin' me like that." He said, before he reached in his middle desk drawer and took out a envelope, which he handed to me.

"What's this, Yo." I was baffled.

"Your 'real' passport to the good life, Champ ----open it up."

I swallowed the last drop of my drink and sat the empty glass on his desk. I tore open that joint, at that point, knowing what was probably inside, that's why my hands shook, a little. Even moreso, once I pulled out a joint from Mutual Insurance Company for six 'hunnet' Gs. Plus the joint had my full name printed in bold letters on it. Without me knowing I was talkin' out loud, I said, "Dammmn ..... Yo!"

I looked at Bay-Bay and he was smiling his ass off when he said, "You owe me six hunnet grand, Champ.

I was cheesing like a mufucka, myself, once I responded, "You guts that, Yo." Because, indeed, that nigga had just given me the ticket I needed to step my game up --- to the next level........

CHAPTER 30

It was late Saturday night of the Fourth of July weekend. The moon was bright and full and pretty as a mufucka. I was sittin out in the 534 Club parkin' lot. That bitch was packed! So I knew niggas was deep up in that jaunt. But I wasn't feelin' that shit. Too much crazy shit was on my dome.

No bullshit.

Like my 'flav' was movin' slow as a mufucka. Most of the cats I had in my click before the drought, had bounced on a nigga. Mufuckas like Mario, Tre, Tree-Top, Pancake, Cash, and that bitch, Fame. That foul-ass shit had me contemplatin' 'bout doin' some treacherous shit to all they bitch asses.

Especially that coward-ass nigga, Popcorn.

He didn't think I knew he was the one steppin' on my mufuckin' toes ---- but I knew. I peeped it fo sho that day I cruised thru Gilpen Court, and saw his bony-red-ass kickin' it wit Tiny's big bitch, Tracy. 'Cause, it was that cocky look that stuntin' ass nigga wore when he looked at me. He didn't know how close I had come to jumpin' out my whip, and puttin' som'um tough on his ass. But I saw those twins, too, and I knew I'd have to put one slug in each of their domes, right out there in broad daylight ---- and I wasn't that pressed 'bout gettin' at that nigga.

Not yet, I wasn't.

It might didn't seem that way to a lotta mufuckas, but I was patient as shit. Being that way lets a mufucka creep a nigga.

It's just that I had thought, when I had that nigga Silk blazed like my connect had told me, I had kilt the source of all that extra 'yay' that that fool had flooded the city wit, durin' the drought. But I was wrong as shit. That nigga Popcorn, to my understandin', was puttin' down a vicious lick, twice as strong as his brother was. Of course, I knew what that shit was suppose' to mean ---- he was tellin' whoever got at his brother, that they hadn't stopped nothin'!

It was some shady-ass shit, but since that nigga was hurtin' my pockets, I didn't see a damn thang to laugh 'bout.

I had the window down in my Lex. Therefore, I could hear the loud-ass music blastin' from the inside of the club. In fact, that vicious joint by Akon,, 'I'm Locked-Up', started to crank; right when them niggas I was laying on, pulled up.

I watched'em park they shit, before I got out my whip and strolled over to where they were still duckin' in they joint. Once I got up close, I could see that they were sniffin' some Raw-dope, as they always do. That had been one of the reasons that I didn't really fuck wit'em , forreal, they asses stayed skeed all the mufuckin' time. In spite of that drawback, however, they were still two of the most notorious stick-up boyz in the city.

Bullshit won't nothin'!

244

I mean them niggas 'bout they work. 'Cause there have been times when they have snatched mufuckas in broad daylight ---- or jacked niggas for all they shit in the wee hours of the night. They didn't give a fuck! In otha words, them mufuckas were exactly the kind of 'jackas' I would've been had I been on some different shit. Except, I wouldn't be sniffin' up Peru.

"What'sup 'Neg-gas'!" I barked as I stood by the door of that STS Cadillac they was pushin', wit my arms folded.

"Creepin', Shauty, you know our M-O." The one named Dirty, replied wit the corners of his motif' turned all the way down.

"I'm feelin' that, Mufuckas. That's the reason I'm posted up on you niggas."

They both looked at each otha, as if they were tryin' to figure out if they had accidentally jacked somebody who was on my team. Bein' that I had forewarned they ass, if they ever violated, it was gon be pure drama. Apparently, they decided that they hadn't crossed a nigga, so the one named Body spoke up and said, "What 'cha mean by that, Hustler?"

I was smiling inside, because I enjoyed spookin' niggas.

I' m just sayin', Neg-gas, a lotta shit don' happened since the last time I saw ya'll ---- - so I wanna make sho ya'll hip to shit. That's all!"

That must've gave both those mufuckas a feelin' of relief, 'cause they each took a quick one-on-one of that 'missle' they had folded in fifty dollar bills. Then, Dirty said, "That's what I'm talkin' 'bout, Shauty ---- give it up, 'cause you know a nigga tryin' to stay on top of game."

In otha words, he was sayin' he didn't want no conflicts wit a nigga.

None!

Therefore, I said, "Four-five of them mufuckas that use to be in my click, ain't in it no mo'. So how eva shit go down wit'em, it ain't on me." I still had my arms folded. Plus I was grittin' hard as a bitch, so they knew I was serious and salty as a mufucka at each of them bitch–ass niggas.

"Oh yeah!" They both let fly at the same time.

"Straight up!" I barked. "Niggas like Mario, Pancake, Tre, Cash, Tree–op, and that stankin' ass bitch, Fame --- they on they own. I dismissed all they asses." They knew that part was a mufuckin' lie, but I tried my hand, anyway.

I heard the wheels churnin' in those nigga's heads, immediately. But I merely smiled to myself, before I eventually said, "I gotta bounce. I just wanted ya'll to know where I stand. 'Cause I ain' t tryin' to stop anotha nigga from gettin' his ---- long as that mufucka ain't tryin' to put his mitts in my mufuckin' pockets."

I turned and started walkin' back toward my shit. But not without hearin' Body when he shouted, "Good lookin', Shauty!!"

'You mufuckin' right it is.' I thought to myself as I climbed back into my whip and cruised off. But there was no doubt in my mind, I had just unleashed some vicious mufuckas on them nigga's. That much, I was sho of.

◆◆◆◆◆◆◆◆◆◆◆◆◆◆◆◆◆◆◆◆◆◆

Yolanda

Thank God that Popcorn was out of town for the whole damn holiday last night while Patrick and I were gettin' our freak on. With that shit out the way, I plan on devoting all of Sunday, toward dipping into everyone of those 'keys' of coke that was still up in that bedroom.

I told Tinia, yesterday, what my plans were for Sunday, and that I wanted her ass to come by and help a sista out. That bitch showed up at my crib at five o'clock in the damn morning. I started not to let her ass in. But since Patrick had already gone home and I was in a position where I really needed her half-runk ass, I let her in and bombed her out, just the same.

She hadn't paid any attention to that shit I talked. She merely staggered up the stairs and virtually crashed on the bed that was in the same room as all those bricks of drugs. But I got her ass back, good as shit, when I marched into that room at nine-thirty that morning and snatched all the covers off that bitch and demanded that she get her ass up, right then and there. She had looked at me like she could kill ---- but fuck that! I wanted to get that shit done, that day, because I didn't have a clue when Popcorn was coming back from his trip.

She was sitting in my kitchen--nook when she said, "Pour me some mo of that damn coffee, Gurl."

"Bitch, do I look like a waitress, or somethin' to you?" I said, even though I got up to hook-her-ass up. How could I not? She looked like her head was killing her. Plus, I figured her pussy was probably still swollen, too. Because I knew she had, no doubt, gotten down last night, before she came to my house.

She watched me pour her a fresh cup of java, with her elbow on the table while her hands held her head. "How much of that shit is up there?"

"I'm not lure, but I believe it's still ova a hundred of'em.

I sat back down, prior to me saying, "I'm mad as hell that I didn't get a chance to get in some of'em, before he took'em out. But that's alright. He got enough up there right now to get us over three 'keys' out of'em. That'll give us another thirty thousand a piece.

That revelation made that bitch sat up straight in her seat And it should've, because we had already grinded forty thousand each off our skeemin' operation. If I know my sister, however, she was probably spending her money, just as quickly as we had been clockin' it.

She lit up one of her stinky cigarettes and asked, "What 'bout that otha thang we talked about? I mean, are we still down, or what?"

I looked off into space like I had done the other day, before I said, "Yeah .... that's a done deal ---- we don't have a choice!" I said in a slightly high pitched tone. "But we definitely can't make no move like that, while he's outta town."

"Why not??" Tinia asked like I had betta have a good enough reason.

I looked at her with her hair matted to the left side of her face, and tried to imagine her asking a trick why was half a man too much for head, with that same bewildered look on her face. Then, I said, '" Cause Popcorn ain't stupid, Girl ---- that's why! He'll see that something was fucked up about that picture, and believe me, he'll see right through that shit, real quick."

"Oh," She said as though she could, at that point, see the logic of what I said, without any further explanation. Still, she added, "You callin' good money, Gurl."

"I know I am. That's why, we gonna wait until after he's back, before we take that shit." I sipped my own coffee and blew out a breath of air, ahead of me saying, "Besides, I'ma need some time to psych myself out."

"For what, Gurl ---- we just do the shit."

I almost laughed at her simple-minded approach to something that was extremely vital to whether or not we came out of that shit with our lives or not. But I didn't crack a smile. I only looked her directly in her eyes and said, "Bitch, don't you understand, if we do this shit, one of two things has to happen to me if we expect to pull this shit off."

"Like what?" She asked and took a toke of her smoke.

I was still holding her gaze as I said, "I'ma have to be shot, or beat within an inch of my motherfucking life."

"What!!" She shrieked. "Are you fucking crazy?"

"No ------ but you are, if you think it can be done any other way."

I saw that her hand shook as she took another drag from her Newport. She blew out all the smoke and asked, "Well which one you gon' do then?"

I was staring out into space when I answered, "It ain't no tellin'.

CHAPTER 31

Peaches

Since yesterday, I've been having the time of my life. It just felt sooo wonderful being in Florida with my man. At first, I thought that bitch, Zesty, was going to spoil my chances of completely enjoying everything to it's fullest. But I was dead wrong. Homegirl and I clicked while she was showing me around their crib, and she noticed that I wasn't a hater, by the way I gave her, hers. I mean, yes, I was trippin' about how she was tryin' to carry a bitch out the gate, but still, while she was givin' me the tour of that huge mansion they was living in ---- I was gracious enough to break the diva off some nice compliments. She had been receptive enough to know that I wasn't tryin' to do shit, but keep it real.

Therefore, she had said, "You wanna walk to the beach and kick it while they in there talking?"

"That's cool." I replied.

She had grabbed two big bundles of grapes, handed me one, and said, "I love eating fruit and walking barefoot on the sand."

I watched her kick off her pink-and white Baby Phat sneaks, and I had done the exact same thing.

We had slowly walked along the ocean front for close to an hour, kickin' it about all sorts of thangs. But the one thing that had stuck with me for the rest of that day, and even when I had awakened the next morning, was when she had said, "You know what, Gurl? When I first saw you and your man at that airport, I was jealous as shit."

Excuse me!" I had said, and perhaps a little too harshly. Because I had wanted to know what the fuck had she meant by that.

She had only smiled from the way I had reacted to her statement, and then said, "Nah ---- I didn't mean it like that. What I meant was, ya'll two look so damn perfect together. It's like ya'll fit!"

I had blushed while saying, "Well thank you ---- but 'choo and Bay-Bay do too."

"Uhuh, not like ya'll do. Ya'll made me think 'soulmates' right when I laid eyes on ya'll."

I had thought, *'Dammmn.......!'*, because that was a beautiful compliment, especially coming from someone who hadn't known jack-shit about us.

Nonetheless, that evening, the four of us had chilled out and watched a movie in Bay-Bay's slammin'-ass home theater. I had seen it in Popcorn's eyes that, as soon as we move into a bigger crib, he was going to hook-us-up with one of those state of the art joints. When he does, he wasn't going to get any argument from me, or, I was sure, from Tondra either.

252

After that, Popcorn and I walked the beach, ourselves, holding hands and shit like that. Believe me, it was romantic as hell. Especially when he lured me down upon the sand and made the sweetest love to me.

I cried.

Because it felt like his essence had walked right into my heart, while the moon was smiling down at us --- and the ocean waves rushed to-and-from the shore.

We slept late Sunday morning, which was why we was sitting out on a gigantic patio, seated around a huge umbrella glass table, enjoying a splendid brunch, when Popcorn looked at his two-way and frowned.

So I asked, "Everythang alright?"

His frown vanished like vapor, before he responded, "Yeah, everything straight, Yo."

Still, he got up and walked over to a corner of the patio and talked on his cell. When he returned back to the table, he leaned in close to me and said, "That was Rainy. Moms let her little ass stay at home, alone, because she didn't wanna go to Charlotte wit her and Precious." Then he frowned again, like he was worried about something, before he added, "Ain't that a bitch, Yo??"

I thought about when I was twelve, going on thirteen, and quickly recalled how grown I was at that age. Therefore, I said to him, "Don't worry, she's ok. Girls that age are a lot mature than you might think."

"Phpht " He said, before he continued with, "Yeah, no bullshit! She just proved that shit, by tellin' me just now that 'her friend' wants to take her to a damn motel."

"What!!!" I'm sure I looked like I had been shocked by a thousand volts of electricity. "Bu.... but aren't they a little too young to get a room?"

Neither of us cared at that point that Zesty and Bay-Bay could hear the conversation. They both were even smiling until

Popcorn said, "According to her, he ain't. She told me that nigga was in his twenties."

"Oh my God!!" Zesty let fly.

She didn't tell you who that sick muthafucka was?" Bay--Bay said with all the lights in his eyes turned dim.

"Nah.... and like a damn fool, I didn't try to make her, eitha."

I said, "Why Boo?"

He shook his head a little before saying, "I just felt like if I hadda, she would've tripped out on me ----- and not tell me anythin' else."

"Damn that made sense, Dawg. I guess the call just now proves you made the right decision. Because you damn sho wouldn't know known about what that whacked ass nigga was tryin to do today."

"So what did you tell her? I mean, you know, after she pulled you up."

He reached and grabbed an apple, and began to polish

it off on his wife-beater tee-shirt, prior to him saying," I told her the fastest lie I could think of." We all must've looked like our expressions were saying, 'And!!!', because he went on to say, "I told her it probably wouldn't be a good idea, because the twins were guardin' her for me. They might hurt 'her friend' real bad if they saw him anywhere near her." He bit into the apple as though he was biting that nigga's heart out.

"So, do you think she believed you, Popcorn?"

"True that! Because she shouted, 'Oh no!! I gotta call'em and warn' em ---- bye!!'. Then, she slammed down the phone she was on, Yo, like she believed every word of it."

He was smiling and chewing the hell out that apple like it was good as shit. So the rest of us, we smiled, too. And believe it or not, Bay-Bay, Zesty, and I, we all reached for one of those juicy-ass apples our damn selves.

HUSTLERS

◆◆◆◆◆◆◆◆◆◆◆◆◆◆◆◆◆◆◆◆◆◆◆

Popcorn

Man! That shit wit Rainy had me buggin' forreal, Yo. I'm sayin', if she hadn't fed into that slick-ass lie I had told her, I knew I would've been on the first thing smokin'. Even if I would've had to charter one of those private jaunts, I would've jacked-that-dough-off in a heart beat. Because, wasn't no grown-ass nigga gon' be diggin' my lil' sis back out and fuckin' her world up ----- not if it was somethin' in my power to do about it. In any case, to get that nonsense completely outta my dome, I called the twins and instructed they asses to swing by Momdukes every few hours, to check on shautie. I knew that shit was gon' give her a major attitude ---- but fuck that!! I needed to be fo sho that that shit was dead.

After brunch, Bay-Bay said his Moms and'em wanted to see me, and meet Peaches. So all four of us loaded up in his 600 Benz, lookin' forward to cruisin' across the city, somewhere, to see my mans family. Therefore, you can imagine the ultimate surprise of a lifetime, Peaches and I experienced when Bay-Bay merely drove up the street to one of those 'big joints' he had referred to earlier, and parked in it's enormous driveway.

Before I realized it, I said, "You kiddin', right?"

He wore a sly-fox grin, just before he said, "Nah.... Playa, this her shit. But then, you know a nigga had to set her out proppa' ---- Baby don' paid her dues."

I was feelin' that shit like a muthafucka! Because I felt the same way about mines. I only hoped that Peaches was gon' be strong enough to accept the way I was plannin' on servin' my Moms because, whether she was or not, 'big thangs' was still gon' be jumpin' off for my peeps, regardless. I had to give it to Zesty, however, because she was standin' by her man, lookin' like she wasn't fazed by the fact that Bay-Bay had made it clear, Momdukes get her's off the whistle.

I felt Peaches holdin' on to me a little tighter as I said,

"You damn straight, Fam. That's how I look at that shit, my damn self." I smiled after I flung that out there, because I was conscious of the fact that my bun-bun, who was still grippin' me, gave me a few loving strokes with one hand. I assumed that was her way of lettin' me know she was cool 'wit dat'.

We all got out of the car right when one of the tall double doors of that magnificent home opened, and Ms. Curry appeared in the doorway wearin' a genuine smile and some of the most exquisite jewels I had saw in my whole entire life. Plus, she flanked a Cuban maid who seemed just as pleased to see us, as her employer.

Their glows had the rest of us beaming, too. Yet, for me, that was a special moment. It reminded me so much of, back in the day, when Bay-Bay and my Pops were alive. Because, as long as O'boy and I hadn't done some mischievous shit that Ms. Curry had been aware of before we went by his house, she would always greet us with that same sweet-loving smile. Only, that time, when I walked up close and gave her a hug and kiss on the jaw, I saw a tear at the corner of her eye ---- and that told me that she was being reminded of some pleasant memories, too.

"Boy, you look just like your father---- I can't believe it!!" She said with a voice full of excitement. But she didn't wait for me to respond, because she swung her attention straight to Peaches, by saying, "And who is this pretty young lady?"

She wasn't lyin' eitha, she really thought Peaches was a nice lookin' honie, that much was printed on her face.

I introduced them by sayin', "My bad, Ms. Curry. This is Peaches ---- she's my best friend and my soul mate." I knew that was going to touch Babygirl, and it did.

She was smiling like she had that day I gave her that fly-ass Benz, as she said, "It's nice to meet'choo, Ms. Curry."

Bay-Bay's Moms said, "Boy, you betta marry this woman, quick! She's pretty, she has good manners, and ya'll look like a match made in heaven."

Bay-Bay must've figured that his. Moms was embarrassing both of us, so he said, "Auight Ma, you done made your point, light up on my mans and Peaches. They cool wit what they got." He was smilin' like he and Zesty had heard that same pitch from her, more times than they both cared to recall.

She knew that he was saying, 'Mind your own business, Mom', but she didn't get offended. She merely said, "Oh ... alright, ya'll come on in, then I got some good home cookin' goin' in the kitchen. I'ma see if I can't put some meat on them bones of your's Popcorn."

Everybody laughed, including me. Yet, no one spoke up and said that we had just polished off brunch. I guess they was thinking like I was, that there was no way in hell I was gon' miss out on some of that good cookin' of Ms. Curry's. 'Cause Babygirl use to burn like a mufucka!!

CHAPTER 32

Peaches

"Oh…..my…...God!!" I shouted out above the loud-ass music that was blaring from the speakers. Because right in front of me, a woman was up on stage that connected to the booth we were sittin' in, on her knees facing away from me, grinding her naked-ass, right in front of my face. She was wearing a G-string, true enough, but that damn thang had crawled evenly 'uptween' the crease of her fat-ass pussy lips.

When we had left Bay-Bay's Mom's an hour ago, Popcorn and Bay-Bay had thought that they was gon' brang Zesty and I a move. But we gated that shit, off the rip. We had stood side-by-side, her and I, and told they asses, straight up, that they could go anywhere they pleased and do any thang they wanted, but we was gon' hang wit they ass, too.

They had only looked at each other like they probably had done as teenagers, and said, "Auight!"

The next damn thang I knew, we were all strolling into a joint off of 22nd Avenue, and a Hundred Eighty-Third Street, called the Mint Lounge. I looked at Zesty the instant that it dawned on me that her shoulders gave me a look that said, go wit the flow.

So I did.

That was how I ended up wit that light-brown skin female's big booty, all in my face.

I tried to cover my eyes, but Popcorn pulled my hands down, and said, "Uhuh, you cheatin'. Ya' ll said ya' ll was game ---- so keep it real."

I reached and grabbed my drink, and drained that bitch. Because he just didn't understand. I was covering my eyes, not because I was afraid to check out the show O'girl was puttin' down. I was trying to block my view of the way she was workin' those hips 'only' from the fact that that shit was turnin' me the fuck on. I mean, my pussy was oozin' like honey runs from the core of a beehive.

That's word!

Plus, it was making me think about something that I really didn't wanna remember ---- that night I was with Choo-Choo and Moon. But Popcorn didn't know a damn thang about that. That's why he was grinning his ass off when he said, "Huh, put this in her G-string."

I knew it would've been against the grain to punk out on my man, especially since, at that point, Zesty was sliding a folded bill between the legs of a chocolate female with glitter all over her body, as well. Therefore, I took the twenty-dollar bill from my man's hand and folded it the way Zesty had. I was bubbling with pure excitement as I gripped the stringy material, while the dancer looked back at me and kept right on slow fuckin' the air.

I was careful to lay it right against her pussy lips and hold onto both ends of it while I cut my eyes at Popcorn. It didn't surprise me that he was lovin' me touching another woman.

But why wouldn't he?

Choo-Choo damn sho had. A bastard!

Once I let go of the twenty dollars, I deviously dropped my hand under the table. Then I smiled. Because it was just as I had thought, Popcorn was hard as a brick. Touching him like that out in public, really turned up the heat below. I wanted that motherfucka, right then and there. He may have sensed it, due to the fact that he slob-kissed me like we were in bed or something. I locked my legs together, and creamed on myself in seven seconds flat.

I was trying to catch my breath, before I broke out to the ladies room. Yet, the moment I glanced in the direction of Bay-Bay and Zesty, I got the hell up outta there---- because, those two were wildin' out, forreal! I'm saying, she was up on his lap and everythang. As I walked toward the restroom, I assumed that the people that ran the place must've really known him, because they were watching the show, as well, and smiling their asses off. All I could think was Florida was off the hook!

◆◆◆◆◆◆◆◆◆◆◆◆◆◆◆◆◆◆◆◆◆◆

Peaches

The next morning when I woke up, my head was hurting like hell. That is, until Popcorn announced that we were going shopping. That alone, perked me up a lot. But when a nigga said South Beach ---- I took and forgot I ever had a headache. I was too busy hurrying to get dressed and far too busy thinking about all those damn designer shops and boutiques I heard was in that section of the city.

My Gurl, Zesty, was hyped also. It didn't matter that she had probably shopped at every one of those places a she was visually just as antsy as I was. In fact, neither one of us ate a damn thang for breakfast ---- we merely drank a glass of cranberry juice, and kept rushing Popcorn and Bay-Bay to hurry the hell up.

Finally, we all got in Bay-Bay's Benz and cruised the short distance down ocean Bay Boulevard, over to Biscayne Bay, which ran parallel with the ocean. Popcorn and I were in our own world, kicking it about some of the things we were going to do, once we got back home. Especially since we, at that point, had that check for that six hundred grand.

I couldn't believe it when he first showed it to me, our first night there. It was like, at the blink of an eye, our lives were different. Because, with that money being indisputably legal, we could began to realize some of the things we had already talked about doing. Fo' sho', we could hook up with my sister Toni, and take off with that Real Estate Company. Thinking about it, was a beautiful feeling. I could hardly wait to tell her the good news.

Bay-Bay turned right and floated over to South Beach ---- I knew that's what street it was. Because, right there in clear view, a Gucci Boutique stood out like a beautiful sore thumb. I squirmed in my seat beside Popcorn, and O'girl did a nice little wiggle her-self, up in front of me.

"Ya' ll chill out, and let me park this bitch, first --aught! " Bay-Bay said in a joking tone of voice.

Popcorn pulled out a platinum card, that he had apparently gotten from his mans, and said, "Here you go ----do you!"

'Do me!' I thought to myself, while hoping that neither one of us would live to regret that he ever said those words to me. I mean, I was sensible as shit when it came to spending money and all that. But a bitch could loose it,   under circumstances like the one he was putting me in, by handing me that damn platinum and telling me to 'do me'.

I felt I needed an escort to keep me from going beserk, that's why I asked, with a puppy-look on my face, "Aren't you comin' wit me, Boo?"

He knew I was frontin' ---- and that if he didn't stay close by, I would burn all the plastic off that card, with no regrets. He even smiled before he said, "Yeah, Shautie, I'ma hang. You kept it real, yesterday, so I'ma let'cha torture a nigga, today."

I hit'em on the arm and right at the instant Bay-Bay said, ya'll, lets rent us four of those scooters, over there."

He pointed at some motor bikes with large baskets on the back of'em. I immediately said, "I don't know how to ride a motorcycle!"

They all laughed, including the attendant. Then Popcorn said, "It's easy, Yo. Com'on, I'll show you how one of these jaunts work."

He was right, that shit was nothing. In fact, I was handling mines, better than all of'em, as we cruised the sidewalk back up toward that Gucci Boutique I wanted to start my shopping spree at.

Two hours later, we all came out with enough bags that we had to go straight back to the car, and unload those things into the trunk. I was smiling my ass off, because I had copped me some real fly shit to wear for when we go into business with Toni. From there, Zesty directed us to a designer shop that had it all ---- Chanel, Prada, Dior, Armani, Burberry, Ferragamo, Dolce and Gabbana, Louis Vuitton, and everything else you could think of.

I copped me some of those slick Francis B jeans, and a few pair of those Baby Phat and J-Lo joints too. Plus, I loaded up on hand bags. I grabbed everything from a pink joint by Fendi, a Birkin Calf-skin and Bullcalf, by Hermes, also, I brought one each of Chanel, Prada, and Tod's.

Popcorn, who at that point, still hadn't brought shit for himself, must've thought I was crazy. But the truth was, he was the one who had it twisted. That's why I said, "Com'on, Boo, I seen some nice Iceberg hook-ups on the way ova here."

"Yeah, aught. But you fo sho it's ok for a brotha to pick up a few things for himself?" He was still messin' wit me.

But I didn't feed into it. I merely led the way, as we marched on over to the men's section. And then, I got busy again, because I loved dressing a man. I was surprised by the fact that Popcorn got with the program. He tried on and copped two Armani suits, a Versace, and a couple of those Phat Farm pinned stripped double breasted joints. I ain't gon' front, I had been in awe, because that nigga looked good enough to eat in every one of those suits.

Nonetheless, after we picked out some casual gear for him, he said "Aught, now lets go take care of babygirl, Yo."

I felt a flood of blood rush to my scalp, because I thought he was talking about Yolonda. But then, I felt foolish as shit when he said, "That way, you won't have to worry about coppin' her too much for school." Because it was clear he had been talking about Tondra, instead of O'girl.

I didn't know if we was gonna be able to haul anymore bags, because both our arms were full as shit. But Bay-Bay and Zesty appeared and lifted that burden, being that they only had a few bags between them both. Yet, that wasn't a surprise. From what I recalled from O'girls walk-in closet, she had most of the shit I had looked at. I'm sure, Bay-Bay's closet was just as full and complete as her's.

Zesty and I picked out Tondra some of the hottest gear that was out there for the fall. She was gonna be 'the shit' at her school --- no doubt. I knew I would've been had I been flossin' Polo, Baby Phat, Gap, and Roca Near, when I was startin' second grade.

To prove to myself that I wasn't trippin' off Popcorn and Yolonda's friendship, I suggested, "I seen a nice gator clutch bag Yolanda might like. You should get it for her."

He looked at me with one eyebrow raised, "Oh, yeah ---- and when you start payin' attention to what O'girl likes?"

I looked him squarely in the face, and said, "After that night we had our little talk -- -- that's when!" I didn't try to fake it, I kept it real.

He respected my response, too, because he turned down the corners of his mouth, while shaking his head up-and-down, before he said, "I can feel that. But now that you mention it, we betta pick up something for my Moms, Rainy, Precious, Toni, the twins, and even your girl, Carla, or niggas gon' have a field day wit our asses."

So that's what we did the next hour. He even looked out for Tiny, Tracy, Toi, and some others that came to mind. And that shit felt good, too. But not half as wonderful as I felt when after we stuffed those items in the trunk, Popcorn turned to his mans, and said, "Where that jewelry store at, Yo?"

CHAPTER 33

Popcorn

"What can I do for you today, Donte?" Spoke a well-dressed Cuban who spoke English fluently. He was smilin' at Bay-Bay like a person did who knew that they was about to come up on some serious scratch.

Bay-Bay said, "I'm just here wit my peeps, today, Menquil." He looked back at me, winked and went on to say, "I told'em you'll hook'em up wit some dope shit, at a reasonable price."

He started walkin' toward me and Peaches like he meant everythin' that Bay--Bay had just proposed. "You told your friends right, Donte. I treat them just as I have you all these years." He shook my hand and continued by askin', "Now what can I do for you nice folk?"

Peaches was a trip, Yo. Babygirl was standing there chewing on her bottom lip, excited as shit. But she was trying her best not to show it. That is, until I said, "Let me check out some of your female diamond rings, Fam."

It was at that point, however, that Shautie lost her cool and composure. Fo' some reason, so did Zesty. Because they both started makin' some strange ass sound and huggin' each otha like they was celebratin' som'um that Bay-Bay, the Cuban, or I, didn't understand. For a minute, I even thought that they were gettin' ready to cry, too. Especially, when Menquil led us over to a glass case that was sparklin' wit nuthin' but pure rocks.

I was enjoyin' the suspense of keepin' Peaches in the dark, by not lookin' at her, or askin' her advice. That's why I said, "Let me check out that jaunt, right there. I pointed at a pear-shaped diamond encased in platinum.

He handed it over the counter to me. Bay-Bay feed into my game by eyein' the joint over my shoulder, and sayin' "She might not want nothin' that big, Dawg."

"Just stay out of it, Bay-Bay!" Zesty warned wit a frown on her mug. She was steppin' out there for O'girl.

I almost laughed before I asked, "How many karats is this jaunt?" "Three." Said O'boy, as though he had the characteristics of every item in the store, memorized.

"Hmmmm ---- " I said, ahead of, "Let me see how this jaunt gon' look on your hand, Shautie."

Peaches held out her tremblin' hand and when I slid the ring on her finger, I thought, 'Damn!! That joint looks good as a mufucka!' Plus, that muthafucka fit like she was born wit it on. Therefore, I merely turned back to the Cuban and handed him the platinum card and said, "I'll take it ---- I think my Moms will like it."

"What!!!" Both Peaches and Zesty screamed out at the same time.

"Chill, Yo. A nigga just funnin ---- that's all." Then I looked a little more intently into my girl's eyes and said, "That's just a little som'um to hold you down, 'til we 'do dat'. You feel what I'm sayin'?"

She shook her head, vigorously, up-and--down before she gave me a tender sweet kiss. Far sweeter than the day I gave her that Benz.

The Cuban asked, "Will that be all?" before he rung up the purchase.

After a second of thought, I said, "Nah, hold up ---- I believe I'll take a couple of those Jacob Jeweler's jaunts, too, and a lil som'um for a lil Shautie."

That shit hyped up O'boy to such a degree he said, "Right this way, Fam!" And he said it just like he and I was 'boyz' at that point.

Fifteen minutes later, we were standin' out on the sidewalk with those big-face joints blingin' our wrist, some ice bezzlin' Baby's finger, and a cute lil necklace gift wrapped for Tondra, when Bay-Bay said, Ya'll ready fo some soul food, or what?"

"Hell yeah, Yo!" I said before the females could say anything.

"Word! 'Cause there's a tough muthafucka a few blocks down, called Tony Romans. That nigga's shit off the chain!"

"Say dat then, Yo,.'cause my shit on 'E'."

So we hopped back on our scooters and raced for that soul food joint like we were a bunch a young kids, racin' for home.

◆◆◆◆◆◆◆◆◆◆◆◆◆◆◆◆◆◆◆◆◆◆

Choo-Choo

"What up!" I barked into my cell, while keepin' my eyes on the light flow of traffic along Bowling Green Ave., as I cruised from Church Hill where I had picked up some slow-ass dough from those two youngin's up in Wilcom. Everytime I think about Lil Shautie stampin' that those two mufucka's were official, I fell like drivin' all the way back out to the crib, and burying my mufuckin' foot in that bitch's ass.

That is, if my girl Wyndie ain't got her mufuckin' dome already uptwixt Shautie's lil-bony ass, like where it's been since that night I hooked they two stankin' asses up. Don't get it twisted though, I ain't trippin' off that shit forreal. 'Cause they still be servin' a nigga decent, wheneva I slide thru that tip.

Anyway, that nigga Tree-Tap was screamin' in my ear, "Choo-Choo, 'PLEASE!!', tell' em don't slaughter my Moms. Please!!"

"Fuck you talkin' 'bout nigga, I ain't told no mufuckin' body to fuck wit dat bitch." I said, but I felt I knew what he was insinuatin'. That nigga Body and Dirty must don' put they thang down on his ass.

That bitch-ass nigga was whining like the coward he was, as he said, "Nah, I ain't sayin' that it's you that got anythin' to do wit it. I'm just sayin' can you please call them niggas, Body and Dirty and please tell em not to hurt my Moms --- PLEASE!!"

I was lovin' that nigga bein' on my nuts like that, 'cause I knew his stuntin' ass was open for anythan'. That's why I said, "What's in it for me mufucka? You ain't in my click no mo' ---- 'member!"

"I'll pay you Choo ---- I'll give you every--muthafuckin' thang I got."

That's what a nigga wanted to hear.

"Where you at, bitch?" I wasn't gon' cut that nigga no slack. He had just sold his mufuckin' soul to me, and he had best know it.

"Down the street from my Moms crib, at that convenience store on the corner. They got her held up in the house and they waitin' on me to brang'em a hundred grand, or they say they gon' split her wig." He whimpered a little, before he went on to say, "But you know what them dirty muthafuckas gon' do ----they gon' slump both our asses."

"Just chill out, neg-ga, I'm on my way." I hung up the cell and started bobbin' my head to the beat of that DMX thaw I kept in my cd changer. Mainly 'cause that jaunt kept me in drama mode.

It didn't take me long to get to where Tree-Top was layin' low, wit his mufuckin' dimmers on. I pulled up beside'em and ordered, "Get your stankin' ass up in this joint, Neg-ga!"

He got out his whip and gingerly jumped up in my SUV wit a large leather bag, and said, "I 'preciate it, Choo. I swear I got 'cha! I'm sorry as hell 'bout that misunderstandin' 'tween us. But you ain't gotta never worry 'bout me jumpin' ship again."

That nigga sho knew how to eat-a-dick-up. But lets not get it twisted, whateva his bitch-ass was carryin' in that bag, belonged to me, now. That's why, before I drove from that spot we was settin' in, I asked, "What's in that joint?"

He knew what time it was, because, he stuttered, Uh..uh... that uh ….. hunnet grand they askin' fo."

"Yeah, auight throw that jaunt on my back seat." He still tried to play stuff by sayin', "Thank you, Choo ---- I'ma make it all up to you, I swear! You's a real nigga."

"I know mufucking well you gon' get-it-right wit a nigga. And you gon' start by takin' your mufuckin' mind off them hunnet Gs, 'cause that shit mines, now." He tried to act like he was gon' buck, like he had pretended to do the otha night. So I said, "You got a problem wit that?"

Just like a mufuckin' bitch, he merely pouted his lips a little and said, real soft like, "Nah, Choo, it's your's. Just don't let'em do 'nofin' to my Moms."

"Nigga, chill out ---- I got this shit now. So ain't nothin' gon' happen to that bitch."

I cruised away from the curb and creeped up toward the crib. I parked behind that raggedy-ass joint his Moms used to always be parlayin' in. I figured it might be less drama if I let those niggas see that it was me wit that chump, straight up. Because I knew they was eyeballin' the whole mufuckin' block ---- lookin' for the cross.

That nigga Tree-Top was shakin' like a mufuckin' leaf. I started to bass on his ass, 'cause that shit was erkin' me to death. But I learned a long time ago, no amount of words could make a nigga have heart ---- eitha he had it, or he didn't. That's why I blocked that nigga out and remained focused on what, at that point, I felt I should do. Especially when that shit ran back thru my mind 'bout how Tree, and the rest of them mufuckas tried to diss the O'boy. So to me, I didn't owe that nigga shit! And I damn sho couldn't trust his bitch-ass no mo. So what was the point in me steppin' up to the plate for him, or the othas when they called.

None.

That's why I looked at his faggot-ass and said, "Go tell'em I wanna holla at they ass."

"But what ---- " He tried to say.

"Nigga just do what the fuck I said!" I knew my eyes was red as shit, because that was how they got when a mufucka was pissin' me the fuck off.

He glanced back at that leather bag full of scratch, before he even had the lack-of-good-sense to look back thru the open window at me, wit the saddest lookin' mug I ever saw. But I wasn't feelin' no sympathy for a nigga that showed me no loyalty, at a time when he should've.

So that he knew as much, I kept lookin' his bitch-ass right in the face, as I put my jaunt in gear --- and slowly drove away from the curb. I couldn't swear to it, because 'X' was bangin' like shit ---- but I believe I heard that nigga scream like he had lost his goddamn mind.

Fo' sho', I didn't care. I had a hunnet Gs lyin' on my back seat and two stankin' ass bitches lying in my mufuckin' bed waitin' a nigga to freak they ass. That's why I was bobbin' my head to beat, and headin' straight for the crib.

CHAPTER 34

Popcorn

"Com' on, Shautie ---- get up! We already runnin' late, Yo-" I said to Peaches.

Bay-Bay had told us, once we got back to his pad last evenin', that he had 'big thangs' planned for the next day, being that it was the Fourth of July. He had also said, be sure to get some sleep, because we was headin' out early and would be on the move, all day long.

But picture that.

What kind of sleep was I gonna get that night, after coppin' those three karats for babygirl? None!! That's how much. She was all ova a brotha at the restaurant, in the backseat of the Benz, and had virtually tore my shit off once we got behind closed doors. But that shit was all good, that she was demonstratin' her gratitude, like she always does.

That mornin', I had already taken a shower, before I woke her. That's why I looked and felt fresh as shit, as I stood ova by the slidin' doors that led to a private balcony, and said, "Come ova here, Yo, and check this out!"

She must've heard the excitement in a niggas voice, because it appeared that she came all the way out of her sleep-walkin'-state-of-being, and hurried ova to where I stood, before she shrieked, "Oooh shit!!"

"No bullshit." I said, because we both were starin' at one of those big-ass yachts we had saw cruisin' up-and-down the coast line, the whole time we'd been there.

"You think that's his?" She asked wit wide eyes. "I'on know, but it's damn sho docked at his pier."

Before I could finish my statement she was pacin' for the shower. I smiled, because she had made a point that she planned not being left behind, from wherever that big pretty muthafucka was suppose to be takin' us.

I put on one of those Iceberg jaunts I scored yesterday, with matching flavs, and she wrapped her luscious body in a Gucci lemon-lime mini skirt, and in one of those tops that looked like a damn bra, to me. Plus, she wore some cute lil' Baby Phat sneaks, with ankle white footies.

She crammed a lotta shit into the shoulder bag she was gonna carry, includin' her swimsuit and a pair of swimming trunks for me, prior to saying, "You ready?"

I had been sittin' in an armchair watchin' her the whole time, so of course I was ready. But I didn't trip, I only said, "Yeah, I'm straight."

When we walked down stairs, we both were obviously surprised by the amount of people that were down there already. The only ones I recognized was J.R. and Big Titty Rose, who were walkin' our way, smilin' like Peaches and I were their long lost children, or sum'um.

"Hey Popcorn!" Big Titty Rose said, and gave me a too--close-hug, before she turned to O'girl and said, "You must be Peaches?"

"Yeah, that's her fo sho, Yo." I knew, at that point, Peaches was baffled like hell, that those two seemed so familiar wit me, so I turned to her and said, "This is J.R. and Big Titty Rose.

I had told her about them, but I never mentioned the fact that they were old enough to be our grandparents ---- or that Rose was 'phat' as all out doors! Still, Peaches took it all in stride, by sayin' , "Nice meetin' ya'll ---- I like ya'll's tans!

I didn't really care for the way J.R. was eyefuckin' her wit his eyes up-and-down her body as he said, "Nah, it's our pleasure, Shautie.

I almost laughed, especially when Big Titty Rose said, "I told'choo J.R., I told'choo Popcorn probably had a dime-piece at home."

In otha words, it must've been clear to them at that moment why I never fed into the different approaches they both had made toward me dickin' down grandma.

"What up Dawg ---- ya' ll ready?" Bay-Bay said from behind where I stood.

"No doubt!" I volleyed back. "Especially if we gon' be stuntin' on that big boy jaunt."

Bay-Bay only showed that sly-grin he published the otha day when he first parked in front his Moms 'big balla' pad. Then he turned so that he could gather everybody's attention, befo' he said, "Aught, errybody, let's do this!"

Without a backwards glance, they started filing out while they continued to kick it and laugh and sip on the bottles of champagne some of 'em was drinkin'. Peaches and I, we fell in pace with my mans, but I was extremely conscious of the fact the J.R. and Big Titty Rose were walking behind us. And that they were probably eyballin' Peaches' ass --- and mine too, for that matter. Because those two oldheads were nothin' but straight up freaks………..

◆◆◆◆◆◆◆◆◆◆◆◆◆◆◆◆◆◆◆◆◆◆

Peaches

"Does all this seem real to you, Boo?" I asked Popcorn, as he and I stood at the bow of that double-decked yacht.

A truly warm and sensational breeze was caressing our faces and bodies, when he replied, "It doesn't matter if it does, or if it doesn't, because it is. "

I looked up into his suntanned features, and saw the absolute truth of words. Being that no matter how surreal that moment had appeared ---- I was in fact standing against the railing of that magnificent cruise ship looking into the face of my man and feeling more loved than I had in my whole entire life.

After a moment more of solitude, we walked slowly along the starboard side, back to where everyone else was hanging out, eating from the elaborate buffet that was already set-up when we came aboard. I wasn't sure, but I believed that it was well over forty or fifty people in our party. Plus, everyone seemed to be paired off, even those two guys who were wearing some of those 'come fuck me' swimming trunks. Yet, there was this one female, who was taller than both Popcorn and I, that looked like one of those females you see shaking see shaking her ass on BET, that stood alone from the crowd. Like all the other men on board the yacht, I knew that Popcorn had gotten a real good look at her, because ---- the bitch was like that! I wasn't bothered by that fact at all.

However, the one thing that was causing little beads of sweat to form across my upper lip, was the fact that every time I glanced in homegirls direction, I caught her staring at me. But, not just that. Also, there was something very familiar gleaming from eyes

Her lust.

That shit was affecting me in a most incredible way, because she was high-yellow and just as freaky looking as Moon had been. I kept telling myself not to look at her, again, but my eyes seemed to have a mind of their own. Because the next thing I knew, they were staring right back into her's.

I was hoping that Popcorn hadn't caught on to what was transpiring between O'girl and I, right when he said, "I think one of us has an admirer, Yo."

I blew it off, however by saying, "Com'on, lets go change into our swim gear."

He had been cruising toward our destination for about an hour, at that point. According to Bay-Bay, it was gonna take anotha half hour before we touched down.

But Popcorn wasn't going for the blow-off. He said, "Don't be actin' like you ain't hear a nigga."

"I heard'cha!" I snapped, because I was buggin' a little from wondering, once again, if I was 'on' females.

He only laughed that time. Probably from the belief that O'girl was spookin' me. That made me think, what would he say if he only knew I wasn't scared of that fine-ass bitch but instead ----- I was turned the fuck on!

CHAPTER 35

Popcorn

Is that your jaunt?" I asked Bay-Bay. We was lookin' at a small island that was out in the middle of nowhere.

He showed that sneaky-ass grin again, before he said, "Nah, Playa, that shit belong to some otha business men, too."

'So what' cha sayin' ---- you down wit it, though, right?"

"Betta say that! That island, this yacht, one of those six passenger jet jaunts, and some otha shit, too." He said it, not like he was boastin' or anything like that. He was just clearing up thangs fo a nigga. "That shit be on time, too ---- that's how a nigga got to your brothers funeral so quick."

I looked at that brotha wit nothin' but pure respect, ahead of sayin', "Your Pops would've been proud as a muthafucka, Yo. 'Cause you don clearly carried this shit to the next level --- fo sho!"

"Fuck that Dawg, I ain't gon' be feelin' this shit until it's me and you that's got our names side-by--side on that kinda shit." He turned and looked down at everybody on the lower deck from where he and I was standing, and said, "Com'on, Dawg, they waitin' for me to set it off."

I didn't understand what he meant by that, but I heard him loud as a muthafucka on that otha shit he said. Still, I followed him, wit nothin' but love fo' that nigga.

We all unboarded the jaunt with Bay-Bay and Zesty leading the way. Peaches and I was right in step wit'em. I was smilin' from the fact that J.R. and Big Titty Rose was dead on our heels. As far as that broad that had been eye-fuckin' my girl Peaches [that's right I was hipped to who she was beckin' at all along] she wasn't playin' us too close. Which told me evenmore, babygirl was smooth and 'bout her shit. Bay-Bay had given me the 411 on her, earlier. He said her name was Dream and that she was holdin' down a section of ATL that her nigga had had on locks befo' he caught a life-bid in the FEDs. Bay-Bay had also made it a point to say, Baby was cool as shit. That's what had made me wonder if he had been hip to O'girl peepin' my bun-bun, too. And to the fact that I was lovin' that shit.

What!!

I wasn't no different than a lotta otha cats that thought two women sexing each otha was sexy as shit. In otha words, if Peaches wanted to spread her wings and get her eagle on ---that was cool wit me. But, make no mistake about it, the O'boy had to be in whateva went down. Ya heard!

We walked a trail that was flat at first, then that joint started to incline like a muthafucka. Next thing I knew, we all were huddled up on a flat round cliff wit nothin' but a huge pool of water below. I looked aroun' at all the excitement printed on everybody's face and was tryin' to figure out what the fuck was the big deal.

But Bay-Bay answered that.

He and Zesty held hands ---- smiled at each otha, and leaped off the bitch like they were birds or sum'um. After that, the rest of'em started buggin' too, Yo. Even J.R. and Big Titty Rose, those two old muthafuckas screamed and jumped off that joint holdin' hands, also. In no time flat, the only ones left standin' up on that cliff was Peaches, myself, and Dream.

"You can go "head." Peaches made clear, wit the most frightenin' look I'd eva seen on her face.

"I would," said Dream wit sincerity in her voice, "But Bay- Bay's tradition is that if you're alone, you can't jump until all couples have. Sorry".

I was feelin' Peaches like shit, because I didn't wanna jump off that muthafucka, eitha. But who were we to fuck up my mans tradition. That's why I looked at my girl and said, "We can do it Baby."

She was shakin' like her nerves were shot all to hell, as she said, "But I'm scared, Popcorn." I kept my eyes glued to her's and said, "So am I. But in my heart, I know that you and I can do 'anythang' togetha!" I then stuck out my hand and waited for her to give me her's.

She was lookin' at a nigga like she was searchin' for sum'um in my eyes, like she had don' that night she and I talked and carried 'our thang' to the next level. Just like then, she must've been feelin' me. Because the fear had vanished from her face, at the split-second she placed her perfect hand in mine. She even smiled before she said, "Yeah...... Babee, we can do anything."

Without anotha grain of thought, Yo, we leapt from that joint ---- hollerin' our asses off. And on all I love, that shit was beautiful!!

◆◆◆◆◆◆◆◆◆◆◆◆◆◆◆◆◆◆◆◆◆◆◆

Peaches

After we all made that incredible leap from that tall-ass cliff, we all swam ashore and laid around like a bunch of lazy-ass whale's laughing and enjoying the fact that we had done somethin' so daring. In a strang' sort've way, it bonded our clan like nothin else could've. Yet, there are no words for what it did for Popcorn and I. I only knew that, as we strolled back to the part of the beach where the yacht was anchored, my heart was on fire. Plus, I knew that his was, too.

The late afternoon sunrays were cooled by the gentle breezes that flowed evenly from across the ocean. It was as if nature was the only air-conditioner that little island would ever need. In any case, we ate, played volleyball, and took to the water. Some of us, like Popcorn and I went snorkling, jet-skied, or just played around in the water. But Bay--Bay, Zesty, Dream, and a couple who had flew in from Chicago, they boldly strapped up in some gear and went scuba-diving. But more power to'em, 'cause I wasn't doin' no shit like that.

Ever!

It wasn't until around six that evening that everyone began to really get their drink on. I mean bottles of Cristal, Moet, and every kind of hard alcohol you could think of, was flowing as if there was an endless supply. I ain't gon' lie about the shit, I was twisted! So much so, that I was dancing my ass off, nonstop. But so was a lot of the other females, including Big Titty Rose and Dream.

Popcorn, on the other hand, he didn't care a lot about dancing, but that was cool! I was just lovin' the way he was watching me shake my phat ass, especially to that Juvenile, 'Slow Motion'. 'Cause he and I had made love off that joint, more times than I could count. Therefore, with that Moet in me, I knew I was movin' my hips in such lascivious manner that told his ass, he was gon' have to brang all he had, if he planned on takin' me there, that night.

Finally, the party was over. I couldn't believe it!

But there we were, all boarded back up on that yacht, cruising away. I almost felt like crying ---- but, I didn't. I was with my man, and I was fo' sho' that there were a lotta more days like that one ahead. How could it not be ---- me and that motherfucker had jumped off a mountain togetha.

"I see your friend still can't take her eyes off you, Yo." Popcorn said while I was standing in front of him slowly moving my body to Usher's,'Let it Burn'.

"Yeah ---- I know." I replied, because that Moet had me feeling myself, like alcohol usually did. "But she can't handle this." I made clear and then smacked my own ass.

Popcorn's eyes was shining with mischief. His ass knew I was a little tipsy, just like I knew he was. Plus he knew, at that point, I was vulnerable to a lotta shit that I wouldn't be affected by, normally. Still, his ass said, "How do you know what she can handle?"

At that point, I decided to call his hand. That's why I walked up closer to where he was propped against the ship's railing, and looked him squarely in his eyes, and said with a mischievous glow of my own, "You wanna bet!" After that, I gripped sides of him and began to slow grind on him.

It was just like I thought.

That nigga's dick was hard as granite rock. That's what drove the nail in the coffin. My man wanted me to freak with another broad. He had dropped a subtle hint the other night at the strip club. But right at that moment that I had his ass pinned to the railing, there was no doubt, he was down.

My pussy started throbbing a lot more than it already had been doing, because I wanted that bitch. I wanted her just as much as he wanted me to be with her. It was at that point that everyone started staring up at the top deck of the cruiser -------- even Popcorn. So I turned around, right as Alicia Keys began blaring from the speakers. She was blowing that joint, 'Secrets'. It fitted so perfectly well with what we were all looking at. Because Bay-Bay and Zesty stood out against the blackened sky, like silhouettes. At first, it looked as though they were naked. But they wasn't. Because it was at that moment that Bay-Bay reached up and peeled Zesty's one-piece from her shoulder; and she smoothly pulled down his trunks, that's when we knew that they were fo sho, in they birthday suits.

After that, they started circling each other, real slow. And all the males on the lower deck, including Popcorn, started barking like a pack of dogs in heat.

"Wroof ..... wroof .....wroof .... wroof!!!"

Bay-Bay and Zesty must've felt that shit, too. Because she locked her arms around his neck, before he picked her up. I could tell from the image of their bodies that O'boy was heavy between his legs. Therefore, when he entered her, I was imagining, as I'm fo sho every female was, that Zesty felt good as shit at that moment Especially with all of us watching'em 'get theirs'.

It was no surprise to me that the barking sounds stopped abruptly after that. Or that Big Titty Rose was the first female on our deck to peel off her bathing suit, and grip the rail. The female from Chi-Town was so fired up ----- she flung her's off the ship, In no time flat, everyone all around us was butt-bald-naked and getting their freak on.

Except us and Dream.

I didn't know about her, but I knew that Popcorn's dick was so hard, I thought it was gonna break right in two. And me, my cheeks, ass, and my pussy was burning. I knew I wasn't gonna take my swim-suit off out there in front of everybody ---- I wasn't feelin' no shit like that! That's why I grabbed Popcorn's hand and said, "Let's go below."

We walked over to the opening that lead down to the cabins, and stopped. I looked up at Popcorn and his glare said it all. So I then turned my head very slowly in the direction of Dream, untied and pulled away the canary-yellow wrap I wore over my swimsuit, and awarded her 'that look' before he and I disappeared thru the hatch.

We landed in what was probably the main cabin. But at that instant, we didn't give a fuck if it had been the boiler room, we started kissing and pulling at each other's gear like we had lost our muthafucking minds. All of that raw freaking up stairs us afire. Yet, and I'ma be straight--up with ya'll, nothing I had ever seen or experienced so far in life, was more electrifying for me than when I looked down and caught sight of Dream as she crawled over to where we stood, and wrapped her luscious lips around my man's dick.

All I could think was 'Florida is off the muthafuckin' hook!!'

CHAPTER 36

Popcorn

We arrived back in Richmond the next day aroun' two, that afternoon, Yo. It was rainin' like a muthafucka when we touched down. I told babygirl to hold tight with all the stuff we brought back wit us, while I dashed over to the long-term parkin', and snatched up her Benz. Durin' the ride home, we both were probably feelin' the same shit. That is, that our trip to Florida had shown us, we had a long way to go ---- and a lotta work that needed to be done if we really wanted a betta life than what we already had.

The first place I stopped, even before we went to the crib, was the bank. We opened one of those joint blickies where I laid five hunnet Gs in, and split the otha hunnet in each of our checkin' accounts. That shit did wonders, in terms of perkin' a nigga up.

I dropped Peaches at the crib and told her I was gonna scoot-aroun' a little. I knew she was still trippin' about us freakin' that broad, Dream, last night. I felt she was worried about a nigga buggin' out 'cause she had indulged in a little kinky sex wit a broad. I had heard that most females was like that, and when I really thought about it, they had reason to feel like that. Being that a rack of niggas did go out like that. They'd take and ask, coerce, or simply trick their honies into freakin' wit anotha broad, then trip about it afterwards. That kind of shit only told a nigga like me that half the niggas out there didn't know what the fuck they wanted or had.

But I did.

Plus, I knew what all I was askin' fo' when I indicated to Peaches to go there. The fact that she gave it up like that, didn't fuck wit my love or respect for her. If anythang, it made me wanna give her more of both. That's why I went straight to the flower shop over on Broad Street, and ordered up a truck of shit to be special delivered to her, right then and there. On one card, I merely put, 'Ms. Curry was right, you are a gift from heaven!'

I left there and went to the apartment in Gilpen Court. It was strange-as-shit bein' in that city without the twins watchin' my back like hawks. But that feelin' left me the instant I pulled up and parked. Because Donte was posted out on the stoop like he had known I would be there at any moment.

I hadn't noticed it at first, but Toi's Escalade was parked a few spaces down from were I had parked. That puzzled a nigga.

"How was your trip, Boss?" Donte asked while he and I shook hands and embraced like brothas do.

I almost flipped the script on'em 'bout that boss-shit, but I figured, what would be the use. Therefore, I merely said, "It was off the chain, Fam." Then I looked over at O'girl's truck and asked, "What'sup wit that?"

290

"She's in the crib wit Donnell and that soft-ass nigga, Tree-Top." He started muggin' afta that.

"Hey Boo!" Toi said.

"What up." I returned while looking at Tree. Because he was standin' and rockin' from one leg to the otha, like he had don' that day at his Moms crib.

Toi even looked ova in his direction before she said, "Some stupid shit."

"Oh yeah ---- give it up."

She didn't waste no time or use any cut-cards, "This damn fool don' tricked your shit off ---- that's what!" Before I could ask for an explanation, she continued by sayin', " Those two dope sniffin' niggas, Body and Dirty, held his Moms hostage while he was suppose to brang them a hunnet grand. But this idiot, he called Choo-Choo, instead."

I looked at that muthafucka, before I said, "And?"

"Choo-Choo came auight, but he only took the hunnet Gs from his ass, and left'em standin' out by the curb, lookin' like the damn fool that he is." She started poppin' some gum she was chewin', after she set'em out.

I squatted on the sofa and crossed my legs, prior to lookin' at that nigga and askin', "Is.that shit true,` Yo?"

"Yeah, but -----"

"AINT NO MUTHAFUCHIN' BUTS!!!" I screamed. Then I said in a much settled tone, "I simply asked if you fucked wit that nigga, Choo, afta I asked you not to."

He was rockin' like he was ready to fall off to one side, when he said, "Yeah, I called'em."

The room was quiet as shit, except for that smackin' Toi was makin' wit that gum. Then she stopped while I just stared at that nigga, tryin' to decide how I wanted to handle the situation, and said, "After Choo took that money and peeled off on'em niggas, that's when he went back and got the rest of your scratch, and gave it to them niggas." She chewed a little mo' befo' she said, "But by then, them niggas was fucked up at his ass for tryin' to brang Choo-Choo in to the situation. So they forced him and his Mama to suck they nasty ass dicks ---- and he ain't don' shit to straighten that shit, eitha."

Donnell and Donte looked at that nigga wit pure disgust. In fact, they were mean-muggin' O'boy as if he had disrespected every componerit of a man.

I didn't feed into that part of it, I only said, "I tell you what, Fam, since I'ma fair muthafucka, I'ma give you seventy hours to scramble up my dough."

He looked relieved, a little, from knowing I was gonna allow his ass to walk up outta there wit his life. But he must've figured I was sweet, forreal, when he cracked, " I can get it fo sho, Popcorn, if you'll just trust me, one mo time, and give me anotha ten of those thangs on my face."

I almost lost my cool, and slumped that nigga on the spot. But I wasn't a complete fool as he was implyin' ----- no way-was I gon' put in work in front of Toi. Therefore I smiled and said, "Not today, Fam, you don' burned all your bridges, here. The best I can tell you, is get at'cha boy, Choo. I'm sho he'll be glad to have you back on his team." Then, I shifted my attention back at Toi and said, "Toi, wheneva you get time, stop by the crib, Yo, 'cause Peaches picked you up som'um nice from Florida."

Toi was smackin' away on that gum, as her eyes widened she said, "Really! Ya'll didn't have to do that, bro-in-law."

I swallowed the urge to smile, because that bitch-ass nigga was still standin' in the crib. "Shhhit .... you would've been fucked-up at a brotha, if we hadn't."

"Boye, you crazy!" She replied, prior to her turnin' toward Tree-Top and sayin', "You ready, Boo?" As if she hadn'said a damn thang that could've gotten O'boys wig split.

Yet, more bizarre than that, was the fact that he actually stepped-off as though he didn't have a mufuckin' clue that niggas like him was the reason the city remained rated in the top five for homicides. Because at that point, it didn't matter if he came up wit that scratch ----- ' cause. I was gon' still rock his dome.

After Tree-Top and Toi jetted, I dismissed that nigga from my thoughts, and got at all my otha peeps. To my surprise, every last one of'em, had my ends, and had been waitin' for me to touch back down and get at they asses. Therefore, before the evenin' was over, I had smashed Peewee off wit thirty jaunts, and scooped that six hunnet and ninety Gs he had owed from the thirty he had already pushed. I gave Mario and that female, Fame, twenty ---- and I kept Tre and those otha two cats, on a dime.

Plus, I placed anotha order to my mans.

By the time I had.gotten to the crib, my muthafuckin' leg was achin' like a bitch. I had always heard that wet-weather was a shot-up niggas worst nightmare. I never believed that shit until that night.

But it was all good. I knew I would rather for my leg to ache on a rainy day, than to have had to wear a shit-bag like my stickman was stuck wit, for only God knew how long. Or to have been restin' six feet under where my brotha was. That's why I laid in bed beside Peaches, not complainin' at all.

"Popcorn, you should've seen Toi's face when she came up in here and saw all those flowers you sent me. That crazy fool acted like she couldn't breathe or som'um, while she looked around at'em. Peaches was smilin' like she felt special as shit, Yo, as she asked, "Guess what she said, Boo, when she could finally talk?"

"What?" I fed into her lil' game.

"She said, 'Dammmn…..... Peaches, Gurl you must got the bomb!'" Peaches' glow got a little brighter, befo' she said, "Ain't that girl crazy, Popcorn ----- ain' t she?"

"I'ma have to stamp that, Yo."

I watched her ebony cheeks burn like her sister, Toni's had done on several different occasions, as she said, "Oh, so 'I got that bomb, huh?"

I saw where that was goin'. But before I could respond to her invite, my cell rang. I gave her a smirk just ahead of me pickin' up the joint and sayin' "What up?"

"Boss, we just peeped a grown-ass nigga sneak up in your Moms pad. What'choo want us to do?"

I bolted up, straight otta the bed. I could tell by the way Donnell was breathin' in my ear, he wanted the ok to get at that nigga.

But I didn't give the word.

Instead, I said, "Don't let his ass leave ----I' m on my way out there!"

I jumped up like I had forgotten my leg was hurtin' a moment ago, and started throwin' on my gear as if I meant business.

Peaches had gotten up, too. So I asked, Where you think you goin' Yo?"

"Wit'choo!!" She said, while pullin' up her jeans.

"You don't even know where a nigga goin', so how you gonna invite yourself?" I asked, but I wasn't angry. Because, forreal, forreal, I was glad that she was comin' along. That way, she could brang Rainy's grown ass back over to the crib, like I shoulda don' as soon as I got back.

"How come I don't? That call was 'bout Rainy, right?"

I was headin' down the stairs at that point, wit her on my heels. "Yeah, the twins said they think O'boy don' showed his hand's."

"Oh my God ---- ---- we betta hurry, then."

All I could think to say was, "No doubt!"

CHAPTER 37

Yolanda

"Yeah, they back in town, Gurl. I said to Tinia ova the telephone. "He came by and dropped a gift he brought back from Florida."

"Oh yeah ------ what was it?"

"Will you stop poppin' that damn chewin' gum in my ear, Gurl?" I said, because that shit was pissin' me off. Then in a much more civil tone I said, "A gator clutch-bag. It's aught, but I'm not feelin' it, forreal."

"Why?"

"'Cause I know that bitch probably picked it out."

So what!!" She virtually shouted in my damn ear. And then, so as to make sure she was on point, she asked, "Who's it by?"

"Prada." I responded, before shifting my position in bed.

"Well, if you buggin' like that about that joint, you can pass it off on the O'girl. 'Cause I'm feelin' it like a muthafucka!"

She must've lit up a cigarette, after that, because it sounded as though she was blowing out smoke, as I said, "Yeah, whateva, Tinia. Anyway, the other thing I wanted to tell you, is that he did exactly what I thought ---- he gave out every one of those bricks we been in already."

"That's good, ain't it?"

"Of course! Because that means his ass'll be getting a new shipment some time this week."

"Does that mean we gon' put our lick down, soon. 'Cause, forreal Gurl, I'm tired of waitin'. That shit startin' to get on my nerves so bad, I ain't had a good night's sleep in a few days."

Who was she trying to bullshit?

I bet her ass done slept like-a-log. But I didn't bust her bubble. I merely went on to say, "Yeah, but probably not until the first of the week."

That must've been all that 'huzzy' was interested in hearing. Being that she said, "well look, Ms. Thang, a trick who's been circlin' the block, and eyeballin' a bitch, just pulled up on the curb, so I'll holla at'cha'!"

I hung up the telephone and turned off the bed-lamp. After I wiggled around and got comfortable, it dawned on me that I was the one who hadn't had a good night's rest since Tinia and I had begun skeeming on a way to jack Popcorn for his stash. Furthermore, I knew that sleeping was gonna be the last thing I would do that night, as well. So I turned back onto my back, stared at the ceiling, and started contemplating how I was

gonna spend some of that money I was getting after we sold all
of that dope……

♦♦♦♦♦♦♦♦♦♦♦♦♦♦♦♦♦♦♦♦♦

Choo-Choo

The first mufuckin' thang I did, after I ruffed that hunnet
Gs from that bitch-ass nigga, Tree-Top, was get straight at my
connect wit his ends. I had already been a little long-winded wit
that niggas shit, but that G-money from Tree, had put a nigga
back in good graces. Therefo' I decided to return the favor, by
givin' O'boy anotha shot at gittin it' wit a balla. That's why I was
standin' in his Moms crib, wit five jaunts for his stuntin' ass.

I knew Popcorn wasn't gon' put that nigga back on, not
afta' he had fucked-up his last pack. Plus, I knew there wasn't
gon' be any static behind it, eitha.

How could it have been?

Popcorn was a straight bitch, his damn self. Since my
suspicions had been proven, I figured, at some point, I might
start strong-armin' that nigga on the strength of him fakin' like
he was som'um, he wasn't.

"Nigga, you know what's gon' happen to your ass if you
let sum'um happen to my shit ---- don' t' cha! "I barked at Tree-
Top's scared-ass.

He was doin' that old bouncin' around shit he always
done, as he said, "Yeah Big Choo, but you ain't gotta worry
'bout no shit like that."

"Who said I was spooked Neg-ga ----- you the one betta
be worried." Then I looked ova in the direction of his Moms,
who was sittin' on the sofa tight-lipped, as hell. I knew she
didn't like a mufucka, but like everythang else, I didn't give a
fuck, eitha. That's why I went on to say, "'Cause I'ma do alot mo
than make both ya'll mufuckas eat this big dick up ---- you
feelin' me nigga??" I screamed.

His Moms, a freaky lookin' bitch, looked down at my mufuckin' shit like she was hopin' that nigga jacked off my shit. That told me that those fools, Body and Dirty, hadn't done nothin' slick when they made that toothless broad slob they joints. If anythang', they did that bitch a favor.

Anyway Tree-Top was shakin' his head up-and-down, as he said, "I feel you, Big Choo, but you gon' be glad you put me back on ---- you'll see."

I wasn't tryin' to hear no mo of that ass-kissin' shit he was talkin'. I flung those five joints at his ass, and got the fuck outta there. 'Cause time was gon' tell if I was gon be glad, as he claimed, or his worst mufuckin' nightmare……..

CHAPTER 38

The twins were parked down from my Moms crib, in my beat-up truck. I parked Peaches' Benz directly behind them. We all got outta the whips at the same time, and started pacin' toward the house. The moon was ridin' high up in the blue-black sky. Yet, there was a thin imagery of a lone cloud floatin' across it's translucent glow, makin' it seem more erry than it already was, as we approached the front steps.

"Huh, Boss, here you go." Donnell said, and handed me the 50 Cal. Desert Eagle I had said I liked from the hardware Tiny had sent ova.

I looked at Peaches as I chambered one in the head wit my jaws set as though I was upset with the whole muthafuckin' world. Then I unlocked the door and placed my finger to my lips, as a way of tellin' the rest of'em to be quiet. He walked into the tiny foyer, and the first thang we heard was, "Let go of my head ----I don't wanna put that damn thang in my mouth!"

Blood shot so fast to my head, I thought that joint was gonna explode. That didn't stop me from takin' those steps, three at a time. In the meantime, I heard a familiar voice say, "You ain't nothin' but a dick.-teaser ---- you lil' Bitch!!" After that, it sounded like he gorilla slapped her.

I heard it loud and clear, as soon as my foot touched the top landing. I knew, at that point, I was gon' tear that niggas heart out. Yet, I knew it even more when Rainy said, "Ooow!! You hurt me. Let go of me, and get out!"

We rushed into Rainy's bedroom and all of us stopped in our tracks. I didn't know if it had been the shock of seeing a grown-ass man tryin to muscle his-rock-hard-dick into such a little person's mouth ----- or the undeniable fact that it was Smokey tryin' to dick-feed his shit to my lilt sister.

His ass must've been in a zone, because that triflin'-ass nigga didn't know we were in the room until the twins had him danglin' in the air. That's when he started hollerin', "Wait, wait-a-minute ------ I can explain!!"

Rainy ran ova and started huggin' me real hard. I had a huge lump in my throat from imaginin' what the hell may have happened if the twins weren't 'bout their business. But then, I swallowed that jaunt, and told Peaches, "Take her to the crib."

Peaches was lookin' distressed as shit, probably from the realization that somethin' just as crazy and perverted could happen to Tondra. Perhaps that was the reason for her givin' Smokey one of those I--ate-your-guts looks, before she departed wit her arm around my lil' shautie's shoulders.

I turned back in Smokey's direction, and he must've saw his fate being reflected from my eyes. Because that muthafucka had the nerve to bitch-up, start cryin' and slobbin' at the mouth, like he thought that weak-shit was gon' spare'em.

But nothin' was gon' save his ass that night.

To prove it, I looked at the twins and saw that they were pleading wit their eyes for me to turn'em loose on that niggas ass. So without the slightest degree of remorse, I nodded my head at'em, and them two muthafuckas went crazy! They treated him like he was a goddamn punchin' bag, because I could hear the sounds of every bone break in his face, both his arms and legs. They stomped, kicked, and crushed his ribs through the skin of his body Then, they threw him thru and outta the window that overlooked my Moms backyard. And to prove that they were 'bout their business --- they both leaped from that bitch, right behind'em.

By the time I got out there, they were high-fiving each otha and smilin' the way they use to smile after one of their own scuffles. But me, I still hadn't saw nothin' to grin about, not wit that nigga still lyin' there breathin' and fightin' for his life. So I pulled that 50 Cal. from my waistband, walked ova to where he was, and pumped slug afta slug in his dome.

After that, the whole neighborhood got quiet as shit. I mean the dogs had stopped barkin', the crickets had surceased in makin' their racket, and even the streetlights had stopped their humming. I looked up at the moon to see if it was still there, and saw that the formation of that one cloud made it seem as though that jaunt was winkin' at me.

I ain't lyin', Yo!

I figured that was a sign that, from that moment forward, I wasn't goin' for a muthafuckin' thang.

I turned to the twins, who were lookin' at me as if they were lookin' at a brand new nigga, and said, "Grab that blanket off'a Ra ny's bed, Yo. We gon bury this nigga in the James River.

◆◆◆◆◆◆◆◆◆◆◆◆◆◆◆◆◆◆◆◆◆◆◆

Peaches

When Popcorn came home last night, I hadn't asked him nothin' 'bout what they had done to Smokey. But in the darkest

301

recesses of my heart, I had hoped they handled their business. Because, in my eyes, Smokey wasn't shit! I mean, how could he have tried something like that with such a young girl, and from knowing that he had been disrespectin' Popcorn in the worst way possible.

I just shook my damn head, after I had served Rainy her breakfast in bed. Because I had always heard that it's the ones whom you let get in the realm of your circle, that'll always be the ones that'll hurt you the quickest. I had never really understood it's full meaning until I had witnessed that shit with Smokey last night.

It was around ten o'clock in the mornin', and Popcorn was already out on top of his business. That's why, when the doorbell rang, I was hoping it was Toni and not Carla. I just wasn't in the mood for her shit, at that time,

I peeped thru the snitch-hole and saw that it was my sister. That shit made me smile, because I wanted to kick it with her badly. Not just about business, but some sisterly shit, too.

"Come on in, Gurl." I snapped the moment I opened the door. "How was the trip?" She asked as we hugged.

"Wonderful!! The best trip I ever been on. I mean -- you wouldn't believe it if I could put it all in words." I said that over my shoulder as I lead the way back toward the kitchen.

She frowned her nose in a playful sort of way, before she asked, "Is that a clever way of telling me that you're not going to give me all of the sordid details of your vacation?"

"Shoo! I'm dying to tell you. I was just sayin', I don't even know if I can put it all in words." I had poured us both some grape juice, while saying that. So I handed her the glass and squatted before I lit up and said, "But maybe this will give you an idea. Then I flashed those three karats for her to feast on.

She placed her hand on her chest, as though she was trying to keep from loosing her breath, and prompted, "That's beautiful!!"

"Ain't it though." I agreed.

"Girl, don't you let that man get away ---- he's in love with you." Her eyes were still caressing that ice-in-platinum.

"I love him, too, Gurl."

"I don't doubt that, but ------"

"But what?" I got all defensive. Because in my mind, there were some 'buts' that I didn't eva want to confront.

And she touched on one of'em when she said, "There's something that's been bothering me ever since that night you called me when he had gotten shot-up."

"And what's that?" My voice sounded nervous, even to me.

"Where were you? I mean, you know, when lil' Rainy was calling." A moment of silence hung between us for a prolonged period. She became affected by it, because she said, "I already know it's none of my business. So you don't have to answer me, if you don't want to."

'Where in the hell did that come from?' I thought to myself, while being unaware of the fact that I had started to twirl the glass of juice between my hands. She had caught a sista completely off guard, therefore, I didn't have an appropriate enough answer for her, other than the truth. Something that was makin' me sick to the stomach at that moment. Especially when how, a moment ago, I had been angry about the way Smokey had mistreated Popcorn, after all the love my man had shown him. Yet, what I had done was far worst than anything anyone could do to him. After all, I had been fuckin' the man that had been responsible for him being shot-up and his brother being killed. But what was beatin' my conscious, more than that, was the fact that when I had the

opportunity to open all the way up and pour it all out to him .....
I didn't.

I lowered my eyes and slumped my shoulders some,
because I knew it was time to let it all out to somebody. It may
as well be to her, since she had me cornered and choking for
relief. Maybe then, I could find the courage to look Popcorn in
the face and show him mad love..........

CHAPTER 39

Popcorn

"Com'ere and give Julie a hug. She said, after openin' her door for me.

I couldn't believe that she didn't ask for a kiss, or that she looked like she had aged like a muthafucka, since the last time I saw her on the day of Silk's funeral. Still, I walked up and gave her a genuine hug as she requested.

"Are they comin' in?" She was talkin' about the twins.

"Nah .... they gon' chill out there."

She closed the door and said, "I've been waiting on you to come by."

"Why is that, Yo." I was puzzled.

"Come on back here, you'll see." She walked back to the bedroom that was on the first floor of her townhouse.

When we stepped into the room, I knew it was Silk's old bedroom by the sight of a big bulky lookin' water-bed that took up most the space in that joint. She opened the closet and that confirmed it even more. Some of his gear was still hangin' from the racks. I figured she was gon' offer those jaunts to me, until she briskly pushed them all to one side, exposin' the back wall.

Just like I thought.

Because, the wall was fake as shit. She bent down and pulled something up that looked like a latch of some type, before she straightened back up and ordered me to grip a strip-of-wood and slide it off to the left. When I did, she turned on a light and there stood the biggest goddamn safe I had ever saw close up. Plus, that bitch was old as shit, but the kind that was probably more secure than any of the ones built at that time.

I looked at her and she said, "That was your fathers. He used to keep it at the other house I use to have, before I moved here." She looked thoughtful for a moment before she went on to say, "He kept it behind a secret wall in my closet. So, when I moved, I had someone to hook something up for it, here. Because, I knew, one day, Silk was gonna need it. I just didn't have an idea that it would only be for such a brief moment."

She touched my heart wit that pitch, because it made me feel like my brother's death was my fault. Therefore I said, "I'm sorry about everything, Julie."

She looked like herself for the first time since I arrived when she quipped, "Boy, shut your mouth ---- you don't owe me no apologies. We both know Silk brought things on himself. What you did for him, was a blessing in a lot of ways. She smiled. "Because, at least he got the chance to touch some real money before he went."

She lifted my spirits wit those words, because she was keepin' it real, by lookin' at shit the way it was. I appreciated it like a muthafucka, being that I liked her and I didn't want Silk's death to cause hard feeling's between us. That's why I served her some shit straight from the gut. "I see why my Pops was feelin' you Julie, you real as they come, Yo!"

"Whatever I am, it was because of him ---- he gave me realness! That's why I kept right on loving him, even after we parted." She turned toward the safe, as she said, "Now enough of that. Be quiet, while I try to open this damn thang." She smiled lightly and started to spin thru the combinations.

That big-ass jaunt made a funny-ass clickin' sound while she pulled on the handle to pull it open. She then stepped back from it so that I was able to see the stacks of money lined across the second shelf, evenly. Yet, I was very surprised to see that there was also four joint's of flay lyin' at the bottom of it.

That's why I said, "Why you didn't call me, I could've gotten rid of that stuff for you, Yo?"

She shrugged her shoulders and said, "I guess I just didn't think about it, that's all."

"I'll take it when I leave."

"If you want to, but this safe and this hidden room is yours, now." She reached back behind the row of dough, and handed me somethin' wrapped in a clothe, before she said, "And so is this."

I uncovered it and was surprised when I saw that it was Silk's knife stuck snugly in it's case. "Thank you, Yo." Was all I could think to say. I placed that jaunt at the small of my back, where I knew my brother kept it stashed on him. After that, I looked at the safe again, as it dawned on me that Julie had offered me a secure place to bama my drugs and money. Yet, in my mind, there was one little kink in her offering. That's why I said, "What about Mr. Cool ----- won't he trip if he finds out I'm layin' work down in your crib?"

She eyed me like I was crazy or som'um, before she said, "First of all, this house is mine. If I say it's ok for you to do something------ bank on it!" For a split-second, her eyes had that crazed look to'em that Silk's use to have when he had gotten pissed about anything. But it vanished as she went on to say, "And besides, he hardly ever comes to this house, anymore ----- I always go to him."

I wasn't convinced enough to jump all out there, at that time. Therefore, I said, "I appreciate it, Yo, but I'm jive straight right now, anyway. But if you don't mind, I'ma leave them jaunts there, for the time being."

"Like I said, it's yours to do whatever you want." To make it even clearer, once we walked out of the closet, she picked up a set of keys that was on Silk's dresser, and said, "Huh, take these just in case I'm not here ---- you can always get in."

Her generosity was blowing a nigga away.

We walked back toward the living room and I was glad that she hadn't tried to hit-on-a-nigga. Especially after I had glanced down at her phat ass, when she bent ova in that closet to unlatch that wall. Because, I probably would've went with the flow.

Phew!

"Oh damn!" I said, "I almost forgot my main reason for comin' out'chere, Yo. Hold tight, auight?" She looked puzzled as shit, as she watched me dash out the door.

"What's that?", she asked, wit a beautiful smile printed on her face.

"A. little som'um we got'cha when we was down in Florida." I was returnin' her glow.

She was gettin' ready to open it, but I stopped her. "Hold up, Yo! Don't open that joint until after I'm gon'."

She didn't trip, she just held it close to her heart and said, "Com'ere and give Julie a kiss"..........

◆◆◆◆◆◆◆◆◆◆◆◆◆◆◆◆◆◆◆◆◆

308

HUSTLERS

Peaches

After I finished telling Toni 'everything', I cried and she hugged me until I calmed down. What amazed me, however, was that I felt like the weight of the world had been lifted. Maybe because my sister had been such a good listener. She never, not once, looked at me like she was judging me, like she and the rest of my family had done when I had gotten pregnant with Tondra. Instead, her eyes had been alive with utter compassion.

In fact, the only thing she had said, afterwards, was, You see how easy that was, to let it all out." I had shook my head up--and-down, before she had went on to say, "It'll be easier when-ever you decide the time is right to tell Popcorn. Don't worry about what'll happen after that, because ya'll a get thru it."

That had made me think about him and I leaping from that cliff after vowing that we could do anything' together. I had smiled. Toni was right, I needed not to worry. Plus I had agreed, when the timing was right, I was gonna give it all up to'em.

"Now tell me about the trip!" She had said, as though none of what I had said, had altered her outlook of me.

I loved her for that.

Also, I gave her the whole run-down. Except about what had transpired with Dream. I figured that was something that should stay between my man and me. Anyway, she smiled and laughed and loved it all. Even more, once I went upstairs, got her gift, and gave it to her. I honestly didn't know what Yolonda had thought about that gator clutch-bag we brought her, but Toni was off the hook about hers.

Finally, while I was fixing up a tuna salad for us, I approached the subject about her going into business with us.

Are you happy with your job, Gurl?"

"Yeah, it's alright." She said in a way that meant just that. "But do you ever think about doing som' um different ---- som'um that you can call your own."

She eyed me suspiciously, before asking, "What're you getting at? You got something in mind?"

I was dicing some boiled eggs, as T said, "Yeah .... sort of. He was thinking, maybe you was interested in branching out on your own."

"Well, ya'll read me right. But what was it ya'll had in mind?"

I didn't bite my tongue, "A realty company."

She looked like she was giving it a lotta thought. Then she said, "You know what would really be cool?" Before I could answer, she said, "Construction and developement. A good friend of mine is into that. He has a company and connections. But he's running short on cash, because he spreaded himself too thin. If I had the cash, I would hook up with him ----- that's where the money's at.

"Oh really!" I said. "How much money would be needed?"

"A lot more than we have, I'm sure of that."

I laid down the knife, and asked her again, "How much?" She noted how incredibly serious I was, so that time she gave the best answer she could, "Well, let me see. I'm not certain, but I would have to say, around a million dollars."

'Humph!' I said to myself, before I picked the blade back up and said, "Well, find out exactly what he wants and let me know." She was astounded. "But to what end?"

I looked her straight in the face and said, "Because, Sis, ain't no tellin'."

CHAPTER 40

Popcorn

"You gon' tell Mama what happened, Popcorn?" Rainy asked, as I was drivin' her home, Friday morning.

That whole scenario about Smokey's bitch-ass, ran back thru my mind, even that vicious ass-whuppin' the twins had put on'em ---- and how I blew his shit all ova my Mom's backyard. That's not to say that T had been undecided about whether or not I was gonna bust Rainy out. Because, in my mind, that fucked-up shit that O'boy had tried, was not worth gettin' Momdukes upset. So I looked ova at my lil' sis, and said, "Nah Shautie, that's gon' stay our secret, aught?"

She looked relieved. Yet, she said, "But what if he comes back?"

I hoped she couldn't see that devilish gleam to my eyes, when I said, "That ain't gon' happen, Yo. His ass don' got ghost."

"You made'em leave town?" She said while she sat up in the seat of the truck.

"Yeah! What'choo think ---- I would let that nigga fuck wit heart' and stay in this jaunt?"

She loved it!

Enough that she stopped asking me anymore questions about shit relatin' to that nigga.

When we got to my Mom's crib, I told the twins to stand fast. Because I knew there was goin' to be some questions that my Moms wanted answers to. I didn't need them around throwin' my concentration off.

I wasn't wrong, eitha, because as soon as Rainy and I walked in, my Moms asked, "What's been going on?"

I looked down at her, because she was sittin' on the sofa, wit her hands restin' in her lap. "Not a lot. How was your trip?"

She narrowed her eyes at me, which informed me that she was already hip to that new window I had a jack-leg replace in Rainy's room. Plus, it wasn't no tellin' what else she knew. Because she snapped "Boy, don't play with me. I asked you a question ----   and I want some answers, right now."

At that point, I guessed it wasn't gonna be as easy as I had imagined. Therefore, I turned to Rainy and said, "Give Mama the gift I brought her back from Florida, Yo, and then let her and I kick it."

My Moms was furious, fo' sho', but she was gracious enough to accept the present from Rainy. Although she quickly laid it to the side. And as soon as Rainy got outta earshot, she said, "Hell, T'm waitin'."

I felt like I was standin' between a rock and a hard place, because I didn't wanna lie to my Moms. But with the same breath, I didn't wanna set it out about Rainy and what that perverted ass nigga had tried, eitha. Therefore, I walked over and sat down beside O'girl and looked her in her eyes for a long moment, hoping that would soften her some, before I said in the most comfortin' tone I possessed, "You know, when Pops died, I didn't have anyone but'choo who I felt I could trust and confide in about anything. To this day, Mama, you have not let me down. As far as I know, you have neva' told me anything that was wrong. You have never held any of my mistakes against me. Nor have you ever told anyone any of the secrets that I have shared only wit'choo."

She was feelin' me, I could tell by the way her eyes sparkled. And by the fact that she was holdin' her lips tightly togetha, to make certain that I knew she was listenin' and had no intentions of interruptin' the O'boy's speil. That's why I went on to say, "But sometimes, there are people who are more fortunate than I was, because they're lucky enough to have more than one person whom they can trust, believe in, and share their secrets wit. To me, Mama, that doesn't say that they have more trust in one person than they do the otha. It only means that they trust everyone equally." I was holdin' her gaze the whole time, but felt that I was lookin' at her more intently, when I said, I said all of that to say, I have my responsibilities as your son, as a brotha, and as a man. I hope you can respect that, and leave things as they are. "Because," I smiled. "Everythang is cool as shit, right now." Afta that, I merely kissed Babygirl on her cheek and walked real slow toward the door.

I was expectin' her to say somethin' before I could get thru that door, but she didn't. She had felt the brotha. She knew I was protectin' Rainy and one of her secrets and that was cool, because, at that point, she wasn't gonna make a nigga give-it-up.

◆◆◆◆◆◆◆◆◆◆◆◆◆◆◆◆◆◆◆◆◆◆

The twins and I left Moms and I drove us straight ova to the apartment. We was gon' chill until I got hit from J.R. and Big Titty Rose, because I was expectin' them at any moment. In fact, I had Bay--ay's ends, packed and ready to go. Plus, I had gladly thrown in the six hunnet I owed for that blessin' he gave me from the insurance Company.

How could I not?

That shit had put me on 'swoll', somewhere it may have taken a nigga forever to get.

Peaches had run down to me what Toni had told'er. And to be perfectly honest, Yo, I was ready to give that shit up, from the word go. Because, as soon as I scooped my scratch from everybody, I was gon' be sittin' on ova a mil, wit no problem. But I liked Peaches' idea betta. Bein' that she suggested that we do like her father use to do, wheneva he invested in som'um.

Borrow that shit from the bank.

According to her, since we had a half-a-joint already sittin' in that blickie, those muthafuckas would be delighted to front us the whole mil. Especially since we was investin' in a sound business, and we gon' use that five hunnet Gs already lyin' there, for collateral.

As soon as Toni do her thang, as far as doin' what Peaches called a in-depth investigation of O'boy's company, then we was gon' put on some of that fly-ass shit we copped from down the way, and get at them crackers.

The twins and I had only been in the crib a few shakes, befo' somebody started to knock on that damn door like they had lost they muthafuckin' mind. Donnell done exactly what I would've done, he snatched that bitch open like he was ready to break them twelves off in a niggas ass. Or, throw'em outta a window.

But to all of our surprise, it was Tiny standin' on the stoop wit a fresh cut, wearin' new gear, and jive grittin' like he was darin' anybody to trip 'bout that shit-joint, I could tell he was still wearin'.

"What'sup, Fam!" I asked as he stepped thru the door carryin' a bag.

"Back at it ---- that's all." He stood a few feet from where I was squattin'

"Oh yeah." I said, because 1 didn't have a clue what he was rappin' about. Still, I asked, "When you get out, Yo?"

"Long enough to handle that shit wit them dope-fiends, that's fo sho." After that, he sat the canvas bag he had been holdin', on the floor beside my feet.

"What 's dat? "

"Som' of dat shit them stiff's took from dat bitch nigga, Tree." That shit made the hairs stand on the back of my neck. That O'boy had only been outta the hospital, no more than a few hours, yet he had hunted down and cold-bloodedly slaughtered Body and Dirty. I knew the twins were buggin', too. Plus, admirin' that lil' muthafucka, as I was. Because, both their eyes seemed to reflect their respect for Tiny.

Nonetheless, I said, "Why you didn't holla at a nigga befo' you stepped out there, like that?"

He shrugged his shoulders, a little, ahead of sayin', "I guess I just blanked-the-fuck-out after Toi told me 'bout dat shit."

I knew he had simply needed to do sum'um in order to get that thang wit Silk off his mind, temporarily. Therefore, I said, "Yeah, auight ----- but don't do no shit like that again, Yo, without pullin' me up first.

"I'm feelin' dat, dats' why I'm here, now. I wanna know when the time fo' dat nigga, Tree, comin' up wit dat dough?" He was muggin' a little harder, at that point.

I didn't stutter, I said, "He got 'til tonight, Yo."

"Yeah, auight." Tiny said, while pullin' out twin Glock 19's from beneath his shirt, prior to sayin',"Because dat shit got to be handled, so nigga's a'no we ain't stuntin' 'bout ours." Then he turned to Donte and said, "Get me a fresh box of them hollowpoints, Playa and sum'um to drank."

I smiled because Shauty was flexin', some, and lettin' it be known he had rank. And even moreso, due to the fact that they was ready to give'em his……..

CHAPTER 41

Popcorn

Aroun' eight-thirty that evenin', I was down at that mufuckin' crap-joint on First Street. Niggas was huddled aroun' the big-ass pool table wit fists full of dough, bettin' and sweatin' and talkin' mad shit. But me, and a few otha niggas that suppose to have been ballin', our mufuckin' selves, was posted by the bar, sippin' on som' gin and juice.

This ole black-ass nigga name, Quiet, was taking his shots straight to the dome, and makin' the ugliest mufuckin' faces a nigga eva saw, every time that shit burned it's way down his throat. He was already gettin' the fuck on my nerves wit that bullshit. But when he slammed the jelly-jar he had been drinkin' from, on the makeshift bar, and said, "I'm glad both them niggas got smoked, at the same time. Fuck' em!!"

My ears perked, 'cause I was the kinda nigga that loved hearin' that a mufucka got burned. As much as I wanted to know who that fool was talkin' 'bout, I wasn't gon' ask. But I didn't need to, because anotha stunna cracked, 'Who dat?"

Quiet looked at that nigga like he was on dope or som'um, before he snapped, "What ----- you ain't heard, nigga? They found Body and Dirty shot-the-fuck-up slumped, this mornin'."

"Get the fuck outta here!" Said the otha nigga, like he was happy 'bout it, too. He even said, "Hey bartender, give these niggas a roun' of drinks, on me."

That shit fucked me up, though. In fact, I wasn't seein' a mufuckin' thang to celebrate about. Unless, I was ready to admit that, maybe, I had that nigga Popcorn, twisted.

That was som'um I wasn't prepared to do.

Yet, as I looked aroun' that crib we were up in, and saw the bullet holes that were still in the walls, I felt myself swallow real hard like I was forcin' sum'um large and painful down my windpipe. Because, no matter how I chose to look at it, that shit wit Dirty and his mans, Body, sounded like sum'um that nigga Silk would've don'. Only he would've don' it sooner. In my mufuckin' mind, the fact that Popcorn hadn't acted too swiftly, made him more of a threat than his mufuckin' brotha was.

I wasn't gon' accept the drink that that stunna brought. But on second thought, I turned to that funny lookin' bartender and said, "Fuck that juice, Nigga, give me that jaunt ---- straight-up!"

♦♦♦♦♦♦♦♦♦♦♦♦♦♦♦♦♦♦♦♦♦♦

"Yeah, but I thought you wouldn't mind if I took a little bit longer." Tree-Top said, as he stood between between Donnell and Donte, bouncin from leg-to-leg.

He was lookin' pitiful, on top of that, but I wasn't seein'.

none of that shit. He should've never taken my shit. And fo sho, he should've never put himself in a position for Choo-

Choo to muscle him outta some of it. That was the part that had me more fucked-up, than all the rest, Yo. Because, now, he got that joker thinkin' that he got ups on a nigga. When as it stood, only thang that was stoppin' me from gettin' at his big black-ass, was because, deep down inside, I hadn't felt like he had actually violated me. What he had done was between him and Tree-Top, bein' that Tree had virtually called him up and freely handed that muthafucka, my ends.

That's why I said, "You thought wrong, Yo. Then I looked at Tiny, who was posted beside that nigga's Moms, and nodded.

In turn, Tiny tripped me the fuck out, because it looked like I had awarded that fool a piece of sunshine, or som'um, His face lit up wit a indescribable glow, and he started whistlin', of all the things a muthafucka would do at a time like that. Tree's Mom looked at his crazy ass, right when he placed the barrel of one of the Nines, inches from her dome ----- and cut loose.

The sight of that shit was disturbin' as hell, especially for Tree. That weak-ass-nigga almost fainted, but the twins held him and slapped him back to life. Once he realized where he was at, and what was fittin' to happen to 'em, that spineless muthafucka had the nerve to lick his lips like he was ready to suck all our dicks, before he begged, "Please don't kill me, Mr. Popcorn!! I know I fucked-up. But I swear, I'ma make it up,! Please!!"

I looked at that nigga's dead-Mom lyin' on the sofa wit her shit peeled back, and thought about how he was still all on my dick, regardless. That shit made me sick to my stomach. Because, I knew if a muthafucka slaughtered my Moms, any kinda way, but especially in my grill, he would have to bang that thang whether he planned on it or not.

Any man would feel that way.

That's why I spit in that nigga's face and said, "You ain't shit muthafucka!!" I picked up that sack wit Choo-Choo's money and flay, and then, purposely blew out Tree-Top's muthafuckin' brains…………..

CHAPTER 42

I spent Saturday mornin' at a Jeep Dealership, on Broad Street with the twins. I upped they shit to ten grand a week, yesterday, so they both decided they wanted to cop whips. Since I had all that scratch in the bank, and was at thatpoint, official, I co-signed for both of 'em and they burnt-out pushin' twin Grand Jeep Cherokee's.

As soon as we arrived back at the apartment, I told they asses thar they was gon' start makin' all the drops and pick-ups for a nigga. In otha words, they was gon' earn they keep. Because, anywhere in America, if you make more dough, you gotta have more responsibility and shit.

"What'sup Fam!" I said to Lil Rob.

I wasn't surprised by the fact that it was him who showed up at the crib in Gilpen Court, rather than any of the othas that worked on my old landscapin' crew. Or, by the sight of him lookin' like he was pissed when he said, "Man, I jus' need to know if I still gotta damn job ---- that's what'sup!"

I'm saying, Shauty, we done showed up for work three days in a row, but Smokey ain't been no where to be seen. "He slid his hands in his pockets, addin', "You should've sold me that joint, 'cause that nigga bullshittin'."

I suppressed the urge to smile, because I didn't want Lil Rob to become discouraged toward tryin' his hand. He was gettin' at Smokey's slumped-ass with no cut-cards. "What's wrong wit' em? Have you called'em to find out what the deal is? "

"Hell naw, I don't think it's my job to make that nigga come to work. To me, he's one of those cats that don' let ownin' a business, go straight to his dome! "

I acted like I was pissed, before askin', "So what'choo sayin', Yo, is that you can handle that shit the way it's suppose to be handled?

"You muthafuckin' right!"

My eyes was shinin' where I said, "But'choo don't even have a truck, so how you 'gon function without that'

"Damn! I hadn't thought 'bout that," He said,' soundin' a little defeated.

Therefore, I said, "Since Smokey beens fuckin' up and not on top of his business like he told me he was gon' do, I' in cancellin' that agreement we had. And I'ma let'choo run the jaunt for me for six months. If you about your's, I'ma give you a sweet deal if you wanna still cop the joint ------ auight! '

"That's cool wit me." He said it like he was still tryin' to figure out where he was gon' get a truck.

"So here you go, Fam, take my pickup----- and handle your's. " I gave 'em the keys to my F-150.

"I won't let'cha down, Popcorn," he said, while he shook my hand.

That time, I smiled openly. Because he didn't know it at the time, but he had already proved that much by showin' face at the crib, to put in his bid for a dead man's job.......

♦♦♦♦♦♦♦♦♦♦♦♦♦♦♦♦♦♦♦♦♦

Choo-Choo

"Why you keep hollerin' at her like that Choo ----- 'cause I don't like it! " Wyndie had the mufuckin' nerve to say to me.

"Bitch! You betta check yo self. I can talk to that lil' stankin'-ass trick, any mufuckin' way I wanna. Fuck wrong with'choo!

That stankin'ass bitch must've thought because I'd been lettin' her and my lil' bitch freak, that lil' shautie was hers now.

But picture that.

She huffed and puffed, but she got the fuck outta my damn face wit that shit. Especially since she knew a nigga well enough to know, if she hadda opened her grill one mo time, I was gon' break my foot off in her mufuckin' ass.

Shit, I had too much otha shit on my mind, than to have to put up wit her and that crazy-ass shit she was kickin'. Like for instance, I had just got wind of the fact that some mufuckin' body don' slumped that nigga Tree-Top and his Moms ---- and strong-armed my mufuckin' shit from that nigga. That shit don' hurt my mufuckin' pockets bigtime! All I could think was, his ass betta be glad them niggas slumped'em. 'Cause I would've been nothin' nice, if I could've gotten at his ass first.

But fuck that!

I know that nigga, Popcorn and 'em don' that shit. In my mind, that bitch-ass nigga don' violated me in the worst way. If I don't get at his mufuckin' ass, nigga's gon' think I'm the one that's soft. And I ain't havin' that! That nigga stole from me ----- so I'ma start puttin' my mufuckin' foot down on his ass too.

After settlin' that shit in my dome, I barked, "Sheila-----
get your stankin' ass in here, and take that goddamn shit off, like
I told'cha ------- Bitch!!"

◆◆◆◆◆◆◆◆◆◆◆◆◆◆◆◆◆◆◆◆◆◆

Yolanda

I was wearing some thin tight-ass silk pants, with some
skimpy-ass thongs beneath them, so I knew my ass was clappin'
as I strolled into the bedroom where Popcorn was handling his
business. Plus, I had on a matching top with no bra under it.
Just feeling that material brush against my nipples and knowing
what I was trying, had me moist below.

"When you gonna slow down long enough to kick it
with me, like you use to? I mean, you been zipping in-and-out
of here so damn fast, you haven't even taken the time to tell a
sista about your trip to Florida. What'sup wit that, Popcorn?"

I could tell that I had touched the right spot with those
words, because he looked defenseless as hell once he turned and
faced me. Still, he tried to clean up the fact that he was ne-
glecting the O' girl, by saying, "That's cold, Yo."

"No it ain't, it's the truth." I said as I walked pass him
and pretended to look out the window. When in fact, I was
merely making sure he got a nice whiff of that same perfume I
wore the last time he and I were in that room alone. Also, I
knew he was gonna look at me salt-shake and wonder what it
would feel like with both his hands on it.

"My bad, you right, Partna. I'm in straight violation like
a muthfucka. "By the time I turned away from the window, he
was leaning up against the dresser, with his arms folded, as he
went on to say, "So what's been happenin' wit'cha ---- you not
goin' anywhere on vacation, yourself?"

'Partna!! Why did he have to go there in his statement?
Was that his way of telling me to "back off'?' That's what I had
been thinking, whil I smiled and said, "Tsk…. I doubt it. "

I made a playful, but pitiful looking expression appear on my face, prior to me adding, "It just isn't alotta fun going anywhere without a man, you know what I mean?"

He acted like he was considering it. Then he said, "If you feel. that way, why you ain't got one? "

Ouch!

That nigga was hitting me below the belt with his smart-ass remarks, but that shit wasn' t dampering my spirits. It was too much at stake. I wanted toget his ass in bed, and I felt the rest would be easy as hell. Because, there was no doubt in my mind, Peaches couldn't get in my business when it came to sexing a man. I was more sure about that, than I had been that Popcorn was leaning against my dresser with a semi-hard-on. And I was looking at that with my own two eyes.

Nonetheless, I walked up closer to him and responded, "Maybe it's because all the good ones are taken --- especially what I want. "

"Oh yeah." He said it like my bluntness had tripped his ass out.

I didn't see how it could, after all, I knew he was feeling me, too. That's why I had said to myself, 'Fuck it! I'ma just tell his ass straight-out, where my head at. Then, the ball will be in his court. Therefore, I placed my hands on my hips and said, "Look, let's stop -----"

But that muthafucka cut me short by saying. "Oh shit! I gotta bounce, Yo. I forgot, I gott do sum'um really important. "

He started gathering up the canvas bag of shit he had loaded, before he said, "Don't be mad, aught:? "

That shit infuriated the hell out of me, but I forced a smile and said, "That's ok, I'll just settle for what I got."

He did that damn kissing-on-the-forehead shit again, and then he left. I merely looked at my watch with evil intent brimming from my eyes. Because at that moment, my mind was made up ---- Tinia and I was taking that shit, tomorrow. Since I.

felt that he wasn't gonna return that night, and probably not before we brought him the move, I began to stuff them kilos of yayo back into the canvas bags he had stored in my closet. That way, they would be ready to go. In either case, it"ll make a bitch sleep better, knowing that the shit was actually in motion.......

◆◆◆◆◆◆◆◆◆◆◆◆◆◆◆◆◆◆◆◆◆

Yolanda

Monday, the next day at lunch time, I was sitting at a table in Ms. Maggie's Soul. Food Restaurant, across from my sister, Tinia. The lunch crowd was light, but the food was as good as ever.

I watched Tinia light up a damn cigarette, before she asked, for the fifth time, "So it"s on for today, huh?"

I turned up the right corner of my mouth, and said, "How many times you gonna ask me that same question?" I sipped my water and pacified her ass, again. "Yes! We gonna do it today, alright? Just make sure you bring those things I asked for. "

Don't be so touchy, Gurl. I'm just tryin' to make sho we on the same page, that's all." She took a drag from her Newport and while she blew out the smoke thru her mouth and nose, she said, "Fuck his ass, Londa! Anytime a nigga turn down some prime pussy like yours, somethin' wrong wit his ass, anyway."

Lord ...... I should've never told that bitch about me throwing myself on Popcorn, twice, and he brushed me off both times. Because, I'll never live that shit down ---- every chance she gets, she'll bring it up. I was sure of that as I swallowed my pride and conceded, "You probably right. But after today, it won't make any difference, anyway, because I'ma be able to buy niggas like him.........a dime a dozen.

CHAPTER 43

Peaches

"What the hell is wrong wit'choo, Gurl? You look a mess," I said to Carla, who sat at my kitchen table, Monday afternoon.

She blew out a stream of breath, like she was tired from runnin', or som'um, before she said, "Tre got tore off last night."

"What!! I shouted. "Is he still locked-up? "

"Yeah, but Gurl, that nigga talkin' 'bout doin' some fucked-up shit." She said with a distasteful look on her face.

My heart was racin' at that point, because it was clear that she meant he was plannin' on snitchin'. Still, I asked, "What'choo mean?"

She looked at me with dark eyes and said, "You know what I mean ------ don't play stupid."

"Oh my God!" I said without realizin' that I was sayin' it out loud. "I gotta tell Popcorn!" I jumped up to get my telephone. "Wait-a-minute." She said. "It didn't sound like he was talkin' 'bout goin' there wit Popcorn."

"Wit who, then?" I was shakin' like the punk I was. I didn't want no harm brought to my man.

She was still wearin' that same discolorful look on her face, when she said, "That Ho, Tinia, that he claim he been scorin' that otha shit from."

"What'choo mean, claim ----- if he's gon' bust her ass out, than it must be true."

She thought about it for a moment, then said, "I guess you right. But I still can't stamp him doin' no shit like that. Some niggas did that shit to my damn brother, and. got him all jammed up in the Feds." She shook her head before she said, "I wouldn't have thought Tre was weak like that ----- I thought his ass was a man. But if he plannin' on settin' up a female, then he's mo' of'a bitch than she is."

I didn't hear any of that shit she was talkin' at that point, because I was thinkin' about how to get rid of her ass. Yet, when she said the last part, I shrieked, "Say what!! He gon' set her up? How? When!"

Carla said, "Pump yo brakes Gurl, what's wrong wit'choo. T don't know none of that shit ---- and I told his ass, I don't wanna know. But why you worried, I told'cha he wasn't kickin' 'bout doin' nothin' to Popcorn?"

I faked like I had regained my composure, and said, "You right, my damn nerves are shot all to pieces." I even showed her a weak-ass smile, before I said, "Well, I gotta go. I got an appointment to do some hair, in a little while." She looked like she was ready to question me about whose hair it was I was suppose to be doin', so I swiftly said, "If you want to, we can hook-up later, and go to the Mall."

That shit worked like a charm. In fact, it brought her completely out of her previous miserable state, because that bitch started smiling and prompt, "Fo sho, Gurl! Maybe that's what I need to get my mind off that damn snitchin' shit Tre talkin' 'bout doin'."

I walked her to the door. As soon as she rolled out, however, I broke my muthafuckin' fingers punchin' in Popcorn's cell digits. Because, in my mind, that shit Carla talked, didn't mean jack-shit. If that nigga'll tell on one person, nobody could make me believe that he wouldn't snitch about everything he knew............

♦♦♦♦♦♦♦♦♦♦♦♦♦♦♦♦♦♦♦♦♦♦♦

Peaches

"Whoooa .. .. Shautie, slow ya roll. I can't understand nothin' you sayin', Yo." Popcorn said.

I had rushed up on Tiny's truck, as soon as they had pulled the otha shit that I had been savin' until I was sho about it. At that point, I was sure as hell about the fact that that bitch Yolonda was hittin' his head in for his stash. So, I waited until we got inside and sat in the front room.

Then calmly I said, "Tre got tore off last night."

Popcorn's brow was furrowed when he said, "I'm hip to that, Yo."

I knew he felt like I had disrespected him by tellin' him that, but I only wanted to make certain that he knew. Yet, that didn't stop me from giving him some mo shit he may have already knew. That's why I remained facin' him as he and I sat on the sofa, and said, "Well Carla just told me that he's plannin" on snitchin'."

I went from Popcorn's face to Tiny's and neither of their features changed. But still, I could tell, they didn't know that part. But I didn't want'em to be trippin' about the wrong shit, like I had done in the beginning, so I said, "But accordin' to her, he claim he ain't gon' set-you out, regardless." I made sho he understood what my feelin's were about that bullshit, by the manner in which I relayed it.

"Then who the fuck he suppose to be 'goin' on'?" Popcorn's voice was hard, but he still had no expression on his face to match the tone of his speech.

I waited about five clicks of the clock. Because I wanted to be sho that he was ready for the bomb I was about to drop.

I knew that Tiny was anxious too, because I heard a pooting sound as his colon dumped into the colostomy-bag. Therefore, I said, "Tinia."

"That nigga's buggin', Yo. The only muthafucka he can set her up wit, is a undercover pretendin' to be a trick." He said that shit like he believed it, and like he hadn't even considered the notion of her gettin' his drugs from her sister. He even smiled.

And that pissed me off!

So I told'em everythin' that Carla had told me. Yet, none of what I said was able to wipe that fuckin' grin away. That's why I screamed, "What the hell is so goddamn funny!! Those bitches been cuttin' yo head off behind your back ----- and sellin' yo shit to that nigga. Now, he's talkin' about settin' them up and you're smilin' like somethings funny!"

"You trippin', Yo" He said as he stood. "Because whateva Tre's bitch-ass plannin' on doin', I'm fo' sho' it ain't got a muthafuckin' thang to do wit Yolonda ------ believe dat!"

"Wha….What!!!" I couldn't believe that every goddamn thang I said had fell on deaf ears.

But he made it that much more clear when he turned to Tiny and said, "Let's bounce, Fam."

330

HUSTLERS

I merely sat right there in that same spot, rubbin' my hands together in a fretful manner. I knew there was nothin' else I could've done. After all, he had made it abundantly clear that Yolonda had a bigger hold on'em, than I had been willing to accept.   I only hoped that it wasn't goin' to cost us our future.....

CHAPTER 44

Yolanda

When I got home from work, Tinia was already there, waiting on my stoop. She was popping her gum and looking like she was in a daze. Which meant, she was probably sitting there spending money in her mind, like I had been doing my damn self.

But it was all good.

We were getting ready to 'get down' for our's. I just needed to get pass the worst part of it. That's why, as soon as we stepped into the crib, I said, "You got what I asked for?"

"Baby pleez!" She said like she was insulted by the question. "You know ain't nothin' slow 'bout me. Huh!" She prompted after pulling a bag from that big-ass purse she was carrying.

I kicked my shoes off, before I dug into the bag and pulled out the pain pills I felt I would need ----- plus a cheap bottle of gin. Yet, I felt my hands began to shake the instant my fingers touched the brass knuckles that were at the bottom of the sack. I even heard a voice at the back of my mind, attempting to talk me outta it ----but I turned that shit off and unscrewed the top off that Gordon's Gin.

Tinia looked at me like I was crazy, before she asked, "What're you doin' ----- aren't we gon' pack that shit up, first?"

"Tsk! I did that shit last night, Gurl. Now get me a glass, and stop trippin'."

"Here you go, I brought you a big one." She said as if that was suppose to comfort me. Shit ...... she wasn't even at ease, her damn self ----- the way her hands shook, too.

Nevertheless, I downed a nice stiff one, prior to swallowing three of the funny looking pills she brought. Then, I took another drink from the glass, before I ordered her, "Alright, now rip my top off, like you mad-as-hell."

She kicked off those damn high-heels she was wearing, gripped the top of my thin blouse and gave a little pussy-ass tug to it. Enough that she popped one of the buttons. "Damn Guurl, Don't'choo have som'um else you can put on that's a little easier to tear?"

The alcohol had started to take affect, at that point, so in a slightly slurred tone of voice, I piped, "Bitch, if you want that shit up there ------ you betta fuckin' act like it!!"

That huzzy narrowed her eyes at me, and gripped my shit, that time, like she meant business. All of the buttons went flying in different directions, and the weak seam of my left shoulder gave, as well. I smiled probably the way a drunk would. Because I was twisted by then, and feeling no pain!

"That's more like it." I said, "Now slap me a couple'a times, so I can get use to it."   She didn't hesitate ----- she slapped my head back-and-forth like I was that bitch who had sliced her with that razor.

"Could you feel it?" She asked.

I wiped at the dribble of blood at the corner of my mouth, before I said, "Not really. So let's stop fucking around. Put those things on and beat the shit outta me, Bitch! I don't care what I say or how much I cry ----- don't let up until I'm out cold and completely fucked up. You hear!!" I screamed and staggered around a little.

"If you say so."

She knew, after that, she was to load that shit up in the car, and get the hell outta there. Therefore, she tore into my ass, with what seemed like, no regrets. Plus, the bitch was landing them hay-makers upside my head and face, like she had mad skills. Especially when she cracked my damn ribs, on both sides of my body.

I was yelling my damn head off, pleading with her to stop ----- I couldn't take it no more. But do you think she payed me any mind?

Hell Naw!!

The most she did, at one point, was take her a breather, to catch her breath and take a few tokes of a smoke. But then, she laid that damn thing in the ashtray and punched me so hard in my eye, I saw stars with blood on each one of'em.

Then, the telephone rang, and I was one happy bitch. Because she decided to answer it. If for no other reason, than to take a few more drags off'a her cigarette before it burned out.

"Hello." I heard her crazy-ass say.

"Oh, she can't come to the phone, right now, Popcorn."

I was lying there thinking, 'You damn right, I can't. I'm too goddamn busy, counting all these knots on my damn head, face, and body -----   Plus, I'm bleeding like a slaughtered pig.'

335

"You wanna leave a message?"

I could barely see thru the swollen slits of my eyes. But for some reason, I saw the panic on her face, crystal-clear. I even saw her drop the telephone and race up the stairs. That was when my heart began to speed up. Because, I didn't know what was going on nor did I care. My eyes were heavy as shit, so I closed them. Yet, I still heard Tinia screaming at the top of her lungs, "OOH HELL NAW!!!", before I fell off the cliff, into a black sea of darkness........

CHAPTER 45

Popcorn

When I left the crib yesterday, I was confused as a muthafucka. Because, I wanted to believe that shit Peaches was kickin' about Yolonda, but sum'um unexplainable was preventin' a nigga from entertainin' that O'girl would do any of the cruddy-ass shit that my shautie was implyin'.

However, before Tiny had driven a full two blocks in the opposite direction from Yolonda's townhouse, I had quietly said, "Go back the otha way, Yo." Because, my Pops use to always say, whenever you're havin' a difficult time believin' your broad about som'um ----- just go wit the flow. If the shit proves otherwise, then you can put a straightnin' on that shit at that time. Besides, I knew that the main reason I wasn't tryin' to get wit that oke-doke rap Peaches was pushin' about Yolonda, was due to me strongly believin' that Yolonda was all out there ova a nigga. Therefore, in my mind, she wouldn't have dared brang me any moves, Peaches had said Carla stated.

Yet, one quick glance in Tiny's direction had told me that he was sold, emphatically, on everythan' my bun-bun had said. That's when I had known, even more, I had betta pull my head from between Yolonda's phat-ass and put some insurance on my shit.

Once Tiny and I walked up into that spare bedroom, and I saw that my bama had been violated, I had experienced a moment of paranoia. Then, I had gotten mad as a muthafucka that somebody had touched my shit without my muthafuckin' permission. Nevertheless, Tiny and I hustled those jaunts down to his whip, and drove straight ova to Julie's. After all, she had said that a brotha could 'do dat'.

So I did.

Later, I had called Yolonda, for two reasons. First to let her know that I had moved my work and   secondly,   I   had wanted to know who in the fuck had packed my shit up. I'm not gon' front, Yo. In the darkest corner of my mind, I had been hopin' that she was gonna tell me that it had been that insurance-man-lookin'-muthafucka that had stepped out there like that. 'Cause, I still had been searchin' for a reason to 'see that nigga', anyway.

So you can imagine how surprised I was that her sister had answered the telephone, instead of her. Plus, she had fed me some shit about O'girl bein' too busy to holla at a nigga. But I had decided not to trip about it. Because, at that stage of the game, my shit had been safe-and-sound in that big-ass safe my Pops use to bama his shit in, back in the days..........

Aroun' eleven o'clock, Tuesday mornin', Carla showed up at the apartment in Gilpen Court. I figured that Peaches had sent her around there to holla at me. Because I hadn't said anythin' else about that situation wit Yolonda, when I returned to the crib last night. In fact, she and I, we hardly kicked it at all. Which had been cool wit me, because I had had a lotta shit on my dome, anyway. That's why when Carla strolled up into the jaunt, wearin' hip-huggers, and a white top that was so sheer, I could see the chocolate tips of her breast ---- I was fo sho that Peaches had put her up to it.

Especially when she said, "Popcorn, did Peaches tell you what I said?" I looked a little confused, just to fuck wit her dome. So she added, "You know, 'bout Tre?"

"Yeah, she pulled a nigga up." I said, before addin', "When he get back at'cha, ask'em I said, what'sup." I knew he would know I was referrin' to my shit, just like the twins, who were standing behind Carla, knew it too.

Apparently, she knew it, as well, because she turned up the corners of her mouth, and said, "You can ask'em, yourself. "Cause he got out this mornin'."

"Where he at?" I promptly asked, from thinkin' I should've been the first muthafucka that nigga was tryin' to get at.

She started examinin' her fingernails, while she said, "I'on know ----- and I'on care eitha. 'Cause it's like I told Peaches, I ain't feelin' that shit he talkin' 'bout doin'." She had the nerve to look down at my joint, in a obvious sort of way, before she said, "I ain't feelin' his ass eitha."

At that point, it was clear that Peaches hadn't sent her as I had thought ------- Baby was there to put her bid in. But that shit wasn't gon' happen. It didn't matter that she had the kind of looks that told a nigga that she was a straight freak-a-leek. Or that that tongue ring she was flashin', would probably have a nigga caught out there from slidin' up-and-down a nigga's jaunt. In eitha case, that shit she was proposin was some straight triflin' ass shit, fo'real, Yo. That's why I said, "You gotta back the fuck up off me, Shautie, wit that bullshit. 'Cause, I'on get down like that, Yo."

I knew she was offended, because she got straight on the defensive wit a nigga. "Oh so you tryin' to tell a bitch you don't like what'choo see?" She was still standin' up, so she did a smooth turn so that her phat-ass was right directly in my face.

"I didn't say that, Yo. I'm just sayin' that I don't fuck aroun' on my Shautie, that's all." I held a straight face, but that scene wit Dovia was runnin' all thru my mind.

I saw the devil, himself, bein' reflected from her eyes as she said, "Too bad Peaches don't feel the same way 'bout ya'lls relationship, as you do."

"Is that right?" I said wit a smile on my face.

"That's right, 'cause her and Choo -------"

"YO CARLA!!!" I shouted above her pitch. "You outta pocket, Shautie. I didn't ask you none of dat so step off, 'cause this conversation is ova!"

"But ...." She tried to repair the damage.

I wasn't tryin' to hear anymo' of her shit, though. I looked in the direction of the twins. And ' right-off- the-bat' her feet were off the ground and she was bein' muscled up out there like she had failed an audition for the mob. On a lotta levels, she had. After all, what was she good fo'. She didn't know what loyalty was as a friend or companion. Fo sho, what that nigga Tre was plottin' on doin' was fucked-up and didn't deserve nobody's respect. But Peaches hadn't don' anythin' but be a good friend to her ass. So regardless of what, she didn't deserve for Carla to be tryin' to get at her man.

Or straight settin' her out.

But she had. What's more, I had heard that shit, loud and Clear..........

340

CHAPTER 46

Choo-Choo

"Where your Moms at Shautie?" I asked a evil lookin' lil.' bitch, that couldn't have been no mo than twelve or thirteen. Yet, she had her damn lips twisted like she had a beef wit the whole damn world, or sum'um.

"She's back in the kitchen ----- why! What'choo want wit her?"

I was standin' there thinkin', 'Who the fuck did this lil' mufuckin' ho think she was talkin' to?', right when a olda broad came up behin' where shautie was standin', callin' herself blockin' the door. The first thang I noticed about Moms, was that babygirl had some of the most serious mufuckin' eyes I eva saw. Those jaunts seemed as though they were lookin' right thru a mufucka when she said, "Who you lookin' for, my son?"

"Yeah, is he here?" I flung back at her ass wit a penetratin' look of my own.

"He don't live here." That lil' pint-size broad butted-in.

"You must don't know'em. 'Cause if you did, you wouldn't be lookin' for'em."

Good point.

Still, I had taken all that I was gon' take from her mufuckin' grown-ass. So, and to both their surprise, I back handed her lil' frail-ass, so hard, she fell backwards into her Moms, and almost knocked them both down. After that, I stepped inside the crib wit lightnin' speed, and slammed the mufuckin' door behind me, before I said, "That mufucka don't know me, eitha!" I heard a sound to my right, so my head snapped into that direction. I was relieved like a mufucka to spot anotha lil' tiny bitch posted-up on the sofa wit her barefeet tucked under her ----- lookin' scared as shit. Like always, that shit gave me a mufuckin' rise.

Yet, I kept my mufuckin' cool and stayed focused on the main reason I was there. That's why I barked at the two that was huggin' each otha and shakin' wit fear, "Both ya'll get your stankin' ass in that mufuckin' room. Right now!!" I shouted, when it appeared they was draggin' they ass.

"But what on earth do you want?" Momdukes asked, like she was hopin' I whatn't gon' rape her stankin' ass.

"My mufuckin' ends, Bitch!!"

"Ends, what the devil's that??" She asked, with her mufuckin' voice quiverin'.

"He means money, Mama." The lil one that I had slapped already, said. Then she rolled her mufuckin' eyes at me, while she wiped blood from her nose and mouth. That's when I got tired of slow walkin' that shit. I pulled my Beretta, and snatched that lil' bitch from Momdukes grip. I smashed the barrel of that jaunt right at the base of shautie's skull and shouted, "I'ma smoke this lil stankin' bitch if you don't call that nigga and tell'em I want' my mufuckin' ends-right now!!

The lil' Shautie had lost all her mufuckin' heart, at that point. In fact, she had started to cry and whimper, while her Moms stood huggin' the otha lil' broad, and pleaded, "Don't hurt her ----- please!!"

I was in love wit those mufuckin' eyes of Momdukes, but that shit didn't stop a nigga from tightenin' his grip on Shautie's shirt, and yellin' back, "I won't my mufuckin' ends, Bitch!!! You betta call'em or I'ma dump all in her mufuckin' dome!"

"I got money ---- you can have all of it! Just don't hurt my baby."

"Take your stankin' ass and get that then ---- hurry up!!" I barked.

I watched her run her old ass up them damn steps like she was a teenager or sum'um. That shit made me wonder if O'girl had that kinda energy in bed. But I couldn't enjoy my thoughts 'bout Momdukes, to the fullest. Because that otha lil' bitch who had been holdin' on to the Moms, was cryin' and whimperin' right in tune wit that lil' trick I was still holdin' on to. That shit was erkin' the fuck outta me. So I barked, "Shut that mufuckin' noise up!"

It was a good mufuckin' thang that O'girl came runnin' back down them steps, 'cause I might've slumped both those lil' bitches.

"Here you go ----- that's all of it!" She said, after handin' a nigga a hat box full of dough.

I had shoved the lil' shautie toward the otha one, before I took that jaunt. 'Cause seein' all that grip had put a mufucka in a good mood. I knew it was ova a hunnet Gs, enough to make up fo that shit of mine Popcorn and 'em had gorilla'd Tree-Top for. So in my mind, his debt had been collected. As far as the aftamath that might come from violatin' that nigga's family -----

he could brang it. That's why I told his Moms, who was bear huggin' her daughters and still puffin' and puffin', 'You can tell that nigga that I was here, and if he fuck wit my mufuckin' shit, again   I ain't gon' be so mufuckin' nice the next time."

I turned and walked out that bitch. I wasn't the least bit worried 'bout Popcorn ------ that nigga was a coward. The fact that I heard his Moms tellin' his sistas not to tell'em anythan' 'bout what I had jus' don', proved that she knew he was a stunna, too..........

CHAPTER 47

Yolanda

"Oh God ------ please help me!" I shouted out from my bed, where I was lying with my head and upper body bandaged tight as shit. No one was in my house, but me. I just needed to scream out my pain. Because every inch of my head, face, and body was aching like I never knew a person could hurt. That bitch, Tinia, had beaten the living daylights out of me.

Just like I had told her to.

It was almost funny to me, at that moment, that Popcorn had out-foxed us both.

I didn't wanna face it, but I knew part of the reason why things had turned out like they had. It was because I tried to do some grimey shit. Popcorn had been good to me. He didn't deserve none of what I had done, or what I had been trying to do. Thinking about it as I laid there staring out thru the swollen slits of my eyes, had me feeling like taking my own life.

But those thoughts were interrupted by the sound of someone walking up my stairs. So I shouted, in spite of my pain, "Who is it??"

"Jus' me, Gurl!" My sister prompted as she walked into the bedroom.

I couldn't believe that she had asked me some stupid-ass shit like that. Because how did she expect a bitch to feel after that vicious ass whuppin she had served me. If I didn't know any betta, I would've swore that she enjoyed landing those blows the night before. But I swallowed my anger and suspicion. Because no matter how I looked at it, I needed her at that point more than I ever had in life. Therefore, I said, "Not too good."

"Aaaah .... Poor baby." That hooker had the nerve to say 'Let me handle this bizness wit Tre, right quick. And then, I'ma come straight back ova here and nurse you ----- okay! "

I gave her the best smile I could give with swollen lips, and said, "Kay!" Because it sounded nice that she was going to be there with me. Plus, that she was selling one of the three bricks of cocaine we still had left.

"Where that stuff at?" She asked and started smacking on some damn chewing gum as though she knew it was getting on my nerves ----- but didn't give a fuck!

"In that black bag on the shelf in the closet, right there." I said, indicating the one in my bedroom.

She started walking toward it, right when we both heard a loud explosion of metal against wood. In fact, it sounded like something had tore out all the walls on my first floor. That shit caused me to sit straight up in bed, and forget all the excruciating pain I felt.

"What the hell was that?" Tinia said, with her eyes the size of saucers.

"Call 911!!" I shouted at her. I heard footfalls coming up the steps, so I screamed, "Hurry up!!!!"

Yet, before Tinia could take a full step toward the telephone, the Feds came storming into the room. They had their pistols drawn, and trained on both of us, as they ordered, "Get down on the floor ------ now!!!"

I watched thru the slits of my puffed-up-eyes, my sister, as she layed down with her hands extended out from her body. So, I raised mine, too. But all the while, I was saying to myself, *'What the hell have I gotten myself into ......'*

CHAPTER 48

I ain't gon' front, that shit that Carla had kicked about Peaches fuckin' wit that nigga, Choo-Choo, had fucked wit my head, all muthafuckin' day. But not to the point of me rushin' to the crib and diggin' in Peaches shit about it. I didn't wanna play myself out like that. I knew I needed time to get shit clear in my dome before I stepped to her for some understandin'. Because I really needed to know what kind of games she was playin'.

Did she know she was gamblin' wit her life?

Because, that's where my head was at. How could it not have? I Broke her off a piece of some straight fabulous shit, and promised the best was yet to come. Only to discover that she had been playin' the O'boy like a straight sucka.

'Damn!'

At that moment, Tiny and I were cruisin' Lee Street toward the Townhouse. We hadn't been raisin' a whole lotta hell, so I was just gon' lay it down at the crib and get in my girl's dome. 'Cause, more than eva, I needed to know where she was that night I got oiled-up.

I got outta Tiny's Jeep and said thru the open window, "I'ma holla back at'cha, Fam."

"Yeah, auight. But I'ma ride aroun' sum'mo to see if I can catch that nigga, Tre." He was grillin' as he said it.

Therefore, "I fixed my grill, as well, before sayin', "That's cool, Yo ----- but don't fuck wit' em til you hit me first.'

I slammed the truck door, and trooped for the front door of the Crib. When I walked in and shut that jaunt, I was startled by the sight of Peaches and Rainy sittin' on the sofa huggin' each otha. Plus, there was som'um highlightin' their features that I didn't catch, at first.

Fear.

That's why I rattled out, "that the fuck is goin' on, Yo? Why you ova here, Rainy?" Before she had answered eitha of those questions, I had gotten close enough that I saw that her upper lip was swollen. So I barked like a two-hunnet-pound Bull--Masstif, "Fuck happen to your lip, Yo!!"

She still had her arms locked around Peaches, when she said, "That man that came to our house lookin' fo' you hit me." The top of my head was blazin' like a furnace. Because I just wanted to know who in their right mind would put their muthafuckin' hands on my sister ----- for any reason. I didn't intend to, but I screamed at her, "WHAT'S HIS GODDAMN NAME!!!"

"Popcorn, please ---- don't upset her more than she already' is." Peaches said, and it made sense.

But fo'real, Yo, I wasn't tryin' to hear shit outta Peaches' mouth. Not until she answered my questions.

Besides, Rainy didn't look like she was upset. In fact, she looked vengeful as hell, as she said, "All I know is, he was big and black and mean lookin'. He slapped me wit his rough-ass hands and made my mouth and nose bleed." She saw me snatch out my two-way and hit the twins, and I used my cell to call Tiny's ass back to the crib. But none of that stopped her from settin' that nigga's ass, all the way out. "He put his gun at the back of my head and told Mama to take her stankin' ass upstairs to get all her ends, or he was gonna smoke my lil' stankin' ass. Plus, [sniff!!] he called Mama, Precious, and me a lotta bitches."

"How you get ova here ----- is Mama and' em auight??"

She shook her head up-and-down vigorously, before sayin', "Yeah, she's betta than she was when he first left."

"How you get ova here?" I repeated.

She let Peaches stroke her pretty hair, before she said, "I ran all the way ----- I was scared. That man told us, if you fuck wit his shit again, he was gon' kill all us. Mama told us not to say nothin' to you about it, 'cause she afraid you gon' get trouble. But I couldn't keep sum'um like that from you Popcorn ----- that man was crazy!!!" She said with her eyes wide open. "Did I do the right thang, Popcorn ----- didn't'choo wanna know?"

The doorbell rang. I opened the door and saw Tiny standin' out on the stoop, lookin' crazy as hell. At first I thought he already knew what Choo-Choo had done to my Moms and lil' shauties, until he opened his mouth and said, "Looks like O'boy sent them folks at'cha girl, fo'real. 'Cause I just rode by there, and they deep as a muthafucka at her jaunt."

"I ain't got time fo' that shit right now, Fam ---- that nigga Choo-Choo don' violated my Moms and'em. So, I gots to sce that niggga, befo' the sun comes up."

I was expectin' that that fool to start grittin' even more.

But, and I should've been hip to his ass, by than ----- he started smilin' instead. Then he said, "I bet I know exactly where his ass at, too. So let's do dat!"

I stepped back inside and told Peaches, "Take Shautie home."

"Ok." She said. But she had some questions of her own in her eyes about us.

I saw them, clear as day.

But I turned and peeled out. There would be time fo dat'shit, afta I handled my business. That's why I got'up into Tiny's jaunt and said, "I told the twins to meet us at the apartment."

He looked at me like I was crazy, befo' he said, "Fo what??" Like their presence was gonna jack off his groove.

I didn't answer'em. I only said, "But go by that jaunt where I store my equipment at, first."

He didn't respond. We rode in complete silence for about fifteen seconds. Then he started whistlin' that whacked-out-shit I had never heard before. But after a few moments, shit --------- that joint started soundin' nice as shit ....

CHAPTER 49

Choo-Choo

"You did what!!" My connect shouted like a mufucka was tellin' him they fucked his Moms or sum'um.

"Ain't nothin' to worry 'bout, that nigga a straight-bitch. "I said, hopin' that shit would calm'em down.

But it didn't.

That mufucka got up out his seat and walked around his desk to where a nigga was squattin' and bitch-slapped the mufuckin' shit outta me. I ain't gon' front, that shit hurt my mufuckin' pride. That mufucka had been like a father to me ----- and was one of the only mufuckas in that city that I admired and respected. But I wasn't gon' let'em carry me like I was a ho or sum'um. That's why when he tried to backhand my mufuckin' face, again, I caught and locked his wrist like a mufuckin' vice, that time, and said, "Mr. Cool, you try that shit one mo time, I'ma fo'get how much I dig your mufuckin' ass ---- and break your ole-ass up!"

No sooner than I had spitted that threatnin' remark to the O.G, did I hear the loud undeniable click of a burner, befo' I felt the barrel of that bitch press against the back of my mufuckin' dome. The fist thought that jumped in my head was, "Ooh shit!! These old mufuckas gon' slay my ass up in here.'

But Mr. Cool said to his mans, "Hold fast Chubby, he didn't mean what he just said." Then, he leaned down toward my face wit a smile on his mug and a unlit cigar stuck between his lips, and asked wit a buttery voice, "Did you?"

"No sir, Mr. Cool, a mufucka would neva do nothin' to hurt'cha."

"That's what I thought?" He said, befo' he hauled off and slapped the goddamn shit outta a mufucka, again.

Only that time, I held my composure, and my tongue. 'Cause those O.G's had the ups on a mufucka. But on all I love, I was gon' get at they mufuckin' asses. Wasn't no mufucka gon' treat me like a bitch and get away wit it.

He stood in front of a nigga and stared down at me. Once he was satisfied that I wasn't gon' jump out there again, he walked back around and squatted behind his desk, and said, "Now here's what you gotta do. He paused and rolled that mfuckin' cigar aroun' on his lips, befo' he went on and said, "The same thang I had done to his father, and what you had done to his brother ----- you got to pay a nigga to take Popcorn out."

I hoped I wasn't lookin' at that mufucka like he was crazy, 'cause that's exactly what I was thinkin' ----- that he was whacked the fuck out. After all, I had already tried that contract killin' shit, and those mufuckas was fakin'. This time, I was gon' put in my own work, like I had been doin'. But Mr. Cool was gon' find out, soon enough. Him and that albino-lookin' mufucka that stood behind me. Still I lied, "Ok, Mr. Cool, I'ma get right on it."

"In the meantime, make sure you lay low, because that stupid shit you done today could have that nigga out gunning as we speak." He was thoughtful lookin' for a moment, then he said, "If you continue to do what I say ----- the way I tell you to, you gonna be sittin' where I now sit, one day, passin' the game to a youngen." He must could tell I wasn't feelin' non'of dat shit he was talkin', 'cause he took that fat-ass cigar outta his mouth and pointed that jaunt at me as he said, "Don't get it fucked-up, young nigga ----- no matter how much money you make, and how successful you might become, you'll always be in the game. He leaned back in his chair, and asked, "You know why?"

I played along wit his mufuckin' game. Why?"

"Because…....you just like me. You love power, Muthafucka. Now get the fuck out my face!"

I got the fuck up, as he ordered. But only because I was just anxious to get the fuck outta there, as he sounded like he wanted a mufucka to be gon'. Yet, when I looked ova at all those mufuckin' bottles of alcohol on that shelf behind him, I knew I wasn't goin' no mufuckin' where to 'lay-low'. 'Cause I was goin' ova to my mans and get me a mufuckin' gin and juice.

Chubby was posted at the door. I couldn't resist fuckin' his dome, by sayin', "Goddamn, Unc, was you gon' slump yo favorite nephew?" Don't get it twisted, though, I was cheesin' when I said it.

He smiled, too. But fo' only three mufuckin' seconds, then it seemed like that mufucka was lookin' at me like he didn't see me no mo'. And fo'real, that shit shook a nigga. I tried not to show it. Because I pulled out the cigar Mr. Cool had given me when I first got there, like he always done ---- lit that bitch, and got the hell up outta there…………..

CHAPTER 50

Yolanda

Tinia and I were sitting on the sofa. She was hugging me like she was trying to protect me from the world. I loved her for that, because she had shown nothing but pure strength the whole time the Feds had busted into my house. Yet, what surprised me the most was when a pale-looking muthafucka walked down the stairs with the black bag that contained those three kilos of cocain. Tinia had promptly turned toward the one that appeared to be in charge, and made clear, "That's my shit!"

"You expect us to believe that?" The Charge-Agent said.

"I don't care if you believe it or not ---- it's the truth! Ask

O'boy. He know I get my shit from a balla up-top." She wetted her lips after that, just to flash that damn tongue ring, I'm sure.

"What is it doing up in her closet, than?" He looked at me, and I lowered my swollen eyes.

"'Cause I put it there ----- duh!! " Tinia said.

"Well, you gotta tell that to the judge. Because, both of ya'll are bein' charged with Conspiracy and Possession with the Intent."

I was shaking so hard after that, I thoughtt my bones were gonna start rattling. I didn't want to go no where near a jail cell. But who could I blame?

Nobody but myself.

The Charge Officer looked at me and must've felt he had me spooked well enough to say, "Unless ya'll can give us the big fish."

"Oh hell naw, muthafucka ----- you talkin' to the wrong bitches for kinda shit. That nigga will slaughter my ass and feed me to those big-ass dogs he got." But then, Tinia crossed her legs like a frishy ho would do, and said, "But if ya'll want som'um else, I'll be glad to accomodate you, anytime you want.

O'boy started fumbling with the knot of his tie, and turned beet-red, before he told the pale-looking agent to cuff Tinia and take her on out to a car. Then he swerved his attention to me, "What about you, Ms. Franks, you haven't said anything all evening. Do you want to help yourself, by helping us?"

I swear, I didn't know what had gotten into me at that moment, but before I could comprehend what it was I was doing, my head was nodding up-and--own like I was eager as hell to help them.

That made that muthafucka happy, to see that I was weak and ready and willing to do his goddamn job for him. He even slid to the edge of the chair he was sitting on, and said, "Ok now, I need a name. If you can give me that and a promise that you'll help us up, I won't take you in."

I felt tears swell and spill from my puffy- -eyes. I didn't care how I looked, at that moment. Because I was hurting inside, and I needed to let it out. That man wanted me to snitch on someone whom I had forgotten how much I loved, until that very second. It was too hard for me to bear, and far too difficult for me to do.

But I didn't want to go to jail.

Therefore, I sat up straight with a determinate look plastered on my face, and said, "His name is Patrick Williams. And yes, I will be more than glad to help ya'll set'em up." I lied on my fuck buddy.

It was about five agents standing around in my front room, at that time. When they heard me say that, it looked like they were ready to start high-fiving each other, but they fought to maintain their composure. The one in charge did stand up, however, and said, "Alright than Ms. Franks. You just gave yourself a get-out-of-jail--free card. We'll be in touch, in the next day or two. Until then," He handed me a card. "If he shows up before than, give us a call and let us know what's going on. Ok!"

Again, I shook my head in response.

As soon as they left, I went straight up stairs and ran a full tub of bath-water. I wrote out a note to Popcorn. I even said a prayer asking for forgiveness. Then, believing I had no choice.... I cut both muthafucking wrist and slid down into the soothing warm water.........

CHAPTER 51

Popcorn

I was posted on the wooden steps that lead up to that crap jaunt that Tiny had felt Choo-Choo would be at. But he wasn't. Still, I decided to post-up at that blickie, just to see if O'boy would eventually come thru. I had been layin' for ova thirty minutes, and was beginnin' to feel that perhaps that nigga had taken his ass straight home ----- after he violated my Moms and robbed her for her dough.

That is, until I finally looked up and saw that nigga's Lex glide up to the curb and park. I glanced up-and-down the block. It was only about ten forty-five at night, but the avenue was quiet and dark and devoid of any movement whatsoeva.

I was quite certain that that muthafucka recognized who I was. But just to be fo'sho that he knew, I stood the fuck up and gritted in a way that told that fool, I was fittin' to be his worst muthafuckin' nightmare…….

◆◆◆◆◆◆◆◆◆◆◆◆◆◆◆◆◆◆◆◆◆◆

Choo-Choo

'Will you look at this mufuckin' shit. That bitch-ass nigga scopin' a mufucka like he want some mufuckin' drama'. That's what a nigga was thinkin' as I took a nice long toke of that mufuckin' cigar, my mans, Mr. Cool gave a mufucka. Then I smiled at that nigga, Popcorn, 'cause 1. was gon' tear his mufuckin' ass up.

To prove just how serious a mufucka was 'bout skinnin' his ass up, when I got out my mufuckin' whip ------ I slammed my mufuckin' door so hard, I was half expectin' the glass to shatter in that jaunt. But I wasn't stuttin' that shit ------- I was seein' nothin' but that nigga's blood.

I kept my mufuckin' stogey clinched in my grill, as I strolled up and stood 'bout ten feet facin' his ass. He didn't have a burner in his hand, and that surprised the shit outta me.

So I didn't whup my joint. Instead, I almost laughed out loud at the thought of that nigga thinkin' that he could get in my bizness without sum' mufuckin' heat. But that jaunt got caught in my mufuckin' throat, once I looked down and saw three mufuckin' infra-red beams dancin' on my chest. The first thang I thought was, 'A mufucka!!'

Then, I saw those otha cats come from each side of that crib O'boy was posted in front of. They didn't try to walk up close to a nigga, they kept they distance wit those kingsize jaunts locked in on me. But I wasn't gon' bitch-up like a lotta niggas would've done. I held my own, and said, "What'chall hos gon' do?"

"You know what it is, Yo.", that nigga Popcorn said.

I dragged my mufuckin' cigar and said, "Whateva you do, Mufucka, ain't gon' change nothin'." I blew out a rack of smoke, and added, "It ain't gon' change the fact that a mufucka don' freaked your mufuckin' ho, while my niggas was bangin' on you and your peeps. It ain't gon' change the fact that me and my connect was just kickin' it 'bout how he had the same mufuckin' thang don' to your bitch-ass Pops. Or that your Mom's phat-ass got my mufuckin' man hard ----- her and your li'l sisters, Mufucka!"

I got my shit off, good. Yet, he puzzled the shit outta me, 'cause that mufucka only smiled and said, "I ain't tryin' to change none of dat, Yo. But you can't change the fact that your muthafuckin' ass, belongs to me now." He then looked at the twins, who's eyes appeared to be red as fire, and ordered them mufuckas, "Pin that nigga to the ground, Yo!!"

I thought to myself *'Shhhit!!'* 'Cause, in my mufuckin' mind, I was gon' dust off both they asses. Bein' I figured that they was gon' try circlin' a mufucka, and brang it to a nigga real slow. But I had it twisted.

Them mufuckas charged my mufuckin' ass like twin freight trains. Only, one of'em hit my ass up high, and the otha tried to break my mufuckin' legs. But what took all my fight game was, them niggas started bitin' and chewin' on my mufuckin' ass like they were a pack of angry ass dogs…….

◆◆◆◆◆◆◆◆◆◆◆◆◆◆◆◆◆◆◆◆◆◆◆◆

Popcorn

I stood there wit Tiny at my side, and watched the twins tear that nigga's ass all to pieces. I had seen in Choo-Choo's eyes that he thought he stood a chance wit those two brothas 'cause he out-weighed each of'em by 'bout sixty muthafuckin' pounds. But what he didn't know was that they been tastin' his ass since that night of the shootin'.

And so had Tiny.

Because, as soon as Donnell and Donte had Choo-Choo pinned to the ground and blood runnin' like a bloody pussy,

Tiny walked back aroun' to the side of the crib. When he returned, he was draggin' the long handled axe that I scooped from my storage jaunt. He walked ova to where O'boy was lyin', spent of all energy. He looked ova at me.

On err-y-thing I love, Yo, I wanted to slump that nigga, Choo-Choo, myself, Yo. But one quick glance at that shit-bag that was bulging from under my mans shirt, and rememberin' just how much Silk had meant to Tiny, prompted me to nod at'em as I said, "Do you, Fam --------- do you!"

And he did.

He started whistlin' and smilin' and swingin' that jaunt like Choo-Choo's big black ass was the trunk of a tree that he was intent on choppin' into chunks of firewood. I never knew that a muthafucka could scream and sound like raw thunder, until the sharp blade of that axe separated that nigga, Choo's big-ass feet from his ankles. But his howlin' didn't mean a thang to Tiny ----- his smile just got brighter, and the tune he was blowin' seemed that much more bizarre. Especially when, after choppin' every limb from that nigga's body, he gave a mighty swing and tore away Choo-Choo's muthafuckin' dome.......

CHAPTER 52

Popcorn

I walked into the bedroom. Peaches was lying on top of the covers, wide awake. I was tired, completely exhausted as I squatted on the side of that joint. But my heart felt like it was cryin', also, when I turned and looked Shautie in her mug and said, "You know shit is all fucked up 'tween us, don't'choo, Yo?"

I wanted to turn away from her, because her plead for forgiveness was alive like a muthafucka, in her eyes. That shit was makin' my soul crumble, 'cause I knew I still loved her. But at that point in time, my feelin's for her, were irrelevant.

I was glad that she didn't try to insult my muthafuckin' intelligence by fakin' like she didn't know what a nigga was talkin' 'bout. I even respected that she held my gaze and said,

"Yes, I know." Then, she placed her hands ova her face like she was tryin' her best to hold back the flow of tears, but they flowed anyway, as she said, 'I fucked-up......I made a terrible mistake by not tellin' you about it, when I had the chance that night we talked."

"Fo' sho', Yo. If you hadda told me everythang, yourself, instead of me hearin' shit from your friend and that nigga ----   it might've made a difference. But now," I shook my head a little, "All of this shit don' destroyed a nigga's trust and belief in you"

"But do you still love me?" She asked as though that was supposed to be the magical solution to solvin' our problem.

"No doubt, Yo." I made clear. Fo' me, that was no time to play games. "But you see Shautie, love ain't got a muthafuckin' thang to do wit it. Because, you was lovin' a nigga when you went behind my back and freaked wit O'boy. You was lovin' a nigga when you chose to keep all that shit from me. And I know that'choo love a nigga, now. Even though you know I would have to be a goddamn fool to spend anotha night in your world ------- wit'choo afta what that nigga did to my Moms and 'em."

Her tears were thick and glistenin' on her cheeks, as she said, "Popcorn, pieeez, Babee, jus' give me one mo' chance. I won't eva let you down again. I promise!!"

I ain't gon' front, Yo, there's a part of me that wanted to get wit dat. But there was a greater part that was tellin' me I couldn't afford to take that chance. I stood up befo' I said, 'I still care 'bout your and Tondra's well-bein', so I'ma look out as far as leavin' enough dough in that bank account for you to take your shit to the next level. You just gotta do it wit out me."

I turned to leave, but she stopped me in my tracks when she said, "Wait if we try, we can get pass it, Popcorn. Because, we jumped off that cliff, together ------ remember!"

I turned partially aroun' and said, "Yeah, I remember, Yo. But the way I feel right now, we could've jumped off the

366

muthafuckin' world, togetha, and that wouldn't stop a nigga from steppin' up out'chere."

I walked out that room, out the front door, and completely outta Shautie's life...............

CHAPTER 53

Popcorn

When I left Peaches last night, I chilled at Momedukes. She never said anything about that shit wit Choo-Choo, but she saw it in my grill that that nigga was slumped somewhere dead and stankin' when I walked in her joint and told'er that I would be crashin' there fo' a few days. Nor did she ask my reason for bein' there.

Neither did Rainy or Precious.

They all were just glad to have me around.

On a lotta levels, I was glad to be there wit'em after what they had been thru. And fo sho, I felt lucky as shit that none of'em got seriously hurt by that episode wit that fool.

The next mornin' afta a huge-ass breakfast my Moms hooked up for me, my two lil'shauties, and the twins, my homies and I jetted straight down in Gilpen Court to the apartment. At first, shit was slow motion, like a muthafucka. But then, that aftanoon, erry-thang started poppin'. Toi lead off wit about six different phone calls 'bout niggas that was tryin' to plug wit a nigga. Apparently, word had got out that Choo-Choo was slumped and floatin' in the James River, wit Smokey, Tree-Top and his Moms. Plus, accordin' to the twins ---- Tre was swimmin' wit the fishes, too.

In eitha case, the twins got at all those knuckle heads Toi had lined up ------ gave'em the spill, and set it out. Why not ---- I was goin' for the gold!

Behind that, I got a call from Toni informin' me that the guy she had spoken about to Peaches, who was into Construction and Development, wanted to meet wit me. She said from her investigation into his affairs, the nigga's credentials were impeccable. It was like she had said, at first, he had merely spreaded himself a little to thin. Therefore, a nigga could become his partna for eight hunnet and fitty Gs. That is, if I was interested.

Picture that!

You muthafuckin' right I was. Yet I said, "That shit sound good, Yo. But I gotta tell you this, so you'll know. Peaches and I are chillin'. So you might not want that shit to go down wit O' boy and me ---------   I' ma let that be your call, Yo. Eitha way, I ain't got nothin' but mad love fo ya."

She was quiet on her end for a second, then she said, "I'm sorry to hear that. I personally think it's a tragedy, because I feel that the two of you are sooo perfect for each other. But that's something that's between you and my sister ----- it has nothing whatsoever, to do with business. So I'll set up a meeting next week, and we'll go from there. Ok!"

"Fo sho!" I replied wit a smile.

Shortly after that call from Toni, Carla walked into the apartment, smilin' like that shit yesterday, never happened. Shautie was lookin' good, too. But still, I couldn't go out like that. That's why I had my grill set in stone when I asked, "What'choo wont Yo?"

"You so crazy, Popcorn. Stop trippin'!!" She snapped, "A bitch heard what'choo said yesterday, Boye. I just came around here to tell you, I think sum' um happened to Tre. They found his car shot-up, wit blood all ova the seat."

"Oh yeah." I said. But she saw what she wanted to see, standin' tall in my eyes.

That's why she tried to cover it up by sayin', "But I know you ain't have nothin' to do wit it. They haven't found his body yet, but they sho he's probably somewhere slumped."I didn't respond that time, so she went on to say, "Anyway, I'm still. sittin' on sum' of dat stuff he had of your's. You can send somebody aroun' there to get it anytime you want."

I knew O'girl was hopin' that I showed up my damn self to get it ---------- and what she had packed in those tight-ass jeans she was flossin'. But I didn't bust her bubble. I just smiled and "Good lookin' out, Yo. I'ma do dat."

She turned and threw that phat-ass all ova the front room I was chillin' in, as she strutted toward the door. Yet, when her hand touched the knob, she spun back around, and said, "Oh yeah, you know that dirty bastard took and set that female up --- and her sista."

Ouch!

That shit hurt, all ova again. That Yolonda had carried a nigga greasy, especially when I thought of how good I had been to her. And how I had thought she had the same kind of feelin's for me, that I had for her. I guess that shit proved even more that feelin's and love and friendship, jus' didn't mean a muthafuckin' thang to most people.

But I ain't gon' front, I still was thinkin' 'bout clockin' both those bitches a top-flight mouthpiece. But only because that was the kinda nigga I was. Carla iced all that shit, though, when she said, "Too bad the youngest one killed herself.

Because they might've beat that shit, now that Tre's gon'." She eased on out the door.

I was too stunned to move. It had never crossed my mind that Yolonda would do something like that. But then, when I really, really thought about it, Yo ----- what choice did she have?

None.

That's why I got the fuck up off that sofa, wiped that shit from my mind, and kept right on handlin' my business.........

CHAPTER 54

Yolonda was buried on Saturday. The sky was full of gray clouds that made that occasion appear that much more sadder and blue. At least, for me it did. Fo sho, Babygirl had violated a nigga, for no otha reason, than greed. Therefore, in my mind, she shitted on our friendship and tore my heart apart in ways that only someone whom I had thought I could trust, could do. Yet, as I wal.ked away from the hole she was lowered into, wit all the other mourners, I knew in the deepest recesses of my soul, was gonna miss Shautie, alot. That knowledge, along wit the continual ache I felt for Peaches, had a niga feelin' fucked-up.

Fo'real, Yo.

Perhaps that was the reason, once I got in the back seat of Donnell's Jeep, I told'em to take me down to Blends. I felt I needed to kick it wit the O.G., Mr. Cool.

"What'sup Chubby!" I said as soon as I walked into the shop. "Mr. Cool in?"

He looked at the twins, and then back at me, before he said, "Yeah, Young Prince, he back there."

I didn't give'em the chance to tell me that the twins couldn't go in the back, because I promptly said, "Ya'll chill out." Then, I walked on back thru the beaded curtains. I cursed myself for not rememberin' to brang that twenty grand wit me, but I made a mental note to do it next week. Nonetheless, I stood in the doorway of Mr. Cool's office and waited like I always don'. "What'sup Mr. Cool ----- you got a minute?"

He was scribblin' on a pad, but he sat that jaunt to the side and said, "Sure, come on in, Young Prince, and have a seat."

I squatted and. said, "I hope I ain't interruptin.' anythang'," "Of course not!" He replied while taking a cigar out of his cigar box. "What' s wrong?"

"Jus' a lotta crazy shit, Yo."

He smiled and shook his cigar at me, as he said, "So you havin' female problems then, right?"

He read the O'boy like a book. "Yeah, sort of. I don' had some fucked-up shit to happen to me, afta I put my faith and belief in two different broads. I remember my Pops tellin' me that sometimes, you gotta forgive they ass, even when you don't want to. Because, in the long run, it could be the best thang a nigga could eva do." But then, I leaned forward, before askin', "But what I wanna ask you, Mr. Cool, is how do a nigga know who to forgive ----- and who not to? 'Cause, that's the kinda shit that got me twisted."

Mr. Cool had a smile playin' on his lips, before he crammed that unlit cuban jaunt in the corner of his mouth, and said, "That's easy, Young Prince. You just gotta listen to your heart ----- and be mindful of the woman that'll try to speak it.

Not with her mouth, Young Playa, but with the sneaky-sweet-shit she'll do to try and win you back."

"I'm feelin' dat." I said while noddin' my approval.. Yet, somethin' else was tryin' to gain my attention, as I was watchin' him roll that funky jaunt around between his lips.

Then, it hit me like a thousand volts, and I almost bolted up out of the chair I sat in. It was what Choo-Choo had boasted about with that cigar in his mouth, that night befo' he got slayed......'me and my connect was just kickin' it 'bout how he had the same mufuckin' thang don' to your bitch-ass father.'

"You alright? Is it anything else I can help you with?" Mr. Cool asked, because I must've looked like I was starin' at my father's blood smeared all ova his hands.

"Nah, not not fo'real, Mr. Cool." I said, before addin', "It's just that my connect don' jacked his prices, sky high.

And I'm trying to find me a betta plug ---- that's all." I stood up afta that, because he was studying a nigga, and that shit made me feel uncomfortable as shit. That's why I went on to say, "Anyway, Yo, I'm not gonna take up no mo' of your time."

I was surprised, but I should've been, that he didn't bullshit aroun'. Instead, his eyes turned black as mud as he asked, "What kind of price you lookin' for?"

I knew him or no one else in the area could stand up to that eighteen thousand dollar ticket I was gettin' from my mans, so I kept it simple, by sayin', "Shit, I'll be cool if a nigga showed love at twenty-three, twenty-four, or som'um like dat."

He slow-twirled that cigar between his lips and said,"'I might be able to do something for you, Young Prince ------ jus' give me a few days."

I acted like I was grateful as shit, prior to me sayin', "But I thought'choo was retired from the game, Mr. Cool." He showed me his perfect white teeth, and said, "I am, but you know how the game goes."

"That told it all, Muthafucka!!" I barked, while pullin' Silk's knife and rushin' ova to where he sat.

At first, his eyes registered an utter and complete glow of shock. Then, that old muthafucka tried to fade a nigga, by reachin' for a jaunt he apparently kept under the center of his desk.

Yet, at that point, I didn't give a fuck if he had a army tank stored there, his ass was mine. I was fo sho he understood that shit, too. Especially when my first stab at his ass landed on the top of his shoulder blade, and forced his cool ass to screech like a oldhead bitch. Plus, he must've dropped whateva he had reached for, because his right hand came out from under that jaunt empty ------ as he tried to use it to block my next assault.

But picture that.

That muthafucka had had som'um to do wit my father gettin' slumped, and probably my brother, as well. Therefore, he could've used a steel plate to try and save'em self from my downward thrust wit that blade, and I'm fo' serious---- it wouldn't've done any muthafuckin' good.

Word, Yo!

Because I drove that joint thru his hand and skull, so far, the tip of it was protrudin' out the socket of his left eye. I backed up off his blood soaked ass, wit'em still screamin' and jerkin' aroun' in his chair. Then finally, he slumped forward and cried out no mo', Yo.

I stood there motionless for an instant, to savor the sweet taste of revenge. That is, until I heard the twins out front growlin' and diggin' in Chubby's ass. I smiled and picked up that sterlin' silver cigar box from Mr. Cool's desk, a bottle of that 'gnac' from the shelf, and rolled out ....

CHAPTER 55

Popcorn

The next week went by in a blur. I went to that meetin' wit O'boy that Toni lined up. She was there, also. And at the end of that jaunt, I walked outta there ---- legit as a muthafucka. Especially since my banker wired that eight hunnet plus to my mans business account, on the spot.

Afta that, I was feelin' so nice, I splurged a little on myself. Meanin', I copped one of those Chrysler 300M joints, and set that bitch on twenty-fours. I even went to Wallers Jewelers, down on Broad Street ----- and picked up some phat-ass ice for my lobes. I wasn't trying to raise no whole lotta hell, not until that business started blessin' a nigga. But I felt I was entitled to som' little kibbles-and-bit shit, until my legit bankroll started readin' otherwise.

Now, it was Saturday night. I drove up into the parkin' lot of 'After-Six', a classy night club in the fashionable section of Shockoe Bottom. Toi dropped by the apartment on Tuesday, and told us she was throwin' herself a birthday party. I wasn't tryin' to fuck wit no shit like that. But since she had rented that After Six jaunt and had been down fo' a niggga, I couldn't refuse her invitation.

Neitha could the rest of my 'click'.

Because, as soon as I parked and got out my new whip, I heard a whole rack of otha car doors openin'-and-closin', also. The parkin' area was huge and jam-packed wit nice shit. But still, I could see that it was errybody on my team who was raisin' up out them whips, too. That shit made a nigga feel special, fo'real Yo, that my peeps had been layin' fo' the O'boy.

I walked toward the entrance wearin' a mustard-colored Armani, white pin-stripped button down, and a pair of eeggshell white flays. Plus, my dome was tapered to the tee.

When I got to the glass doors, Donte opened that joint wit a perfect smile on his face. Inside the door I was greeted by a balla named Les from Highland Park, and anotha money getta named Ty Peete from Church Hill. All I could think was, Toi knew some good niggas.

Yet, once I got deeper up in that jaunt, my antennas went up, because first, I saw my moms and Julie standin' togetha smilin' at me. Then, I glanced my mans, Bay-Bay and Zesty doin' the exact same thang. That's when I thought, 'OH SHIT!!!' Because, I knew what was comin' next.

"SURPRISE!!!!" Everybody screamed. "Happy Birthday!!!"

My damn birthday was still ova a week away, but they had got a nigga the only way they could've. But no matter, I fed into that shit like a muthafucka, Yo, by sayin"This shit is beautiful, Yo!!"

Then came the hugs and kisses.

378

When I got to my mans, Bay-Bay, he said, "Happy Birthday, Dawg! Looks like the stunna set'choo out, Playa."

"She sure did." Zesty chimmed in, while holdin' onto his arm, and smilin'.

Toi was still huggin' me, so I said, "Peaches didn't do this shit, Yo ------ Shautie did."

Toi broke free and said, "Uhuh ------- no I did'n, Peaches don' all this, herself. She just asked me to give ya'll the invite and act like this joint was for me." Then she started smilin'.

Bullshit ain' t nothin', Yo.

When Peaches came struttin' toward a nigga wearin' a form fittin' mini dress, she copped at that Gucci jaunt down the way ---- and a pair of those Manolos, I began cheesin' my muthafuckin' self. Especially when she handed me a gift wrapped jaunt and said, "Happy Birthday, Babee." Then she kissed me lightly on the lips.

And I let'er.

Plus I said, "This is som' fabulous shit, Yo ---- thanks!"

I looked down at the gift and asked, "What's inside?"

She merely smiled and said, "One part of your gift."

"Oh yeah ----- well what's the otha part?" I figured she was kickin' it 'bout herself.

But she gave me 'that look', before she slowly turned her eyes in a direction across the room, and landed at a table where Dream was sittin' wit her legs crossed, starin' at us.

My smile was pure sunshine. Because if all of what she had don' was not som' sneaky-sweet shit, than nothin' eva was.

Alicia Keys' *'I Don't Want Nothing'* tune, started blarin' from the speakers. Gently, Peaches gripped my hand and said, "Com'on Babee, they playin' my song."

I followed my heart and strolled wit her toward the dance floor, only to hear Toi yell out, "Ya'll gettin' back togetha??"

I looked at Peaches, felt her eyes touchin' a nigga's soul, then I responded to shautie, "Ain't no tellin'.........." - THE END...

"CRUNK"
DESCRIPTION

Imagine a Thug-World divided by the Mason-Dixon Line........

After the brutal murder of four NYC ganstas in Charlotte, the climate is set for an all-out Thug Civil War – North pitted against South!

Rah-Rah, leader of NYC's underworld and KoKo, head of one of the Durty South's most ferocious Crunk-crews are on a collision course to destruction. While Rah-Rah tries to rally his northern Thugdom (Philly, NJ & NY), KoKo attempts to saddle-up heads of the southern Hoodville (Atlanta, South Carolina & Charlotte).

Kendra and Janeen, a southern sister-duo of self-proclaimed baddest b*****'s, conduct a make-shift Thug Academy to prepare KoKo's VA-bred cousin (Shine) to infiltrate NYC's underground, as a secret weapon to the impending battle.

The US Government, well-aware of the upcoming war, takes a backseat role, not totally against the idea that a war of this magnitude might actual do what the Government has been unable to do with thousands of life sentences -- Rid society completely of the dangerous element associated with the Underground-World.

Suspensfully-Sexy, Erotically-Ghetto and Mysteriously-Raw. CRUNK will leave you saying, Hmmmm?

"Get Ready For A Wild & Sexy Ride! Twists & Turns Are Abundant! An Instant Urban Classic Thriller! Tariq, Rudd & Jones Are Definitely Some BAD BOYZ! Errr'body Gettin' CRUNK!"

"Hustlin' Backwards"
DESCRIPTION

Capone and his life-long road dawgz, June and Vonzell are out for just one thing.... To get rich!....By any means necessary!

As these three partners in crime rise up the ranks from Project-Kids to Street-Dons, their sworn code of "Death Before Dishonor" gets tested by the Feds.

Though Capone's simple pursuit of forward progression as a Hustler gains him an enviable lifestyle of Fame, Fortune and all the women his libido can handle – It also comes with a price.

No matter the location – Miami, Charlotte, Connecticut or Puerto Rico – There's simply no rest for the wicked!

WARNING: HUSTLIN' BACKWARDS is not the typical street-novel. A Unique Plot, Complex Characters mixed with a Mega-dose of Sensuality makes this story enjoyable by all sorts of readers! A true Hustler himself, Mike Sanders knows the game, inside and out!

"Fast-Paced and Action-Packed! Hustlin' Backwards HAS IT ALL -- Sex, Money, Manipulation and Murder! Mike Sanders is one of the most talented and prolific urban authors of this era!"

"Wild Thangz"
DESCRIPTION

Jazmyn, Trina and Brea are definitely a trio of Drama-Magnets - the sista-girlz version of Charlie's Angels. Young & fine with bangin' bodies, the three of them feel like they can do no wrong – not even with each other.

No matter the location: Jamaica, Miami, NYC or the A-T-L, lust, greed and trouble is never far from these wanna-be divas.

Jazymn has secret dreams that if she pursues will cause her to have mega family problems. Though the most logical of the group, she can get her attitude on with the best of them when pushed.

Trina wasn't always the diva. Book-smarts used to be her calling-card. But, under the tutoring of her personal hoochie-professor, Brea, she's just now beginning to understand the power that she has in her traffic-stopping Badunkadunk.

Brea has the face of a princess, but is straight ghetto-fab -- without the slightest shame. As the wildest of the bunch, her personal credos of living life to the fullest and to use *'what her mama gave her'* to get ahead, is constantly creating drama for Jazymn and Trina.

When past skeleton-choices in Brea's closet places all three of them in an impossible life-and-death situation, they must take an action that has the most serious of consequences, in order to survive!

The very foundation of their friendship-bond gets tested, as each of them have the opportunity to sell-out the other! The question is, Will They?

Wild Parties, Wild Situations & Wild Nights are always present for these Wild Thangz!

Best-Selling Author of "Caught Up!", Winston Chapman weaves yet another suspenseful, sexy-drama tale that's a Must-Read!

"Wild Thangz is HOT! Winston Chapman shonuff brings the HEAT!"
-- Mysterious Luva, Essence Magazine Best-Selling Author of *"Sex A Baller"*

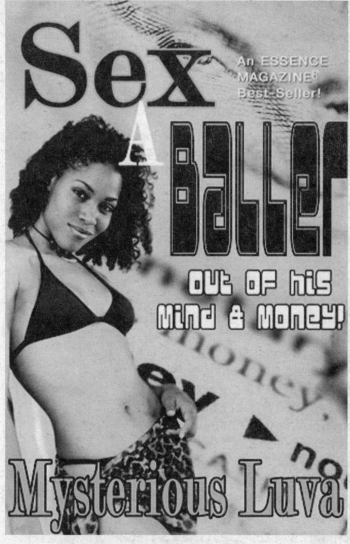

"Sex A Baller"
DESCRIPTION

Mysterious Luva has sexed them all! Ball players, CEO's, Music Stars -- You name the baller, she's had them. And more importantly, she's made them all pay......

Sex A Baller is a poignant mix of a sexy tale of how Mysterious Luva has become one of the World's Best Baller Catchers and an Instructional Guide for the wanna-be Baller Catcher!

No details or secrets are spared, as she delivers her personal story along with the winning tips & secrets for daring women interested in catching a baller!

PLUS, A SPECIAL BONUS SECTION INCLUDED!

Baller Catching 101

- Top-20 Baller SEX POSITIONS (Photos!)
- Where To FIND A Baller
- Which Ballers Have The BIGGEST Penis
- SEDUCING A Baller
- Making A Baller Fall In Love
- Getting MONEY From A Baller
- What Kind Of SEX A Baller Likes
- The EASIEST Type of Baller To Catch
- Turning A Baller Out In Bed
- GAMES To Play On A Baller
- Getting Your Rent Paid & A Free Car
- Learn All The SECRETS!

BY THE END OF THIS BOOK, YOU'LL HAVE YOUR CERTIFIED BALLER-CATCHER'S DEGREE!

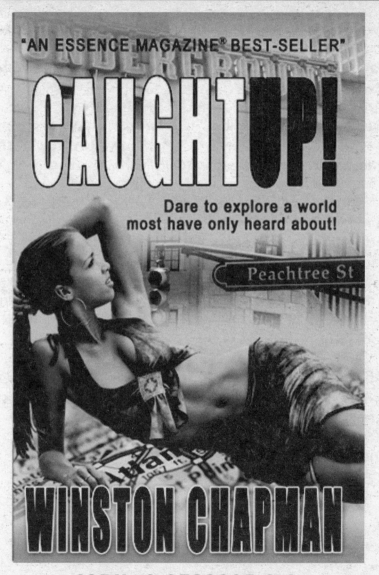

"CAUGHT UP!"
DESCRIPTION

When Raven Klein, a bi-racial woman from Iowa moves to Atlanta in hopes of finding a life she's secretly dreamed about, she finds more than she ever imagined.

Quickly lured and lost in a world of sex, money, power-struggles, betrayal & deceit, Raven doesn't know who she can really trust!

A chance meeting at a bus terminal leads to her delving into the seedy world of strip-clubs, big-ballers and shot-callers.

Now, Raven's shuffling through more men than a Vegas blackjack dealer does a deck of cards. And sex has even become mundane -- little more than a tool to get what she wants.

After a famous acquaintance winds-up dead -- On which shoulder will Raven lean? A wrong choice could cost her life!

There's a reason they call it HOTATLANTA!

" S l i c k "
D E S C R I P T I O N

Dana & Sylvia have been girlfriends for what seems like forever. They've never been afraid to share everything about their lives and definitely keep each other's secrets ... including hiding Dana's On-The-DL affair from her husband, Jonathan.

Though Sylvia is uncomfortable with her participation in the cover-up and despises the man Dana's creepin' with, she remains a loyal friend. That is, until she finds herself attracted to the very man her friend is deceiving.

As the lines of friendship and matrimonial territory erodes, all hell is about to break loose! Choices have to be made with serious repercussions at stake.

If loving you is wrong, I don't wanna be right!

"SLICK!!! .... Ain't That The Truth! Brenda Hampton's Tale Sizzles With Sensuality, Deception, Greed and So Much Drama – My Gurrll!"

- Mysterious Luva, Best-Selling Author of
Sex A Baller

"HYPED"
DESCRIPTION

Maurice LaSalle is a player – of women and the saxophone. A gifted musician, he's the driving force behind MoJazz, a neo-soul group on the verge of their big break. Along with his partner in rhyme and crime, Jamal Grover, Maurice has more women than he can count. Though guided by his mentor Simon, Maurice knows Right but constantly does Wrong.

Then Ebony Stanford enters Maurice's world and he begins to play a new tune. Ebony, still reeling from a nasty divorce, has just about given up on men, but when Maurice hits the right notes (everywhere) she can't help but fall for his charms.

While Maurice and Ebony get closer, Jamal is busy putting so many notches on his headboard post after each female conquest, that the post looks more like a tooth-pick. When a stalker threatens his life, Maurices warns him to slow his roll, but Jamal's hyped behavior prevails over good sense.

Just as Maurice is contemplating turning in his player card for good, stupidity overrules his judgment and throws his harmonious relationship with Ebony into a tale-spin. When it appears that things couldn't get any worse, tragedy strikes and his life is changed forever!

A Powerfully-Written Sexy-Tale, *HYPED* is a unique blend of Mystery, Suspense, Intrigue and Glowing-Sensuality.

"Buckle Up! HYPED Will Test All Of Your Senses and Emotions! LUKE Is A Force To Be Reckoned With For Years To Come!" -- Winston Chapman, Essence Magazine Best-Selling Author of "Caught Up!" and "Wild Thangz"

"STILL CRAZY"
DESCRIPTION

Kevin Allen, a rich, handsome author and self-reformed 'Mack', is now suffering from writer's block.

Desperately in need of a great story in order to renegotiate with his publisher to maintain his extravagant life-style, Kevin decides to go back to his hometown of Chicago for inspiration. While in Chi-town, he gets reacquainted with an ex-love (Yolanda) that he'd last seen during their stormy relationship that violently came to an end.

Unexpectedly, Yolanda appears at a book-event where Kevin is the star-attraction, looking every bit as stunningly beautiful as the picture he's had frozen in his head for years. She still has the looks of music video model and almost makes him forget as to the reason he'd ever broken off their relationship.

It's no secret, Yolanda had always been the jealous type. And, Kevin's explanation to his boyz, defending his decision for kicking a woman that fine to the curb was, "She's Crazy!".

The combination of Kevin's vulnerable state in his career, along with the tantalizing opportunity to hit *that* again, causes Kevin to contemplate renewing his expired Players-Card, one last time. What harm could one night of passion create?

Clouding his judgment even more is that Kevin feels like hooking-up with Yolanda might just be the rekindling needed to ignite the fire for his creativity in his writing career. But, there are just two problems. Kevin is married! ....And, Yolanda is *Still Crazy!*

"Darrin Lowery deliciously serves up…..Scandal & Sexy-Drama like no other! *STILL CRAZY* has all the goods readers are looking for!" -- *Brenda Hampton, Author of "Slick"*

" S H A K E D O W N "
D E S C R I P T I O N

Paris Hightower, is a sexy young thang who falls in love with the man of her dreams, Tyree Dickerson, the son of very wealthy Real Estate tycoons. But there's a problem.... Tyree's mother (Mrs. Dickerson) thinks that her son is too good for Paris and is dead-set on destroying the relationship at all costs.

After Mrs. Dickerson reveals a long-kept secret to Paris about her mother (Ebony Hightower), a woman that abandoned Paris and her brother more than fifteen years ago when she was forced to flee and hide from police amidst Attempted-Murder charges for shooting Paris' father --- Paris is left in an impossible situation.

Even though the police have long given-up on the search for Ebony Hightower (Paris' mother), the bitter Mrs. Dickerson threatens to find her and turn her in to authorities as blackmail for Paris to end the relationship with her son.

Paris knows that Mrs. Dickerson means business – she has the time, interest and money to hunt down her mother. Left with the choices of pursuing her own happiness or protecting the freedom of her mother, a woman she barely knows, Paris is confused as to the right thing to do.

As the situation escalates to fireworks of private investigators, deception, financial sabotage and kidnapping, even Paris' life becomes in danger.

Just when Paris feels that all hope is lost, she's shocked when she receives unexpected help from an unlikely source.

"Be careful who you mess with, 'cause Payback is a ......! *Shakedown* combines high-drama and mega-suspense with the heart-felt struggle of the price some are willing to pay for love!" -- Winston Chapman, Best-Selling Author of *"Wild Thangz"* and *"Caught Up!"*

"DYME HIT LIST" DESCRIPTION

Rio Romero Clark, is an Oakland-bred brotha determined to remain a Playa-For-Life!

Taught by the best of Macks (his Uncle Lee, Father and Grandfather), Rio feels no woman can resist him. And he knows that his game is definitely tight, considering that he's as a third-generation Playa.

It is Rio's United-Nations-like appreciation for all types and races of women, from the Ghetto-Fab to the Professional, that leads him to the biggest challenge of his Mack-hood, Carmen Massey.

Carmen, a luscious southern-Dyme, at first sight, appears to be just another target on Rio's *Dyme Hit List!* Possessing a body that's bangin' enough to make most brothas beg, mixed with southern-charm that can cause even the best playa to hesitate, Carmen's got Rio in jeopardy of getting his Playa-Card revoked.

Burdened with the weight of potentially not living-up to the family Mack-legacy, Rio must choose between continuing to love his lifestyle or loving Carmen.

Unexpectedly tragedy strikes in Rio's life and a dark secret in Carmen's past ignites a fire that threatens to burn-up their relationship, permanently.

"*Dyme Hit List* is On-Fire with Sensuality! This story is pleasingly-filled with lotsa lip-folding scenes! Curtis Alcutt is a bright new star in fiction!"

-- Winston Chapman, Best-Selling Author of *"Wild Thangz"* and *"Caught Up!"*

"T W I S T E D"
D E S C R I P T I O N

Nadine, a sultry, ghetto-fine conniving gold-digger, will do whatever it takes to make sure that she is financially set for life -- even at the cost of breaking-up a family.

When Wayne, Nadine's man since high-school, is sentenced to two years in prison for a crime he did not commit, he's betrayed by the two people he trusted the most—his woman (Nadine) and his cousin (Bobo).

Asia, a curvaceous diva and designer-clothing boutique owner with a wilder-side sexual-preference becomes an unlikely confidant to her best-friend Nadine's man (Wayne) during his incarceration.

Meanwhile Bobo, one of VA's most notorious and most successful Street-Entreprenuers, manages to hustle his way into staring down a possible life sentence.

Now that the roles are reversed, it's Bobo who's now facing some serious prision time, as Nadine tries to do whatever it takes to keep her hands on the secret stash of cash hidden in a suitcase that Bobo left behind.

Money, greed and sex always have as a way of gettin' things **Twisted!**

"Daaaaayummmmmm! Holland Jones brings it! A hood-licious story that combines deceit, murder, freaky sex and mysterious-twists! You gotta get this one!"

-- Winston Chapman, Best-Selling Author of **Caught Up!** and **Wild Thangz**

"LEGIT BALLER"
DESCRIPTION

Jay Bernard has been dedicated to his craft as a baler. That is, until his deeds land him a 14-year bid in the Federal Pen on drug-charges.

Kim, Jay's supposed 'Bonnie' to his 'Clyde' wastes no time in cutting ties after his sentencing by moving her game to the new Baller-Kint (Paris).

During Jay's incarceration, sexy Summer Foster, proves to be a better friend than anyone who'd benefited from Jay's life-style. Though from the same hood, Summer has managed to rise-up, earning a college degree and currently an M.B.A. student at Harvard.

After his early-release, Jay finds it hard to avoid the only life he knows, even with the love and encouragement from an old-friend (Summer) for him to go 'Legit' – Old habits, just seem to die hard!

The complete opposite of Jay's gangsta, Summer views him as much more than just hard-rock – but a true diamond-gem! However, Jay's past and the streets keep calling him.

Paris views himself as a street-rival of Jay's even before his stint in prison, and now feels threatened that Jay may want to re-claim everything back – his drug territory and his woman (Kim)!

When the inevitable confrontation arises between Jay and Paris, the next move could be the last!

*"Gritty Urban Realism At Its Best!
... Legit Baller Is The Truth!"*
Lynne D. Johnson, **VIBE MAGAZINE**

Black Pearl Books Inc.

ORDER FORM

Black Pearl Books Inc.
3653-F Flakes Mill Road- PMB 306
Atlanta, Georgia 30034
www. BlackPearlBooks. com

YES, We Ship Directly To Prisons & Correctional Facilities
INSTITUTIONAL CHECKS & MONEY ORDERS ONLY!

TITLE	Price	Quantity	TOTAL
"Caught Up!" by Winston Chapman	$ 14. 95		
"Sex A Baller" by Mysterious Luva	$ 12. 95		
"Wild Thangz" by Winston Chapman	$ 14. 95		
"Crunk" by Bad Boyz	$ 14. 95		
"Hustlin Backwards" by Mike Sanders	$ 14. 95		
"Still Crazy" by Darrin Lowery	$ 14. 95		
"Twisted" by Holland Jones	$ 14. 95		
"Slick" by Brenda Hampton	$ 14. 95		
"Hyped" by Luke	$ 14. 95		
"Dyme Hit List" by Curtis Alcutt	$ 14. 95		
"Busted" by Rhonda Swan	$ 14. 95		
"Shakedown" by Nubian James	$ 14. 95		
"Hustlers" by Ronald Quincy	$ 14. 95		
"Legit Baller" by Jerry Blackshear	$ 14. 95		

Sub-Total	$	
SHIPPING: ___ # books x $ 3. 50 ea. **(Via US Priority Mail)**	$	
GRAND TOTAL	$	

SHIP TO:

Name: _____

Address: _____

Apt or Box #: _____

City: _____ State: _____ Zip: _____

Phone: _____ E-mail: _____